Rhiannon

Sonja Collavoce

This novel's story, characters, and many of its buildings are fictitious. Certain long-standing institutions, agencies, and public offices are mentioned, but the characters involved are wholly imaginary. Any similarities the reader may discern must be attributed to the reader's vivid imagination!

Copyright © 2022 by Sonja Collavoce

All rights reserved.

No portion of this book may be reproduced in any form without written permission from the author.

Rhiannon

The sleepy Welsh village of Llannon has remained resolutely untouched by the advent of the swinging 60s. Forty-three year old Mavis Watton's life is superficial, her marriage cold and passionless.

When bohemian Irishman Seamus O'Brien leaves the cultural metropolis of London, seeking tranquillity in Llannon, he has no intention of creating havoc, but then, he has yet to meet the captivating Mavis.

Contents

1. Full Circle — 1
2. The Great Pretender — 7
3. The Maverick — 13
4. Strategic Schemes — 25
5. The Fosterling — 35
6. The Green-Eyed Monster — 45
7. A Voyage of Discovery — 57
8. Repercussions and Revelations — 69
9. Broadening Horizons — 85
10. The Progress of Summer — 95
11. The Silky Threads of the Web — 105
12. Submission — 117
13. The Ways of a Child — 137
14. Dunes — 151
15. The Ebb and Flow of Summer — 167
16. The Swirling Tide of Life — 185
17. Altering Roles — 203
18. Subtle strategies — 221

19.	The Elevation of Status	237
20.	The Serpentine Way of Things	257
21.	The Sacking of Jezebel.	275
22.	A Month of Missives.	279
23.	A season of change.	291
24.	Noel	309
25.	Parturition	319
26.	Introductions	327
27.	Cruel Tricks	339
28.	Survival	357
29.	Resolution	369
30.	The Finale.	373
Acknowledgments		387
About Author		388

Chapter One

Full Circle

The nurse bustled efficiently around the room as she cleared away the dressing packs and soiled bandages from the trolley, the powerful smell of Hibitane antiseptic filling the room, her broad backside swaying in time to the music playing unobtrusively on the radio in the corner. Despite a song playing which urged everyone to feed the world, Mavis could see that Sister Davies probably needed no further feeding at all.

"Well, Mavis, that's your leg ulcer done for another day." The nurse smiled patronisingly down at her patient. "See you tomorrow, then? And do be a good girl for the care staff, won't you?"

My name is Mrs Watton, you insolent woman, thought Mavis furiously, watching Sister Davies leave the room. I am not allowed to address her by her Christian name, I don't even know it, yet she treats me like a child and calls me Mavis.

Maybe it was the constant pain from her leg, but Mavis Watton was rarely in a good mood these days. Christmas was only a week away, but Mavis felt sad and lonely. The tiny, sparsely-lit tree on the window sill seemed a pathetic representation of the excitement and joy that everyone else seemed to be feeling. Her small room seemed to her like a prison cell, for she could not leave it without summoning help. Her increasing frailty and arthritic joints rendered her chair-bound for most of the day, and, being the proud, stubborn woman that she was, she felt it quite beneath her to join the other residents in the day room. No indeed. Bingo and communal sing-songs were not for Mavis Watton. She had her own radio, and a tiny portable television, but neither held much entertainment value for her. I just sit here, she thought, I just sit.

She looked out of the window. The sky was darkening already, and it wasn't even four o'clock. Rain was beating a relentless tattoo on the pane.

The park-keeper was closing the gates of Parc Hardd, and the leafless trees were dancing about wildly in the wind. It all seemed so bleak and cold. Mavis remembered looking out of the same window, so many years ago, holding her newborn son, when the care home was a maternity hospital. And she had come full circle...from his cradle to my grave, she thought, grimly. She supposed she should be glad to be tucked up safe and sound in Brynglas Residential Home, but she missed her independence terribly. It had been her decision to come here, she hadn't wanted to be a burden on her late husband's family. Sometimes, on those rare days when she was well, it felt as though she was still young. Mavis wondered what the staff saw when they looked at her? Was she just a tiny, bird-like woman, with what they called "attitude" (yes, she had heard them whispering in the corridor) who was practically disabled? Another geriatric to help wash, feed and medicate? With the exception of young Stacey, a kind-hearted junior carer who was always deferential and respectful, the staff seemed to her be in a hurry, to go back to their little office and gossip. Or was it purely in her imagination? But maybe she was indeed "difficult." There was so much time, these days, to allow her thoughts to run riot. She closed her eyes and sighed, wishing she could turn back the clock to happier times. The clock at her bedside ticked loudly, lulling her into a soporific state. Just as she was drifting off to sleep, there was a knock at the door.

"Mrs Watton?" A uniformed young woman with black, curly hair tentatively stepped inside.

"Stacey?" Mavis opened her eyes wide. "It isn't tea-time yet, surely?"

"No, it's only a quarter past four. But you have a visitor." Stacey stood back to allow a slim, elegant woman enter the room.

"Aunty Mavis?" The visitor rushed forward, enveloping Mavis in a warm embrace and a cloud of Amarige.

"Wendy!" Mavis hugged her, clinging to her as if she would never let her go, tears starting to her eyes. "What a wonderful surprise!"

Wendy sat on the bed, putting a beautifully wrapped present on the side-table.

"I've brought you a little something. I'm down from London for a few days, as Coppelia doesn't start until Boxing Day and I had this week off."

Mavis took time to regard her. What an astoundingly graceful and attractive woman she had become, so far removed from the naughty, playful six year old Mavis remembered so well. Her blond hair was gathered up into a bun at the nape of her neck, her pretty face was perfectly made-up and her figure was the stuff of dreams.

"I can't even make you a cup of tea, Wendy. I have everything done for me these days, it's so frustrating." Mavis took Wendy's long, slender fingers in her own small hand.

"Well, it's just as well you can't make me tea, Aunty, because that's why I'm here! To take you out to tea! You will come, won't you?" Wendy smiled impishly, reminding Mavis of the exuberant little girl who could be simultaneously cheeky and charming.

"But I'm not ready! I haven't got any make-up on, and my hair is like a rat's nest!"

Wendy giggled at Mavis' horrified expression. "As vain as ever, I'm relieved to see! Don't worry, I'll sort your make up for you, and all you have to do is tell me what you want to wear and I'll help you dress."

Ten minutes later, Mavis was standing shakily at her Zimmer frame, wearing a blue velvet dress and her best black patent shoes, the pain from her leg ulcer forgotten in the excitement of the moment.

"Where are we going?" She narrowed her eyes and frowned anxiously at her niece.

"The Stradey Park Hotel. I've booked us a special Christmas afternoon tea at half past five. So we've plenty of time. Where's your coat?"

Mavis paused, considering this information, a new determination filling her tired mind.

"Open the wardrobe, Wendy. At the far right you'll find a fur coat. Pull it out. I don't care if it's raining. I'll wear that. I never get a chance to wear it any more, and the staff here disapprove of it so I hide it away....I will give it one more outing this afternoon."

The beautiful coat completely swamped Mavis, but she stroked it affectionately, closing her brown eyes in appreciation. Wendy clapped her hands in delight.

"You look lovely, Aunty Mavis. Now, I'll get the wheelchair!"

Mavis had never travelled in such a smart car before, and clung to the edge of her seat as Wendy steered the shiny BMW out of the car park and onto the main road. It was completely dark now, and

Mavis could see all the brightly lit Christmas trees in the bay windows of the houses in Felinfoel Road as they drove past. Families would be gathering together, students returning home from college, present wrapping would be in progress. She thought wistfully of her own son, far away in Paris, unable to return home this year as the new baby was expected any day.

Wendy pulled up directly outside the hotel's main entrance, where a kindly porter helped Mavis into a waiting wheelchair, all the while staring enviously at the car.

"See? I thought of everything!" Wendy laughed, as she turned the BMW around to park it in the nearby car park.

By half past five on the dot, the pair were sitting in the beautifully decorated dining room, with a deferential waitress hanging on their every word. Mavis gazed around at the bright chandeliers, and the immense Christmas tree, ablaze with a thousand fairy lights. The hotel had changed a great deal since her last visit here, so many years ago, at her step-daughter's wedding. Everything in her world had changed, it seemed.

"I'll never be able to eat all this!" Mavis looked anxiously at the heaps of hot mince pies, smoked salmon sandwiches and miniature Christmas cakes laid out before them on the pristine white tablecloth..

"Yes, we will! At any rate, we'll give it a bash!" Wendy poured the tea. "I told Mam and Dad that I won't be wanting any supper this evening!"

"So, how is the job going?" asked Mavis, nibbling on a sandwich. "How do you like teaching and not performing any more?"

"Oh, it was time for me to quit the limelight." Wendy smiled sadly, sipping her tea. "I have hung up my pointes and put away the greasepaint for good. I have had a good innings in the Royal Ballet, principal dancer for ten years and goodness knows how many years in the corps. Now I am content to teach, choreograph and help direct the performances."

Mavis smiled mistily. "You were such a beautiful dancer, Wendy fach."

"And you helped me on my way!" Wendy patted the old lady's arm gently. "If it hadn't been for you, I wouldn't have achieved anything half as wonderful. Anyway, how about James? Is he coming back to Wales for Christmas?"

"Not this year. The baby is due on New Year's Eve, and he and Simone have so much to do, with the other two being quite young as well." She looked up at her niece. "Do you mind never having had children, or being married?"

Wendy sighed. "I was married to my vocation, Aunty Mavis. It took over my whole life. And now I am a woman of a "certain age," time has run out. I do have a boyfriend, you know. He's a lot older than me, is Keith, and he's been married before, but no children. My pupils are my children, I suppose. I enjoy teaching and choreographing so much, getting to know the youngsters, helping them with all their little problems..." Her voice trailed away, wistfully.

They were suddenly distracted by a commotion at an adjacent table. A vastly overweight peroxide blond woman in her seventies was trying to squeeze her large bottom onto one of the rather delicate chairs, and had knocked over a bottle of sparkling wine in the process. Her brash exclamations carried loudly through the crowded room.

"Well, I don't believe it!" Mavis chuckled softly. Wendy looked quizzically at her aunt, raising a well-defined eyebrow. "That's Gladys Williams," Mavis explained quietly, "she used to be a bit of a man-eater in her time. Now she must be over eighteen stone! And she's twice divorced!" It was all Mavis could to do to stop herself staring over at the unfortunate Gladys, who, thankfully, seemed quite unaware of the interest from the other table.

At half past six, Mavis felt tired and said so.

"That's fine, Aunty Mavis, I'll take you back right away. I'll just ask for the bill, first." Wendy searched in her bag for her cheque book.

Mavis watched proudly as Wendy signed her name with a flourish on the cheque. Wendy Wainwright.

"You still use your stage name, then?"

Wendy grinned. "Yes! I'm so used to it now. I doubt anyone would pay attention at all to a Wendy Watton!"

As Wendy pushed the wheelchair to the front entrance, Mavis couldn't resist having a look back at Gladys, who was now busy stuffing cream cakes into her cerise-lipped mouth as though they were going out of fashion, a blob of butter icing hanging decorously on her triple chin. Mavis chuckled inwardly. She had really enjoyed her outing.

Wendy helped Mavis remove her fur coat and shoes before easing her aunt back into her armchair. Mavis adjusted the cushion behind her. She sighed with sheer tiredness. Her body ached so much.

"Don't put the coat back in the wardrobe, Wendy. I want you to have it. You've just the right look
about you to wear it, and just the right height."

Wendy sat on the bed, still holding the coat.

"Me? But it's so expensive! And what about your daughter-in-law? Wouldn't she like to have it?"

Mavis smiled. "No, Simone is too, what is the word - casual - .grungy, I think? Yes, that's the right word. I've heard the girls here use it a lot. She wears jeans and jumpers all the time, and never dresses much at all. And French as well! I realise fur is despised these days, and you won't want to wear it out, but maybe, from time to time, you can just put it on and think of me? And I don't want the staff here to send it to one of the charity shops after I...." Mavis faltered. Wendy hugged her. "Well, if you're sure....but won't you want to wear it again, perhaps?"

Mavis looked away, through the window to the pitch black park, thinking back to another time, another season, when her world was full of hope and the park was sunny, full of laughter.

"No," she shook her head sadly, "I won't be needing it any more."

Chapter Two

The Great Pretender

Mavis Rhiannon Hughes entered the world on a snowy night at midwinter, the unexpected and unplanned addition to the two daughters Mr and Mrs Hughes already had. The wind howled around the street of terraced houses where they lived, and the village of Llannon was covered in white drifts three feet high. The baby's arrival was fast, furious and unequivocally dramatic, as the Llannon midwife had not been able to reach the house through the snow, resulting in an ashen Mr Hughes having to deliver his own child. It may not have been the Nativity scene his older daughters were hoping for, but the child's birth, in the middle of the worst snowstorm in living memory, seemed to herald the delivery of an exceptionally special individual. Or so Mr Hughes thought, in his tired, yet excited mind.

The subtle glow of the candles illuminated the pale, exhausted face of Morfydd Hughes, as her anxious husband wondered desperately what he should do with the bloody remains of this precipitate birthing, especially as it was still attached to the baby.

Common sense prevailed, however, and under his wife's tremulous direction, he tied the no-longer pulsating cord in two places with some string, before cutting it with a pair of scissors which he had boiled in a saucepan. Feeling quite pleased with himself, he then disposed of the placenta on top of the coal fire, whereupon it let out a merry, festive hiss. He could see that the infant was pink, warm and alert, as she rooted instinctively for her mother's nipple, wrapped up warmly in a flanelette sheet, so he began to relax. Time to celebrate, he thought, bringing out a bottle of stout from under the stairs, after telling the other daughters to go to bed. Mr Eric Hughes was a gentle soul, and worshipped his rather delicate wife. This had been the most terrifying experience in his entire life, so he felt this decadent beverage was perfectly justified.

The five pound Mavis was an angelic looking baby, with glossy black hair, and huge dark eyes. She even smiled at two weeks old, charming her mother and father into doting, parental submission. Her elfin beauty also ensured that her besotted mother abandoned any thoughts of a feeding regime, and breast fed the tiny baby on demand. Unfortunately, this resulted in little Mavis being labelled by her sisters as demanding for the rest of her childhood. She grew up cosseted and pampered by her parents and the extended family, much to the chagrin of her older sisters, Enid and Evelyn, who took every opportunity to inflict their jealous spite on their small sibling when no-one was looking. So many times they waited until Mavis was alone before pinching her, or pulling her hair. Worst of all was the name-calling and insults. Mavis lost count of the number of times Enid and Evelyn called her a midget, or the runt of the litter. If she had dared to complain to her parents, Mavis knew the consequences would be even more dire – her head would be pushed down the outside toilet bowl, or spiders would be put in her bed. At the tender age of nine, Mavis knew she had but two choices: accept defeat and a subsequent lifetime of submission, or develop a tough skin, and fight back. Which is exactly what she started to do.

Unfortunately, Mavis' most staunch supporter, her father, was killed in a farming accident when she was just ten years old, leaving her to fend for herself against Enid and Evelyn's vitriol, her mother being prone to taking to her bed on account of various psychosomatic illnesses. This resulted in the young girl developing a hard outer shell, and a tough, resilient character. Her mind was sharp, and young Mavis suffered no fools gladly. She soon developed the knack of answering back, with slick sarcasm and biting barbs, which frequently floored her sisters. At sixteen, she was small, but beautiful, so her sisters' jealousy knew no bounds. Mavis, suffering their torments on a daily basis, grew into a sharp-tongued, spirited young woman, and her acerbic attitude became second-nature, even when not warranted.

One rainy afternoon, Mavis, having sustained yet another spiteful attack from her sisters, rushed up to her bedroom, a tiny boxroom at the back of the house. Locking the door, she flung herself on the bed, her thoughts in a turmoil.

Why do they do this to me, she wondered furiously, I don't deserve this. Angrily, she punched the pillow before bursting into tears, being careful to weep quietly. Mustn't let them hear me, she warned herself, they mustn't know. The protective shield was developing. Unbeknown to the rest of her family, Mavis rescued chicks fallen from nests, wandering baby hedgehogs and even injured toads, feeding them and nursing them back to health in the shed at the top of the steep garden which backed on to the hills behind the village. She guarded them fiercely, bestowing on them the love and affection which she yearned for herself.

Her widowed mother took in lodgers. Their comfortable four-bedroomed terraced house in the middle of the village was kept like a shiny new pin, and the 'professional' men who stayed there were uncomfortable most of the time, afraid to sneeze, cough, or pass wind. Young Mavis fascinated them, to her sisters' intense annoyance. But she was oblivious to the lodgers' attentions, setting her teenage heart on greater things than tradesmen and salesmen.

The Second World War soon halted Mavis' marital ambitions, and she decided to volunteer as a farm worker nearby, along with her sisters. This proved too strenuous for the compact Mavis, so, shrugging off her sisters' ridicule and sneers, she secured a temporary job in the General Post Office down in Llanelli, where she worked three days a week. The war ended, and consequently, so did her rather enjoyable position behind the post office counter, and Mavis resumed her position as a dutiful daughter in the Hughes household.

However, Llannon after WW2 was even more bereft of eligible men. The local boys who had fought in the war had either met their wives in the forces or had been one of the many sad casualties.

The years crept by, the village stagnated and Mavis seethed with frustration. What can I do, she would ask herself, I can't leave the village, there's nowhere I can go, no job I can do.

Mavis was an extremely well-preserved spinster when she reached forty, having a taste for smart suits which she wore to Evening Prayer with all the flamboyance of a bird of paradise amongst a flock of crows, forever hopeful of attracting a man. Mavis was not popular amongst the other hopeful women, for her alluring, dark features and slim figure set her apart from them; her sharp tongue had inflicted verbal wounds on many of them, and the memory still smarted.

There may well have been a shortage of marriageable men in the village, but there was one possibility. Mr Ernest Watton, the deacon.

Mr Ernest Watton lived an exemplary life, and after the war ended, he left his job in the local munitions factory, and returned to Llannon as caretaker of the local school. He lost his first wife to tuberculosis and his second wife as a result of a premature heart attack. Fortunately, his two children survived and lived mainly with Ernest's sister down in Felinfoel. He was a staunch Baptist and a hard-core teetotal, even declining sherry trifle at Christmas. He concentrated his energies on the Bible and breeding large dogs, in particular Labradors and Alsations. Eventually, Mr Ernest Watton became the deacon at the village chapel, to his mother's great delight.

Having been widowed for a second time, Mr Watton started to feel lonely after a while. So many of the spinsters and widows of Bethel chapel had their predatory eyes on the stern, devout minister, each hoping his piercing blue eyes would in turn meet theirs. However, no-one was more predatory or cunning than Mavis Hughes. From under lowered eyes, she watched the tall, white haired minister as he delivered his fire and brimstone sermons each Sunday, his handsome features forbidding and hard, only rarely softened by a smile.

Mavis did believe in the Lord, but her fervour knew no limits when she decided she wanted Mr Ernest Watton for her husband. Used to attending chapel three times each Sunday, she suddenly joined the Sisterhood, went to Prayer Meeting each Tuesday, Bible Study every Friday and even enrolled in the choir.

Mr Williams the choirmaster soon developed a crush on the adorable Mavis, and pestered her endlessly to accompany him on outings to Carmarthen in his brand new car, showering her with invitations to visit him and his elderly mother for tea. Mavis ignored his advances, all the while playing the coy, innocent woman, hoping that Mr Watton would take note of her virtuous rejection of Mr Williams.

And notice her he did. Mr Watton was quite taken by this feisty yet modest lady, and invited her to Sunday lunch at his mother's house.

Mrs Annie Watton was a formidable character, living in splendid solitude on the top of a hill, with only the trees and her cats for company. She viewed this new pretender to the crown of wife number three with predictable scepticism. However, Mavis proved a worthy contender, and Mrs Annie Watton was soon won over by her future daughter-in-law's charm and determination. At eighty-three, she seemed content that her son had yet again found himself a suitable woman.

Mavis travelled to Cardiff to buy her wedding dress, with her friend Eiddwen Lewis for company. Mavis had the unconscious knack of surrounding herself with women far less attractive than herself, so that she would appear even more appealing.

Poor Eiddwen, dressed in serviceable brown crimplene, was no rival at all. Her mousey brown hair (by no stretch of the imagination could it be called dark-blonde) surrounded her plump face in tight, permed curls. She visited Barbara's in Tumble regularly for this coiffure, always hopeful that, one day, she would be transformed into an attractive woman. Eiddwen was only too grateful to bask in Mavis' reflected glory, unaware how the contrast disadvantaged her.

The pair arrived in Cardiff, and spent four hours traipsing from shop to shop, Mavis trying on a variety of suitable dresses. Of course, to walk up the aisle in a full-length white dress would be quite inappropriate for a woman of her age, but cream, or even the palest pink would be perfectly acceptable.

Eiddwen's cheeks were aching by the end of the expedition, having had to smile constantly, and reassure Mavis as to how beautiful she looked. Luckily for Eiddwen, Mavis found her perfect dress fairly easily. Even the most cynical parish widow would have had to agree that it could have been designed and made just for Mavis.

As she tried the pretty blue dress on, Mavis caught her breath as she twirled delightedly in front of the mirror in the bridal shop. Eiddwen's eyes misted over with tears as she watched the glamorous spinster admiring herself. How fortunate she was to have such a beautiful friend!

The wedding took place in Bethel chapel, a stone's throw from Mavis' house. The early spring sun shone warmly down on the couple; the severe winter's snow had finally disappeared.

Nearly the whole village turned up to see the enigmatic deacon and the notable Mavis join together in holy matrimony. Fake and bitter smiles were de rigeur amongst the remaining lonely ladies of the parish, and many teeth, false and otherwise, were gritted as the rapturous Mavis Watton exited the chapel on the arm of the proud Ernest.

The reception was held in Llanelli. An Austrian restaurant, The Vienna, had been booked for the thirty-five guests who had been deemed of high enough social status to be worthy of an invitation.

Despite her husband's extreme disapproval, Mavis had ordered Harvey's Bristol Cream sherry to be served on arrival, and the guests glasses were kept filled with Mateus Rose wine. Ernest turned a blind eye to all this wicked behaviour, but vowed inwardly that on no account would his beautiful little wife be allowed to drink in future. The celebration was quite a jolly one as a result, and nobody minded the overcooked Wienerschnitzel, the limp broccoli or the rather cool boiled potatoes. Ernest's son, Fred, drove the couple down to Llanelli railway station to catch the train downline, where they honeymooned in Tenby.

The sunny weather continued, and the newly married couple spent each of the four days exploring the town, sitting on the beach and discussing the Old Testament over fish and chips. Ernest was too tired to make much of an effort to relieve Mavis of her virginity during the holiday, and merely contented himself with a kiss and a cuddle before turning the light out in their modest hotel room at ten o'clock on the dot. Mavis, knowing no better, assumed that this was the norm, so was appalled three weeks later to find that her new husband suddenly became rather more energetic in the bedroom. However, she bore it all magnificently, never complaining or withholding her charms.

Secretly, she was puzzled. What pleasure was in it for her? Her strict Baptist upbringing discouraged any discussion about such intimate matters with her mother or her friends, so Mavis continued along her married life, completely ignorant of the true joys of the flesh. Inexperienced in the game of love, she sometimes remembered a fumbled encounter behind the Sunday School girls' toilets when she had been sixteen. Emyr Thomas had been considered quite a catch at eighteen, and working in the bank, he had seemed sophisticated and worldly-wise. It had been on Christmas Eve and had been raining. Emyr had kissed young Mavis with all the skill and tenderness of an adolescent dog chasing a bitch. He certainly hadn't lacked enthusiasm, and his next move was to grope her breasts and attempt to undo her brassiere, earning him a hard slap on the face. The experience had left Mavis wondering what all the fuss was about. Sex. She could do without it, she'd reckoned. She went to her wedding night a virgin, and remained so until about three weeks later, when Mr Watton had finally managed to deflower her.

Ernest was a cold, unresponsive man, his moods changing as quickly as the Welsh weather. He expected the cottage to be run efficiently, and was of the opinion that women should, like children, be seen and not heard. It was fortunate for Mavis that she had learned emotional self-defence throughout her childhood and teenage years, for it stood her in good stead during the early months of her marriage. Ernest seemed quite different from the fiance she had been so desperate to marry. Had she even known him at all?

Being deprived of any warmth or fondness in her married life, Mavis turned her attention to worldly possessions, collecting jewellery and expensive clothes like a little magpie. She had her own part-time job in the local sweet shop, as well as some money left to her by an aunt, so felt perfectly justified in these purchases. Ernest never commented on her materialistic extravagance, maybe it absolved him of any emotional responsibility.

Three years later, Mavis travelled to London to purchase a fur coat. It had been her ambition to own one for a long time, firmly believing that only people with high social or economic status were privileged enough to wear mink fur. The ownership of such a garment would therefore elevate her into that elite group.

Having chosen and paid for the beautiful garment, Mavis returned to Llannon, where she anxiously waited for its delivery the following week.

A week which would tip her world upside down.

Chapter Three

The Maverick

The moon suddenly appeared from behind a cloud, illuminating the big house and accentuating its deep shadows. The artist paid the taxi driver and looked up at his new home. Grinning in satisfaction, he hauled his suitcases and boxes up the rough path before sitting down on the doorstep to survey his new kingdom. The April night was cold, and a slight frost sparkled on the fields. Not many lights were on in the village, as it was just past midnight. He heard the melancholy hoot of an owl drift across the distant woodland, and felt that his decision to leave the bright lights of London had been the right one.

"Perfect," he murmured to himself, lighting a cigarette. Turning his attention to the left, he could see a small cottage with a tree-filled garden. But it was in darkness.

Tomorrow, he told himself, I will see it all tomorrow. With a contented sigh, he put the key in the lock, and after struggling with its rusty mechanisms for a minute, eventually opened the creaking old door, and entered his new house.

Early May in Carmarthenshire could be either a slap in the face or a kiss on the cheek, depending on the weather. This year, the sun shone warmly, the blackthorn blossomed in white and bridal beauty over the hills which cradled Llannon, and bluebells started to carpet the secret valleys of the woods. Mavis Watton cursed the sweetness of the season, as it made it absolutely impossible to find a reason to wear her new coat, which had duly arrived a few days ago.

Her part-time job in the sweet shop was not exactly taxing, and Mavis had plenty of free time in which to polish and dust her cottage within an inch of its life. The mahogany sideboard reflected Mavis' satisfied smile as clearly as the gilt-edged mirror above the fireplace. No smudge or smear would dare show itself in Mavis Watton's house, and her housekeeping was legendary, if rather regimented. Eira Jones, who lived down the road, would have been seriously concerned if she'd failed to see a line full of white shirts blowing happily on a Monday morning in the Watton's garden, as that was when Mavis did her boil-wash.

She sighed as she folded the towels away in the airing cupboard. How abrupt Ernest had been to her this morning. Why, he didn't even greet her when he got up, just ignored her and went about saying his prayers. Tears pricked her eyes, but she refused to let them flow down her cheeks.

"What am I doing wrong?" she asked her reflection in the hall mirror in a whisper. "Why is he so cold?" But mirror Mavis had no answers for her.

However, today was Friday. Her husband was away in nearby Felinfoel, conducting a funeral, so Mavis decided to walk down to Eiddwen's house in the village, in the hope that she would be offered a cup of tea and a chance to gossip.

The weather remained determinedly balmy, and Mavis had no need of a coat or jacket, so she pulled on a scarlet angora cardigan over her navy dress, and set off in good spirits. Mavis walked confidently down the lane, her head in the air. Despite her annoyance at being unable to wear her fur coat for the foreseeable future, the spring day soon soothed her irritation. The May sunbeams glossed her dark hair, and brought a rosy pink tint to her cheeks. She felt good, smiling as she watched Pili-Pala's new foal nuzzling up to the mare, seeking milk.

However, Mavis had never felt maternal in her life, had never felt the heart-pull of motherhood when a cousin or friend had given birth. No, she was content with her life – well, more or less.

Half way down the lane, Mavis was slightly surprised to see a "Sold" sign on the old Richards house. It had been empty for years, as no-one seemed to wish to move to Llannon. It was a huge, rambling pile of pale, grey stonework, with strange turrets and more windows than Crystal Palace. She wondered who had bought it.

"Hello," came a voice suddenly. Mavis jumped. She couldn't see anyone. Then, just as unpredictably, a man scrambled out of a gap in the hedge.

"Er, hello," she replied, looking at the man curiously. He was tall and slim, but well-built. Mavis thought he looked about fifty, but his rather long hair was still brown and his deep blue eyes were scrutinising her, taking her in. Splashes of brightly coloured paint decorated his torn, grey shirt, and his baggy green trousers were held up by a piece of string. Despite his dishevelled appearance, the man had an assured, confident air. His wide mouth seemed to be perpetually smiling at her.

"Seamus Declan O'Brien." He held out a paint-stained hand to her. Mavis took it, gingerly. Her small, child-like hand was crushed by his long, slim fingers.

"And you are...?" he continued. Mavis realised she was staring at him with her mouth open.

"Um, Mavis, "she replied, "Mavis Rhiannon Watton. I live in the cottage back there. You're Irish, aren't you?"

"To be sure I am," he laughed heartily. "I bought this place just last week. Bought it for a bloody song! Couldn't wait to move in. Such light, such wonderful light."

Mavis couldn't imagine for the life of her why the light was of such importance, but didn't comment, not wishing to betray any ignorance in front of her new neighbour.

"Rhiannon, you said?" He suddenly looked excited."The Welsh goddess of the horse?"

Mavis looked puzzled. "I don't know, actually. It's quite a popular name around here." Hastily, she changed the subject. Goddesses, indeed!

"I suppose you are busy decorating, is it?" she asked, her big brown eyes taking in all the violet, yellow and crimson marks on his hands and clothes. What gaudy colours with which to paint your house, she thought privately.

"Oh, no no no," laughed Seamus, his eyes crinkling engagingly in his tanned face. " If you're wondering about all this paint, 'tis because I paint. For a living. Pictures."

Mavis' eyes opened even wider."You mean, you're an artist?" she smiled. "What sort? Do you paint pictures of the countryside? Or of the sea?"

Seamus laughed again."Perhaps," he chuckled, "But then again, maybe not!"

Mavis laughed uncertainly, but Seamus was so friendly, so relaxed, that she couldn't help but open up and warm to his effervescent charm.

"So where's the pub around here, then?" he asked, his hands on his hips, looking about him as though he expected one to be hidden behind the hedge of Eira Jones' garden.

"Pub?" repeated Mavis , incredulously. She was amazed at this newcomer's direct and frank questions.

"Yes, the pub! Surely to God there is one in Thlannon?"

Mavis smiled at his attempt to pronounce the village's name correctly."Well, seeing as you are so keen, our one and only respectable pub is the Golden Hind (the Dappled Horse is nothing but a den of iniquity,) and it is just in front of the Protestant church in the centre of the village. It's terrible, really, some of those church-goers spill out of church after Holy Communion on a Sunday, and tumble straight into the pub! It isn't even supposed to be open! Shocking, if you ask me."

"I'm not." His reply was dry, to say the least, but his lips were twitching, amused at Mavis' intense disapproval.

Mavis blushed. "You see, I'm Baptist, and we don't drink — well, except at weddings."

"Ah," came his enigmatic reply, "well, I am neither Protestant nor Baptist, so would very much like to find this pub of yours. Care to join me?"

Mavis stared at him in disbelief. "At eleven in the morning?! And I am a married woman, who most certainly does not accept invitations from strange men!"

"Please yourself," he shrugged, and with that the charismatic stranger sauntered off down the lane, leaving a stunned Mavis watching him as he went.

His appearance was certainly bohemian, and his manner maverick in the extreme, but there was something very appealing about this man that Mavis couldn't quite explain. His gait was loose-limbed and graceful, his air was carefree and nonchalant. But terrible clothes. Mavis shook her head, and followed him at a much slower pace down the lane, keeping a wary distance between them both.

Llannon was particularly quiet this Friday morning, hardly any cars disturbed the tranquil village, and sleepy spring lambs lay down in the meadows alongside the main road, lulled into a soporific nap by the warmth of the sun, their fussy mothers keeping a watchful eye as always.

Eiddwen lived on the main road, in a small terraced house, the same house in which she had been born, and would probably die, alone and lonely.

Mavis knocked on the highly polished brown door, and went in. Her relationship with Eiddwen had developed over many years, and both women were used to this comfortable familiarity. The scent of lavender polish filled the air, and despite the sunny day, the house was dark and cool, being north-facing and overshadowed by the ancient oaks across the road.

"Hello!" called out Mavis, " It's me!"

A clattering of pots and pans heralded Eiddwen's entrance into the hallway. Her round face was flushed and she was wiping her hands on her apron. Friday was cawl-making day, and there were mountains of vegetables to be peeled before it could be started. Eiddwen, although a spinster, had a multitude of cousins, aunts and uncles, and provided their main meal most days of the week.

"Well, fancy you coming this morning!" she exclaimed, smiling happily, "Shall I put the kettle on?"

"That would be lovely, Eiddwen," Mavis replied, going through to the back-kitchen, the gegin fach.

As was typical of small Welsh houses, the front room was called the parlour and never used; all the best china and crystal was kept there and the odd coffin would lie in state there, when a death occurred in the family. The room beyond that was usually called the middle-room, where guests would be received, and a television, if one was wealthy enough to have one, would hold a position of great importance in the corner. The gegin fach, or kitchen, provided the house with a comfortable, womb-like warmth, and was usually heated by a coal fire or a Rayburn. A big wooden table ensured that everyone could be accommodated at mealtimes.

There was no need of a new-fangled refrigerator, as the pantry under the stairs was as cool and dark as was necessary. Lastly, the bathroom completed the downstairs layout, with sky-blue being considered the height of sophistication.

Mavis sat down on the ancient armchair next to the kitchen window. The sun streamed in, its beams making tiny particles of dust dance and twirl around in the atmosphere. Eiddwen busied herself with making the tea, and Mavis idly thumbed through last week's copy of the Llanelli Star, only interested in the marriages column.

"The old Richards house has been sold, then," announced Eiddwen, pouring boiling water into the huge brown teapot.

Mavis smiled to herself. "Yes," she murmured, "I know. In fact, I just met the new owner."

"Well, i Duw, Duw! You never did!" Eiddwen's eyes couldn't have opened any wider. "How much did it go for? What's she like?"

"I have no idea what it sold for," replied Mavis, then added smugly, "And she is in fact a he."

"Ooh!" squeaked Eiddwen in excitement, dropping the tea-strainer, giving Mavis her undivided attention.

Mavis said nothing, but continued her perusal of the newspaper. She laughed inwardly, knowing that Eiddwen would be unable to contain herself for much longer. True to form, Eiddwen abandoned any further tea pouring or vegetable peeling and sat down opposite Mavis.

"So what's he like, then?" she demanded, eagerly. Mavis paused for greater dramatic effect, then glanced slyly up at Eiddwen from under her long, dark lashes.

"Middle-aged, tall and as crazy as any Irishman could be."

"Irish?! He's Irish?"

"And what is more," continued Mavis, smiling, "He is an artist." Eiddwen gasped in astonishment, all attempts at hospitality suddenly and completely abandoned. Such devastatingly exciting news!

"Married?" she asked, breathlessly.

"How should I know, Eiddwen?" remonstrated Mavis, "Anyway, where's my cup of tea?" She didn't want to give away too much information too soon to Eiddwen. She may be married, but she didn't want to share this romantic newcomer with anyone else, not just yet.

Eiddwen knew that she wouldn't get any more titbits out of Mavis now, judging by the pursed, pink lips on her friend's closed face. She sighed, poured the tea, and cut a couple of slices of bara brith for the two of them.

"Don't butter mine, Eiddwen," ordered Mavis imperiously.

"Why ever not?" protested Eiddwen, the butter knife half-way to the slices of tea-bread.

"A moment on the lips, a lifetime on the hips, Eiddwen. You know that. Nobody else is going to look after my figure, so it is up to me to do so." Mavis smoothed her hands over her slim waist, to emphasise the point.

Eiddwen looked down at her own ample hips in sorrow. She had no will power whatsoever. Maybe, if she gave up butter, she would have a figure like Mavis, and would get herself a man.

The golden butter glistened temptingly in the dish, and any self-control that Eiddwen may have had went flying out of the kitchen window. She buttered the tea-bread thickly. Her diet could start tomorrow.

The two women continued to discuss the latest gossip, Hannah Evans' new Mini car (bright red, such an ostentatious colour,) that hussy Mab Price's dalliance with the milkman (everyone was talking about them) and the Davies children having whooping cough.

At half-past twelve, Mavis got up to go. "I can't stay any longer, Eiddwen," she announced. "Ernest wants us to go down to Llanelli to visit his son this afternoon, and see the grandchildren. His daughter-in-law isn't well. Influenza, I think."

"Oh, all right then," replied Eiddwen, disappointed at the brevity of the visit, yet relieved she could get on with the cawl-making. "Still, should be a nice afternoon out, it's such a lovely day."

"Yes, it is," agreed Mavis, although she was not looking forward to the planned trip at all. She did not get on terribly well with her husband's family. His son Fred had married a Llanelli girl and the pair and their two young children lived with his in-laws in the town. Mavis did not like or understand young children. They either reproduced their insides over one's expensive clothes, or they screamed incessantly, disrupting adult conversation and making a mess, which Mavis was most certainly not going to clear up.

As Mavis walked home, huge grey clouds were gathering in the western sky, and a chill wind started blowing along the lane to the cottage. There was no sign of her new neighbour. Mavis assumed he was in the pub, drinking......

She sighed. Such decadent behaviour. And yet..... Part of her longed for some decadence, to be wild, excited and, if she was honest with herself, free.

By the time she arrived back at the cottage, the sky was leaden , and spring had disappeared, it seemed, forever. The wind had whisked itself into an uncertain turbulence, and the temperature had plummeted . Mavis rushed to light the coal fire, ready and waiting as always, the neatly folded newspaper placed at the bottom of the grate and the carefully stacked sticks and coal on top.

It was now almost two o'clock. Ernest would be home shortly. The funeral had been at eleven, and Ernest would have stayed a little while for the tea and sandwiches in the Sunday School hall, but he would have disliked having to make pointless conversation with all the mourners. Privately, Mavis thought that the mourners should be called the "moaners" as all they did was complain and make irritatingly depressing remarks about the quality of the tea provided by the bereaved. Still, it was none of her business. As long as her husband continued to sustain his esteemed position in village society, and they remained prominently respectable, she was happy enough. Or was she? All too frequently her restless mind considered her relationship with Ernest. Was it right to live her life stifled and suffocated, having exchanged one unyielding lifestyle for another? Mavis shook her head, turning her attention instead to the footsteps on the garden path. Ernest was home.

He entered the kitchen by the back door, wiping his black-booted feet fastidiously on the coconut mat before entering the cool, dark room. His serious expression lowered the temperature even further, his cold blue eyes a reminder of the recent harsh winter.

"How was the funeral, cariad?" asked Mavis, tentatively, unable to read her husband's mood.

"It went." His terse reply discouraged any further conversation. Mavis busied herself with applying the bellows to the infantile fire, although the brisk wind outside should have provided enough stimulation. Ernest removed his black coat and hung it up on the back of the mahogany carver chair at the kitchen table.

"Would you like me to make you some sandwiches?" volunteered Mavis, refusing to be intimidated by Ernest's froideur.

"No need," he replied, "I have eaten already. Mrs Williams, the widow, invited me back for lunch." Mavis said nothing, but felt surprised. This was unheard of. Ernest never accepted invitations to dine or lunch with the bereaved. Still,

Mrs Williams was sixty-five, and as round as she was tall, no threat to the pretty Mavis. However, Mavis was puzzled at this strange behaviour of Ernest. She would tackle him about this later, choosing her moment carefully. Having finished making the fire, she turned to her husband and asked, "What time do you want to leave for Llanelli?"

Ernest glanced at his pocket-watch, a beautiful gift from his mother when he became deacon.

"We shall leave at three o'clock," he decided, "Fred has to go be at the police station at six o'clock, he is on nights, so we can't leave it any later." Mavis nodded in agreement.

"It's very cold out there," he added, "you'll want to wear more that that cardigan."

Mavis smiled at her good fortune in the change in the weather. "Yes, I will have to wear something warm."

At half-past two, Mavis retreated upstairs to the bedroom. Taking her new fur coat out of the wardrobe, she slipped it on over her shoulders, looking with satisfaction at her reflection in the mirror. The door opened behind her and Ernest entered the room.

"Very nice," he commented, stiffly approving of his wife's appearance. "Now will you be ready to leave at three?"

"Of course," reassured Mavis, "Just let me comb my hair and put some more lipstick on, and I will be ready." Ernest frowned at the latter. He disapproved of make-up almost as much as he disapproved of alcohol. But Mavis was always discreet in her application, and he had to admit, it did suit her incredibly well. She may be of a rather frivolous nature, but Ernest remained proud of his wife's appearance, despite her occasional lapses from his strict Baptist ideals.

At three o'clock on the dot, Ernest and Mavis set off for Llanelli in their three-wheeled white Reliant Regal. The wind was howling by now, but thankfully it didn't rain. Mavis snuggled cosily into her coat, grateful for its warmth. The heater in the car had ceased to work about two years ago. Ernest did not think it was an essential function, so did nothing about it. The trees blew about alarmingly, and in the distance the water of the Burry Inlet was an angry, sombre grey. Just like Ernest's mood, thought Mavis to herself.

By twenty-past three, the car pulled up outside Number Ten, Victoria Street. The neat terraced house was just like all the others in the street; net curtains graced the bay window, and the small front garden was filled with orderly tulips and marigolds. Not a single weed dared show its face. The front step was well-scrubbed and the empty milk bottles sparkled with cleanliness. The door was opened by a sweet-faced woman in her late forties. Fred's mother-in-law.

"Hello," she greeted them, warmly, ushering them inside, "I thought I had heard the car. Come in."

"Good afternoon, Mrs Baker," replied Ernest, removing his hat and putting it on the banister.

"And how is poor Margaret today?" asked Mavis, solicitously.

"Oh, a little better, thank you," answered Gwyneth, "The doctor called this morning and has ordered her to stay in bed until her fever goes. And she should have peace and quiet, he said. Easier said than done with these two little blighters." And with that, two little girls came hurtling around the corner of the hallway, shrieking and laughing. Mavis cringed inwardly at the noise, thinking that it was just as well that these two children were blessed with astonishingly good looks, or they would have been utterly unbearable.

Aged six years old and eighteen months respectively, Wendy and Julie Watton were lively and excitable, particularly Wendy, the six year old. She had blonde curls, her grandfather's blue eyes, and a merry smile, whereas Julie was dark, rosy-cheeked and more serious. Just as the latter seemed poised to launch herself and her naked Sindy doll at Mavis' silk-stockinged legs, she was expertly scooped up by her grandmother.

"Sorry, Mrs Watton, she hasn't been out today, she's all wound up; I haven't had time to take her anywhere, there has been so much to do here, looking after Margaret." Gwyneth Baker was very flustered now, a striking contrast to Mavis' sleek appearance. Mavis didn't reply, but waited for Gwyneth to comment on her new fur coat. Gwyneth, however, seemed oblivious to the garment, and was paying more attention to the antics of Wendy, who was now trying to do forward rolls down the two bottom steps of the staircase.

"For goodness' sake, Wendy," remonstrated Gwyneth, her freckles disappearing under the
embarrassed flush that was spreading across her pale, plump cheeks, "Behave yourself, now, there's a good girl. Your Aunty Mavis has come to see you, and your Grandpa as well!"

Wendy stopped mid-forward roll, and looked up at Mavis, challengingly.

"Can you do a roly poly, Aunty Mavis?" she demanded, her piercing blue eyes meeting Mavis' directly.

"I most certainly cannot," replied Mavis, trying to smile at the cheeky six year old.

"Come in to the middle room," beckoned Gwyneth, anxiously. She was only too aware of her own appearance, her auburn hair escaping from its bun, damp tendrils framing her hot face, her apron straining at the waist.

Mavis' cool composure was in a different league to Gwyneth's distressed anxiety. Mavis regarded the whole scene with detachment, unwilling to become part of this domesticity, this chaotic and humdrum activity. She felt distanced from the family into which she had married.

Ernest and Mavis moved forward into the middle room, darkened by the lack of sun, gloomy and full of shadows. The important television stood in splendid and imperial isolation in the corner, its silent screen a muddy green, redundant during the day.

"Fred will be down in a minute," explained Gwyneth, " He is getting ready for work. Margaret is asleep. I was just going to bath little Julie." She looked extremely harassed.

There was a silence. Mavis resisted catching Ernest's eye, and avoided Gwyneth's look altogether. She had no intention whatsoever of assisting in the ablutions of young Julie, which would no doubt involve the possibility of getting splashed with water, the folding of nappies, safety pins, messy talcum powder and the application of Vaseline onto various infantile parts, which was best left to mothers and grandmothers.

"We will wait here until Fred comes down," announced Ernest, solemnly, taking a seat on the beige armchair, settling his head comfortably against the brightly embroidered antimacassar. Nobody asked Mavis to sit down. She remained standing, undecided as to whether she should remove her fur coat.

"Ooh! I like your coat, Aunty Mavis," announced Wendy, moving towards Mavis, her jam-covered hand outstretched to stroke the garment. Therefore the decision was simple. Off came the coat, and Mavis pointedly took it out into the hallway to hang it carefully on the banister along with her husband's hat.

"Yes," answered Mavis, returning to the middle room, "it is new. I went all the way up to London to buy it."

"How much did it cost? Did it cost hundreds of pounds?" demanded Wendy, her wicked blue eyes sparkling with mischief as she danced a jig around the unresponsive Mavis.

"Wendy!" scolded her grandmother, "Don't be so rude! That's a very naughty thing to ask!"

"Why, Nana?" she persisted, dancing all the while, "Why is it naughty?"

"Because little girls should be seen and not heard," interjected Mavis, feeling a slight headache developing as a result of all this boisterous and childish behaviour

"I would make some tea," apologised Gwyneth, "but I really must bath young Julie first. Please, come and sit in the gegin fach, at least I will be able to talk to you while I sort this little devil out." Mavis thought privately that of the two girls, Julie seemed the least devil-like. She watched Mavis solemnly out of dark green eyes, no smile on her chubby face. Into the kitchen they trooped. Mavis and Ernest sat down at the table. Wendy stopped jigging about and settled down quietly to play with her doll, dressing it in an old yellow duster. There was an awkward silence.

Gwyneth busied herself with filling the big pink plastic tub with water, and set it down in front of the coal fire. The kitchen door opened, and a slim dark man in his late twenties walked in.

"Hello, Fred!" greeted Gwyneth in relief. "We have visitors and your two little scamps are being as naughty as they possibly can!"

"Afternoon, Dad," he greeted his father, "And how are you, Mavis?"

"Hello, Fred," replied Ernest, "Been busy this morning?"

"Been busy painting the new house. We hope to move in next month."

"Where is your new house again?" asked Mavis, "I can't remember where it is."

"Oh, you probably don't know the street, Mavis, but it is down past the railway station gates. Number eighteen, Nightingale Street," answered Fred, shortly, turning his attention away from Mavis, who felt slighted at his abrupt reply.

"Would you like to go upstairs and see Margaret?" asked Gwyneth, keen to be rid of her prim and disapproving audience.

"Oh, I don't think we had better," decided Mavis, with a concerned look on her face, "She needs her rest, I don't want to disturb her."

Ernest and Mavis continued to sit and watch while Gwyneth struggled to bath an objecting Julie; Fred made some tea and ham sandwiches for the guests.

The visit lasted just over an hour, and at last the Wattons got up to go.

"Well, it's been lovely to see you," said Gwyneth with as much honesty as she could muster.

"When are you going to come and visit us?" asked Mavis. She liked having visitors, even if it meant the two children coming too, as there was nothing she enjoyed more than showing off her pretty little cottage, with its expensive furniture and immaculate garden. An unspoken, unacknowledged battle was constantly being fought between the Mrs Baker and Mavis Watton as to who could be the most house proud.

"Well, Raymond will be receiving his new car next week," announced Gwyneth, proudly. At last a chance to outshine that snooty Mavis! "We shall visit you as soon as it arrives!"

Mavis' eyes narrowed. Nothing could persuade Ernest to part with his three-wheeler. She resigned herself to the fact that the Bakers had the upper hand here.

"We shall look forward to seeing you, then." Her smile somewhat lacked sincerity.

The journey home passed in silence, Ernest gripping the wheel tightly as the rain beat down on the windscreen, the wipers monotonously sweeping the heavy drops away relentlessly as curious thoughts kept on invading Mavis' mind. Her monotonous life seemed to be choking all the joy out of her. Things seemed so complicated today. She used to be satisfied with being the Queen Bee, viewed and regarded by the village as the smartest, prettiest woman in Llannon, envied by her spinster sisters and the other single women.

But is that important, she asked herself, is that what I want? Do I need more than this? Is it right that I live in this cold prison of a marriage? The Bakers seemed so happy and content, warmth and love seemed to radiate from their chaotic home. Why can't Ernest and I be like them? What is wrong with my life?

What she didn't realise was that her life was actually just beginning.

Chapter Four

Strategic Schemes

The unseasonally cold May weather continued for the next few days, with rain thrown in for good measure, so Mavis' activities were significantly curtailed . The little cottage was festooned with damp laundry, the smell of detergent filled the air, and any hopes of a sociable walk down into the village remained unrealised. Mavis hated going out in the rain, aware of the unflattering effect it had on her smooth, dark hair. Like a cat, she made only necessary excursions, and these were usually as brief as possible. Ernest didn't believe in taking his car out for short trips, so if Mavis wished to go out, she would have to walk. The rain poured down incessantly, shrouding the cottage in a grey, miserable curtain, rendering the village invisible, making Mavis feel lonely and isolated.

At nine o'clock on Tuesday morning, she was due to go to work, so set off down the lane, valiantly battling the downpour with a smart red umbrella, patterned with white flowers. She cursed as she dodged the puddles, not wishing her shiny black patent shoes to be spoiled.

As she passed the old Richards house (she supposed it should now be called the O'Brien house) she glanced up at the front windows, furtively scanning them in case Seamus could be seen, using her umbrella to shield her inquisitive eyes.

However, there was no sign of him. No dishevelled head was visible through the dusty windows, no lanky figure was moving about, doing whatever artists did....

Mavis sighed. Then she shook herself impatiently. Why on earth should she care? He was only a newcomer. But a rather romantic rogue, she thought, smiling again, as a marvellous idea popped into her head.

Of course, she must act like the kindly neighbour she was! She would bake a cake (or rather, get Eiddwen to make one for her) and take it round to Mr

O'Brien, to welcome him to the village. Thus inspired, she continued her journey to the sweet-shop, entering its spicy-smelling depths with a satisfied smile upon her face.

"Bore da!" she called out, cheerfully, shaking her wet umbrella outside the door.

"Bore da, Mrs Watton," replied Mr Griffiths, the shopkeeper, immaculate as ever in his white shirt, protected by his brown dust coat, "Dreadful weather for the time of year, isn't it?"

"Yes, terrible, Mr Griffiths," she agreed, removing her bottle-green PVC mackintosh and hanging it up behind the blue curtain which separated the shop from the rest of the house. As she donned her floral pinafore, she looked quickly at the list Mr Griffiths was reading at the counter.

"What time can I expect the delivery this morning?" she asked, pinning up her dark curls into a neat chignon.

"Around eleven, I expect," he answered, "I have to go down into Llanelli today, I have an appointment with the bank manager. Can you manage on your own?"

"Of course," replied Mavis confidently, starting to open up the till, emptying last week's takings into little bags. Griffiths' sweet-shop was thriving, the post-war desire for sweet and toothsome confectionery was more than evident in Llannon. Jar after jar of boiled sweets, winter candy, sherbet lemons and Everton mints stood in perfect, sparkling order along the shelves, like a regiment of Welsh Guards awaiting inspection.

Mavis enjoyed her part-time job. Mr Griffiths was easy-going, his wife worked as a district midwife, and out more often than not. Like Mavis, the Griffiths couple didn't have any children. However, the hordes of hungry youngsters which poured into the shop, particularly after school, more than made up for that.

As well as selling sweets, Mr Griffiths also sold tobacco and cigarettes, something Mavis disapproved of. However, she was paid to work, and if that included the sale of tobacco and the like, so be it. Ernest remained unhappy about this aspect of his wife's job, and every so often could be heard muttering to himself, "Tobacco is a filthy weed, and from the devil doth proceed, it stains your fingers, burns your nose and makes a chimney of your nose!"

Mr Griffiths left for Llanelli at ten o'clock, braving the rain on his scooter, his wife having started her rounds two hours earlier in their grey Morris Minor.

Mavis busied herself with dusting the counter and sweeping the floor, mindful of the fact that come four o'clock it would be patterned with the muddy footprints of the schoolchildren during their sweetshop expedition on the way home. As she organised and cleaned, her thoughts wandered, meandering in particular around Seamus O'Brien. Mavis couldn't understand why he should keep on creeping into her daydreams all the time. Yes, he was quite good-looking, in an untidy, carefree sort of way, but not her type at all. Obviously he wasn't short of a bob or two (as Eiddwen liked to put it) or he wouldn't have been able to afford the Richards house. Mavis remembered those twinkling blue eyes, as warm and friendly as her husbands' were cold and remote. She recalled the way those wicked eyes had scanned her completely, up and down, taking her in, assessing her....she wondered what he had thought of her.

Reluctantly, her thoughts returned to the present, and the imminent arrival of the delivery man, but not before she remembered her husband's unexpected lunch with the widow the previous week. Now why on earth had he done that? It was so out of character, Ernest really disliked socialising after a funeral. Mavis decided to pursue this line of enquiry after supper that evening, when Ernest would be well-fed and in a reasonable mood.

At eleven o'clock on the dot, the door opened, and a man's cheerful voice called out,

"Delivery for Mr Griffiths!"

"Come in, come in out of the rain!" replied Mavis, hurrying to hold the door open for the delivery man.

A splatter of raindrops accompanied the man as he staggered in with two large cardboard boxes.

"Put them on the floor, if you don't mind," she ordered bossily, "I have just polished the counter."

Irritably obeying her command, the delivery man dropped the boxes in front of Mavis, saying "Alright to leave them there? Are you sure you don't want them delivered around the back?"

Then he looked up and saw Mavis properly, appreciating her hourglass figure, which even a pink flowery pinafore couldn't disguise and he smiled. Mavis stood there, like a miniature Venus, her hands on her hips and her dark eyes sparkling with annoyance at the casual attitude of the delivery man, who seemed to have total disregard for her newly swept floor.

"Very well, bring them around the back if you want." replied Mavis ungraciously, turning around with her nose in the air, and leading the way through the blue curtain, " Follow me."

Like a hound tracking a scent, he followed Mavis, peeping over the top of the boxes at the undulating hips and the shapely legs as she strutted into the storeroom behind the shop.

"Put them on the floor, please," she instructed, pulling out the order sheet from her pocket, "I will check it all before you leave."

"No chance of a cup of tea, then?" asked the man, hopefully, removing his cap and shaking the raindrops onto the storeroom floor. Mavis looked at him disdainfully. She did not consort with delivery men. Who on earth did he think he was?

"This is not my house, I'm afraid," she announced briskly, "And I have a lot of work to do, so if you'll excuse me...." She turned away and started to open one of the boxes.

"You married?" came the next question.

Mavis swung round, her mouth a pink and perfect 'O' as her fury exploded. "What an impertinent question!"

The delivery man laughed. "Well, are you or aren't you?" he persisted, smiling craftily.

Mavis was taken aback. She had expected the man either to make a hasty retreat or to offer some retort himself. She looked at him more closely. He was quite tall, heavily built, with light green eyes and a mop of sandy hair. His cheeky grin practically split his ruddy face in two. As for his accent, Mavis reckoned he must be from Swansea, judging by the length of his vowels.

"Well, since you seem so interested, yes I am married," she stated, glaring at him haughtily.

"Lucky bloke, your other half!" laughed the man. "He certainly wouldn't be happy if he knew you were entertaining delivery men in dark storerooms!"

Mavis gasped at his audacity, but had no time to reply as he grabbed her waist and pulled her to him quickly, pressing his lips to hers, forcing his tongue into her mouth. His other hand swiftly found its way to her left breast and squeezed it hard. Gasping for breath, Mavis wrenched herself away, and slapped his left cheek hard.

"Stop it!" she hissed, "I will scream for help if you do that again!"

But the man just laughed, rubbing his cheek slowly. His right arm continued to encircle her waist, and he held her tightly. His hot breath smelled of cheap mouthwash and onions, and there was a determined look in his pale eyes.

"Oh, I'm not going to let you go that easily," he murmured, "And don't pretend you didn't enjoy it, Everyone knows what you village women are like, a shortage of men around here, and given half a chance you'd all drop your knickers for any Tom, Dick or Harry!" And he stroked her hair roughly, swiftly pulling out all the pins.

Furiously, Mavis tried to bite his hand, but in doing so lost her balance, falling down onto a pile of sacking. She shouted in pain as her wrist knocked against a wooden case.

"C'mon, you little tease," he laughed, "You know you want it!"

"Leave me alone, you idiot!" Mavis felt a wave of panic surging through her, "Mr Griffiths will be back soon! He will catch you and report you!"

"Mr Griffiths won't catch you, but I certainly have!" An angry voice from the doorway stopped the delivery man in his tracks. Swinging around, panic replaced the lust on his heavy features. Mavis took a sharp intake of breath, for standing there, with a furious look on his face, was none other than Seamus O'Brien.

"Piss off, you fecking bastard!" Seamus took a few steps closer, his manner threatening and angry. The delivery man lost no time at all in trying to beat a hasty exit back to his lorry, but not before Seamus lunged towards his retreating back, grabbing his collar and his arm, forcefully throwing him out of the door, sending him crashing into the rubbish bin outside, denting it and tipping it over.

The man scrambled hastily into the driver's seat of the lorry, all the while muttering,

"She was asking for it, the bitch..." He drove away, grinding the gearbox, keen to put as much distance between him and this angry Irish giant.

Mavis was mortified. What a state to be found in. Seamus looked at her intently. Her dark hair was cascading around her shoulders, her skirt was rucked up, revealing the most delectable legs encased by sheer silk stockings, with the tiniest glimpse of bare, white flesh visible. God, she was lovely.

"Are you all right?" he demanded, going over to Mavis and helping her up to her feet. Breathlessly, Mavis turned to him, attempting a smile.

"I'm fine." she lied, feeling sick inside. "But I promise you, I did nothing at all to encourage him. He just launched himself at me out of the blue!"

Seamus looked concerned. "Did he, I mean, did he manage to...?"

Mavis blushed furiously. "No! Of course he didn't!" She was trembling, he noticed.

"Just as well I happened to walk in then, isn't it?" he responded, with a wry smile.

"It most certainly was." Mavis struggled to maintain her composure, tugging down her skirt and pinning up her hair.

"Don't do that," said Seamus unexpectedly, "it looks much better loose."

Mavis looked at him in surprise, but allowed her hair to remain curling around her shoulders, framing her heart-shaped face. There was an awkward silence between them, and Mavis looked away eventually, feeling the colour rushing to her face again.

"Shouldn't you go and have a lie-down?" asked Seamus solicitously, "Have a cup of tea or something? Do you want me to report him?"

"No, I'll be all right," replied Mavis bravely, "No harm done really. I doubt he'll be back, not if he values his job." Inside she was a quivering wreck, and she longed to rush home and brush her teeth. Hard. But her determination to deal with and forget the unfortunate event was foremost in her mind.

"Anyway," she continued, briskly, "You have obviously come in here to buy something, and I shouldn't be keeping you waiting like this." She led the way back into the shop, with Seamus following her, appreciating the same view as the delivery man had done only ten minutes earlier.

Safely behind the counter once more, Mavis regained her authority. She stood up straight and tossed her head.

"So," she began, "How may I help you, Mr O'Brien?"

"Oh, no no no!" he laughed, "Please! Call me Seamus! Seeing as we are to be neighbours!"

"Very well, Seamus," she smiled, "What is it that you require?"

"Some cigarettes." His sharp blue eyes scanned the shelves and the counter. "I can't see any Gauloises, do you have any?"

"Gauloises?" asked Mavis, rather puzzled, "What are they?"

"Cigarettes," he explained, "French."

"Oh, dear me!" Mavis looked dismayed. "We don't sell those, I am afraid!"

Seamus looked mildly irritated. "I thought it would be pretty easy to get Gauloises here," he grumbled. "What do you suggest instead?"

"Pall Mall is a very popular brand around here," suggested Mavis tentatively, reaching for the distinctive red packet in the glass cabinet behind her, "Go on, 'Reward Yourself!' That's what it says on the advert!" She giggled wickedly. Seamus grinned back.

"They'll do," he decided, "All I know is I haven't had a bloody fag all morning, and I am fecking gasping for a drag!" Mavis felt shocked at this total disregard of polite speech. However, she hurriedly pretended not to appear shocked at all, keen to seem sophisticated and mature after her disappointing ignorance of French cigarettes.

"That'll be one and six. Would you like a paper bag for them?" Mavis assumed that it was indeed a shameful activity, and that Seamus would prefer to conceal his decadent habit from the rest of Llannon's chapel-going community.

"No need for a bag," he replied, putting his money on the counter and taking the cigarettes. "I'll be off then, see you around!" And with that he sauntered out through the door, ignoring the downpour as if it wasn't happening at all.

"Goodbye," whispered Mavis forlornly, disappointment filling her heart. Strange, she thought, how only five minutes ago she felt ecstatically happy, and now she was feeling melancholic.

Sighing, Mavis set about the mundane task of opening the newly-delivered boxes and stocking the shelves, trying with some difficulty to put Seamus O'Brien to the back of her restless mind.

Mr Griffiths returned at lunchtime, and the rest of Mavis' working day passed uneventfully. She did not mention the incident of the delivery man. The hordes of noisy children came and went, leaving a trail of raindrops and black footprints in their wake.

At five o'clock, just as Mavis was setting off for home, the clouds dispersed and a watery sun put in an appearance. Shaking her unrestrained hair, Mavis headed west and walked up the hill towards the main road and home. Home. To Ernest and whatever mood he happened to be in.

The struggling sun soon warmed up the wet grass, and Mavis watched the steam rising in hopeful spirals as she trudged up the lane to her cottage. Early bluebells, recovering from the deluge, lifted their drooping heads once more, as though forgiving Nature for her unkindness.

Mavis' eyes were unable to resist the temptation of glancing surreptitiously at Seamus' house as she walked past. There was no sign of him. Mavis wondered where he could be in that great pile of stone, which room was he in, what he was doing...? Was he painting? Smoking? Drinking? Or even all three?

Just as Mavis was about to drag her thoughts away from the Irishman, she caught sight of someone hurrying down Seamus' garden path. Instantly, Mavis' radar was on full alert. A fair-haired woman was making her way towards the gate, saying goodbye to whoever stood at the door.

Mavis quickly hid herself behind a convenient lilac tree, in full bloom at this time of year. As the heady scent of the flowers filled her senses, Mavis was also filled with an overpowering feeling of jealousy. Who could this woman be? A stab of envy pierced her heart. She continued watching, as Seamus' visitor continued her walk down the lane, turning to wave as she went.

The woman appeared to be in her mid-thirties, with bobbed blond hair, lots of pale pink lipstick and lashings of thick black eyeliner. She was taller than Mavis, and quite plump. Mavis observed the mystery woman as she reached the main road, swinging her curvy bottom from side to side in a very wanton manner, or so was Mavis' opinion. Not wishing to be discovered, she waited until the woman had disappeared around the corner and Seamus had retreated inside.

Continuing her way home, her thoughts were reeling. Surely Seamus wouldn't have got to know a local woman so quickly? He had only moved in the previous week. Never in her life had Mavis experienced such a wave of alternating emotions. It made her feel quite exhausted, and she was glad to arrive at her garden gate.

Ernest was already home, his muddy boots were on the back-door mat. Mavis opened the wooden door, firstly removing her erstwhile shiny patent shoes, which were now also mud-splashed, matching Ernest's boots quite nicely. Entering the dimly-lit kitchen, Mavis found Ernest sipping tea by the fire, sitting in his favourite armchair, the Watton family Bible open on his lap.

"Preparing for Sunday already, cariad?" asked Mavis, removing her coat and tying an apron around her waist. Ernest peered up at her from over his spectacles.

"Of course," he replied, pompously, "It's always a good idea to be well-prepared. What's for supper?" Mavis paused. She had originally planned to throw together a quick ham salad with new potatoes, but, knowing her husband's weakness for comfort food, she decided instead to make a beef stew with mash, in order to appeal to his better nature.

"Beef stew and mashed potatoes!" she announced cheerfully, watching his reaction. Ernest brightened visibly.

"Excellent!" he responded, "just the thing."

She felt surprised, as Ernest never praised her much. It was short-lived, however, and he soon became absorbed again in next Sunday's sermon.

By seven o'clock, supper was ready, and the couple sat opposite each other at the heavy kitchen table, the setting sun casting a rosy glow on Mavis' face, which was already flushed from cooking. The silence was only broken by a rogue bumble bee, which had found its way into the Watton's cottage and was now trying to escape through the net curtains at the small window. Ernest clasped his hands together and closed his eyes.

"For what we are about to receive, may the Lord make us truly thankful. Amen."

"Amen, "repeated Mavis dutifully, thinking privately that Ernest should thank her instead, after she had sweated an hour over a hot stove. How glad she felt that Seamus couldn't see her right now, with her hair tied back in its customary bun, damp tendrils escaping and framing her hot face. They ate without speaking, as was their habit. The grandfather clock ticked away on the wall. Putting his knife and fork together, Ernest finally looked up at his wife.

"Very nice, my dear, you certainly know how to satisfy a man." Mavis smiled wryly. Do I, indeed, she thought to herself. Taking advantage of Ernest's good mood, Mavis got up to pour him another cup of tea, solicitously putting two sugars in his cup and stirring it for him.

"So," she started, smiling sweetly, "Any news from the widow last week? You said you had had lunch at her house."

"Oh, yes," he replied, "I had quite forgotten. Pleasant lady, Mrs Williams. Not a very good cook, though. Her potatoes were like bullets and the mutton was as tough as an old boot." Mavis peered at her husband over her cup of tea, trying to read his mood. Ernest seemed happy enough, so she continued her line of enquiry.

"So what did you talk about, then?"

"Oh, Mrs Williams, poor soul, she wanted to know if her daughter could take up the vacancy of organist at the chapel. Gladys is an accomplished organist and has passed many examinations."

"I see," responded Mavis, carefully, " Have you heard her play?"

"Of course." Ernest looked rather more irritable now. "She played at the funeral." Mavis looked aghast.

"At her own father's funeral? How could she?"

"She played very well. A cool and collected young lady is Gladys Williams."

"Young, you say? How old is she then?"

"Now how would I know?" Ernest was getting quite cross at this interrogation. "All I know is that she went to school the same time as Eiddwen's niece, Angharad."

"That would make her about thirty-five, then," pondered Mavis aloud

"So it would seem," said Ernest firmly, ending the conversation as he got up from the table. "I'm going to go down to make sure that the caretaker has locked the cemetery gates. He left them open last week. You cannot trust people these days, I don't know..." And with a heavy sigh, Ernest put on his jacket and shoes, and set off down the lane, leaving Mavis to deal with the washing up and the whirlpool of thoughts that were racing through her mind. She gazed with huge, puzzled brown eyes at the dying embers of the spring sun, trying to understand her turbulent emotions, her wild and wonderful thoughts.

Outside in the garden, a couple of hopeful blackbirds continued their symbiotic duet. Dusk settled like a deep, rosy veil over the apple trees, rendering the blossom a vivid and passionate flamingo pink. Mavis switched on the table lamp. Ernest disapproved of unnecessary waste of energy, and the cottage was often cold and dimly lit. Shivering slightly, Mavis took a final glance at her pristine kitchen, then turned and climbed the narrow staircase to the bedroom. Slowly undressing, she watched her refection in the wardrobe mirror. Who was she, this woman who stared back at her? Mavis dragged her reluctant eyes away and she pulled on her white cotton nightdress, buttoning it to the chin.

Maybe, she thought to herself, it would keep out the draft and the icy blast she so often felt from her stern and devoutly-religious husband. Putting her red dressing gown on, Mavis crept downstairs once more. It was now half-past eight and getting darker in the gloomy kitchen. So many lofty trees guarded the little cottage that it was frequently curtained in a secretive and dappled twilight. Despondently, she put the milk to heat on the Rayburn, preparing two mugs in readiness for Ernest's return. Putting the cocoa powder into the blue and white striped mugs, she added an extra sugar for Ernest, for that was how he preferred his bedtime cocoa. The moon shyly put in appearance in the rear kitchen window, and Mavis hurriedly looked away - bad luck to see the new moon through glass. However, the gentle moonlight persisted in finding a wistful Mavis; despite its sliver of silver, Lady Luna found enough power to caress that stubborn and proud little face, softening it, bathing it in a glow that maybe was already there...

Ernest returned ten minutes later. There was a scuffling, a strange whimpering. Mavis rushed to the back-door. To her amazement, her husband stood there, clutching a small ball of white fluff, which displayed a shiny nose and a small pink tongue.

"Oh, Ernest," she sighed, "What have you done?"

Chapter Five

The Fosterling

Mavis looked at her husband in astonishment, unable to believe her eyes. In his arms lay an adorable white Alsation puppy, its pink tongue hanging out, licking Ernest's hands and chin at every opportunity.

"Where did you get him?" asked Mavis, clutching her red dressing gown closer around her shivering body. The warmth of the May evening had evaporated as soon as the sun had set behind the hills of the Gwendraeth valley. Ernest clasped the puppy closer to his chest, as though afraid he would be stolen from him.

"Llew the Coal," came the curt explanation, "He was parking his lorry outside the Bowen's farm. Found this poor little blighter tied up to the gate. No-one else around. Yelping and whimpering. So he's ours, now, Mavis, and he shall be called Dai."

And that was that. Ernest strode into the cottage, holding Dai tightly to him. Mavis scuttled in after him, unsure of the situation. She knew nothing about dogs, although she was well aware that Ernest was an experienced dog handler, with an established fondness for white Alsations. Privately she wished that he was rather more experienced and loving in other ways...

"Where will he sleep, Ernest?" she enquired anxiously, looking around the small kitchen. Her desire for an orderly, tidy house was uppermost in her mind, and here was Ernest, bringing a potentially messy puppy into her pristine domain. Ernest, however, only had eyes for the little dog, nestling in his arms.

"Oh, he will sleep by the fire," he replied, absently, "As long as he is warm and fed, he will settle in well enough. Now, fetch me an old blanket, and an empty biscuit tin. And are there any leftovers from supper? I expect this little chap could do with a bite to eat."

Mavis sighed and turned around, rolling her eyes behind Ernest's back, and obediently rushed off to the outhouse, where she kept sacks of potatoes, the clothes horse and various unsightly items which were not considered attractive enough to keep in the cottage itself. She rummaged around amidst the old newspapers and discarded curtains, and succeeded in finding a large, grey towel and a battered saucepan.

"They'll do," she murmured to herself, and with pursed lips and an air of martyrdom, she returned to the kitchen, where her husband was sitting in his favourite chair, stroking the puppy and talking to him softly.

"If only Ernest would treat me like that," thought Mavis wistfully. Aloud, she said, "I hope he is house trained, Ernest, I don't want a mess on the floor tomorrow morning."

Ernest ignored her, and busied himself with preparing a bed for Dai, folding up the towel and placing it close to the fireplace.

"This towel is a bit hard," he grumbled, "What about the rug that is on the settle in the parlour? That is a great deal softer."

That was the final straw. Mavis flashed a spirited glance at her husband, saying, "The towel is perfectly suitable, Ernest. The dog will be quite comfortable on the towel. He is a dog, not a human."

Ernest did not challenge her, and continued to fuss over the puppy, putting leftover beef stew into the old saucepan, which Dai inspected carefully, sniffing it cautiously, then, happy that it seemed very nice indeed, gobbled it all up, splashing drops of gravy on the tiled floor. Ernest observed the young dog with distinct pleasure, his normal fastidious manner seeming to have evaporated with the arrival of the little stray animal.

Mavis sighed inwardly. How could she possibly compete with this cute newcomer? Leaving Ernest to his canine attentions, she climbed the narrow staircase to the cold and unwelcoming bedroom, forgetting the cocoa in her desire to seek sleep and oblivion.

Looking out through her bedroom window at the garden below, she watched a fox slowly slink out of the hydrangea bush, sniffing the grass, looking around nervously. An owl hooted through the spring twilight. Peace reigned over the valley, and all was quiet, but Mavis' heart was in a turmoil.

Eventually, rearranging the crisp cotton pillowslip for the umpteenth time, sleep overcame her, and she dreamed of puppies, organists and castles in Ireland.

It wasn't the spring sun which woke Mavis the next morning, but a cacophony of whining and barking. Ernest lay with his back to her, snoring gently, oblivious to the sounds drifting up the stairs from the kitchen. Mavis slipped like a wraith from the bed, putting on slippers and dressing gown, then she quietly crept downstairs to the kitchen, glancing briefly at the landing clock as she went.

Six o'clock. She usually rose early. This was her favourite time of day, the quiet and solitude were her close companions. Her bedtime hair hung in a dark, unruly plait over her slim shoulder, and her unmade-up face was pale and strangely childlike in the embryonic light of the new day. With extreme caution, Mavis entered the kitchen, uncertain and a little anxious about what may await her eyes. However, she smiled when she saw the comical scene in front of the fireplace. Dai was sitting bolt upright on the towel, his pink tongue hanging out joyfully, with all the cushions from the kitchen chairs arranged in a neat circle around him. He had certainly had a good night's sleep. There was no mess to be seen, and no malodorous scent reached Mavis' sensitive nose. Dai's long, plumy tail beat a steady tattoo on the floor. He seemed very pleased to see her. Mavis felt she should let the puppy out into the garden, so he could do whatever puppies needed to do, but she was afraid he would run away. Resourceful as ever, Mavis rummaged around in her "odds and ends" drawer, and, having found a length of string, she tied it around Dai's soft, white neck, put on a pair of Ernest's old boots, and led him out into the sunlit garden, stumbling slightly as her size three feet slopped about in the size nine boots.

Mr and Mrs Blackbird were rehearsing their early morning duet, and the sweet perfume of apple blossom filled the air. However, Dai was oblivious to the beauty of the scene, and busied himself with snuffling about on the damp grass, excited no doubt by the scent of the fox from the previous night. Mavis hung on to the string, patiently waiting for Dai to perform. Finally, her patience was rewarded.

"Good boy, Dai!" she exclaimed, patting the young dog on the head. Dai looked up at her adoringly with his big brown eyes, panting slightly. Mavis decided that Dai wasn't too much of a problem after all.

Her new-found pleasure in the little fosterling was short-lived, though, as Dai spied one of the Wattons' resident squirrels who had dared to climb down from the apple tree. Without any warning, and with incredible strength, Dai launched himself at the pesky squirrel, pulling Mavis after him. The grass was still quite wet, and Mavis suddenly slipped in her ill-fitting boots, landing in an undignified heap on the muddy ground, her dressing gown flying open, and her nightdress flapping open at the neck.

"DAI!" she shrieked crossly, "You stupid dog!"

"Now what's that poor dog done to warrant such a vitriolic response from its owner?" came a familiar Irish voice from beyond the hedge.

Mavis gasped in horror, for there was the amused face of Seamus O'Brien peeping at her, his eyes crinkled up with laughter at the sight of Mavis sitting on the wet grass, and Dai panting and straining at the leash.

"Er, hello..." she stammered, embarrassed at being caught once again on the ground with her clothes in disarray. Mavis clambered to her feet, trying to regain her composure.

"Um, your nightdress...?" remarked Seamus, grinning, his merry eyes fixed on her chest. Mavis glanced down, only to see that her nightdress had now become even more undone, and the Irishman was being treated to the unexpected view of Mavis' small but pert breasts bobbing about in unrestrained freedom. She hurriedly grabbed the neckline of that problematic garment closer to her.

"Well, I'll be getting back in the house, now," she announced decidedly.

"You do that," laughed Seamus, "Tis a wee bit cold to be gadding about in your nightwear, don't you think?"

"Whatever are you doing wandering about at this hour, anyway?" flashed back Mavis with spirit, "Spying on your neighbours and mocking them!"

Seamus merely chuckled to himself, waved his hand cheerfully at her, and sauntered off down the lane, leaving a furious Mavis behind him.

She returned to the cottage, fed the puppy some more leftovers, and went upstairs to get dressed, her thoughts in a whirl. How very unfortunate to have been caught in an embarrassing situation by Seamus for the second time within a few days!

The rest of the week flew by, Dai settled in nicely with the Wattons, and Ernest took the lion's share of looking after him.

Mavis paid Eiddwen another visit on Saturday afternoon, and asked her to bake her a cake. She mentioned nothing about Seamus's chivalrous rescue in the sweetshop, and did not tell Eiddwen about last Wednesday's early morning fall in the garden.

"Well, Mavis, what sort of cake did you have in mind?" asked Eiddwen, all agog, sitting on the edge of her chair in the warm, snug kitchen. Mavis sat back comfortably in her armchair, and sipped her tea thoughtfully.

"I suppose it is too late to make a fruit cake by Monday, is it?" she asked, hopefully, thinking that she would be able to pop the cake down to Seamus' house after Ernest had left for a chapel meeting on Monday morning. "You are such an angel with your cakes, I could never make one as well as you!" The reality was that Mavis had never baked a cake in her life, and neither had she any plans to.

"It is a bit short notice, Mavis," replied Eiddwen anxiously, not wishing to disappoint her friend. "I don't have all the ingredients I need, and it would need a week at least to mature. Plus..." and here Eiddwen lowered her voice to a whisper, "...I would need to go into Llanelli to buy the sherry to add to it!"

Mavis sighed. A plump, juicy fruit cake with a hint of spice and plenty of sherry would have been just the thing for an Irishman who liked his drink.

"Never mind," she relented, "A Victoria sponge will do just as well."

"Oh, but I could make some bara brith." suggested Eiddwen, excitedly, "Or what about some Welshcakes?"

"No," said Mavis decisively. "A Victoria sponge will be better, it will seem more of an occasion cake, especially if you dust the top with icing sugar, won't it?" Mavis was of the opinion that it would seem quite provincial to arrive at Seamus' house clutching a basket of Welshcakes. "And I will pay you for the eggs and butter, of course."

"Very well, Mavis," agreed Eiddwen, meekly, pleased to be included in one of Mavis' schemes.

Mavis drained her tea, and got up to go.

"Stay a little longer, Mavis, don't go yet! You haven't told me anything else about Mr O'Brien! Or about your little newcomer, Dai!"

"There really isn't a lot more to tell, Eiddwen," replied Mavis, vaguely, " Mr O'Brien is from Ireland, an artist, and smokes like a trooper!" And swears like one too, she thought to herself, smiling naughtily. "As for the dog, well, he's fine. I have to dash now, Eiddwen, Ernest wants to have cawl for supper, and I haven't even peeled the vegetables yet! I will call for the sponge after chapel on Sunday morning, is that all right?"

"Yes, of course, Mavis," came Eiddwen's obedient reply, "I will have it ready for you."

"Bye, then!" Mavis airily waved goodbye to her friend, and sailed out of the house with a satisfied smile on her face, happy in the knowledge that come Monday morning, she would have a good excuse to pay a visit to the enigmatic Seamus O'Brien.

Trudging up the hill towards home, a lively breeze teased the roses into her cheeks, and the afternoon sun made her eyes crinkle against the light. Half a ton of vegetables waited for her in the kitchen of the cottage, and she groaned inwardly at the thought of all that drudgery. Her fingers would be sore and her nails ruined after that peeling marathon.

She glanced swiftly at Seamus' house, but there was no sign of life there today. The front garden was rather wild and unkempt : just like Seamus himself, she thought. The grass was nearly a foot high in some places, and bluebells ran riot in a glorious wave of Wedgewood blue across what could be seen of the garden path. A big weeping willow shielded the big parlour window from prying eyes; Mavis remembered visiting the house as a child, at Christmas time, when the Richards family held wonderful parties for their neighbours and friends, and a huge Christmas tree would stand in that window, lit with a hundred tiny candles, filling her with awe and excitement.

Reluctantly, Mavis brought herself back to the present, and the onerous task ahead. She sighed, and continued her journey home to the cottage. The cottage was empty, as Ernest had taken Dai out with him to visit the Bowens in their nearby farm. Putting on a blue and white striped apron, Mavis set to work preparing the carrots, parsnips, swede and potatoes for the cawl. She would leave the leeks until later, and add them when the stew was nearly ready, as Ernest preferred them crunchy. The problem with the monotonous task was that it set her mind free to roam, and Mavis nearly chopped the end of her finger more than once, as she daydreamed about Seamus and the chance she would have of seeing him on Monday.

Sunday morning dawned grey and cold, and this pleased Mavis immensely, as it meant she could wear her new fur coat in public for the first time. After their Sunday breakfast of bread and cheese (Ernest insisted that no unnecessary work should be done on the Sabbath) the Wattons got ready for chapel. While her husband donned his austere black suit, and combed his snow-white hair, Mavis selected a dove-grey linen dress and matched it up with some beige patent shoes.

"Won't you be rather cold just wearing that dress?" observed Ernest, "There's an easterly wind blowing."

"Oh, I'll be warm enough wearing my new coat, won't I?" smiled Mavis, applying her pink lipstick with more care than she usually did.

Ernest flashed a disapproving look at her, which Mavis subsequently ignored. She applied a quick splash of Avon's Topaze, and she was ready. Ready to show the world (well, the whole of the chapel congregation, anyway) her beautiful new fur coat.

At ten o'clock, the Wattons set off for Bethel chapel. The service was due to start at ten thirty, but Ernest had to prepare the papers for the sermon, and finalise the choice of hymns for the service.

As they approached the stern, grey building, sounds of organ music could be heard from within.

"Ah!" remarked Ernest with satisfaction, "It seems as though Gladys has already arrived. Excellent." Mavis was puzzled for a moment, then remembered the widow's daughter, who had now become Bethel's new organist.

They entered the chapel via the vestry. It was dark and musty, with piles of old hymn books and music sheets on the ancient desk. Strains of Bach's "Toccata" filled the air.

"She plays very well, doesn't she, Mavis?" observed Ernest, going through into the chapel itself.

Mavis followed him dutifully, murmuring her agreement. Organ music did not really excite her, if truth be known, Mavis much preferred to listen to Pick of the Pops on the radio when Ernest was out. However, her disinterest melted away when her eyes fell upon the organist who was sitting with her back to them. The music stopped, the woman turned around. Mavis breathed in sharply. She could not believe her eyes. The blond hair, the made-up eyes, the ample hips spilling slightly over the stool - she was none other than the mystery visitor to Seamus O'Brien's house.

Speechless, Mavis continued to stare at the woman.

"Bore da, Miss Williams," greeted Ernest, "Wonderful to see you here so early. This is my wife, Mrs Mavis Watton." Gladys Williams looked up at Mavis, smiling like a cat who had got the cream. Her sly smile spread over her face, her pale green eyes cool and calculating.

"Pleased to meet you, Mrs Watton." She spoke with a slight lisp, and held out her hand to Mavis.

Mavis reluctantly took Gladys' hand, and shook the plump, white fingers briefly, forcing herself to smile sweetly, thinking to herself that, whereas Gladys may say she was pleased to meet Mavis, Mavis was not at all sure if felt likewise.

"How do you do, Miss Williams," she replied politely.

"Oh, please call me Gladys!" gushed the new organist, simpering but Mavis had turned away, her emotions in a turmoil, and unsure as to how to compose her features. But, being of a stoical and resilient nature, Mavis held her head up high and swept away into the front pew, enjoying the feel of her fur coat as it swished luxuriously against the backs of her legs.

Settling down in her seat, Mavis was able to assess Gladys Williams at her leisure. As was the saying in Llannon, Gladys Williams did not seem to "dress" very well. Her navy blue suit was demure enough, but far too tight. She exuded a wanton opulence, yet maintaining a brittle and shallow veneer of ladylike good manners.

The service passed in a haze for Mavis. She was vaguely aware of admiring glances from the rest of the congregation, but was unable to enjoy the attention due to the unwelcome and intrusive distraction of the new organist.

At eleven o'clock, the service ended, and the congregation gradually left the chapel, chattering amongst themselves as they usually did, the conversation being centred around the sermon and what meat they had roasted the previous day in readiness for Sunday lunch.

"Oh, Mavis, how beautiful you look!" exclaimed Eiddwen, rushing up to her at the chapel door.

Mavis smiled in satisfaction, stroking the soft sleeves of her coat.

"Thank you, Eiddwen," she replied graciously. "And what do you think of our new organist?"

"Oh, she is wonderful, isn't she?" gasped Eiddwen rapturously, "Such an accomplished musician! Such expertise, such -"

"Such obviously bleached hair," interrupted Mavis, acidly, turning away from Eiddwen abruptly, fury surging within her. Eiddwen trotted after her friend into the courtyard, a puzzled look upon her face.

"But Mavis, she is rather good, isn't she?" insisted Eiddwen, "She was in school with my niece, I remember her as a little girl, she always played in the Eisteddfods, talented then, she was....."

Her voice trailed away, as she became aware of an icy expression developing on Mavis' face.

Mavis forced a smile. "I will call around at ten o'clock tomorrow morning instead for the sponge. Good morning to you, Eiddwen." And with that, Mavis stalked away to the vestry door, to meet her husband.

They walked home slowly, Ernest reflecting on his sermon and Mavis pondering on her intense and unfamiliar jealousy over the advent of this younger rival for the attentions of Seamus O'Brien. Why should she care? She hardly knew him, and anyway, she was married...

She felt ashamed of her unfair coolness towards Eiddwen, and resolved to make it up to her at the earliest opportunity. Passing the artist's rambling house, she refrained from looking up at it, and strolled past, her arm through Ernest's, nose in the air.

Seamus O'Brien moved away from the window, having followed the Wattons' progress up the lane. I wonder what the set up is there, he pondered, idly tapping a paint brush against the palm of his hand. They seemed a rather incongruous couple, the stern, God-fearing husband with his alluring wife. Yes, she was certainly alluring, he thought, that tiny pocket Venus, with her bewitching brown eyes and her glorious smile....

Pushing away any further thoughts about Mavis Watton, he returned to the canvas he was working on, painstakingly applying the carefully mixed paint to the next strand of hair on the portrait.

Normally in possession of a healthy appetite, Mavis found that she was not hungry at all at lunchtime, and could only pick at her roast chicken, toying listlessly with her vegetables. As for the rice pudding, well, Dai was in for a treat tomorrow morning.

By half past one, Mavis had cleared away the dishes, and Ernest was getting ready to go to Sunday School.

"Aren't you coming, Mavis?" asked Ernest, surprised that his wife still wore her apron and did not seem to be making any attempt at preparing for the afternoon chapel trip. Normally, she would be ready promptly at a quarter to two, relishing her job of being in charge of the Collection.

"I am sorry, Ernest," she sighed, "I really feel so tired. I won't come today."

"Hmph!" snorted Ernest, disbelievingly, putting on his jacket. "Well, I suppose I will have to ask young Gladys to take the children's collection today. She works in a bank during the week, so will be well suited to the task, I am sure." And with that he strode out of the cottage, leaving a furious Mavis scowling at her reflection in the hall mirror. Hastily, she composed her features into a smooth mask. No point in encouraging any wrinkles to appear, just because of that yellow-haired minx.

Mavis was glad that, this evening, there would be a visiting choir, who would be accompanied by their own organist, thereby rendering Gladys redundant for the Evening Service.

Less than twenty four hours remained before she could make her neighbourly visit to Seamus O'Brien. Maybe she would take a little nap and catch up on some beauty sleep. She mounted the stairs to the bedroom, and without bothering to remove her dress, she lay down on the bed and closed her eyes. Sleep washed over her in soothing waves, dreamless, restoring her strength. Tomorrow would bring new encounters, different challenges which Mavis would meet and, hopefully, enjoy to the full.

Chapter Six

The Green-Eyed Monster

The longed-for Monday morning finally arrived, accompanied by a brisk, spring breeze, with cotton-wool clouds scudding across a pale blue sky. Good, no rain, thought Mavis happily, waving goodbye to Ernest as he left for his chapel meeting.

Rushing upstairs, Mavis decided to forego the sensible blue skirt and white blouse she usually wore to do housework, and instead donned a brightly printed dress, with puffed sleeves and a sweetheart neckline. Mavis was no slave to fashion, and the emerging trend for shorter skirts had completely passed her by. She dressed to complement herself, and if it suited her to wear daring colours to chapel, such as a 1940's crimson frock which became her complexion, so be it.

She carefully fastened her stockings and smoothed her petticoat under her pretty dress, looking at her reflection in the wardrobe mirror. Mavis saw a small, dark woman, of uncertain age, with huge, dark eyes and a figure that most women half her age would sell their souls for, be they Baptist, Methodist or even, God forbid, Roman Catholic!

Before she could go visiting she needed to collect the cake from Eiddwen, so set off down the lane, deliberately avoiding looking over at Seamus' house, butterflies fluttering around in her stomach and her heart thumping.

Eiddwen was as pleased as ever to see her, having forgotten Mavis' coolness towards her the previous day.

"You will tell me what he says, won't you, Mavis?" she asked anxiously, handing over a perfect Victoria sponge, wrapped in cellophane and tied with a blue ribbon.

"Of course," smiled Mavis reassuringly, carefully taking the cake and placing it gently in the wicker basket she was carrying. "Thank you so much, Fiddwen, you are such a good friend! I am entirely grateful to you. I'll settle with you tomorrow for the ingredients. I only have a ten shilling note in the cottage."

"Pay me whenever you can," gushed Eiddwen, "But be sure to stay a while to have a nice chat!"

Waving goodbye, Mavis walking back up the hill towards Seamus' house, her mouth dry and those pesky butterflies dancing a veritable Irish jig inside her. The sun shone brightly, and birds sang their spring anthems as sweetly as a wedding choir.

Arriving at the big, old house, Mavis made her way carefully up the garden path, avoiding the overgrown shrubs and blossoming rose bushes, which would snag her stockings. She stood before the door, her heart in her mouth, pausing for a moment, silently rehearsing her greeting. Trembling slightly, she lifted up her hand to knock, but to her astonishment, the door suddenly opened, and there stood Seamus, grinning from ear to ear, holding a paintbrush in his hand.

"Why, if it isn't my ravishing neighbour!" he exclaimed, laughing, "Come in at once! I saw you through the window! What's that in your basket? Is it for me?"

All this was delivered at top speed, leaving Mavis no time to reply, so she merely entered the dark hallway, clutching her basket as if her life depended on it. There were boxes and crates everywhere, and what was once a red carpet lay in dusty tatters on the floor. Huge cobwebs graced the ceiling, wafting slowly as the breeze accompanied Mavis' entrance. She shuddered. Cobwebs meant spiders, and Mavis detested them, nasty scuttling creatures.

"I haven't had time to unpack yet," explained Seamus, seeing her look of distaste as she took everything in.

"Oh, I'm sorry!" murmured Mavis, colouring, "I didn't mean to stare, it's just that I don't like spiders, and it would seem that they have made themselves very much at home here!"

"Ah, to be sure, I can tell you right away that I can cure you of that fear!" he replied, smiling down at her.

"Anyway," stammered Mavis, a little uncertainly, "I have indeed brought you a present. A house-warming present." And with that she shyly gave Seamus the cake.

He gasped in delight, and, putting the basket on the floor, suddenly scooped up Mavis into the biggest hug she had ever had in her life. She breathed in a heady mix of paint, whisky and fresh male sweat.

"Why, that's wonderful!" he exclaimed, finally putting her down. " To be sure, such a fine gift! You are so clever! Thank you, sweet Mavis!" Mavis basked in his delight and approval.

"Where are you, Seamus?" A female voice suddenly called out from within the house.

Mavis stared at Seamus, puzzled, but he was not at all fazed, however, and ushered Mavis towards a half-open door.

"We have a visitor," he announced happily, gently pushing Mavis into a large, unfurnished room.

Unfurnished, that is, except for an easel upon which rested a large canvas, several crates, two empty whisky bottles, and a blond woman lying full length upon a chaise longue. Mavis blinked, unable to believe her eyes. The woman was none other than Gladys Williams, and she was draped rather inadequately in a white sheet, her rather pendulous left breast completely exposed.

"Hello, Mrs Watton," smiled Gladys, slyly, sitting up, allowing the sheet to fall away totally.

Mavis, never having seen another naked woman before, could not help but stare. Gladys was certainly voluptuous; her large breasts hung heavily towards a thick waist, and were tipped with pale brown nipples as big as saucers. Her curvy white thighs were modestly crossed, but not well enough to hide the dark V between them, proving beyond all doubt that she was not a natural blonde.

Mavis swallowed hard, her thoughts racing. She must not, at all costs, appear shocked. That would make her seem terribly inexperienced and unsophisticated. However, as a wave of jealousy swept through her like a white-hot shower of brimstone, she had difficulty maintaining her composure. Turning to Seamus with a fixed smile, she managed to murmur, "Miss Williams and I have already met."

"Why, how splendid!" he laughed, hands on hips, "Shall I make some coffee?" Mavis could not believe he was offering her coffee, when a naked organist was wantonly spread out over his couch, a woman who only the previous day had been piously thumping out hymns and psalms in Bethel chapel.

"No, I won't be staying," whispered Mavis, "Clearly you are busy." And with that she turned to leave the room, gathering as much dignity as she could muster. Seamus followed her, a rather puzzled expression on his face, halting her exit in the doorway.

"Are you sure you don't want some coffee?" he persisted, "We could cut into that divine looking cake as well!" Mavis nearly imploded with seething anger. What? Have that scheming flaxen-haired hussy sink her greedy teeth into

Eiddwen's cake? And have to watch as well? And would the tubby little tart deign to put her clothes on for the occasion?

"The cake is for you, Seamus," she said, primly, "Just for you. If you ask me, young Gladys would do better than to eat too much cake. It would seem she has eaten rather too many rich things in the past." She flashed her eyes angrily at Seamus, who continued to appear quite confused.

Mavis turned around, casting a backward glance at Gladys.

"Be sure to wrap up well, cariad. There's a biting little breeze blowing outside." And with that, she flounced out of the room, Seamus following her.

"What's the matter?" he asked, "Why won't you stay a little longer?" For once, Mavis was at a loss as to what to say. How could she possibly tell Seamus the truth? How could she admit, even to herself, that she kept thinking about Seamus when she shouldn't. She was a married woman. And how could she tell him that she was consumed with a burning jealousy about the fact that Gladys Williams, a single woman almost ten years her junior, was lying naked on a couch in Seamus' house.

"I can't stay, Seamus," she mumbled, her eyes downcast, "I can see I am interrupting something. I have no wish to do that."

"Oh no! You have completely the wrong idea!" said Seamus, suddenly serious, putting his hands on Mavis' shoulders, "Gladys was posing for me. I needed a nude model for some work I have been commissioned for. That's all."

"I see," she replied, quietly. Seamus gently lifted her up chin and looked at her intently.

"Come back tomorrow," he whispered, "Come back, won't you?"

"I will try." Her mood lifted. "I will try and visit you after I finish work, if that is convenient."

He grinned happily. "That'll be grand!"

Opening the door for her, he handed her the empty basket, and their hands touched briefly. Mavis started; it was as though an electric shock had shot through her. Smiling shyly up at Seamus, she took her basket and set off down through the garden, waving goodbye to him as she went. Reaching the gate, she turned around. He was still there, waving. Gratifying though this was, Mavis was even more pleased to catch a glimpse of a sulky, pale face peeping through the window, a scowl furrowing the bland, white features.

Back at the cottage, Mavis changed reluctantly into her work clothes, and set about the mundane task of sweeping the kitchen floor. However, her heart was light, and the work was soon completed. A whimper from the outhouse reminded her that Dai hadn't been walked as yet. It was such a lovely day, thought Mavis, why not take the puppy for a walk?

They set off at a gentle pace, heading up towards the old track that wound its way from the coast at Llanelli, up through woods and quarries, passing rivers and ponds, until it reached the village of Cross Hands, just north of Llannon. Dai was well-behaved, and didn't pull or tug at the lead. Despite the fact that he had only been a resident at the cottage for just over a week, Ernest had successfully trained him, and Dai really was the most loveable, obedient little fellow.

The pair climbed up the steep, slippery steps which led up to the bridge which lay over the lane up to the track. Mavis paused, uncertain whether to go north or south. The track was quiet, there was no-one else around. Not wishing to encounter any other dog-walkers, Mavis decided to head north.

The midday sun, although strong and reasonably hot, failed to penetrate the leafy, emerald shade of the ancient oaks and towering pines which lined the path. Mavis shivered, and wished she had worn her red cardigan.

The trouble with a solitary walk, she considered, was that it allowed her thoughts to run riot, enabling her worries and insecurities to play havoc inside her head.

Mavis encountered no-one as she walked, just a few dare-devil squirrels who taunted Dai boldly, then ran away up into the trees. She wondered what her mother and sisters would say if they knew all her secret thoughts. They would be shocked beyond belief. She would be disowned, cast out, considered a scarlet woman at the very least, and told never to darken their door again. Mavis glanced up at the trees. They seemed so solemn and serious, as though even they disapproved of her wicked and wanton daydreams. Mavis tossed her head defiantly; she wasn't actively seeking anything. She was merely being neighbourly. Sociable.

However...why should she have these feelings of repression and of being unloved? Was it her? Or Ernest? But this was all in her imagination, surely, she was being silly.

Satisfied with this analysis of recent events, Mavis quickened her step cheerfully and Dai fell in with this increased pace with alacrity. Her thoughts then turned to the subject of Gladys Williams and her indecent presence at Seamus' house. Of course, that was what artists were like, she supposed. They were liberated and hedonistic, caring nothing for public approval, and did exactly as they pleased. Despite Seamus' permissive behaviour, however, there was a child-like innocence about him, a total lack of guile. Gladys Williams, on the other hand, had probably given up all hope of innocence when she had stopped believing in Santa Claus. Mavis did not think for one second that the organist was saving herself for an unlikely marriage, and was of the opinion that those sly cats' eyes of hers hid a multitude of extremely sinful memories. She wondered idly what a man would find attractive about Gladys. She realised that most men secretly admired a large-breasted woman, but for the life of her she could not consider Gladys' droopy attributes alluring. She seemed overblown, overfed and lacking in any subtle chic. And with regards to that peroxide blond hair....well, any man who didn't require spectacles would soon realise that Gladys' attempts at innocent Nordic beauty did not extend to her nether regions. Mavis sighed. Who could possibly know what went on inside a man's mind.

She for one had yet to fathom out what intricate and complicated things traversed the stern and iron cold mind of her husband. Did Gladys' rather obvious and overt manner render her irresistible to the opposite sex? What did Ernest think of her? And did she, Mavis, actually care?

Passing somnolent cows, indifferent sheep and the odd braying donkey, Mavis reached the next exit of the track. This would take her, if she so wished, to the group of terraced houses where her mother and sisters lived in blissful and cloistered godliness. She hadn't seen them for over a fortnight, as her mother had taken to her bed on account of a spring fever, and her sisters had stayed home from chapel in order to fuss over and care for the seventy-five year old matriarch.

Carefully climbing down the steps which led down to the country lane, she headed for her mother's house.

Passing the Bowen's farm, she wondered who had left poor Dai tied up to the gate. Despite the fact that she was no great dog lover, Mavis couldn't bear the thought of a creature suffering pain or distress. She wrinkled her nose in distaste. Mr Bowen had been muck spreading. She was so grateful that she had moved from this end of the village three years ago!

The midday sun shone warmly down, and there was no longer any need for a coat or a cardigan. However, her sisters' absence from chapel had meant they hadn't been able to appreciate her beautiful fur coat. She would have to remedy that very soon.

Mavis soon reached number eighteen, Cae Mair, and knocked tentatively on the highly polished brass knocker.

The heavy oak door was opened by her sister Enid, a short, plump woman of forty-seven.

"Well, look who it is!" greeted Enid, rather frostily, "We thought you had forgotten where we lived!" Her petulant expression told Mavis she was in for a difficult visit.

"How is Mam?" asked Mavis, struggling to stop Dai from rushing into the hallway.

"Fully recovered, if you really wish to know," replied Enid, "not that you have been to visit her." Enid had never really forgiven Mavis for flying the nest, for finding a man and succeeding where she had failed miserably. She glared beadily at Mavis through her unflattering, thick-lensed glasses. "And don't think you can bring that messy dog in here, either," she continued, her venom gathering momentum. "Evelyn and I have slaved here over the past two weeks, looking after Mam, fetching and carrying, and cleaning the house. We couldn't leave her at all. I only washed the hall floor this morning, so don't you go thinking you can let that dog in here." She scowled at Dai, who looked up at this ranting harpy with beseeching brown eyes.

Mavis bridled. She may be the youngest daughter, but she refused to be intimidated by Enid.

"Fine," she snapped. "As you wish. I will tell Ernest that I called, but was refused entry. Please be sure to let Mam know I came to see her." And with that she turned around, pulling a confused Dai behind her. In her temper, Enid shut the door rather too loudly, and Mavis could hear her mother's voice call out feebly,

"Who is there, Enid? Are they coming in?"

But Mavis didn't wait to hear any more, and ran swiftly down the past the other terraced houses, to join the main road which would lead to the turning to Bethel Lane. She felt sorry for Enid, in a way. Her older sister had no redeeming features, and always seemed angry at some real or imagined slight. She also suffered from the middle-child syndrome, never enjoying the privileges of the oldest child, nor the cosseting which she, Mavis, had received from the extended family. Mavis had always preferred Evelyn, the oldest sister, as she was quick-witted, occasionally humorous and marginally less spiteful than Enid.

Mavis felt it was as though she had escaped from a glass prison which had separated them from the outside world. All her sisters could do now was to watch her from their own, introspective microcosm, and think longingly of what might have been.

Returning home to the cottage, she gave Dai some water, then started preparing the potatoes for supper. Mavis suddenly realised she was hungry, not having eaten anything since breakfast, and now it was almost two o'clock. She was just settling down to a quick lunch of bread and ham, when there was a knock at the front door.

Who could that be? Hardly anyone she knew in Llannon used the front door, all her friends and family automatically used the back kitchen door.

Sighing irritably, she got up and went reluctantly to open it. To her intense annoyance, there stood Mr and Mrs Baker and the two grand-daughters, all dressed up in their best clothes, smiling and hopeful of an afternoon's entertainment.

She forced a smile onto her face, and held open the door for them, thankful that all the necessary cleaning had been completed, and that Gwyneth Baker would therefore be unable to find any fault whatsoever with her housekeeping.

"Come in, come in!" she greeted, cheerfully. "What a surprise! How lovely to see you all!"

"Thank you, Mrs Watton," replied Gwyneth, stepping into the darkness of the rarely-used hallway. It smelled of lavender polish, beeswax and pride.

"We were just going out for a spin in Mr Baker's new car," explained Gwyneth, "We had thought we would go to Carmarthen for the afternoon, but as I have to be back for Mothers' Union at six o'clock we thought we would pay you and Ernest a visit instead."

Mavis realised what was now expected of her.

"Ernest hasn't come home yet," she explained, "but I would very much like to see the new car. Shall we go outside?"

They all trooped dutifully out into the drive, and stood in a line to admire the shiny, new Morris Minor Traveller. Its wooden frame gleamed in the spring sunshine, and the green paintwork was glossy and sparkling. The new car was clearly Mr Baker's delight, judging by the rapt expression on his face.

"What a roomy car!" exclaimed Mavis, unable to think of a better compliment.

"Yes!" agreed Gwyneth in satisfaction, "Plenty of space for us all. We will be able to go for picnics over the Gower, to Port Einon or Oxwich Bay!"

"Yes, Nana!" shouted Wendy gleefully, jumping up and down, her blond pigtails flying about, "And we can build sandcastles and go paddling!"

Mrs Baker laughed indulgently, patting her granddaughter's head fondly.

"Julie was sick in the car yesterday," continued Wendy, giggling, "She doesn't like going in cars!"

Mrs Baker looked embarrassed, and hastily changed the subject.

"We are looking after the girls so that Margaret and Fred can carry on with decorating their new house," she explained. Mr Baker said nothing, but stood quietly smiling. He had no wish to engage in the women's talk. Julie also stood silently, clutching her grandfather's hand, solemnly watching the whole scene and sucking her thumb.

"Shall we go in?" suggested Mavis, having had quite enough of motor admiration. " I was just making some tea."

They all returned to the house, and sat down on the uncomfortable armchairs in the parlour, Wendy wriggling and fidgeting, and Julie settling down placidly on Mr Baker's knee.

"No school today?" enquired Mavis casually, casting an eye on the active Wendy, who was now executing cartwheels in the doorway.

"The school has been closed," explained Gwyneth, "Measles. I hope little Julie doesn't catch it. Wendy had it last winter."

Mavis attended to her hostess duties in the kitchen, hoping that Gwyneth Baker's parenting skills would extend beyond those of a warm, loving grandmother, and also ensure that reasonably strict discipline was kept. Mavis' best china and her aunt's handmade antimacassars were in the parlour. A rug from South Africa, sent by Ernest's daughter, Audrey, a nurse in Johannesburg, graced the hearth. She fervently hoped that the two children wouldn't spill anything on the beautiful cream rug, and that Wendy's acrobatics wouldn't result in the smashing of anything delicate and precious.

As she was cutting up the angel cake and pouring boiling water into the teapot, the kitchen door opened, and in walked Ernest.

"We have visitors, I see," he observed gruffly, taking off his flat cap and putting it down with some force on the table. "I am too busy to talk to them right now, Mavis, I have to address some financial chapel issues. Please apologise to them for me. I must go upstairs to write a letter and will be down as soon as I can." And he stalked upstairs, leaving an astonished and furious Mavis open-mouthed in his wake.

How could Ernest behave like that, she thought, angrily. The Bakers were his relatives, after all.

Gathering her composure as best she could, Mavis carried the tea tray back into the parlour.

"Ernest will be down presently," she explained, hastily, "Something has occurred in the chapel. Please help yourselves!"

Wendy's eyes lit up with delight. Angel cake! Such a treat! Her grandmother Gwyneth was an excellent cook, and was considered the local expert when it came to bara brith, Welshcakes and the like. But angel cake was always shop-bought, and a luxury not often affordable. Mavis wondered if her visitors knew the real reason why she was serving them this highly coloured, expensive confection - she could not bake a cake to save her life!

Tea passed relatively uneventfully; thankfully, the two little girls had been well disciplined and ate their cake without any misdemeanour. Ernest reappeared after half an hour and joined the party, without any apology or excuse. Mavis fumed inwardly. As always, Ernest prioritised chapel affairs above everything else.

Presently, Mr Baker took Ernest outside to look at his new car, leaving the women and children to their own devices.

"Young Wendy will be starting piano lessons next week," announced Gwyneth, proudly.

Mavis looked surprised.

"Isn't she rather young?" she asked. "I would have thought it necessary to be able to read and write really well before it would be possible to learn piano."

"Oh, our Wendy can read and write better than most children in the class above her!" replied Gwyneth, sighing with satisfaction. "And the stories she writes! She has Mr Baker and me in stitches!"

"Well, Wendy, you are indeed a clever little girl," acknowledged Mavis reluctantly. "Maybe you can read something out of the Bible for me?" Dai whined in objection from the kitchen.

Wendy's wicked smile flashed at the grown ups. "Can I play with the puppy instead?"

Ernest strode into the room, smiling indulgently. "And why not? I'll take you out into the garden in a few minutes and you shall learn how to make him sit!"

This was a side to her husband she had never seen before. It surprised her and puzzled her. She doubted she would ever really understand him. Mrs and Mrs Baker smiled uncertainly, relieved that Ernest had not taken Wendy to task for her blatant refusal to read from the Bible. They remained seated on the stiff, brown armchairs, their empty tea-cups lying high and dry on the shiny occasional table, while Wendy played with Dai in the garden, her young sister clinging closely to her grandmother's knees.

A formal and stilted conversation followed, weighing up the merits of individual wine glasses for Holy Communion, preferred by the Baptists, and the Chalice as used by Protestants.

"Well, time to be on our way," decided Gwyneth, finally, gathering up the placid Julie in her capable arms, and ushering the nimble Wendy towards the door. "Thank you so much for calling by," sighed Mavis, with a thankful smile on her face, "it was lovely to see you all. Have a safe journey home." The children and their grandparents piled into the car, and slowly disappeared into the spring afternoon, Mavis and Ernest waving goodbye on the stone doorstep of the cottage.

" Clever little girl, that young Wendy." sighed Ernest. "She will do well, I'm sure. I can see her working in a bank, or even as a teacher." "Yes, I suppose she is," replied Mavis, resignedly. Personally, she thought the child over-active and rather insolent. " Her grandmother would have liked her very much indeed," he continued, looking away, as if harbouring fond memories. He fell silent. A skylark soared overhead, its song exquisite in its solitude. Mavis felt that familiar pang of exclusion, feeling yet again an outsider, not quite part of Ernest's family.

But she did not feel the pain as acutely as before. Something was blunting the barb, cushioning and softening the blow. Her horizons were broadening, her outlook expanding, and she didn't really know why.

Chapter Seven

A Voyage of Discovery

Tuesday morning dawned, misty and silent. Mavis couldn't even see the apple trees at the bottom of the garden, let alone the woods to the west or the main road to the east of the cottage. There was no spring sun to lift the spirit, the light remained uncertain and shifting.

She shivered, drawing her red dressing gown more closely around her slim shoulders. Ernest snored peacefully, lying on his back on the hard, high bed. Mavis couldn't remember if he had a chapel appointment today, or if he had agreed to help Mr Bowen with the installation of a new water pump at the farm. But that was his own problem. She decided to let him sleep on, as it was only half-past six.

Downstairs, the kitchen felt cold and miserable. Dai was whining in the outhouse, wanting to be let out. Mavis sighed. So many mundane tasks to be completed before she went to work. Then she remembered – today she would, once again, pay a visit to Seamus, and this time, that annoying little trollop Gladys Williams would not be there to spoil things. Thus cheered, she flew through her early morning housework with a lighter heart, and by a quarter to nine she was hurrying down the lane to the village. The mist was beginning to lift, but the treetops were still delicately veiled with floating white tendrils. An increasing brightness over the eastern horizon indicated that the sun was trying to

break through and warm the May morning. Mavis was pleased that she'd chosen to wear a bright and cheerful yellow dress, which enhanced her olive skin and clung to her tiny form enticingly. She giggled inwardly, thinking that Mr Griffiths would be quite surprised at her appearance.

Remembering Seamus' opinion on her hair, she had left her dark hair loose, and it hung in glossy curls over her shoulders.

When she arrived at the sweet shop, Mr Griffiths did indeed glance in quiet astonishment at Mavis.

She was always smart and efficiently dressed, but today there was a new softness about her, a carefree, almost girlish air.

The day passed slowly, or so it seemed to Mavis, the only customers being old Frank Bennet who called in to buy Golden Virginia tobacco, fat Bessie Thomas buying some illicit Dairy Milk chocolate, and Mr Williams the choir master, her erstwhile admirer, buying some even more illicit rum and butter toffees to suck during next Sunday's sermon.

At last five o'clock came, and, saying goodbye to Mr Griffiths, Mavis left the shop behind and headed up the hill towards Seamus' house.

By now the sun was shining brightly; Mavis enjoyed its warmth on her bare arms, but her heart was beating uncomfortably. As she walked westwards towards her destination, she noticed groups of bluebells cuddling each other in familial isolation under the canopy of protective elms and oaks.

How briefly but gloriously they lived, she thought, a beacon of spring and a hope of fine weather, just like the struggling forget-me-nots which vied for attention besides their more showy companions, the toxic, purple foxgloves. The front of Seamus' house was shaded from the sun, facing north-east, and Mavis suddenly felt cold as she opened the rusty gate and walked up the untidy garden path. More rogue bluebells gathered together in secret clumps between the rose bushes, unhindered by any orderly gardening. Dandelions grew tall and proud in the cracks of the path, with a sprinkling of daisies lending their shy support. Beautifully coloured butterflies flitted from flower to flower, enjoying this abundant harvest. Ordinarily, Mavis would have felt intense disapproval of such a disorderly garden, but somehow, this riotous explosion of weeds and wildlife simply represented Seamus' general approach to life. Wanton, wild and wonderful. Mavis felt a wave of terrifying, yet exciting anticipation wash over her.

A sudden burst of birdsong interrupted her anxiety. As Mavis raised her hand, for the second time in two days, to knock on the door, she glanced up at the joyful blackbird, singing its heart out on the branch of an ancient, towering oak which cloaked this side of the house in its protective shade.

Lucky bird, she thought wistfully, it has no concerns other than to provide for his wife and protect its own little nest. Mavis lifted the old, brass lion's head, and knocked tentatively on the door. She heard footsteps inside, and the door opened.

Seamus stood there, a glass of whisky in his hand, and a huge smile on his face. Come into my parlour, thought Mavis in panic, feeling suddenly reluctant.

"How marvellous!" He exclaimed in delight. "You came!" He stood back as Mavis entered the dim hallway.

"Isn't a bit early to be drinking alcohol?" Mavis whispered, shocked.

"Not at all!" He laughed wickedly. "Would you care to join me?" Mavis looked up at him in horror.

"Oh, goodness me, no!" She protested. "I don't drink, you see - "

"You're a Baptist!" Seamus finished for her, a wry smile playing around his lips.

"Er, yes." Mavis looked away, avoiding his scrutiny, and followed him into the room where Gladys had lolled about in all her blond opulence yesterday.

"Welcome to my studio," he announced theatrically, "I own but one item of furniture in here, and you may sit on it if you wish!"

Mavis sat down gingerly on the chaise, remembering its previous occupant, and her lack of clothing.

Seamus perched on a large wooden box.

"I paint in here," he explained, taking a sip of whisky, "because the light is so clear in the morning. At this time of day it's not so good, but I still like the room, it has potential, don't you agree?"

"Yes, I suppose it has," murmured Mavis, looking around at the heaps of dust sheets, boxes, paintbrushes, blank canvases and easels, and the bare, wooden floor. " I quite like the wallpaper, too, "he continued, oblivious to Mavis' lack of enthusiasm, and pointing to the ancient, peeling blue flocked paper on the wall above the fireplace, "it has a charm all of its own. I think I will leave it alone, there's no need at all to decorate, don't you think? You know, you look really lovely in that yellow frock of yours!"

Mavis looked up in surprise at this seemingly random compliment, and saw he was watching her intently, his friendly blue eyes concentrating on her face. She said nothing. Seamus smiled.

"Are you local?" He drained the rest of his whisky.

Mavis burst out laughing. "Of course I am! What a strange thing to ask!"

Narrowing his eyes, he lifted her chin in his fingers. "Well, you see, sweet Mavis, you most certainly don't look local. Here's the thing: you look positively Mediterranean. Your complexion has that hint of the exotic, you really are a "dusky beauty." If I was to paint a portrait of you, and nobody knew you, they would think you were from Sicily, or even North Africa. A little Bedouin woman. Would you like some coffee?" Mavis marvelled at the way he could abruptly change the direction of the conversation. She also liked the way he talked, his Irish accent, his inability to say "th" which resulted in his amusing here's de ting.

"Yes, coffee would be nice," she replied with a smile, "plenty of milk and one sugar!"

"Okey dokey, I'll be just a minute, have a look round."

With that, he leapt energetically to his feet, and loped off in the direction of the kitchen, reminding Mavis of an enormous Irish wolfhound. She started to wander around the large, unfurnished room, which for her was filled with memories of parties and fun from long ago. Her kitten heels clicked quietly on the floor boards. Her mind drifted back in time, to the 1930's, when the Richards family held sumptuous parties and was the most prominent family in the village. Such wonderful entertainment, someone always playing the piano, young and feisty Hannah Richards (she must be well in to her sixties now and living in Australia) singing her brilliant solos, and old Uncle John Richards, long dead and buried, reciting Welsh poetry in his musical, melancholic voice. Mavis sighed, dragging her mind back to the present, and the untidy room as it was now. There may have been little in the way of furniture, but in the corner there was a bookcase, rammed full of books. She approached it curiously, wondering what sort of books Seamus enjoyed reading, and whether they would give her an insight into the mind of the man she was starting to think about only too often. There was no order to the collection, no method or anything remotely organised.

"Lady Chatterley's Lover" rubbed incongruous shoulders with an ancient copy of the King James' Bible. Several issues of the Readers' Digest lay at a forty-five degree angle to a bundle of children's comics. A vegetarian recipe book jostled for space with several copies of Famous Five books, and a myriad art journals and magazines were heaped in an undignified pile on the bottom shelf. A biography of C. S. Lewis claimed sovereignty on the top of the bookcase. Mavis warily reached for "Lady Chatterley's Lover," but before she could open it, Seamus returned with the coffee. She replaced the book hastily, but Seamus' sharp eyes had caught her in the act. He chuckled.

" ' A woman has to live her life, or live to repent not having lived it.' Are you of a mind to heed Mr Lawrence's words, Mavis? But I have to say I much prefer "The Virgin and the Gypsy," it's earthier and more passionate, don't you agree?"

"Um...I haven't read either," she admitted, embarrassed. All she knew was that she was once caught in Llanelli Library by her sister Enid, secretly trying to read the first chapter of the controversial book, even though it was just an abridged version, and was given such a scolding by her mother, she had never attempted it again. She took her coffee from Seamus, surreptitiously checking if the cup was clean. No saucer accompanied it. She took a small sip, and found it surprisingly good. Her eyes widened. Glancing up, she saw that Seamus was grinning at her wickedly.

"Now then, Mavis Watton, you weren't expecting that, were you? You didn't think that a crusty old bachelor like me could make a decent cup of coffee, did you? And before you ask, I don't believe in saucers, a total waste of time, they just clutter the place up and make for extra washing up." He grinned again, clearly pleased with himself.

"And how often does that rare event take place?" teased Mavis, playfully. " Once a month? Anyway, I think it's time I asked you a question now."

"Ask away!" Seamus laughed, finishing his coffee in just a few gulps. Mavis wondered if he had slipped some whisky into it.

"Well," she started hesitantly, "you mentioned you are a bachelor. Have you never been married?"

There. She had said it. She bit her lower lip, waiting for his response.

"Nope." His reply was slightly terse and to the point. "I nearly got caught once, but thanks be to God I escaped in time." He looked sideways at Mavis, as if wondering whether he should continue. Seeing her intent expression, he carried on.

"I was in art college in Dublin, she was a waitress, and the prettiest little thing you ever did see. Eyes of the clearest turquoise, the palest skin, long red hair – and a temper to match, she was just twenty-one." Seamus stared into the distance, and lit a cigarette.

"What was her name?" Mavis wanted to know more.

"Carmel. Carmel O'Donnell. She was a struggling dancer, actress, not enough jobs around. The war was just starting. She waitressed in Temple Bar to make ends meet. I was besotted with her. We got engaged secretly, as her parents disapproved of my wild ways! I was a bit of a hellraiser in those days, and I was a good few years older than her!" He smiled wryly.

Mavis was intrigued. "Go on."

"She ran off with my best friend," he said simply, "my so-called best friend Willie Brennan. They got married immediately, she was pregnant by him."

"Oh no!" gasped Mavis. "How terrible!"

"She died in childbirth," he continued bleakly, "such a very young woman. The baby died as well. The sort of poetic justice I could do without." Mavis sat quietly, trying to absorb what she had just been told.

Seamus drew heavily on the cigarette, exhaling slowly, watching the smoke disperse in the silent room. "I swore from then on that I would never allow myself to be hurt again. So no, I have never married, never fallen in love. It only ends in grief, believe me."

The pair sat in silence for a couple of minutes. Mavis twisted her cup around in her fingers, feeling shy and ill at ease.

Seamus broke the silence finally, putting his empty cup on the floor. "Tell me more about yourself."

Mavis looked up at him, her head on one side. "What would you like to know?"

"How old are you? How long have you been married? What did you study at college? Have you ever travelled?"

Mavis laughed. "Now you should realise, Seamus, that a lady never reveals her age!"

"Oh, I'll find out soon enough, to be sure!" He winked at her.

Ignoring this remark, Mavis continued.

"I have been married for just over three years." Seamus raised an eyebrow. "I went to Llanelli Girls' Grammar School, but I never went to college or anything, my mother wouldn't allow it, she said there was no point, that my place was at home with her and my sisters, to help with the lodgers. Do you know, I would have loved to have been able to study English in the sixth form! And my French and Latin were pretty good as well! And then of course, there was the war effort. As for travelling, I went to London on the train only the other day, and on my own too. Apart from that, I haven't been anywhere much, just around here, really. We do go to the Gower in the summer, but only on a Saturday, as my husband is the deacon in the chapel. Now tell me, is that enough?" She smiled up at him, uncertain. How desperately inexperienced she must appear. What a boring life it must seem to him.

Seamus sighed. She couldn't tell if it was out of despair, disapproval or boredom. She twisted her hands tightly and bit her lip hard, not feeling any pain. She was aware of the salt, metallic taste of blood on her tongue. The light faded swiftly as the sun disappeared temporarily behind the trees. A shawl of chilly doubt gathered around her.

"Have I said something wrong?" she asked eventually, her thoughts racing , wondering if her lack of higher education somehow rendered her less attractive to this enigmatic, artistic, yet tragically wronged man.

He smiled. "Not at all. Now, if you have finished your coffee, would you like me to show you round?"

"That would be lovely." Looking for somewhere to put her empty cup, Mavis got up.

"Just stick it on the floor, I'll wash it later." His enthusiasm was all too evident, as he sprang to his feet.

"You know, I used to visit this house a lot when I was a girl." She followed him meekly into the hallway. "It's as though time has stood still. Apart from the dust and cobwebs, nothing has really changed."

They stood under an ancient chandelier, Seamus towering over the diminutive Mavis.

"I bet you never went upstairs!" He chuckled, suggestively. "Would you like to see the first floor?"

Mavis didn't quite know how to react to this, but had no time to object because he propelled her around and, with his hand lightly on her back, gently pushed her up the staircase, which, together with the landing, was dark and gloomy. A damp and musty smell hung in the air.

"Don't worry, I won't bite you!" teased Seamus, sensing her reluctance.

"I know that!" she replied indignantly. "I was merely thinking how unloved the house feels now, how empty and sad."

He glanced at her quizzically. " How could a house feel anything? You must be more sensitive than I gave you credit for!" They were now at the top of the stairs, and the landing stretched away into the dim light, the closed bedroom doors uninviting and forbidding.

Anxious to dispel the increasingly intimate atmosphere, she laughed briskly. "Oh, I'm not sensitive at all! I am a sensible married woman, who holds down a job and looks after her husband to the best of her ability."

He bent down to whisper in her ear. "Exactly. A sensible married woman who, of her own volition has entered the house of a strange man, and is now, at this very minute, consorting with him upstairs!" He grinned down at her. Mavis glared back at him, uncomfortable with his implication.

"I am not consorting!" she flashed, crossly. "How dare you! I am just being neighbourly!"

"Of course you are..." His expression gave nothing away.

The landing light fitting was devoid of a light bulb, or she would certainly have asked him to switch it on. Seamus stopped at a door at the far end of the landing.

"This is where I store my completed work," he explained, ushering her inside.

The room was dark, filled with draped canvases, with thick velvet curtains shielding all the paintings from any sunlight which had the audacity to cast its unwelcome beams onto Seamus' work. Mavis moved forward, curious.

"So many paintings," she observed, at a loss as to what else to say, feeling out of her depth and unsure of herself. At the far side of the room stood a large canvas, uncovered, but with its back to the door. Mavis walked over to it, inquisitively, wondering what the painting was.

"Why is this one uncovered?" Seamus was still standing near the doorway, leaning lazily against the wall. "It is finished, but the paint has yet to dry." He watched her expression as she turned to look at the painting.

Mavis felt as though she had been kicked in the stomach. She wanted to hurl the painting out of the window, and would have taken great pleasure in seeing it smashed to pieces on the garden below. For there smirked Gladys Williams, resplendent in all her naked, wanton voluptuousness, mocking her from the canvas. With supreme effort, Mavis composed her features.

"What do you think?" He was smiling, moving some green paint covered cloths from the floor, wiping his hands on them before depositing them on a wooden box. Exercising as much dignity as she could muster, Mavis looked up at him.

"It's very good indeed," she said, a fixed smile on her face, her eyes cold and remote. She turned back to the portrait. Gladys Williams was voluptuous, yes, but on closer inspection was indeed overweight. Seamus had been accurate and unforgiving, and had faithfully depicted the several rolls of white flesh which had folded rather unglamorously over her abdomen. His skilled artist's brush had identified every inch of cellulite, and had brought out the cool green of her cat-like eyes. Gladys was smiling in the portrait, but a closed-lipped smile, full of self-satisfaction.

Really, thought Mavis uncharitably, her only obvious attributes were her large breasts and her blond hair, which she knew by now to be unnatural. She noticed with pleasure that Seamus had painstakingly reproduced the dark hair between her legs, not exercising any artistic license at all. Eventually, her mind brimming with wild, jealous thoughts, she turned back to Seamus, who was still watching her from the doorway, regarding her intently, observing her reaction with interest.

"Why did you paint her?" she asked, eventually, the burning question erupting from her lips before she could stop it. But it was a question which had plagued her for the past twenty-four hours and more.

"Let's go and sit in the garden," he suggested, beckoning her over to the door, "this isn't a good place to talk. Too many others watching, if you know what I mean!"

Mavis followed him like a lamb, down the stairs, through the hallway and out into the rear garden.

The six o'clock sun was filtering teasingly through the blossoming apple trees, dappling the overgrown lawn with golden light. She forgot completely the housewifely duties waiting for her at the cottage, her head was filled Seamus, art and the beautiful spring evening.

There really was nowhere to sit comfortably in the jungle of a garden, but Seamus beckoned to her to join him on an ancient, low stone table.

"I remember this table when we came here to tea with the Richards children. We used to have tea parties, sang songs, laughed out loud!" She sighed, raising her face to the sun. "How I loved this garden, what fun we all had."

"Did you have fun, then? Was that allowed in your strict, Baptist upbringing?" His slight sarcasm stung slightly, but she resolutely refused to react, persisting in her original question.

"So, Seamus, why did you paint that portrait of Gladys Williams?" Again, she bit her lip, not sure if she wanted to hear his response.

"Well, it's quite simple, really," he started, lighting another cigarette, inhaling the smoke with clear enjoyment. "Money." His thoughtful features were illuminated by the sunlight.

"Go on." prompted Mavis, wishing to know more, yet fearful of the truth.

"As I was saying," he continued, "it's quite simple. I was commissioned to produce the painting by Sheik Abdul Al Sabah. He owns several oilfields in Saudi Arabia, has more money than he knows what to do with, and has a penchant for plump, blond ladies. He lives in London most of the time, in a penthouse in Mayfair. I met him at an exhibition last summer. We started talking (through his aide his English is non-existent) and he made me an offer I couldn't refuse. He was quite specific. I had to paint a blond, curvaceous woman in the nude, and complete it by June this year. I put an advert in several local newspapers, stating I needed a model for some art work. Gladys responded and was picked for the job."

"I see." Mavis considered this information. "Is that why you moved to Llannon? Because of Gladys? Is that why you bought the house? Did you pay her?"

Seamus laughed softly. "Why such interest in Miss Williams? She provided me with a subject to paint, and that has been completed. I doubt our paths will cross again. And I paid her fifteen guineas for her trouble."

Mavis gasped. "That's an extortionate amount! Fifteen guineas for sitting still?"

"She sat for me nine times, for over two hours each session and she had to remain perfectly still. She earned every penny, I can assure you."

Thus rebuked, Mavis stood up as if to go.

"Stay a while," protested Seamus, reaching for her hand, pulling her back down.

"I really should go," Mavis explained, anxiously, "Ernest will be home by now, expecting his supper."

"Of course, I understand. Don't worry, you get on home." He smiled at her worried face. "But come and visit me again soon, won't you? And I tell you what, why don't you sit for me? Just for fun! It would give me great pleasure to paint you. Will you let me?" His enthusiasm was endearing and almost child-like; Mavis laughed.

"I'll think about it," she smiled, "and I really should go."

Reluctantly, they got up, and made their way through the house to the front door. Seamus put his hand on her shoulder. Once again, she felt as though an electric shock had surged through her whole body. Breathing in sharply, she looked up at him.

"I really enjoyed our little chat," he murmured, his hand sliding down slightly between her shoulder blades. Mavis wished he would keep his hand there forever.

"So did I." she replied quietly. "Goodbye." And she turned around, making her way down the path, and opening the gate. Glancing back, she was pleased to see that he was still there, leaning against the door frame, watching her, smiling thoughtfully. She raised her hand to wave, smiling back at him, before making her way up Bethel Lane, returning to her reality, her mundane life and her role as a dutiful wife.

There was no sound as Mavis opened the kitchen door, no excited bark from Dai, and no complaints from a disgruntled Ernest. Cautiously, she wandered into the living room, calling out, "Ernest? It's me, are you home?"

"I'm here."

Mavis jumped. Ernest stood behind her, Dai at his side. She couldn't read his expression. Annoyed? Suspicious?

"You're late," he continued tersely, "where have you been? You finish at five o'clock. Did Mr Griffiths make you work late? I shall have to have a word with him, making my wife work above and beyond her agreed hours." He scowled, and stalked out of the room, Dai following, without waiting for a reply. Mavis' heart sank. There would be no mollifying him in his current mood. She followed him into the garden, and began unpegging the washing from the clothes line. Ernest busied himself brushing Dai's white coat.

"So. Why are you late?" he asked eventually, not looking up from the dog.

"I called to see our new neighbour," she explained, rather defensively, folding a pair of Ernest's longjohns and putting them in the laundry basket. "His name is Mr O'Brien and he's bought the Richards house. I took him a cake by way of welcome." Mavis conveniently omitted to mention the exact date and time of her previous visit.

"You visited him alone?" snapped Ernest. "That is most unacceptable, Mavis. People will talk, mark my words."

Mavis swung round, angry at the inference. "For goodness' sake, Ernest! We are living in the nineteen sixties! This is not Jane Austen's era! Eiddwen made a cake and I delivered the damn thing!"

"How dare you swear in this house!" he bellowed, furiously.

"Don't you shout at me!" Mavis was close to tears now, and clutched the two remaining drying cloths to her chest protectively, gripping them tightly in her anger. She turned to go back into the cottage, her cheeks aflame and her heart beating quickly.

"What's that on the back of your dress?" came his next interrogation.

"What d'you mean?" Without waiting for his reply, she rushed inside to have a look in the hallway mirror. Turning this way and that, she was horrified to see a large, green handprint on the left shoulder of her pretty, yellow dress.

Chapter Eight

Repercussions and Revelations

When Mavis woke up at six o'clock the next morning, a thumping headache drummed out a loud tattoo in her tired brain. She turned over to look at Ernest. He scowled in his sleep, his strong jaw jutting out belligerently, even in his slumber. A wild wind howled around the cottage, unseasonal and unwelcome. No work at the shop today, just Wednesday's housework, the beating of rugs, the polishing of silver and the scrubbing of the tiled floors in the kitchen and the tiny bathroom. With a sinking heart, she remembered yesterday's events, and Ernest's fury at her supposedly wanton behaviour. She had gone to bed early, missing supper herself, but ensuring Ernest had plenty to eat, cooking him bacon and eggs. She had had no appetite at all, feeling upset at Ernest's accusations and guilty about her tumultuous emotions. She had explained away the green paint on her dress by saying that some naughty children had come to the shop after school, and had played wicked pranks on her.

Ernest had come to bed around ten o'clock, and Mavis had pretended to be asleep, her brown eyes gazing sleeplessly through the north-west facing window. The May night had been clear, full of stars, and now and again, Mavis had caught flashes of the northern lights, as the Aurora Borealis lit up the sky, projecting the trees on the hill into stark relief. They had failed to soothe her spirit, however, and the cold Gobi desert of marital strife had maintained an arid gulf between the couple.

Blinking her tired eyes against the weak morning light, Mavis went downstairs and into the kitchen, brushing past Dai on the way, her mission being the location of the brown aspirin bottle, securely kept in the cupboard above the stove. Running the cold tap briskly, she retrieved a glass from the draining board, and filled it. How could she have neglected to have dried it and put it away last night! She threw the two tablets into her mouth and swallowed them. Wiping her lips on the sleeve of her dressing gown, she sat down at the scrubbed kitchen table, sighed and put her head in her hands. A warm snuffling at her knees reminded her that Dai had still to be let out and fed. Smiling, despite her forlorn mood, Mavis got up and unlocked the kitchen door, and Dai bolted for his favourite target – the apple tree at the bottom of the garden. Mavis smiled as she watched him balance precariously on three legs for a full two minutes as he relieved himself, panting, but with one eye out for the pesky squirrels.

Not having had any supper the previous night, Mavis thought she had better eat some breakfast. Her usual habit was to make do with some bread, or toast, or whatever she found in the pantry. Today, however, she thought she would have something more substantial. Two of Mr Bowen's chicken's eggs later, Mavis felt sufficiently restored, and returned upstairs to dress. The stairs creaked noisily as she quietly crept up the staircase, and the wind caused the loose tiles on the roof to clatter and chatter as though they were giving away all her secrets. Needless to say, Ernest was awake by the time she entered the bedroom. He was sitting on the edge of the bed, his eyes shut tightly, murmuring his morning prayers to the Lord his God. Mavis knew better than to interrupt him during this routine, so she quietly set about finding some suitable clothes, and retreated to the spare bedroom to get dressed. The window looked southward, overlooking Llanelli town with its houses, shops and factories, towards the valleys and fields, with a glimpse of the Loughor estuary: it gleamed dull and brown in the distance. Mavis preferred to look at it when the sun was full and hot, making the turbulent, dangerous waters sparkle and glitter, like a blue, lurex dress, a dress she could only dream about, and never, ever wear. However, she liked to dream, and imagine that some day, she would gad about down in Llanelli, on a Saturday night, like so many women did, at the Glen Ballroom, and dance the night away.....

The kitchen clock struck eleven. Ernest was busy writing next Sunday's sermon at the kitchen table, Dai was slumbering at his feet, and Mavis stoically rubbed the silver tea set, continuing to dream her wistful dreams and momentarily escape her stunted and restricted life. The silence of the morning was suddenly and abruptly interrupted by a sharp knock at the back door. Peering through the glass panel, Mavis saw the bristly, whiskery face of Mr Bowen, their neighbouring farmer.

"Bore da, Mrs Watton," he greeted her, taking off his hat and stepping inside as Mavis opened the door, "it's a breezy day out there. Is Mr Watton about?"

"Ernest! It's Mr Bowen the farm. Come in, Mr Bowen, and sit down." Mavis set about making some tea, leaving the two men to whatever urgent business had instigated this unexpected visit.

"It's your mother, Mr Watton," explained Mr Bowen. "We called up there just now, me and the boy, to ask if she wanted us to pump water from the lower well, and there she was, sitting on the bedroom floor, been there all night she had, took a tumble when she got up to use the commode. We managed to get her downstairs, but she could hardly walk. She refused to go back to bed."

"Is Mam alright?" demanded Ernest, anxiously, getting to his feet and collecting his hat from the stand in the passage.

"Well, I took the liberty of calling Dr Hodges, and his wife said he would come as soon as possible. Apparently he was attending a difficult birth down at Brynglas."

"Shouldn't we call an ambulance instead?" suggested Mavis, pouring tea into three cups.

"Mam would never want to go in to hospital," snapped Ernest, impatiently, "and we don't have time for tea. Come along Mavis, we have to hurry."

And with that, Mavis and Ernest scrambled into the Reliant, leaving Mr Bowen to cycle his way up to Mrs Watton senior's house, no mean feat, living as she did atop the steepest hill in the whole of Llannon.

When Mavis and Ernest arrived, Mrs Watton was sitting in her favourite armchair, her oldest cat, Ted, a feline lump of spite and hatred, on her lap. She scowled at her visitors, but looked very pale indeed. Ted glared at them with rheumy yellow eyes.

"There's no need to fuss!" she mumbled at them, crossly, "I am perfectly fine. Just a little fall, that's all."

Mrs Watton shifted slightly in her chair and Mavis became aware of a slight smell of urine. Her breakfast eggs churned uneasily in her stomach. Ted heaved his heavy black and white body off his mistress' lap.

"What happened, Mam?" asked Ernest, concern furrowing his forehead. Mrs Watton sighed impatiently.

"I had to get up in the middle of the night, as I often do, and the next thing I knew I was on the floor." Her speech sounded slurred, as though she had been drinking, thought Mavis, knowing that her mother-in-law had never touched a drop of alcohol in her entire life.

"Did you trip over the cat?" suggested Mavis, but was silenced by a glare from Ernest. It was never a good idea to say anything negative about any of Mrs Watton's beloved cats, let alone suggest that the senior cat was responsible for her demise.

"I can't remember much." the old lady continued, hesitantly. "I tried to call out but I couldn't talk. Not that there would have been anyone to hear. And when I tried to stand, there was no strength in my legs."

Mavis and Ernest looked at each other, but said nothing. There was a knock at the door.

"That'll be Mr Bowen," said Mavis, hurrying to open it. However, Mr Bowen was still labouring up the hill, having been overtaken by Dr Hodges in his black Rover.

Dr Hodges towered over Mavis as she opened the door.

"Where's the patient?" he demanded, pushing past Mavis, and striding into the kitchen. Mavis smiled to herself, despite the solemnity of the occasion. Dr Hodges was more than a match for Ernest and his mother, and would tolerate no nonsense from either of them. Mavis had harboured secret desires about Dr Hodges when she had been a teenager, and his dark good looks had only improved with the passing of years. At sixty-two years old, he had the appearance of a man ten years younger, and his thick, black hair had turned a distinguished silvery grey. There was nothing silvery about his bedside manner, however; Dr Hodges was direct and to the point. Having completed his examination of Mrs Watton, he turned to Ernest.

"It would seem that your mother has suffered a stroke. This has affected her mobility and her speech. I would prefer her to go to hospital, but of course, I cannot force her."

"Indeed you cannot!" protested Mrs Watton. The petulant features settled into a more sinister demeanour. The sinister Ted mewed equally petulantly.

"As you can see," continued the doctor smoothly, "her hearing is unaffected, as is her mind. Her memory may seem a little sketchy for a while, but that should return."

Mrs Watton frowned at Dr Hodges.

"Don't talk about me as though I wasn't here!" she objected. Dr Hodges turned back to his patient.

"Of course, if you follow my instructions, then hospitalisation will be avoided."

Mrs Watton's mouth, about to open and hurl more vitriolic torrents at her physician, clamped shut.

Dr Hodges turned to leave, beckoning Ernest and Mavis to follow him to the front door. He paused, and looked searchingly at them.

"She will need to be kept quiet, no stress or shocks. I will prescribe some medication, and will ask the district nurse to call. Your mother may also have problems with incontinence. Someone really must stay with her at all times. I will visit again tomorrow. There is one thing you should be aware of. A second stroke could happen at anytime, and it could be worse. However, she has been a fit and healthy woman all her life, but she is, after all, eighty-five. Good-day."

And with that, he returned to his car, and departed down the lane, passing a sweating, puffing Mr Bowen on his way up on his bike.

It was decided that Mavis would remain with her mother-in-law, while Ernest would return to the cottage to ring Fred. Mr Bowen, feeling he had done his duty, went back to his farm.

"I want Audrey back home." grumbled Mrs Watton, crossly, "What's the point of having a nurse as a granddaughter if she isn't here to look after you?"

" I will send a telegram to her," reassured Ernest, "but she may be unable to come home. Her contract at the hospital in Johannesburg is for another six months."

"I want to go back to bed," said his mother, quietly, "I feel so tired now."

"Help me, Mavis," asked Ernest, starting to get Mrs Watton out of the chair. Mavis considered this, and thought it rather foolish.

"Wait, Ernest," she advised, anxiously, "the bed is upstairs. How on earth will we get Mam up there? I think it would be better to wait for the district nurse to come, then we can ask her what to do for the best."

For once, Ernest heeded his wife's opinion. Settling his mother back into her chair, he said, "Mavis is right, Mam. I'll get your bed brought downstairs. Mr Bowen will help me, and maybe Fred if he isn't in work. You just sit there until we can sort it all out. Mavis will stay with you, and if you need anything, she will get it for you."

Mrs Watton, being too exhausted to argue, sat back in her chair, closing her eyes.

"You will look after her, won't you?" asked Ernest, "I will be as quick as I can."

"Of course I will," promised Mavis, her heart sinking at the thought of being alone with her formidable and now indisposed mother-in-law..

Mrs Watton seemed to have slipped into a deep sleep. Mavis sat down opposite her, unsure what to do next. Her mother-in-law was as fastidious as she was about housekeeping (her cats being the exception) and there was no real housework to be done. Ted stared up at her balefully, as if challenging her to cross his path.

"Shoo!" hissed Mavis under her breath, "Out you go, you mangy animal!" The cat refused to budge, and continued to regard her stonily. Mavis had no wish to touch him, so they sat and tolerated each other for the next ten minutes, while Mavis tried and failed to concentrate on the births and deaths page of last week's Llanelli Star.

She jumped slightly, as she heard the door open, and a cheerful voice call out, "Hello! It's Sister Griffiths! May I come in?" It was the shopkeeper's wife.

Mavis rushed to greet her. Never before had she been so pleased to see someone.

"Why, Eva! Thank goodness you have come so quickly! But I thought you just visited mothers and babies!"

Eva Griffiths smiled wryly. "Sister Cook is on holiday, so, being a registered nurse as well as a midwife, I am covering her work for her. Just as well the recent "baby boom" has slackened, or I would be working twenty-four hours a day!"

Mavis took her coat and showed her into the room, where Mrs Watton was still fast asleep.

"Dr Hodges saw me in the surgery. He said your mother-in-law has had a stroke. Now our main concern is to make her comfortable, keep her clean, and ensure she takes all the prescribed medication." Sister Griffiths smiled confidently at Mavis.

"What do you want me to do?" asked Mavis, anxiously. She had never looked after an elderly person before, and had no clue as to what would be expected of her.

"Don't worry," reassured Sister Griffiths, "We can't do much until the men bring the bed downstairs."

"Downstairs?!" Mrs Watton was suddenly awake again, one blue eye opening and staring ferociously at the two women. A drop of saliva dribbled down her chin. Mavis felt quite queasy.

"Yes," replied Sister Griffiths, firmly, "It would be dangerous for you to try to go upstairs at the moment. Impossible, actually" she added in a whisper to Mavis.

Mrs Watton fidgeted in her chair, and looked uncomfortable.

"I want to go to the toilet," she announced, sulkily, "And my commode is still upstairs."

"Not a problem, cariad." Sister Griffiths bustled efficiently about the room, moving furniture around and creating more room within which to work. Turning to Mavis, she smiled brightly and said, "Let's go up and bring the commode down, Mavis. I am sure that between the two of us we will manage it easily."

"Of course!" Mavis was only too glad to have something useful to do, and somehow, the two women, neither of them at all well built, succeeded in carrying the ancient, mahogany commode down the narrow stairs.

"Now then, Mrs Watton, let's help you on to it." Mavis admired the way Sister Griffiths was completely in charge of the situation, and how comfortingly capable she seemed. Eva Griffiths was also much too glamorous to be a nurse and midwife, with long, coppery hair pulled up into a neat bun, and a neat figure which her navy blue uniform couldn't possibly hide. It must be wonderful to be a nurse.

The two helped Mrs Watton to her feet, and manoeuvred her towards the commode.

"Right Mavis, pull her drawers down while I hold her," instructed Sister Griffiths. Mavis was horrified, but saying nothing, just gritted her teeth and held her breath against the fumes of urine which wafted up towards her nose, as she removed the damp underwear from her mother-in-law's large, white bottom. Thus enthroned on the commode, Mrs Watton sighed in relief as she started to pass urine, then, to Mavis' horror and intense embarrassment, she let go volleys of sulphurous wind, of which she seemed totally oblivious. If this was nursing, thought Mavis, you could keep it.

Twenty minutes later, Mrs Watton was back in her armchair, washed and clean, her snow-white hair brushed and her dentures soaking in a mug, ready to be reinserted. It had been Mavis' task to clean those pink and white beauties, after which she had had to sit down for fear of passing out. If Sister Griffiths was at all aware of Mavis' discomfiture, she did not show it.

" I will be off, now." she announced, returning from the kitchen where she had been washing her hands. "Nothing more for you to do, really, except make Mrs Watton a drink. Fluids are very important, but don't worry if she doesn't want much to eat."

Mavis thought privately that her mother-in-law could probably benefit from a little weight loss, after that gargantuan struggle with the commode.

"I will return this afternoon, around four o'clock, and I will show you how to care for Mrs Watton's pressure areas, and how to give her her medication." And with that, Sister Griffiths put on her coat and left, leaving behind a very anxious Mavis, who was certainly feeling reluctant about her new role as personal nurse to a difficult and demanding Mrs Watton.

"Would you like a cup of tea?" asked Mavis, keen to keep busy and avoid having to make conversation with the cantankerous old lady.

"Feed the cats first, then make some tea!" ordered Mrs Watton imperiously.

Yes, your majesty, thought Mavis, going into the kitchen. Several cats were mewing plaintively outside the kitchen door. Mavis looked in the cupboard under the sink, and found a couple of tins of Kit-E-Kat, which she proceeded to open and share between the three feeding bowls. Opening the door, she placed the bowls on the floor. Immediately, they were surrounded by Ted, then a small female tabby and two ginger toms. Closing the door, Mavis left them to it, not sure which she hated more, the fishy smell of the cat food, or Mrs Watton's drawers.

"Tea will be ready in a minute!" she called out, setting a tray with crockery.

There was no reply.

"Are you alright?" she called again, filling the kettle.

Silence.

Mavis put down the kettle and rushed into the other room.

There sat Mrs Watton, her eyes fixed and staring, her mouth hanging open, her face a mottled purple, her head lolling to one side. Mavis wanted to scream, but no sound would come out. She ran over to her mother-in-law, and touched her arm. It was warm, but there was no doubt at all that Mrs Watton was now very much dead. Mavis had never seen a dead body before, and was sickened by the lurid scene she was witnessing. How could a person look like that? She had always thought that dead people merely appeared to be asleep, yet here was her mother-in-law looking as though she had choked, struggled for breath, seeming to have fought against some evil spectre as it had come to collect her soul.

Panic surged through her. There was no telephone, no way of calling for help. Mavis' instinct told her to remain where she was. Ernest would soon return, surely. At a loss as to what to do for the best, Mavis walked over to the window and drew the curtains. She wasn't sure whether she should touch Mrs Watton, or leave everything as it was – or maybe that was what you should do if you were calling the police. She paced up and down, wringing her hands and praying for someone to arrive.

Fortune was on her side, the Reliant pulled up , and Ernest stepped out. Mavis flew to the front door. "Oh, Ernest, she's gone!" she sobbed wildly.

"Gone? What do you mean? To hospital?" Ernest looked confused, pushing her away from the door.

"No! She's dead! Your mother is dead!"

"Arglwydd mawr!" Ernest pushed Mavis aside and ran into the house. She followed him slowly, dreading his reaction when he saw her. She entered the darkened room. The clock ticked quietly and relentlessly. Ernest was on his knees at his mother's side, holding her cooling hand. He did not weep, but his face was rigid with grief.

"Ein Tad yn y nefoedd," he began reciting the Lord's Prayer in Welsh, "Sancteiddier dy enw..." and beckoned to Mavis to do the same, which she obediently did.

They remained kneeling and praying for a while, then Ernest got to his feet.

"Mavis, I will have to stay here with Mam. It's at a time like this that I wish you could drive. I know it's a long walk back to the village but you will have to do this. Ring the doctor, from the phone box then ring Fred. Ask him to pick you up and bring you back here. Bring my Bible with you." Mavis nodded, quietly.

Leaving a silent, pale Ernest sitting with his deceased mother, Mavis started the mile-long walk back to the village. Dark clouds were gathering, and the wind, which had been gusty, but mild, turned cold, cruelly whipping the trees into a requiem anthem for the departed Mrs Watton. Leaving the wooded part of the road behind, she hurried along, wishing she had worn rather more practical footwear than her black patent work shoes. Before long, it started raining; Mavis lifted her face to the sky and allowed the raindrops to sting her cheeks, wanting to suffer their punishment for allowing her mother-in-law to die whilst in her care. Tears mingled with the rain and her black mascara trickled southwards, but she didn't care. For once, Mavis forgot her appearance, so wrapped up was she in witnessing for the first time the death of a human being. Her dark hair hung in rats' tails over her small shoulders, as she stumbled along the road, reaching the phone box in record time, searching in her pocket for a threepence.

Fifteen minutes later, she reached her garden gate, and, fumbling for the key, she let herself inside, but not before a keen pair of blue eyes spotted her from beyond the hedge. Seamus, back from a ramble, clad in a concealing waterproof coat and a large leather hat, watched Mavis, wild-faced and soaking wet, as she disappeared once more into the depths of her cottage.

The funeral was scheduled for the following Tuesday. Tudor Morris the undertaker had been in regular attendance, and Mrs Watton's body now lay in the chapel of rest at his funeral parlour in Llanelli. Ernest had wanted to have the coffin brought to the cottage, but Mavis drew the line at that. She wished to show her late mother-in-law all the respect possible, but to have her lying in state in the parlour? Out of the question.

Various chapel members and extended family had called to pay their respects. Mavis was kept busy making tea, opening cards and arranging flowers. By the Friday of that week, over fifty sympathy cards graced the sideboard and mantelpiece, and the cloying scent of lilies and chrysanthemums filled the air. Mavis could never bear the smell of those flowers again, to her they would always be the harbingers of death and sorrow.

At half-past three, Mavis was waving goodbye to the last of the day's visitors, looking forward to a quiet five minutes alone. Ernest had gone down to the undertaker's to view the body once more before the coffin was sealed. He hadn't asked Mavis to join him, and she hadn't offered either. She found the whole business ghoulish and unnecessary. With a sigh, she sank gratefully into an armchair, and closed her eyes for a blissful moment. Within a few minutes, her breathing slowed and deepened, and she drifted off to sleep. Just as she was lifting her face to be kissed by a man who looked remarkably like Seamus, she was abruptly woken from her dream by a loud knock on the door, which then opened, and there stood Audrey, Ernest's daughter, back from Johannesburg.

"Aunty Mavis!" she greeted, rushing forward and hugging her stepmother.

Mavis had always liked Audrey, and admired her adventurous spirit. The two women pulled apart, and regarded each other. Audrey's dark eyes, so similar to her own, sparkled with fun and mischief, despite the sad reason for her visit.

"When did you get back?" asked Mavis, happily, "How did you get here from the station? My, you look wonderful, you look so brown!"

"Oh, Aunty Mavis!" Audrey giggled, wickedly. "It's so wonderful to be home. You have no idea how I have longed to get back." She looked more solemn. " I am so sorry Mamgu has passed away. I was coming home anyway, I had sent a telegram, but I don't know if it has reached anyone. I called in to Fred's after we got off the train, and he told me everything."

"We? We got off the train?" smiled Mavis, slyly. "Now who are 'we,' or shouldn't I ask?"

Audrey shook her dark, bobbed hair, and laughed. She looked at Mavis, searching for sympathy and support.

"Oh, Aunty Mavis, you don't miss anything, do you?" Audrey blushed, slightly. "I have a fiance, now. He is from Canada. I met him in Johannesburg, he works for the Diplomatic Service, and his name is John. He's outside. We got a taxi from town. Can he come in?"

Mavis looked at her step-daughter, whose face was slightly flushed from unaccustomed shyness, her smart figure clad in an apricot suit, obviously purchased in some equally smart boutique in South Africa, her big brown eyes hopeful, so reminiscent of Audrey Hepburn, and her heart softened.

"Cariad! Of course you can! Bring him in at once! Your father is down in Llanelli seeing to the funeral arrangements, but no doubt he will be back soon."

Audrey grinned and shouted out, "John! Come in!"

Mavis watched how excited Audrey seemed, how girlish, even at twenty-four, and envied her, briefly. Then her eyes were drawn to the door, as in stepped the most handsome young man Mavis had seen in her life. John was over six feet tall, with kind brown eyes and a tanned complexion.

"Hi, Mrs Watton," he greeted her in a soft, American-sounding drawl. Mavis was delighted for Audrey, and totally enthralled by this captivating young Canadian.

"So what happened exactly?" asked Audrey, after all the introductions were over and done with. "What about the post-mortem?"

"Well, there was no need for one," explained Mavis, "because Mamgu had seen the doctor the day before. She had called Dr Hodges out because of a painful knee. Apparently that dispenses with the need for a post-mortem. But, Audrey, how on earth could she have died so quickly? I only turned my back for a few minutes to make her a drink." Mavis wrung her hands, remembering that awful moment.

Audrey looked her step-mother's stricken face and out her arms around her. "Let's sit down, Aunty Mavis. Maybe I can try and explain." The two women sat down on the sofa, while John hastily went outside for a cigarette.

"You see, Mamgu had a stroke, and maybe there was a clotting problem with her blood, so possibly she either had a heart attack, or more likely a clot on the lung. A pulmonary embolus. It would have been so quick, she wouldn't have been aware, probably. There was nothing you could have done, it wasn't preventable. Honestly."

Mavis looked up at her step-daughter gratefully. "Thank you, Audrey, cariad. That is really helpful. I wish Eva Griffiths had told me that when I saw her afterwards. But maybe she didn't realise how responsible I feel about it." Mavis smiled. "Now go and fetch in your gorgeous young man, and we'll have some tea."

The next half-hour was spent gossiping and exchanging news.

"We will be staying with Fred and his wife, their new house is almost ready now" Audrey grinned at Mavis. "I don't think it would be terribly comfortable for John and me to stay here with you and Dad."

Reading between the lines, Mavis translated this as Audrey being far too free-spirited to endure the cloistered, regimented environment that the cottage offered. She smiled, nodding her understanding.

"But please come and visit us often, won't you?" she pleaded. "And would you like a bite to eat? Eiddwen has made us some bara brith."

As if he had heard the offer himself, the door opened, and in walked Ernest.

"Well, I Duw, Duw!" he smiled. " Dere 'ma, Audrey, come here! And how is my little Staff Nurse Watton?"

Audrey pecked her father dutifully on the cheek, and although there was no hug or embrace of any kind, nothing could hide the pride shining in Ernest's eyes, for once warm and friendly, losing their northern coolness in his joy at seeing his daughter once more.

"I won't be Nurse Watton much longer, Dad!" smiled Audrey, bringing John forward. "Meet John Fediuk, my fiance."

Ernest's face immediately clouded over. He shook hands reluctantly with the Canadian giant.

"Fediuk? What sort of name is that?" he demanded, grumpily. Surely if his daughter was to go gadding about the globe to find a husband, she could have found one with a proper name?

But John merely laughed. "My father was from the Ukraine," he explained. "He emigrated to Canada in the thirties. My mother is actually from Burry Port!" Salvation. Relieved at his future son-in-law's Welsh half-pedigree, he warmed slightly, and the two men chatted amicably.

"I sure am sorry to hear about your mother." offered John.

"Well, she was well into her eighties," sighed Ernest, "And she had been a faithful servant to the Lord. May she rest in peace."

"Amen." responded John solemnly. He caught Mavis' eye, and she wasn't entirely certain if he was being serious or not. Maybe there was more to this clean-cut Canadian than met the eye. Lucky Audrey, she thought. Her step-daughter then went out into the garden with her father to talk about the old Mrs Watton, leaving John alone with Mavis.

Whilst Mavis made the tea, John explained the wedding plans. The engaged couple planned to return to South Africa to complete Audrey's contract, then would return to Wales for their wedding, maybe the following autumn. They hoped to honeymoon in Canada, staying with John's family in Vancouver, before returning once more to Wales to settle in Cardiff, where John would be working in the Welsh Office, and Audrey hoped to find a staff nurse's post at Cardiff Royal Infirmary.

The afternoon passed speedily. How pleasant it was to have the two young people here, thought Mavis, wistfully. She would be sorry to see them leave.

"We had better see about a taxi home," decided Audrey, after tea. "Is there a taxi service yet in Llannon? And is there a phone here yet, or are you still all living in the dark ages!?"

"No need for a phone." Ernest was adamant. "We have managed quite well without one so far."

"I will run down to the Richards' house and ask Mr O'Brien if I can use the phone to call you a taxi," volunteered Mavis. "Do you have a number?"

Audrey fished about in her capacious bag, and handed a slip of paper to her mother-in-law.

"I'll be as quick as I can." Mavis pulled her red cardigan over her shoulders, for the spring afternoon was bright but breezy. She set off down the lane, happy for the first time in days. How eagerly her feet ran down the leafy, sunlit lane. But what if Seamus was not at home? Ah well, it was still worth a try. Reaching his front door, a little breathless from running, she knocked rather timidly. After what seemed like an eternity, the door creaked open, and there stood Seamus, bare-chested, barefoot, with paintbrush in hand, his eyebrows disappearing up into his untidy hair, as he regarded Mavis in surprise.

"Sweet Mavis! And for what reason am I being treated to your unexpected but most welcome appearance?" He grinned at her, holding open the door.

"I hope you don't mind me turning up like this, uninvited!" she began."It's just that I was hoping I could use your telephone. My step-daughter needs to return to Llanelli and I have to get a taxi for her."

"To be sure, that's no problem at all," he laughed, "just be sure to leave the threepenny bit on the sideboard, that's all!"

"Oh dear, I didn't bring my purse with me," apologised Mavis, embarrassed.

"Oh, for feck's sake!" groaned Seamus. "I was bloody joking!"

"Oh. I see." Mavis looked down, avoiding his eyes, then started giggling.

"That's better! Now the phone is in the small room there on the right, I use it for all my paperwork, the work I never, ever do. Help yourself!"

Unaccustomed to using a phone, Mavis spoke very loudly and slowly into the receiver, causing Seamus to smile behind her back. However, Mavis managed to secure a taxi to take Audrey and John back to Fred's house.

Turning back to Seamus, she smiled. "I don't use a telephone very often. Not many people have one here in Llannon. But thank you so much."

Seamus sighed. "So many things you don't know about, yes? Now tell me, Mavis, will you agree to sit for me, for me to capture that wild look in your eyes? That passion in your face? Will you?"

Mavis stared up at him, confused and bewildered. Tiny beads of sweat glittered on her forehead.

"Me? Wild?"

Seamus turned away from her, walking into the hall once more. Without looking back he continued.

"I saw you, I saw you running, racing into your cottage the other day. Tears coursing down your face, panic written all over your gorgeous features. The provincial little housewife proving she had a heart after all."

Mavis followed him slowly. "That must have been the day that my mother-in-law died," she murmured, "and it was a terrible day."

She paused under the ancient, dusty chandelier. The scent of the old house's history filled her senses. The memory of past gaiety and laughter rushed briefly through her mind. How frivolous those days seemed now, how insubstantial and meaningless.

Turning to him, she raised her serious face, her eyes dark with hidden emotion, and said, quietly,

"I dreamed of you this afternoon." She turned away from him, and headed for the half-open front door. Too slowly, for within a second he had grabbed her arm and pulled her close. She breathed in the wonderful scent of fresh, masculine sweat, felt the rough hair against her skin as she buried her
face in his chest.

"Don't do this to me," she whispered, yet all the while not wanting him to let her go.

"Don't do what? What shouldn't I do? What are you afraid of?" He looked down into her dilated eyes, saw her flaming cheeks and felt her breath hot on his bare arm.

"Nothing. I-I....nothing," she finished, lamely, pulling reluctantly away from him. Yet his grip on her arm did not lessen.

"Come back and sit for me, erstwhile heartless woman!" Softly, so very softly, he murmured those words into her ear. Mavis closed her eyes and wished with all her soul she could give in to her desires.

However, a sharp bark brought her back to reality. There stood Dai at the front door, gazing quizzically at the couple, his white ears pricked up, his head on one side.

"Seems like your chaperone has arrived!" laughed Seamus. The moment was gone, the magic shattered by the presence of a young dog. How Mavis cursed that intrusion.

"Dai. You daft, stupid dog." Mavis sighed in disappointment. Turning to Seamus, she said softly, "I have to go. As you said, my little chaperone has come to take me home."

"Of course," he smiled. "but just do one thing for me. Come back here next week, after the funeral - it will be next week, I assume? Come here and sit for me. I want to paint you. I want to do that more than anything. Will you come?"

The sun gleamed through the landing window, setting Seamus' hair on fire, creating a halo around his head until he looked like the angel Gabriel himself, but come to lead her into mischief, rather than proclaim her virtue and chastity. He was irresistible.

"Oh, yes, I will come," replied Mavis, quietly. "The funeral is on Tuesday, and I will have the day off work, of course. May I come on Thursday? There may be a few things to sort out on Wednesday, and I think Ernest has to go to see his solicitor on Thursday - "

"Wednesday, Thursday....whenever!" interrupted Seamus, laughing. "Very well, Thursday it shall be. Come here in the morning, when the light will be good."

"Fine," she smiled back, "I shall see you then." She turned and walked down the path, Dai trotting obediently behind her.

"Hope the funeral goes well." Seamus watched her make her way to the gate, then disappeared once more into the depths of the house.

The following Tuesday was as miserable and cold as a November day. How fitting, thought Mavis, as she buttoned her black dress to the chin. However, it was cold enough to justify wearing her fur coat. The grey, leaden sky would compliment it perfectly.

The funeral would be at ten o'clock and the service in Bethel chapel would last about an hour or so. There would be many hymns, no doubt accompanied on the organ by that minx Gladys Williams, and several eulogies by righteous, upstanding members of the congregation. The burial would follow, but would only be attended by the men. Mavis and all the other women in the family would retire back to the cottage, for the mandatory tea and sandwiches. Everything was ready. Eiddwen had once more proved herself a true friend, and had baked several cakes; a whole regiment of scones and biscuits also lay waiting on the parlour table, resting prettily on the snow-white tablecloth which was reserved for such sombre events.

Mavis looked at her reflection in the dressing table mirror. Hastily, she removed some of the lipstick she had earlier applied. Maybe it wasn't entirely appropriate to look too glamorous this morning. Having pinned up her hair into a casual topknot, she sighed in satisfaction as she retrieved the fur coat from the wardrobe. She never failed to appreciate the sensuous softness of the mink as she put it on. How wonderful it made her feel.

"The car is here!" called Ernest from the bottom of the stairs. Mr Morris' funeral car was parked rather awkwardly in the lane, blocking it completely. Despite the fact that the chapel was only a five minute walk, Ernest insisted that he and Mavis should travel there in the mourners' car.

As she got into the car, Mavis noticed Seamus, walking up the lane, carrying a large bag. Probably off to paint the countryside, thought Mavis. He raised his hand and waved discreetly at her, but did not smile. Mavis caught his eye, and nodded slightly.

The driver managed to turn the car around, almost decapitating Mavis' newly planted magnolia tree as he did so, and the huge, black Daimler purred its way down the lane.

About thirty or forty people were already gathered outside the chapel, all dressed in the deepest black. Obviously the chapel must be full to overflowing. They reminded Mavis of a flock of vultures, ready to pick over the carcass of her late mother-in-law's life. But then she spotted Audrey and John, like twin rays of sunshine on a dull, cloudy sky. The funeral hearse arrived almost immediately. As Mavis and Ernest got out of the car, she could almost feel the disapproval of the women as they regarded her attire.

However, Mavis just stuck her chin up in the air, put her arm through Ernest's, and they followed the flower-covered coffin as it was carried slowly into the chapel, where the late Mrs Watton would have thoroughly approved of her final chapel attendance, with all its religious pomp and depressing Bible readings, full of warnings of burning in hell.

She may even have smiled.

Chapter Nine

Broadening Horizons

The next few days passed in a haze of solicitors' appointments; the late Mrs Watton's estate was fairly uncomplicated, but the practicalities of clearing the house and its contents, as well as the adoption of her various cats to local disinclined families, required a great deal of time and energy. Many dark and introspective conversations with Ernest also took their toll on a disinclined Mavis. To her dismay, Audrey and John only visited once more, then left Llanelli in order to visit John's family in Burry Port. The couple then travelled even further west, to Pendine, to stay in a caravan. The loyal Eiddwen did her best to provide her despondent friend with as much support and succour as she could, but Mavis felt as though she was drowning in a whirlpool of strict, dark Welsh duty. Dark and thick as treacle, but never as decadently sweet.

An eventful May was developing into June. The first of this celebrated and flaming month was also the very day when Mavis was expected to present herself at Seamus' house.

June the first. It arrived with a triumphant blast of gold, burst into glorious, joyful flame with hot sunshine beating down on Mavis' red geraniums, cosseting her tender magnolia tree in its warmth, teasing even the reluctant and exotic oleander into a hint of Mediterranean blossom. At half past nine, Ernest had departed for his solicitor's appointment.

Mavis was alone, apart from little Dai, who was already having a nap under the apple tree. The beauty of the morning lifted Mavis' heart. She longed to escape the cottage, to participate in the season's fabulous celebration. But she would escape only as far as the bottom of the lane, to Seamus' house, to visit the person who had captured her imagination, so much so that he now invaded her dreams, and disturbed her daytime thoughts. Within fifteen minutes, Mavis was walking down the lane, her mahogany curls dancing freely about her shoulders, wearing a plain, cream dress and a defiant look in her eyes. No longer feeling shy or timid, she knocked assertively on Seamus' door. She heard his slow, languid footsteps as he came down the hall, saw his pleased, lazy smile as he welcomed her and invited her in.

The hall was as untidy as ever, but it did not register within Mavis' preoccupied mind.

"Hello." His quiet greeting and the intense look in his eyes spoke volumes. Mavis stepped inside. He circled her, like a great, predatory cat, waiting to pounce. She remained perfectly still, her features composed, like a statue waiting to be brought to life. Or like a lamb to the slaughter? She wondered. Facing each other at last, their eyes locked. They watched each other, and a thousand years passed, as they held each other's gaze, slowly, gradually, surfacing to the reality of the present.

"So," he said finally, "are you ready to sit for me?" He smiled, extending his hand to lead her into the front room, his studio. Mavis returned his smile.

"I am as ready as I can be. But I didn't know what to wear or anything. You never mentioned that. I didn't know how you wanted me to appear." Taking her small hand in his, he drew her into the studio. The early sunshine filtered through the large, dusty windows, filling the room with brilliant light.

"I want you to appear exactly as you are. Little Mavis Rhiannon Watton. Entirely yourself. Do you fancy a coffee?"

"That would be lovely."

Seamus sauntered off to his kitchen. Mavis wandered around the room once more, but this time ignored the eclectic book collection, settling instead on a dusty record player, a Dansette Popular 4 speed model. Several black vinyl seven inch records lay scattered over the floor. Idly, she examined them, finally selecting one. Mavis had never used a record player before, but Eiddwen had one in her house, which belonged to her brother. Before Mavis got married, the two would spend hours listening to Danny and the Juniors, the Poni-Tails and Elvis Presley. She placed the record on the turntable, but didn't know what to do next.

"Don't know how to turn it on?" Seamus returned with two cups, again devoid of any saucers.

"Um, not really," laughed Mavis, apologetically.

"What have you picked?" He switched the machine on. The record dropped noisily onto the turntable, started rotating, and the beautiful, husky voice of Dusty Springfield spilled out.

"Island of Dreams. Do you live alone on your island of dreams, Mavis?" He handed her the coffee, settling back on the chaise longue, leaving her crouched on the wooden floor. He lit a cigarette. She took her time before answering.

Closing her eyes, she deeply inhaled the rich aroma of the hot coffee. Realising that he was aware of her sense of social claustrophobia, of her quiet, personal rebellion against her strict upbringing, she thought carefully, choosing her words judiciously.

"I live my life as I must. I made my bed, and I must lie on it. Any other choices I may have had have gone. My island of dreams is just that. Dreams."

He remained silent, quietly smoking his cigarette, casually flicking the ash into the derelict fireplace. The clock ticked resolutely on, without intruding on the couple's comfortable and companionable tranquillity. Mavis sipped her coffee, looking at the floor. Finally, Seamus spoke.

"Come on then, Mavis, be my muse, my Mnemosyne , for I shall depict your charm in art, so that it shall be remembered forever." He pulled her to her feet and led her over to the chaise longue. "Make yourself comfortable. You will need to be, as you will have to maintain that position for quite some time."

As she sat down gingerly, remembering once again its previous occupant, she looked up at Seamus and asked, nervously, "Will I be allowed to talk, or move?"

He laughed. "To be sure you will! All you have to do is look in the same direction, and keep sitting fairly still, as you are now."

An easel was standing ready at the far end of the room, which benefited from having large, bay windows at the front and the side, allowing the morning light to flood in, illuminating everything in its purity. As he painted, they talked, laughing and teasing each other playfully. Seamus seemed to have lost his sharpness with her, withholding the acerbic comments he once seemed so fond of. She began to relax, to enjoy herself.

"When can I have a peep at the painting?" she laughed, playfully. He gave a little smile, but did not look up from painting.

"Ah, not until it is finished! And then you will see it in all its glory! For it shall be glorious!"

The hours flew by all too quickly. Before she knew it, the clock struck eleven.

"I think I had better go," she announced reluctantly, slowly getting to her feet, her legs and hips a little stiff from sitting still for so long. "Ernest will be home soon, he will wonder where I am."

"He doesn't know you are here?"

"No." Mavis looked anxious. "I will just say I popped down to see Eiddwen or something. But I dare not stay any longer." She stumbled slightly on her weakened limbs as she moved towards the door; he caught her swiftly, his strong arms catching her by the waist.

"Not so fast, my pretty." He looked down at her, holding her close to him. His fingers lightly traced the outline of her face, gently brushing back her hair, lifting her chin up, so her eyes met his.

"Your eyes are beautiful." he whispered. "They speak to me of southern skies. Never hide them. Be true to yourself."

He bent down to her. His breath smelled of tobacco, yet sweet and inviting. Mavis did not resist. Her lips opened slightly, and she felt the warmth of his mouth as he started to kiss her, softly caressing , his tongue tentatively seeking and probing, until she was melting inside. She kissed him back, unable to believe the emotions he was stirring within her. He ran his fingers through her hair, held her face in his hands and carried on kissing her as though he never wanted to stop. She melded into his body, arching her back so her tiny form pressed into his. His immediate response was to cup her small and pert left breast tenderly in his large hand, to hold and stroke it, suspend it whilst teasing her quickening nipple into eager attention. Never before had she felt such passion, such a soft, deep and erotic stimulation of her senses. She felt warm, as though she was being immersed in a pool of pleasure , excited beyond belief. Never before had she experienced such intense tenderness, such natural sensuality. Her head swam. They pulled away. Seamus appeared serious.

"This is a very dangerous game we are playing, Mavis." He looked down at her, and removed a smudge of mascara from her right eye with his thumb. Her face was stricken. Yes, she had dreamed about this moment, and had thought about Seamus constantly, but this was something she hadn't really believed would happen. She regarded him with awe. Was this what it felt like to fall in love?.

"I understand." She looked down at her beige toed shoes, unsure what she should say, what was expected of her. Sensing her uncertainty, Seamus hugged her close.

"Come again, as soon as you can. Pop a little note in, telling me when you can sit for me again. Don't sign it. I will know it is from you. No-one else sends me notes." He laughed.

Mavis smiled back. "I will. Maybe at the weekend?"

"To be sure. That'll do nicely, sweet Mavis."

He opened the door for her, and she stepped out into the hot June morning. He watched her walk quickly down the path, looking back at him, smiling, waving, looking happy and carefree. He waved back, and remained at the door until he could see her no more.

Mavis' head was reeling as she hurried home, she could still feel the heat of his kiss on her face; she relived every second of the embrace, enjoying again and again the thrill she had just experienced. She thought that had birdsong had never sounded so sweet as she opened her garden gate, never had the sky been such a brilliant blue. She sighed with happiness. Happiness which soon evaporated when she entered the kitchen, to find Ernest glowering in his chair.

"Where have you been?" He seemed irritable. Mavis turned away from him to put on her apron.

"Only to see Eiddwen. What do you want for lunch? There's a couple of pork chops in the pantry. Shall I fry them with onion for you? Or I could roast them and we could have a couple of baked potatoes too?" Her voice shook slightly.

"Baked potatoes? Tramps' food, that's what they are!" he spitefully snapped in reply. Mavis was jolted out of her anxiety by his unpleasantness.

"Fine," she retorted, "sort it out yourself. I am going for a walk with Dai."

Removing her apron, she flounced out of the kitchen, exchanged her smart beige shoes for sensible walking brogues and put the lead on the dog. Without another word she slammed the back door, and set off once more, but this time up the lane, to the track, Dai trotting along enthusiastically in front of her. Her bare arms soaked up the warmth of the sun; soon they would be golden brown. She smiled to herself, at least her olive skin tanned easily.

Up on the track, she decided to head south, towards the sun and the farms which dotted the countryside along the way. There was relative silence, apart from some midday bees, industriously and obsessively diving into the foxgloves and fading bluebells in the hedges. How they reminded her of Seamus' tongue delving its way into her eager mouth. Such a blissful, ecstatic morning....

Even the birds had decided to retreat for a while, seeking rest and shade amongst the oaks and sycamores which lined the track. Peace ruled the hour. The smell of hot grass and wild flowers filled her senses. Such a soporific setting, thought Mavis. She would willingly have curled up beneath the trees and fallen asleep, to dream the sweet dreams of a passionate woman.

The footpath ran alongside the railway, used only twice a day by the miners who were transported from the town to the coal mines along the Gwendraeth Valley, and then home again at the end of a shift. Mavis had walked along the track after dark on a few occasions, when she had visited her cousin Glenda, who lived in Felinfoel. Those night time walks filled her with a sense of fear, yet a lurid and strange desire. What if a ghost train hurtled along the railway, late at night, silent and oblivious to the living? Would the long-deceased miners silently ignore their own tombstones in the graveyards which lined the track? Would the cadaverous guard grin evilly at her, his smile never reaching his eyes, hoping to whisk her off to hell....? She shivered. The hot June sun suddenly failed in its intensity as a rogue cloud stole across it, and she quickened her step. Dai fell in alongside her, his only concern being clumps of grass along the track, which other dogs had urinated there previously, and how high he could aim his own stream of doggy urine by way of response.

The walk was downhill, a gradual and deceptive gradient, and fine whilst one was heading south, but a steady tax on the energy on the northbound return. Once she had reached the junction at the lake, Mavis decided to go home. She had been gone over an hour, and hopefully Ernest would be in a better frame of mind once she returned. As she walked back along the track, she realised that she had met nobody at all along the way. Still, that suited her mood. She wanted nobody to intrude upon her secret and delightful thoughts, wishing to savour them at her leisure.

It was a quarter past one as Mavis opened the door, removing her walking shoes before entering the room. Ernest was nowhere to be seen.

"Ernest?" Mavis felt puzzled. She moved swiftly from room to room. There was no sign of her husband. The only evidence of his recent presence was his used plate and knife in the kitchen, where he had made do with some bread and cheese for his lunch. Mavis sighed. Still, she was relieved that he wasn't there to play the Grand Inquisitor and spoil the day once more. Energised by her emotionally charged morning, and her reflective walk with Dai, she set about her housework, attacking the ironing with more gusto that it usually received.

Trouble was, she considered, the monotonous task of ironing set her mind free, allowing it to wander and analyse....

She had read somewhere, (always somewhere, she could never remember where, exactly) that through the ages, women would let their minds wander freely whilst spinning flax, and would frequently see into other worlds....

She knew of no other worlds other than her own, indeed the chapel vehemently prohibited anything other than its own, strict dictum. Even "fringe" beliefs such as spiritualism, Roman Catholicism or any interest in the supernatural, were staunchly forbidden and frowned upon. Mavis herself kept an open mind. Outwardly she conformed and obeyed the rules of her rigid Baptist upbringing, but her mind reached out towards other knowledge, unusual and stimulating ways of thinking and philosophies. She had no idea of what she was seeking, had no intention of being subversive or rebellious, she was merely aware of a secret and personal yearning for more.

Seven Daz-white shirts, four pillowslips, two sheets and seven drying cloths later, Mavis heaved a sigh of satisfaction. There was something to be said for living an orderly life. Seamus may live in a topsy-turvy world, but she was happier when her life was predictable and secure. She sat down in an armchair, sipped a cup of tea and, for a brief while, was at peace with herself and the world.

Further down the lane, at the old Richards' house, an artist was struggling with his thoughts, attempting to rationalise and compartmentalise the simmering passion which was threatening to sabotage his protective barrier. For many years he had sought to secure an armour of iron-clad immunity against the treachery of so-called love. Seamus had had many women, had known them, in the Biblical sense and otherwise. After Carmel had left him, and then died, his heart had frozen. Never again had he entirely trusted women. He courted them, laughed and entertained them, slept with them and played with them. But he never promised them anything, other than a good time and his gregarious company for a short while. His tummy rumbled. Artists also eat. Seamus decided to delve into the cool, dark pantry. He had employed a local woman to do his shopping for him, down at the Co-op in Felinfoel. She drove a car, and delivered his goods every Tuesday morning. Rummaging around amongst the cheese, onions, bread and vegetables, Seamus thought he would construct a pie of a sort. He was seriously hungry. Having brought with him, from his travels, many spices and herbs, he considered his new culinary venture. Oregano from his visit to Corfu, and memories of the midnight view from Bellavista, the sweet smile of Anthousa, the scent of the aromatic herb warmed from the Mediterranean sun…he lost himself in the Ionian islands…

He smiled to himself, enjoying his dreams of the past, and immersing himself in his cooking. Just as he was carefully removing the hot dish from the Rayburn, sniffing appreciatively as the savoury aroma filled the air, his mouth watering, there was a knock at the door.

"Who the feck can that be?!" Scowling, he flung down the drying cloth and rushed angrily to open the door. To his surprise, there stood Gladys Williams, smiling hopefully up at him. With the greatest of effort he managed to mumble a greeting.

"Oh. Hello." What on earth did she want? Seamus struggled to keep the annoyance out of his voice.

"Hello, Seamus." Gladys' words were silky smooth, like the easy smile which she wore with casual confidence.

"Um, did you want something?" Seamus thought longingly of his pie, rapidly cooling in the kitchen. Gladys didn't bat an eyelid at such rudeness, and merely continued in her caressing tone.

"Why, Seamus! Aren't you even going to invite me in?"

"Well, actually I was about to have my lunch." He was getting more impatient by the second.

She raised a well-plucked eyebrow. "Lunch? It's past three o'clock!"

"So what?" shrugged Seamus, extremely frustrated by now. "I eat when I am hungry, not because the clock dictates."

"So are you going to invite me in or not?" She stood at the door, her hands on her ample hips, a beckoning smile on her pale, pink lips.

"Okay, okay." He knew when he was beaten, so turned around, allowing Gladys to follow him into the hall. Before he could stop her, she wandered into the studio, and went straight up to the canvas depicting the first strokes of Mavis' portrait. She gazed at it for a full minute before turning back to Seamus with a strange expression on her face.

"So. Mrs Watton has been sitting for you now, has she? You are scraping the bottom of the barrel, asking a minister's middle-aged wife to sit for you. Did her husband ask you to do it? I can't see any other reason for it. I mean, she's not exactly youthful, is she? And hardly womanly, if you get my meaning. A skinny little thing, she is, no meat on her at all. I doubt your Arab friend would fancy her, would he? You've only painted her head so far. Is she going to get her kit off for you? I can't imagine prim little Mrs Watton doing anything like that! And there wouldn't be much point anyway, nothing much there to paint!" She laughed scornfully.

"My, my, that has upset you, hasn't it?" Seamus shook his head thoughtfully.

"I mean, she is such a bitch, that Mrs Watton." There was no stopping Gladys now. A spiteful gleam illuminated her green eyes as she continued. "Everyone in the village will tell you how horrible she is to her friend Eiddwen. And how she schemed and planned things so she could get a man. There was a word for her before she got married. She was a tease. Accepting invitations from other men, and then rejecting them, just so Mr Watton would notice her. She got him in the end, obviously. Mind you, she is welcome to him, miserable bugger that he is. She certainly has to toe the line where he is concerned. But, having said that, he buys her lots of nice things, like that fur coat, so I suppose it's worth it. But she thinks she's so special, doesn't she? And so vain, the way she struts about like a peacock in those fancy clothes of hers. I can't abide the woman." Her tirade over, she sighed. "Are you going to make me one of your lovely cups of coffee, Seamus?" She walked suggestively into the kitchen, swinging her hips as she went. The pie stood in all its golden splendour on the draining board. Gladys sniffed appreciatively.

"Goodness, that smells nice! I haven't had any lunch either. I had to spend the last few hours tucked up in the vestry with Mr Watton, going over the hymns for next Sunday. And I had to suffer the journey up from Felinfoel in his bloody draughty car. Just as well it's warm today." She moved closer, her hips undulating, thrusting out her firmly-scaffolded breasts provocatively. Seamus moved protectively in front of his pie.

"That's strong language from a chapel organist, Gladys. And you can take your beady eyes off my pie. As the dreadful Mrs Watton herself remarked, you do seem to have eaten too many rich things recently...." Too late. The words were out of his mouth before he could stop them. Gladys glared at him. "That stupid cow is far too full of her own self-importance, in my opinion," she hissed, "and she could do with taking down a peg or two. Prancing around the chapel in a bloody fur coat in May! Showing off to the whole congregation. Who the hell does she think she is?" She stopped suddenly, aware that her angry words would not endear herself to the likes of Seamus. She smiled again, composing her features. "I thought you would be pleased to see me, after our little, er, you know...." Her voice trailed away flirtatiously, she lowered her eyes coyly, putting out a plump white hand to touch Seamus' chest. Seamus frowned, his fair eyebrows meeting each other in the middle of his furrowed forehead. The pie would be bloody cold by now. God, how badly he wanted it.

"Listen, Gladys," he sighed heavily, removing her hand "our little er, you know was nothing more than you posing for me to paint you, for which you were paid, quite handsomely. Now I really must be getting on...."

"But you kissed me!" Gladys was becoming the shrieking harpy once again, unable to stop herself.

"So what's in a kiss?" he shrugged. "You were flirting with me all the time. If I hadn't kissed you, you would have been very upset, and I needed a seductive model, not a bloody weeping willow."

Gladys looked him up and down, rage distorting her bland face into ugliness. "You are such a sod, Seamus." And with that she turned abruptly and stormed out of the house, slamming the door behind her.

"Thank feck for that!" Seamus turned gleefully to his longed-for pie, attacking it with gusto, eating directly from the baking dish with an enormous tablespoon, not even bothering to pull up a chair, but devouring it standing up, like a Hebrew at the Passover.

Dusk descended with almost indecent speed that evening. The heat of early summer was rapidly cooling. Mavis had endured Ernest's petulant mood since he had returned at tea-time. Finally, after supper, she had tentatively asked him where he had been. His terse reply had been that he had been discussing the following Sunday's hymns with the organist, Gladys Williams.

"She gets about a bit." Mavis' words were innocent enough, but the hidden sarcasm was lost on the surly Ernest.

"Yes. She is a very busy woman. Looks after her mother well enough since her father passed away. Holds down a job as well. Very creditable."

"Of course." She murmured her polite reply as she dried and put away the supper dishes, one eye on the apricot sky in the west, feeling the longing for escape surging within her.

"And a damned attractive young lady. Well-fed and robust. Sound of body and of mind." Mavis looked at Ernest in astonishment. She couldn't believe her ears.

"And of soul, no doubt, Ernest," she added softly, her heart set on opening the back door and rushing towards the sunset.

"Oh, she is one devout and committed Christian." Ernest smiled in satisfaction. "She knows her Old Testament as well as I do. She supports her poor widowed mother, financially and spiritually. A gem of a woman!"

Mavis restrained herself from heading for the bathroom in order to regurgitate her supper. Instead she grabbed poor Dai's lead and, having hooked him up securely, told Ernest she was going for a twilight walk, made once more for the track, her thoughts racing madly through her head.

"Make sure you get back before it's dark." He returned to his perusal of the Bible, making notes in pencil alongside particularly relevant verses.

The trees on the hillside beyond the track were silhouetted starkly against the peachy sky, the blackbirds were in full evensong and only a few anxious ewes called plaintively for their erring lambs. Otherwise, silence reigned.

On the eastern horizon she could see the twinkling lights of nearby Swansea: another world from the rural, provincial Llannon. Down on the lane, she could see lights on in Seamus' house. She wondered what he was doing. The lights were only shining upstairs.....maybe he had retired for the night? Woman and dog walked on, southwards. The fading purple light settled like a vampire bat over Mavis' slim shoulders, absorbing light from her soul and feeding her fertile imagination with thoughts of spectres and ghouls. It was time to go home.

She slept heavily that night. No dreams of any sort disturbed her slumbers. Her exhausted mind allowed no intrusion, needing no more than peace, quiet and the comforting restorative powers of the deepest sleep.

Chapter Ten

The Progress of Summer

A lilac-coloured envelope fell quietly and discreetly through Seamus' letterbox on Friday evening at around six o'clock, the sender quietly hastening away into the gloom of the shadowy lane. He caught a glimpse of her, a slight, pale form disappearing into the darkness of the trees which shielded the house from the strong, midsummer sun. Smiling to himself, he carefully opened the note, feeling a thrill of anticipation as he read its contents.

"I will arrive at four o'clock tomorrow." Brief and succinct. The writing was small and neat, just like the writer herself. Folding it in half, he put it away in a drawer, returning to his painting of the woman who had arrived in his life, bringing such emotional turmoil with her.

The following day, Mavis called once more to sit for the fascinating artist, whose arrival in her life had likewise caused such havoc. The afternoon was warm and sultry. However, no sun shone over the old Richards house and pearly grey clouds hung heavily in the skies over Llannon.

Mavis knocked on the front door, perspiring slightly, wondering if her scarlet cheesecloth dress was entirely appropriate for the occasion. Should she have worn the same dress as before? She wore the scantiest of make-up, just a touch of rouge and a hint of mascara. Her emotions were make-up enough, causing her eyes to sparkle and putting a happy expression on her face.

Ten minutes later she was sitting upon the chaise longue, in the same position as she had been three days previously. Seamus was his usual charming self, but politeness personified, with no reference to the events of the previous

Wednesday. Mavis felt relieved, as she didn't know how to behave in such a situation.

"So, sweet Mavis," he began, without looking at her, intent on his work, "how did you manage to escape from your little cottage this afternoon?"

"Well, Ernest has gone to Llanelli, to help his son sort something out in his new house. He said he will have supper with Fred and his wife, so shouldn't get back until about seven o'clock." Mavis shifted slightly, her new lace petticoat scratching uncomfortably on the bare flesh above her stocking tops.

"That's grand! So I have you for three whole hours? We should get quite a bit done in that time!" Seamus grinned happily, mixing a combination of colours on his palette. Mavis looked up anxiously. "Oh no! I had better be gone by half past six! Just in case he returns earlier than expected. Fred and Margaret may decide to make shift for supper and get some fish and chips or something, and Ernest won't like that. He would come home if that happens."

Seamus looked crestfallen. "So you build up my hopes and dash them all to pieces within five minutes!"

Mavis scrutinised his face, and was relieved to see he was smiling at her. "Don't worry. I won't make you late or get you into trouble......or maybe I should..." he added quietly under his breath. He continued to paint for the next half an hour, concentration furrowing his forehead, making his face look unusually stern.

"Time for a coffee break." he announced, putting his brush aside. "It is Saturday after all, and there is no need to bust a gut today!" Mavis smiled at his total lack of conversational delicacy.

Over coffee they continued to talk, Seamus not taking his eyes off her, with Mavis looking desperately around in order to avoid his gaze. Suddenly, she could bear it no longer.

"About last Wednesday....." she began, awkwardly, colouring at the very memory of it. He put down his cup, got to his feet and walked over to her, took her hands in his and pulled her to her feet. "Look at me, Mavis." The tone of his voice demanded her immediate compliance. Slowly she raised her eyes and looked at him directly and unflinchingly.

"Yes?"

His voice softened. "If you have been feeling the way I have over the past three days, then you will have realised that there is nothing to be said about last Wednesday. I have been thinking about you far too much. In fact, sweet Mavis, you are in grave danger of it happening all over again." And with that he bent down and kissed her gently, running his hands through her hair once more, then holding her face in both his hands.

"Oh, Seamus. Of course I feel the same. How could I not?" She buried her face in his paint-splattered shirt, holding him close and relief flooding through her. Reluctantly, they pulled apart. He sat down once more, drawing her to him, taking her onto his lap so she was sitting on his knee.

"You know, you look like a little gypsy woman in that red dress." He laughed slightly, pulling at the puffed sleeve which threatened to descend at any moment down her brown arm. "My little gypsy woman, my little Simza, for you bring me such joy."

She tentatively stroked his cheek, wondering at the happiness she was experiencing.

"Speak to me Mavis, talk to me in that lovely accent of yours."

She sighed. "I don't know what to say." She fiddled absent-mindedly with the collar of his shirt. "I am just so happy to be here."

Once again, he laughed softly. "You know, I am painting you as you are today, as you were last Wednesday. But I have only painted your face, so far. Now the other day, I think it was the day of the funeral, I saw you wearing a fur coat. It suited you so bloody well. Now it would suit me bloody well to paint you wearing that coat. Could we do that, d'you think? Would you sit for me wearing it?"

Mavis looked at him in surprise. "You saw what I was wearing on the day of the funeral? Even though I was sitting in the mourners' car? How could you have seen what I was wearing?" Seamus looked embarrassed. He remained silent for a few moments before replying.

"Actually, I also watched you wearing that coat one Sunday when you walked past my house on your way to chapel. You were arm in arm with your husband, walking with such an air of confidence and self-awareness. You looked so lovely."

"Ah….I see." She glanced up at him with a wicked smile. Then, flinging her arms around his neck, "Of course I will wear it for you! What a wonderful idea! I will find some way of getting it here - it won't be easy, the weather being so kind for once. But it's not impossible." Putting his hands on her shoulders and gently turning her around, he patted her on the bottom.

"Back to work, then, for sinful people like us!"

Mavis resumed her position on the chaise-longue, and Seamus began his work once again. Silence reigned. Seamus was engrossed in his work, and spoke little. Mavis drifted in her mind, in time, in space.....she relaxed into the soft velvet of the chaise-longue, allowing herself the luxury of relishing her new-found sensual happiness, a contented smile on her face.

"You know, it's not absolutely essential that you smile all the time." He looked up briefly, grinning. "You are allowed to relax, occasionally." Mavis instantly looked serious, but burst out laughing within seconds.

"Actually, I had better be going," she said reluctantly, getting to her feet. Seamus looked dismayed. "Oh, not so soon!" he began, waving his paintbrush around in frustration. "It's only -" he looked at his watch, "Oh bugger. It's twenty-five past six! Ah well, what must be, must be."

He put down the brush and wiped his hands carefully on a paint-spattered cloth. Suddenly, his face clouded. Mavis moved towards him, wondering what on earth could be wrong. He flung the cloth on the floor, and sighed loudly.

"Whatever's the matter?" Mavis felt puzzled.

"Oh, it's nothing." He seemed frustrated and worried. Then he smiled once again. "Truly, it's nothing. Honestly. But one last kiss before you go." Once more, he pulled her towards him, engulfing her in his arms and seeking her eager mouth with his. Such tenderness, such warmth. Mavis thought that if she never lived another day, at least she would have had this beautiful experience.

"Send another note when you can, won't you?" he smiled down at her, reluctantly releasing her from his embrace and opening the front door. "And bring that fur coat too?"

"Yes, I will." She turned and once more left the old Richards' house with a spring in her step and filled with happiness, Seamus watching her walk away, back to her strict and stifling reality.

The evening passed uneventfully. Ernest returned home, happy for once, having been well-fed and watered down in Llanelli. No fish and chips for him that evening. Soon after eight o'clock, he retired to the parlour, to settle down and perfect the following day's sermon. Plenty of light remained, and Mavis was still restless. Dai lay asleep upon his grey towel, dreaming the exhausting and exciting dreams of a young dog, chasing imaginary rabbits as his white ears pricked up and his whimpers filled the room.

Impatiently, Mavis pulled on her walking shoes and a cardigan, and quietly slipped out into the fading light, calling to Ernest as she went that she was going for a short walk. Should she go up onto the track? Or maybe walk down to Eiddwen's house for a quick chat? Eiddwen would be up later than usual on a Saturday. She owned a television, and would of course be glued to it at this time of the evening. Mavis turned left at her gate and made her way down Bethel Lane towards the main road and Eiddwen's house. Instinctively her eyes were drawn towards Seamus' house as she approached it. She hoped to catch a quick glimpse of the artist at work, or even a chance meeting....

However, her blood ran cold when she saw a blond woman standing on his doorstep, in deep and earnest conversation with him. Gladys Williams. Had she been visiting Seamus? Had she posed nude for him again? Irrational thoughts raced through her mind. She froze, terrified of being noticed.

Gladys then reached out and stroked Seamus' cheek. Unable to contain herself any longer, Mavis gave a stifled sob, betraying her presence and attracting Seamus' searching glance in her direction. Horrified at being detected, she turned around and ran back up towards the track, unable to believe what she had just witnessed. Wave after wave of despair and jealousy broke over her as she swiftly climbed the damp and slippery steps. It started to rain, lightly at first, then more heavily, drenching Mavis' cardigan and soaking her thin red dress. The wind picked up, rustling the leaves in the trees and whipping Mavis' dark hair around her face. She continued to run, without feeling breathless or tired. All she wanted was to escape this terrible dark chasm of betrayal. Tears poured down her cheeks. How could she have been taken for such a fool? How could she have believed everything he said? Her sobs subsided, and she slowed to a walk, considering everything that had just happened, trying to make sense of it all. Little light reached this part of the track, and dark shadows lurked in the hedgerows. Huge rocks leered down at her, as the track meandered its way through ancient quarries, forming a natural tunnel; her steps echoed eerily as she stumbled along

Suddenly she was grabbed violently from behind, strong hands forced her to turn around, then she was kissed even more violently, and the strong hands, artist's hands, brushed the hair from her eyes, and wiped away the tears from her face. He held her close. Neither of them spoke, allowing Mavis' emotions to settle before trying to talk. He tilted her chin so she was looking up at him. She could barely discern his expression in the dim light.

"What the hell do you think you're doing? he demanded anxiously. "Running up here in this awful weather! What's the matter?"

"I saw you with Gladys," she whispered, "I thought, you know..." Her voice trailed away, miserably, not knowing how to explain her extreme reaction.

"I need to tell you something." Seamus looked at her seriously. "Gladys came by the other day, indeed wanting to start something, as you so quaintly put it. I am not interested in her and told her so. However, she saw your portrait, Mavis, and was as mad as a spurned woman ever was. She turned up just now, trying her luck again. And was given the same response."

"Did she see me?" Mavis looked worried. "Did she see me outside your house just now?"

"I don't think so. She had her back to you. But how could I miss you? You are the woman I have always dreamed of, Mavis. I would find you on the darkest night, even if I was wearing sunglasses!"

Mavis giggled. "Such a romantic thought!"

"But I am more than a little concerned that she could cause some trouble for you over that painting. I thought you should be prepared."

Mavis pondered. All her old fire suddenly returned, and she looked up at Seamus with a determined look in her eyes. "Don't worry. It'll be fine."

The rain suddenly stopped. Seamus put his arm around her. "Time to be going home, I reckon. You're going to have to do some explaining when you get in! Look at the state of you!"

Under the cover of twilight, the couple returned to Bethel Lane, daring to hold each other's hands, but parting without kissing when they reached the steps. Their whispered farewell and intense gaze was enough.

Sunday dawned misty and murky. An emotionally drained Mavis looked up at the nearby hills through the spare bedroom window. "'From whence cometh my help'," she thought to herself. But there was no-one to help her but herself. Ernest had gone to bed when she had returned home the previous night, so her wet clothes had not initiated an interrogation. She'd gone to bed around ten o'clock, and slept heavily.

The low clouds hung delicately along the tops of the pines, like scarves of mist thrown casually and artistically by some ghostly giant. On a day like this, Mavis would often feel a yearning within her soul, a wish to make for the track, and walk for hours in a northerly direction, allowing the damp air to caress her face, meeting no-one and feeling at one with the countryside.

But today was the Sabbath. Chapel at ten o'clock was the rule, and one which should never broken, except in cases of illness.

Ernest walked into the room, buttoning the starched collar of his shirt.

"Would you mind going on ahead of me this morning, Mavis? I have to finish the last paragraph of my sermon. I am not entirely happy with it. It won't take long, and I will meet you in the vestry in plenty of time for morning service. If you could get the prayer books ready and make sure that Gladys Williams has everything she needs, I would be very grateful." All this was delivered like a military command, allowing no room for negotiation and assuming immediate compliance. Mavis nodded, without speaking, reaching for her dark grey jacket. Still officially in mourning for the late Mrs Watton, she dressed soberly.

"You look very nice, Mavis, very smart." His unexpected compliment took her by surprise. Her navy dress was modest, but well-cut, and her new shoes

were black leather sling-backs, a recent purchase at Baker's shoe shop in Llanelli.
 Ernest seemed to prefer it when she wore subdued colours and did not attract attention to herself. He should have married a nun, she thought privately. Although, such was his disapproval of all things Papist, even a nun would have been considered far too frivolous for the pious Ernest.

Mavis set off once more down Bethel Lane, her head down, looking demure and inconspicuous, as befitted the minister's wife. However, her brown eyes could not resist but steal a swift glance at Seamus' house. He was nowhere to be seen, however. Maybe at half-past nine he was still asleep in bed. The damp air caused her hair to form tiny ringlets around her face. How wickedly defiant they seemed, disregarding the need for a prim and orderly appearance.

As she tried the vestry door, she discovered it was unlocked. Surprised, she opened it. Of course. Gladys Williams had a key. There she was, with her back to Mavis, sorting out music sheets and stacking hymn books, her black skirt straining over her ample hips, her overly curvy legs precariously perched on black high heels.

"Good morning, Miss Williams," greeted Mavis with as much sincerity as she could muster. "How are you? Ernest will be along soon. He asked me to help you get ready for the morning service." She bustled efficiently towards the vestry table, starting to put the remaining books in order.

"I am very well, thank you, Mrs Watton," came the slick reply. "And how are you? I must say, you looked very well in that painting I saw of you in Seamus' house the other day, when he so kindly invited me in for coffee. What does Mr Watton think of it?" She turned to look at Mavis, an innocent smile on her bland face.

"Oh, please don't mention anything to Mr Watton!" Mavis feigned horror. Gladys smirked spitefully. "Have you been a naughty girl, Mrs Watton?" There was a deadly silence.

Mavis' eyes narrowed. "How dare you be so insolent, you bold creature?! Who on earth do you think you are talking to?" "Well, I suppose Mr Watton wouldn't be very happy when he discovers his wife is consorting with the likes of Seamus O'Brien." Gladys stood in front of her, challenging and mocking.

"Meaning?" retaliated Mavis, stepping closer to Gladys.

"Well, if he doesn't know, then he will have a big shock when I accidentally let slip that you have been playing away!" Mavis closed her eyes in mock disbelief. "You are such an imbecile, Miss Williams, and a rather fat one at that." Gladys' demeanour changed instantly. She coloured and scowled at Mavis with pure hatred on her features.

"I would, of course, prefer you to say nothing at all to Mr Watton." Mavis continued smoothly. "However, if you choose to disclose the subject of the painting to him, then you will, in all probability, spoil his birthday surprise. I doubt he would be very pleased with you, his protégée, if you display such malice. What do you think?" Gladys glared at Mavis with such venom, it was almost comical. Unfortunately, Mavis was unable to prevent herself from laughing, resulting in Gladys spitting like an angry viper,

"You are nothing but a cheap whore, Mavis Watton! Teasing men and flirting with them! Wearing provocative clothes and flaunting yourself before the whole of Llannon!" Before Mavis could stop herself, her hand shot out and slapped Gladys hard across the face.

"That's quite enough!" she hissed back.

"You bitch!" Gladys put her hand up to her cheek, where bright red fingermarks were beginning to develop. Mavis stood perfectly still, but quivered with rage. At that very moment, in breezed Eva Griffiths, ready to assist with the preparations. Apparently oblivious to the tension between the two women, she opened the cupboard nearest Gladys, who then decided to capitalise on her predicament.

"My face!" she wailed, gently rubbing her cheek. "Oh, my goodness! How can I go out there and play the organ looking like this?" She cast a sly glance at Mavis. Eva looked up disinterestedly.

"Oh, that's slapped cheek syndrome," she observed, drily, "Caused by the parvovirus. You must have been hanging around with some infectious people. Strange to get it at your age, though. But not impossible. It's not dangerous, except in pregnancy." She winked discreetly at Mavis. "You're not pregnant, are you?"

Gladys looked horrified at this suggestion and its implications. "I most certainly am not!" And she stormed out, gathering what dignity she had left, to take her place at the organ.

Eva looked at Mavis' stricken face. "Be careful of that one," she advised, quietly. "She's a dangerous woman. Believe me, I know.

"Thank you, Eva. I think I am beginning to recognise that." Making a huge effort to maintain her composure, Mavis took a deep breath and entered the chapel, waited for her husband to arrive and the morning service to begin.

Gladys churned out "Myfanwy" with a sullen expression on her face, avoiding the curious looks of the congregation. Ernest entered the chapel. Everyone stood up.

Eva Griffiths was later than usual starting her rounds the following Tuesday morning, and was still at the sweet shop when Mavis turned up for work, hastened along by a rogue summer shower of rain, which had caught her unawares.

"Bore da, Eva." Mavis shook the raindrops from her hair, draping her damp cardigan on the back of a chair behind the counter.

"Hello, Mavis." Eva was putting on her navy hat, and getting ready to leave. "Typical! I have got to go up as far as Pontyberem this morning. It's bleak up there when it rains, and the Thomas farm will be a quagmire."

"Well, at least I will be warm and dry in here!" laughed Mavis. Then she became serious. " By the way, what did you mean about Gladys Williams being a dangerous woman when we were in the vestry on Sunday?"

"Ah. I was meaning to talk to you about that." Eva turned to Mavis, taking her time to choose the right words. "I don't want to appear a gossip, and I have no idea what went on between the two of you yesterday, but I think you should know that our respectable new organist was sacked from her last position at a church down in Llanelli." Mavis raised her eyebrows in surprise. "What happened? Does Ernest know?"

"I doubt it. She had a very irregular relationship with the Sunday School teacher, Goronwy Harries. It all came to a head when he refused to leave his wife and run off with her. Gladys took her revenge and went round to his house, spilled the beans to his wife, Sybil. Thankfully, Sybil kept her head, didn't make a scene, but reported her to the church council. She was sacked with immediate effect. It was all kept very quiet, mind you, which is why she was fortunate enough to secure her new position with us."

Mavis stared at Eva in disbelief. "But how do you know? If it was all hush hush and all that?"

Eva smiled slightly. "Sybil Harries is a midwife with me at Brynglas maternity hospital. I know her very well. All is fine with her now. Goronwy had a momentary lapse from the straight and narrow, and has been forgiven. Mind you, his wife may have been understanding about the whole, sordid affair, but the church council exacted their own pound of flesh from the poor man! He no longer teaches Sunday School, and cannot return to that post for another six months. He must 'prove his character,' you see."

"Well!" Mavis gradually digested this information. "What a bad apple we have in our midst, Eva." She smiled at her friend. "I am grateful you told me. I will be very wary of young Gladys from now on."

Eva looked sharply at Mavis, wondering what she could have been implying. However, Mavis was blithely starting to polish the counter, hoping to change the subject, which was beginning to make her feel very uncomfortable indeed. Fortunately, Eva had no more time to quiz Mavis, and left to start her visits.

The morning dragged on, with no customers at all. Mavis was able to while away the hours dreaming of Seamus as she cleaned and dusted, filling shelves and sorting the takings in the till. At lunchtime, the shop door opened and in rushed Eiddwen, her plain little face shadowed with anxiety.

"Oh, Mavis!" she gasped. "I ran all the way from the house! I had a letter this morning, from my cousin in Carmarthen! She is bringing her family up to visit this Friday! And you know what Mair is like for dressing! I have nothing to wear!" She sank down despondently on the one chair in the shop. Mavis giggled, but not unkindly, remembering Gladys' accusations the previous day.

"Of course you have! You looked very nice in chapel yesterday. Why don't you just wear that dress you had on? It really suited you." Mavis felt sure the Lord would definitely forgive this blatant exaggeration, as she had her friend's feelings at heart, a relatively new response in her usual repertoire. But Eiddwen shook her head sorrowfully.

"She has seen my navy crimplene before. I can't wear that. It would never do, Mavis. It would be all round the family in the wink of an eye. I can just imagine it now: Eiddwen wore the same dress we saw her in only in March. Poor woman. Maybe she can't afford anything new. What shall I do?" She sat there, wringing her hands.

"There's only one thing for it." Mavis looked decisively at her worried friend. "We will go to Llanelli on Wednesday. We will go to Paige, Howards, even Renee Gwilym! Ernest cannot take us because he is waiting in for a parcel which should be delivered in the morning, a book about the Reformation or something. But we can go on the bus! Shall we?"

Eiddwen clapped her hands in excitement. "Wonderful! And maybe we can go and see the new Jubilee Swimming Pool! There is a cafe there. Maybe we could have lunch there?" Mavis looked dubious about that suggestion. Have lunch in a noisy cafe, surrounded by hordes of boisterous schoolchildren? She didn't think so.

"Well, we'll see about lunch, Eiddwen," she murmured. Mavis already had designs on lunching at the Blue Orchid in the centre of town, or possibly the Mayfair. With a sparkle in her eyes, Mavis whisked off her apron with a flourish.

"It's my break, now. I will put up the "CLOSED" sign, and we will go down to the bus stop to check the times of the Llanelli buses on Wednesday. We are going shopping, Eiddwen!"

Chapter Eleven

The Silky Threads of the Web

Mavis and Eiddwen waited patiently for the nine-thirty bus which would take them down to Llanelli, through Felinfoel, passing Parc Hardd with its manicured lawns, and Brynglas Maternity Hospital, where Eva Griffiths sometimes worked. The day was pleasant, the sun shone and a light breeze swayed through the trees which lined the main road, lifting Mavis' hair gently, but having no effect whatsoever on Eiddwen's rigidly permed coiffure, held stickily in place by copious amounts of Supersoft hair lacquer.

Mavis hadn't spoken to Seamus since they last met, but had seen him through his window, when she'd walked home from work the other afternoon; he had waved. She knew that the ball was in her court now, and she would need to drop another note in to him, advising when she could next sit for him. He was in her thoughts constantly. She couldn't read a book, or even listen to the radio, without wondering what he would think of it. She hugged her secret to herself.

The two women settled down on the side seats of the bus, all the forward facing ones already occupied by pensioners from Cross Hands holding shopping bags and umbrellas "just in case."

"I hate sitting in these seats," grumbled Eiddwen, "I always feel sick when I look at the scenery flashing by."

"Don't look at it, then," murmured Mavis, "Just look at that woman's earrings instead. How dreadful!" She giggled wickedly. Eiddwen smiled back weakly, glancing briefly at the huge pink plastic monstrosities worn with such pride by the smiling woman sitting opposite. She felt even worse. The bus bumped along the country road, by-passing Sylen and the Swiss Valley reservoirs. The Burry

Inlet was now visible, sparkling and enticing in the June sunshine, the curvaceous hills of the Gower peninsular settling comfortably into the bluest of waters.

"Oh, how nice it would be to go over to Horton today," murmured Mavis, holding on tightly to the metal bar for support. "It would be wonderful to lie on the sand, soak up the sun and do absolutely nothing for the whole day!" She smiled at Eiddwen, who was quite pale by now.

"I haven't been to Horton," she whispered, clutching her handbag into her stomach, "Mam and Dad only ever took us to Penclawdd for fish and chips in the summer." She then regretted the reference to fish and chips, vowing inwardly that on the return journey she would secure a front-facing seat, at whatever cost.

By ten o'clock, the two women were advancing up the main shopping street, glancing this way and that, as the shops and their window displays attracted their attention. Eiddwen felt much perkier, and started to enjoy the expedition, wondering what fabulous outfit she would find, and what her beautiful friend would recommend.

"Shall we have a look in Puddy's" asked Eiddwen, hopefully. She liked going into Puddy's, the curious little draper's shop in the middle of the town.

Mavis looked at her friend despairingly. "If you must, but I doubt we will find anything suitable there."

The two entered the dimly lit shop, staffed by short, serious men, and bespectacled ladies with perms even tighter than Eiddwen's. Mavis disliked the store. It was fine if you wanted to buy a sensible liberty bodice or thick, lisle stockings, but there was no room for frivolity or fun.

"Don't you just love those pullies!" Eiddwen pointed up at the money-carrying pullies, which whizzed to and fro across the ceiling, transporting the correct change from one end of the store to another.

"Fascinating." Mavis was anxious to leave the shop. The looks of disapproval from the prim women behind the counter were almost tangible.

"Can we come back here after we get my dress, Mavis?" begged Eiddwen, squeezing her friend's arm. "I want to get some pink bias binding for a blanket I am knitting for my niece's baby."

"Yes, don't see why not. Now let's go to Renee Gwylim's!" Mavis marched assertively out into the sunshine, heading for her favourite shop. The traffic was heavy that day, with double-decker buses and several cars inching their way up and down the street. The pair managed to cross the road without being run over. Dodging busy shoppers, mothers with prams and the omnipresent pigeons, avoiding the interested glances of several spivs who were selling nylons and cheap scent outside Lloyds' bank, the two women finally arrived at Mavis' preferred destination.

The window display showed a couple of mannequins wearing smart suits, and others showcasing negligees, corsets and the sheerest of stockings. Mavis' eyes sparkled. There was nothing in the world she liked better than pretty clothes, particularly underwear. However, this was Eiddwen's day out, and there was serious shopping to be done. In they went, Eiddwen nervously clutching her brown leather handbag to her as tightly as she could.

"Wouldn't it be better to go to Marks and Spencer's, Mavis?" she whispered. "I could get a lovely crimplene dress there for half the price."

Mavis looked at her friend incredulously, pausing a moment before saying, "Eiddwen, do you really want to look just like everyone else in Llanelli? Don't you want to look that little bit different? This is your chance! For goodness' sake, let me help you!"

Eiddwen looked down, suitably chastised. Of course, she should listen to any pearls of wisdom which issued forth from Mavis' perfectly made-up little mouth. It was just that, maybe, she really did want to look exactly like everyone else, and not be noticed....

After half an hour of poor Eiddwen being bullied and directed by a determined Mavis, having tried on shift dresses, crew-necked tops and pencil skirts, the decision was made. Eiddwen finally emerged from the tiny fitting room wearing a powder blue sleeveless dress with a short fitted jacket and a beaming smile on her face.

"Eiddwen, cariad! You look just like Jackie Kennedy !" Mavis clapped her hands in delight. Even Eiddwen's plain and ordinary features were enhanced by the suit.

"I'm having it, Mavis!" she laughed. "It costs a fortune, but it's got my name on the price tag!" Eiddwen retreated to the fitting room.

Mavis wandered around the shop, looking at the soft, shimmering fabrics and imagining how they would feel next to her skin, how they would flatter her body, clinging to every curve.....she shook herself out of this reverie, forcing Seamus' image from her mind as quickly as she could. Yet, she could not resist lingering over an exquisite pink satin waspie and suspender set. She gently caressed the smooth material, thinking how exciting the lingerie seemed when compared to her demure Maidenform brassiere. Her Majesty the Queen had recently commissioned Rigby and Peller for her own underwear, so why shouldn't she, Mavis, the self-established queen of Llannon, make an illicit and naughty purchase of her own? Thus inspired, Mavis slipped into the next available fitting room, and tried on the beautiful set, gazing at her reflection in the mirror. What would Seamus think of her now? A diminutive form, legs with bow-like curves, a waist held tightly by the pink satin, golden breasts just peeping coyly over the top of the waspie. Indeed, what would the chapel congregation think of her? How could they possibly guess that the minister's wife wore such seductive garments beneath her outer clothes? She caressed her body sensually, her mind made up. If Eiddwen thought the suit "had her name on it," then this darling little set certainly did.

Twenty minutes later, two happy, smiling Llannon ladies continued their way down Stepney Street, clutching large paper bags containing items with which they were very pleased indeed.

"Let's go to Allegri's for coffee, shall we?" Not anticipating any objection from the docile Eiddwen, Mavis forged ahead, down to the eastern end of Stepney Street, with Eiddwen trotting along obediently beside her. Allegri's was one of several Llanelli cafes run by a substantial community of Sicilian immigrants, many of whom had settled in south Llanelli, along New Dock Road, an area into which the snobbish Mavis preferred not to venture. The enticing aroma of Italian coffee filled their senses as they entered the cool, dark depths of the cafe. A marble staircase swept up to the first floor, where wedding receptions and other significant events took place. Mavis sniffed appreciatively, and chose to sit at a marble topped table near the window.

"I want a good view of everything!" She smiled at Eiddwen, who sat opposite her. "I will be able to look down at Market Street, and you will be able to look up at Stepney Street. Now, what shall we have?" Mavis reached for the leather bound menu, scanned it rapidly, and handed to Eiddwen. "Cappuccino for me, I think! What about you, Eiddwen?"

"Oh, I'll just have a cup of tea." Eiddwen had never been one to sample anything more exotic than Tetley tea, or, at a push, a cup of Nescafe. A hovering waiter moved in quickly, having ascertained that the two women were ready to order.

"Si?" His dark Sicilian eyes roved wickedly over her, full of suggestion.

"Er, one cappuccino and one cup of tea, please." She watched his narrow hips, clad in the tightest of black trousers, as he moved efficiently back to the bar, where a more senior Sicilian controlled the hissing, steaming coffee machines. The cafe was filling up quickly, with shoppers tired and hungry, intent on an early lunch. Young children were digging in to knickerbocker glories, the raspberry sauce dribbling onto the tables, and the triangular wafers cascading into a dusting of crumbs on their laps. Mavis looked away in distaste. But at least the ice cream kept them quiet....

"Thank you so much for coming with me to buy that suit!" sighed Eiddwen, almost overcome with gratitude and happiness.

"It was my pleasure!" smiled Mavis, sipping her cappuccino as decorously as she could, trying to avoid the froth making a creamy moustache upon her upper lip. Eiddwen gazed out of the window, hoping that Mavis would suggest they had a custard slice or possibly some soup and a roll. Even the brown sugar cubes were beginning to look inviting. Suddenly, her attention was diverted, her rumbling tummy ignored.

"Who is that, Mavis?"

"Who d'you mean?" Mavis was trying to drain the last of the frothy coffee, and could not see the tall man waving enthusiastically at her through the window.

"That man!" exclaimed Eiddwen, excitedly. "Do you know him?"

Mavis looked up quickly. To her amazement, there at the window was none other than Seamus, a huge grin on his face. Mavis smiled back, and Seamus burst into laughter. She suddenly realised that all her efforts to keep her pretty mouth clean had been in vain, and that he was laughing at the remnants of her cappuccino which remained obstinately on her upper lip. Hastily, she found a handkerchief in her handbag, and dabbed at the offending mark. Looking up, she was disappointed to see that he had disappeared.

"Who was that man, Mavis?!" Eiddwen was beside herself with curiosity. Before Mavis could reply, a familiar voice said,

"May I join you ladies?" And there he was, tall, grinning and totally Irish.

"Yes, of course." Mavis giggled inwardly at Eiddwen's face, a mixture of disbelief, excitement and horror. Seamus sat down with them. He looked marginally less untidy than usual, and was actually wearing a shirt and tie.

"This is Mr Seamus O'Brien, Eiddwen. He is our new neighbour, and he has bought the old Richards house. He is an artist."

"How do you do?" Seamus held out his hand, which the flabbergasted Eiddwen took and gripped rather too firmly.

"Pleased to meet you, Mr O'Brien," whispered Eiddwen, breathlessly, holding his hand all the while.

"Do you reckon I could have my hand back now we are acquainted?" He smiled roguishly at her. Eiddwen was totally smitten, and tittered coyly.

"What brings you into town, Seam – Mr O'Brien?" Mavis struggled to keep the familiarity from her voice. He grinned congenially at the two women, taking a cursory glance at the menu.

"Well, would you believe it! I had an advance from a prospective client, no less than a hundred pounds! So I thought it prudent to make an appointment with the bank and set up an account here in Llanelli!"

"And what sort of client would that be?" Mavis' thoughts turned uneasily to the infamous Gladys Williams, and that particular commission.

"Well!" His voice dropped dramatically, and he put his chin in his hands on he table. "You see, there is this manufacturer of fur coats, and he wants me to depict his luxurious garments in oils!" His bright blue eyes narrowed, and he turned slightly towards Mavis. "Such an offer I cannot possibly refuse!" He no longer smiled, but his piercing look spoke a thousand words, as he watched Mavis' pupils dilate and her cheeks redden.

"That is the most gratifying of news, Seamus." Mavis held his eyes a moment longer than necessary, then lowered her own demurely. Eiddwen had no such composure.

"Oh, how exciting! When will you start? Will your painting be exhibited in Llanelli? Will you mention that it was done in Llannon?"

"Oh, all will be revealed in the fullness of time." He casually lit a cigarette, ending the discussion and ordered a cup of tea from the waiter, who seemed to be efficiency personified.

"Shall we have another drink, Eiddwen?" Mavis was anxious to prolong the meeting as long as possible.

"Yes! And I think I shall have a toasted teacake as well!" Eiddwen's hazel eyes sparkled greedily at the thought of some long-desired sustenance. For once, Mavis did not scold her friend for her self-indulgence, for the preparation and consumption of the teacake would inevitably mean more time with Seamus.

"I am just going to pop to the Ladies." Eiddwen whispered discreetly to Mavis, squeezing behind Seamus as she departed.

"So. How are you, sweet Mavis?" Seamus spoke softly, looking at her intensely, his fingers just a couple of inches away from her hand. How she longed to touch them.

"Fine. How are you?"

"Missing your illicit presence more than I care to admit."

She smiled up at him warmly. "I was going to pop a little note in later this week. What is all this about a fur coat manufacturer?"

" Ah! A ploy! A ruse! Nothing at all in it, really, nothing more than a gentle reminder of what I want from you. I have come into town to pay a few bills and legitimately open an account. And the reason for your own excursion?"

"I assisted Eiddwen in choosing a new outfit. And I made a purchase of my own. We came down on the bus. How did you get here?"

"Well, here's the thing! I was waiting patiently at the bus stop for the half-past ten into town, and who should stop and give me a lift but your kind employer!"

"Mr Griffiths? But he rides a motorcycle! Did you ride on the back?" Mavis giggled at the thought of Seamus clinging on for dear life as Mr Griffiths tore down the country roads towards Llanelli.

"No, no, no! He drove his wife's car, the midwife. She had the day off, so was minding the shop for him. God forbid, the fecking car was full of bloody stuff! Hardly any room for me! Papers and sheets and equipment and God knows what else!"

Annoyingly, Eiddwen took hardly any time in the Ladies and was soon back in her seat, eagerly awaiting her teacake. "This is turning out to be such an exciting outing!" Her apple-cheeked smile dimpled at the others, bewitchingly, she thought.

Seamus and Mavis merely gazed into each other's eyes, without saying anything. Eiddwen rabbited on, ignoring the others and oblivious to any subliminal indicators they may have been displaying, filling the conversational void with trite and random comments about the weather. After what seemed like an age, the teacake arrived, and Eiddwen's teeth settled around the spicy, fruity bread with alacrity, melting butter dripping down her mouth. At least that silenced her chattering.

"Actually, it is quite propitious that I should see you – both - here." Seamus looked from one to the other of the two expectant faces . "I am having a party. Next week. At my house. A little house-warming of a sort. I will send you both invitations, officially. But I reckoned you would like to know in advance, so that you can organise your busy schedules!"

Eiddwen nearly fainted in sheer delight. She had never been invited to a house party before, not as an adult, anyway. Mavis stared at Seamus, her mind working overtime. Who else would he invite? Would Ernest be invited too? Unless he was, she, Mavis, would be unable to accept.

"Why, how terribly kind!" Mavis struggled to maintain her composure, unsure what was coming next. Seamus grinned at the two women and continued. "I am sure Eiddwen will not mind being the sole recipient of an invitation within her household! However, if you should wish to bring a friend…" here he chuckled softly at the blushing and rapt Eiddwen, " please feel free to do so! Of course, Mavis, I will personally hand deliver yours and Mr Watton's invitation within the week!" Mavis sighed inwardly, relief flooding her face and returning her happiness instantly.

"Well, I am sure Mr Watton and I will be thrilled to accept! And of course, dear Eiddwen, you may accompany us if you prefer!"

"Oh, I would so love to go to the party! And I will go with you and Ernest!" Eiddwen knew nothing about the importance of appearing cool and collected, having about as much reserve as a Labrador puppy presented with a rubber bone. "He will accept, won't he?" she added, a little doubtfully.

"Oh, I will make sure he accepts." Mavis smiled with a confidence she didn't entirely feel. But, she thought, whatever Ernest decided, she knew that, come what may, she would most definitely be going to that party. This particular party reluctantly broke up soon after, with Seamus and the two women going their separate ways. Mavis sighed.

"It's almost one o'clock, Eiddwen, and I am tired, now. Let's get the quarter past one bus home." In reality, she wanted to get home as soon as possible in order to scribble a note and pop it through Seamus's letterbox, advising him of her availability the following Saturday, when Ernest would be assisting at a wedding in the town centre. Eiddwen complied without protest, and the two friends once more boarded the bus which would take them back to Llannon. Fortunately for Eiddwen, they managed to secure the very front seats of all, so her return journey was a far more pleasurable experience.

Mavis entered her little cottage around two o'clock, letting an excited and frantic young Dai out to run in the garden. There was no sign of Ernest. His parcel must have been safely delivered; his absence and Dai's imprisonment meant he had probably gone over to the chapel for something. Had he gone over to the Bowen's farm, he would have taken the dog with him. Excellent, thought Mavis. She would write her note to Seamus and then take Dai out for a walk. Reaching into the sideboard for some writing paper and a pen, she caught sight of her reflection in the large mirror. The light in the room was dim, despite the glorious sunshine outside. Her large, dark eyes looked huge, full of longing and repressed passion. There was a new wilfulness to her expression that had never been there before, in her Life Before Seamus, or LBS as she thought of it. Hastily she wrote her message.

Dear Seamus,

It was so lovely to see you today; how unexpected, how thrilling. If it is convenient with you I will call over on Saturday afternoon at half past one. I will bring my fur coat as well, as you have requested.

Mavis

She put the note into a plain white envelope, licked the gummed area to seal it, wickedly imagining how delightful it would be to run her tongue along Seamus' smiling mouth instead.

Ten minutes later, Mavis and Dai walked briskly down the lane to Seamus' house, and, like a child posting her parents' Christmas cards late on Christmas Eve to less than popular neighbours, she swiftly popped the letter through the letterbox and tip-toed quietly away, heading once again to her beloved track, and blissful solitude.

When Mavis returned around an hour later, there was still no sign of Ernest. How unusual, she thought. Nevertheless, she did not allow this to disturb her happy daydreams as she climbed the stairs to the bedroom, to try on her new and exciting underwear. The cottage was as silent as the grave, except for the solemn sound of the grandfather clock, as it ticked away resolutely downstairs. She undressed quickly, discarding her sensible underwear in a carefree heap on the bedroom floor. Holding her breath, she slowly put on the new set, positioning the mirror in order to view herself from the least flattering angle. Mavis privately acknowledged she was probably the most incredibly vain creature west of Swansea, but she never deluded herself, being her own harshest critic. The passing years had treated her well. Her skin was smooth and unblemished; no cellulite dimpled her thighs and her bottom was firm. She ran her hands over her breasts. They were pert and well-formed, untouched by pregnancy or dramatic fluctuations in weight. However, Mavis did wish they were a little bigger....

She sighed, and lay down on the bed, luxuriating in the slippery softness of the pink satin. Glancing out at the blue sky, she wished for freedom, to be at liberty to fly away and have no restrictions within her life. She allowed all the tension to leave her body, her mind started to feel at peace, she closed her eyes. Idly, her right hand strayed down to her knicker line. Her thoughts became focussed on the man whose advent in her life was so exciting. She imagined him slowly undressing her, caressing her....

And what would happen next, she wondered? She desired his touch more than anything, she wanted him to touch her everywhere. She lay back on the pillow, her cheeks flushed, feeling drowsy and relaxed and Mavis drifted off on a sea of sensuality, into a dreamless sleep.

She was woken by the bedroom door being opened. Ernest stood there, a look of horror on his face.

"Mavis!" He thundered, a look of intense disapproval on his face, "What on earth do you think you're doing?"

"Er, sleeping?" Mavis rubbed her eyes, smudging her mascara and giving her face a rather wanton appearance.

"Don't be so insolent! I am referring to your garments! Why are you dressed like a trollop?" Mavis had no energy to retaliate, instead she stretched her arms above her head and yawned lazily. She reached for her dressing gown, and, putting it on as she walked slowly from the room, she murmured,.

"I was just trying on some clothes. Would you like a cup of tea?"

Ernest stared at her retreating form in disbelief. For once at a loss as to what to say, he busied himself with removing his best jacket and followed her downstairs.

The couple were just finishing their tea when there was a knock at the front door.

"That will probably be Mrs Bowen the Farm." Ernest did not look up from last week's copy of the Llanelli Star. "She is bringing the eggs, more than likely. Will you answer the door, Mavis? Although I have no idea why she is using the front door."

Mavis frowned slightly. Ernest sometimes behaved like a sergeant-major. However, anxious to avoid a disagreement, she rose to her feet obediently, pulling her dressing gown more tightly around her small waist. Opening the door, Mavis was both pleased and horrified that it wasn't Mrs Bowen standing there with the eggs, but a tall, grinning Seamus with some envelopes in his hand.

"Good afternoon, Mrs Watton. Have I called at an inconvenient time? Are you unwell, or...?" His voice trailed away as he gazed with amusement at Mavis. "I seem to remember that red dressing gown from a few weeks ago, when you were with your little dog in the garden!"

"Ssh!" Mavis turned around hastily to see if Ernest had heard. In a louder voice she announced

"We have a visitor, Ernest. Do come in, Mr O'Brien. Would you like some tea?" Ernest looked up in astonishment as his dressing gown-clad wife ushered in a tall and rather wild-looking stranger.

"Good afternoon, Mr Watton. Seamus O'Brien's the name. I am new to Llannon. Bought the big house down the lane, the old Richards' house, I believe it is called. Have come to extend a warm hand of friendship and to invite you to a house-warming party I intend hosting next week." Seamus held out a paint-splattered hand to Ernest. Politeness stifled any acerbic remark Ernest may otherwise have made, and he shook hands with Seamus, gruffly muttering, "How do you do? I hope you have settled in well within our community."

"Oh I have settled in very well indeed." Seamus avoided looking at Mavis, who was scrutinising the scarlet mat beneath her feet.

"And some tea, Mr O'Brien?" Mavis brandished the teapot with a fixed smile upon her face. Seamus smiled back at her, holding her gaze just a moment longer than necessary, thankfully unnoticed by Ernest. "In fact, Mr Watton, I have become acquainted with your organist, a Miss Williams. She assisted me with some business I had to conduct recently."

Ernest brightened. "Ah yes, young Gladys. An excellent organist and a fine woman. Well, if you're a colleague of hers then that is no bad thing." Mavis looked as though she was chewing a wasp. If she heard one more word about that evil, sneaky, "fine" woman, she would scream. "And some tea, Mr O'Brien?" Mavis brandished thte teapot with a fixed smile on her face. Seamus smiled back at her, holding her gaze just a moment longer than was necessary, which thankfully went unnoticed by Ernest.

"Oh, no thank you, Mrs Watton, I have to get going. I have left a stew in the oven. In fact, perhaps you could do me an enormous favour and deliver another invitation for me, as I don't know where Eiddwen lives." Mavis held her breath – how could she explain how Seamus knew that Eiddwen was her friend? But Ernest seemed not to have noticed anything at all.

"My sister will be coming down from London as well." Seamus smiled blandly at Ernest. "She lives at the Convent of the Sacred Heart in Pimlico."

"She has taken the veil?" Ernest looked decidedly interested.

"In a manner of speaking, yes, she has. Bridget is now known as Sister Immaculata and she has lived in London for many years."

"I shall look forward to being introduced to her. Good evening, Mr O'Brien. It's been a pleasure to become acquainted with you."

Leaving the two white envelopes on the table, Seamus turned around and walked out of the cottage, followed by Ernest.

"Goodbye, Mr Watton. I look forward to seeing you a week tomorrow, then." Ernest extended his hand, which Seamus took and shook.

"Very well, Mr O'Brien. Maybe you will attend our services in Bethel chapel soon?" Seamus smiled wryly. "Well, you never know, Mr Watton, you never know. Goodbye." Ernest said no more, but silently watched the retreating artist make his way down towards his house.

Peeping through the kitchen window, Mavis watched him saunter down the lane, his easy gait and nonchalant manner making her long for him to turn around. Every fibre of her being longed to see his face, willing him to turn and look at her. Which he did, with seconds to spare. Just as he reached the lilac tree, Seamus looked over his shoulder, and with the cheekiest of grins, gave Mavis a saucy wink. She allowed herself the briefest of smiles by way of return. Roll on Saturday, she thought to herself, roll on.

And Saturday approached with the most languorous lack of haste. On Friday night, Ernest having gone out to a prayer meeting, Mavis ran a bath, filling it with a scented oil called Fenjal, a new product, which she had bought a few months ago in Boot's the Chemist. Relishing in her privacy, she took off her dressing gown in her sunset-filled bedroom, the rosy glow of the departing sun illuminating her reflection in the wardrobe mirror, making her look like a goddess in a movie about ancient Greece. Jason, she thought, I wish you were with me now! Her eyes strayed downwards. She frowned. Being of a dark, almost Mediterranean colouring, Mavis also had to suffer the annoyance of being rather hirsute in certain intimate places. She had always hated this aspect of her femininity. Such a blot on the landscape of her otherwise unblemished womanly form. She considered it for a few minutes, then, seized with an inspired determination, she rummaged in Ernest's top drawer, and finding a seemingly unused blade, hurried into the bathroom, fitting it onto the top of his immaculately placed brass razor which he kept on the bathroom windowsill. Reaching for her bar of Camay, she swiftly worked up a scented lather and set to work.

Mavis considered whether she should attempt a heart shape while she was shaving herself, but thought better of it. What on earth would Seamus say if he saw it? Or even Ernest? The latter, however, was most unlikely, as they had been married for three years and he still hadn't seen her completely undressed. Come to think of it, no-one had ever seen her naked. Satisfied with her handiwork, Mavis rinsed all the soap off, had a long soak in the bath before drying herself in a fluffy pink towel, and heading back to her bedroom. She kept a big tub of Nivea crème on her dressing table, which she kept for her hands in wintertime, but this evening she applied it liberally all over her body. She was unwilling to admit to herself the reason for all her efforts, but, despite never having been a Girl Guide, she was determined to be prepared. Regarding her unclothed body for the last time, she popped her sensible white nightdress over her head and went downstairs to make her bedtime cocoa. She paused before descending the stairs. The landing window looked out over the lane. The early summer evening was pleasant, the sun had set behind the hills and a couple of cautious stars were gracing the eastern horizon. If she leaned out of her window far enough, she could just about see Seamus' house. The light was on in one of the upstairs windows, probably the one where he kept all his paintings. Mavis wondered what he was doing. Tomorrow, she thought, I will be down there, tomorrow I will see him again.

Chapter Twelve

Submission

By one o'clock the following day, Ernest had departed for the wedding and Mavis was alone. Never one to wonder for very long what she should wear, she slipped on her new satin waspie, with matching satin knickers. She fastened her stockings, then chose an understated but well-fitting black dress and stepped into it excitedly. Glancing in the mirror, she satisfied herself that her make-up was just right, then carefully took her fur coat in its protective cover from the depths of the wardrobe, and carried it downstairs. It may have been a rather dull and cloudy day, and the sun would not be shining on the Llanelli bride, but nothing could dim Mavis' joyful anticipation of her couple of hours with Seamus. It had been to her advantage that Ernest was a distant relative of the bride's family, and so he had accepted the invitation to stay for the wedding breakfast.

At half-past one, Mavis locked the kitchen door behind her and set off down the lane, the fur coat draped over her arm, glancing each way, to make sure she wasn't seen. Thank goodness she didn't have to carry it very far, as it was cumbersome. Ernest would be unlikely to notice its absence, and she planned to leave it at Seamus' house until he had completed the painting. Should Ernest unexpectedly query its whereabouts, she would say that she had taken it to Eiddwen's so that a loose button could be sewn on more securely. Mavis had thought of everything.

There was no need for her to knock on the door today, for he was there, holding it open for her, smiling and welcoming

"Come in, come in! Let me take that for you!" He removed the coat from her aching arm. "Jesus, Mary and Joseph! This is seriously heavy! I cannot imagine how a slip of a thing like you could even bloody well wear it!" Mavis looked at him reproachfully, ostensibly shocked at his swearing, but then gave him a radiant smile.

"Oh, Seamus, a woman has to suffer for her appearance. And I can assure you, that coat is worth every single ache it gives me!"

Entering the studio, he reverently hung the coat on its black velvet hanger on the curtain rail at the side window.

"Don't you want me to put it on?" Mavis looked at him, slightly confused.

"All in good time, all in good time. First things first!" He beckoned to her, and as soon as she was close enough, drew her into his arms, ran his fingers through her hair, and kissed her softly, gently running his tongue along her lips, only releasing her when they both had to stop for air.

"Well!" laughed Mavis. "And good afternoon to you, too!"

"Ah, but it's so good see you, sweet Mavis. Very well, put on the coat and take up your position on the chaise, I have everything ready."

"But you've kissed off all my lipstick! Please let me put more on!"

"No point. It'll come off again before the afternoon is over." He looked at her sternly. "Now do as you are told, and I shall begin." Obediently, Mavis put on the coat and sat on the chaise, assuming exactly the same position as she had last time. Seamus frowned as he worked, and there was complete silence, apart from the birds singing in the trees outside. Before long, the sun decided to put in an appearance, and started to shine in through the rear window. Mavis began to regret wearing her black woollen dress as the temperature in the room started to rise.

"May I open a window?" she asked, her face becoming quite pink with the heat.

Without even looking up from his work, he replied, "Most certainly not."

"But I am melting, Seamus, I will pass out unless you can let a little fresh air in. This black dress is far too hot."

He looked up at her sharply. "Take it off, then."

"What?" Mavis smiled in disbelief. Surely he was teasing her.

"I said take it off." He smiled back at her. "You know, you have given me a fantastic idea. Take off your dress."

Mavis felt flustered and uncertain. "I – I don't know. I mean, I haven't ever, you know...." Her voice trailed away. She looked down, unwilling to meet his gaze.

"Haven't ever what?" He was scrutinising her face, now.

"Oh, Seamus, I have never undressed in front of a man before."

"Not even Mr Watton?" Seamus looked incredulous.

"Not really. He would be quite shocked if I did that."

"But you are married! For feck's sake!"

"I know." There was silence for a minute. Seamus put down his paintbrush.

"Take off your dress." He moved towards her, slowly, dangerously, pulling her to her feet. He slipped the coat from Mavis' shoulders, putting it gently on the chaise. She made no objection, but allowed him to turn her around, and unzip her dress. It slipped to the floor, and she stood there before him, blushing and terrified. He took her all in, from her head to her kitten-heeled toes. What a body, such perfection, such glorious delights were presented in front of his eyes.

"Bejesus! Holy mother of God! You are fecking divine." He ran his hands over her satin-clad waist. "So divine, in fact, that I want to paint you with your fur coat slipping off your shoulders, with just a glimpse of your skin visible, that would be so bloody fantastic! You would tantalise the imagination, the painting would hint at so many delights hitherto hidden from the eye, but about to revealed...." He smiled happily at his new idea.

"But what would Ernest say?" Mavis' face clouded with anxiety. "I could just about get away with telling him that the picture was to be a present, when I was wearing the coat properly and appropriately, but to have him see me like this..."

"Do not trouble yourself, sweet Mavis. I will paint two portraits, one official, for the public eye, and the other unofficial, for my eyes only."

Mavis visibly relaxed. "Paint away, Seamus, I am all yours." She sat down once more on the chaise, arranging the coat so it was over one shoulder, but slipping down the other. Seamus set to work, frowning in concentration, allowing Mavis the chance to watch him without him realising it. He really was an incredibly handsome man, although unconventionally so, with his weather-beaten face and long, untidy hair. He moved with the natural grace of a panther, his movements fluid and predatory.

Half an hour into the sitting, he straightened up and rubbed his back. "Coffee time. Come with me into the kitchen and I will make us some." Mavis wandered after him into the untidy centre of all his culinary attempts, trying to ignore the piles of dirty saucepans and empty coffee cups scattered over the table and draining board. They were soon sipping Seamus' coffee, perched on high stools at the overflowing table, Mavis feeling slightly self-conscious at sitting there just wearing her pretty underwear..

"So, how long have I got you for today?" he grinned at her hopefully over the rim of the cup. "Well, Ernest has a wedding down in Llanelli this afternoon, and he will be attending the wedding breakfast, also Mr Grace the photographer is unbelievably slow, so I don't really expect him home much before five o'clock."

"Excellent! I have you for another two hours at least! Time to get back to work!"

They returned to the front room, and Mavis resumed her position on the chaise, Seamus retiring behind the canvas. After about a quarter of an hour, he flung down his brush in exasperation, startling Mavis and making her jump.

"It's no fecking good! I cannot possibly concentrate!"

"Why ever not?" Mavis immediately assumed responsibility for Seamus' artistic demise. She looked up at him, anxiously. He scowled back at her, then, as he walked towards her, his face broke into a wicked smile.

"You tempt me, you satin-clad siren, you tease me with those beautiful eyes; without saying any words, you invite me to touch you.....may I touch you, Mavis?" He sat down on the chaise, removing the coat and putting his arm around her shoulders.

"Professionally?" Her voice was just a whisper.

"Oh, no, Mavis, most unprofessionally, if you will allow it...." He buried his head in her hair, then his eager lips sought hers, his tongue running along her teeth, then delving deep into her mouth. She responded equally unprofessionally, holding his face in her hands, feeling her passion take possession, throwing caution to the winds. His hand ventured lower and lower, cupping and stroking each of her breasts in turn, sliding along her satin waspie, eventually reaching the lacing at the back. He pulled her to her feet, towering over her. "Beautiful though it is, it has to come off," he murmured, as with expert skill he swiftly undid the laces and the waspie fell lightly to the floor. Mavis stood there in just her satin knickers, stockings and suspenders. He stood back, allowing his eyes to travel up and down her body. Then, without another word, he scooped her up in his arms and carried her out of the door, up the stairs and into the huge rear bedroom. His bedroom. She had no time to protest, indeed, she had no wish to. He lay her on his unmade bed, a tangle of bright purple sheets and orange blankets. There was no more talking between them, there was no need of speech. She lay there, stretched out on the bed, her dark hair spread out like Medusa's, her smooth limbs pliant and obedient to his touch. Waiting, expectant, nervous.....shivering with hot anticipation, desiring him. She watched him stand there before her, taking off his paint-stained shirt, showing a bare chest and a taut stomach. Closing her eyes, she caught her breath as she heard him unbuckle his belt and let it fall with a clatter to the wooden floor. He wore nothing beneath his discarded jeans. Then he was upon her, the whole length of his body was on hers.

"Slowly does it, my lovely. Let's not hurry, we have plenty of time."

Mavis did not answer, but allowed his wandering hands free reign, to stray where they wished, do what they wanted. And they strayed so smoothly, so cleverly, so sensually. His fingertips brushed her feverish skin, setting all her senses alight, making her arch upwards towards him, begging for more. He may have been stroking her legs, her arms, but there was a secret place within her that also felt warm and aroused. To her intense frustration, his exploring fingers circumnavigated this forbidden triangle, skimming the delicate lace of her knickers along the waistband, and also along the edges of her trembling thighs, avoiding that very place where she most desired his touch to linger....

When she thought she could bear it no longer, he changed his position. His mouth settled on her breasts, softly sucking and licking her nipples, flicking them with his tongue, rendering them upright and erect beneath the heat of his breath. Moving further south, he brushed his lips along her midriff, slyly licking her navel as he did. He glanced up at her face, saw that her eyes were wide with shock, yet she did nothing to stop him. He laughed softly and adjusted his position again, so his face was level with her hips.

"May I kiss you here?" He did not wait for an answer, but gently ran his thumb and index finger under the rim of her knicker leg, pushed it to one side and then buried his face in the dark, silky V beneath the satin, using his tongue in the most wonderful way imaginable. Such a wicked, decadent feeling. Mavis had never known such sensations could be felt by a human being; she felt herself float outside herself, as wave after wave of incredible pleasure suffused her pelvis. He stopped and looked up at her once again.

"Do you like that?" he whispered.

"Yes! Don't stop, please don't stop!" Her longing was overwhelming, her usual composure lost and she cared nothing for her appearance or what he thought of her. He laughed again, then leapt to his feet.

"Why have you stopped? Where are you going?" She looked in agony at his departing legs, long, lean and well-muscled, his broad shoulders....and wondered what on earth she had done wrong. He chuckled at her discomfiture.

"Need a fag." He grinned as he sat down on a wooden chest, completely at ease with his nakedness. "It is what you might call a fag break." He rummaged in the pockets of his discarded jeans and pulled out a battered packet of cigarettes. Mavis stared at him in disbelief as he settled down next to her on the bed and lit a cigarette. He puffed away contentedly, while she seethed silently. What could he be playing at? Was he toying with her? Spurning her womanly charms?

"What are you concerned about, my darling woman-child?" He smiled down at her, breathing out a silken stream of smoke, all the while fondling her nether regions in an absent-minded fashion, her sensitive flower of desire throbbing relentlessly. "Oh for God's sake, Seamus, finish me off!" He stared at her in complete astonishment, then burst out laughing.

"Well, if you really must..!" Stubbing out the cigarette on a nearby saucer, he grabbed her slim hips, and once more set to work, driving her to that frenzied state of peri-orgasmic pleasure; his clever tongue worked its way upon her womanhood, causing her to convulse and climax in the most fantastic way imaginable. For the very first time in her life. She fling herself back on the indigo pillow, breathless and flushed.

"Was that nice?" he whispered, smiling indulgently at her.

"Oh, Seamus! What a genius you are! Thank you, thank you so much!"

"Whatever for?" Mildly amused, he settled back next to her on the bed, stroking her breasts, casually.

"Why, for making that happen! And in such a naughty, naughty way!" She giggled up at him, self-consciously. "Is it normal to feel like this?"

"Have you never had an orgasm before?" He observed her quizzically, feeling as though he was just scratching the surface of her new-found sexuality.

"Um, not really. No, I must be truthful. Never." She could never lie to him, this man who was opening up a whole new experience to her. Seamus got up once again, then sauntered over to the door. "Where are you going now?" Mavis found his behaviour both confusing and disconcerting.

"I need to take a leak. And when I return, you had better be ready for me, you little tease!" Ready for him, she thought. Oh, she was more than ready for him. Within a couple of minutes he was back, walking slowly and purposefully towards the bed, his lower body indicating that he was also more than ready for her. She caught her breath at the sight of his weapon of seduction, proud and erect, and she knew what was going to happen. He lowered himself onto her, and took her, blissfully and willingly, to paradise once more.

At half past three, Mavis was luxuriating in a steaming bath, and Seamus was massaging her wet back with a huge bar of rose-scented soap. The bathroom was ancient, but in working order. Black patches of mould decorated the walls, and the window refused to open, but there was a copious amount of hot water and Mavis' bath attendant was both attentive and solicitous.

"That soap smells so lovely. Where on earth did you buy it? It makes me want to throw out my Camay and rush to the nearest chemist who sells it!" Mavis smiled up at Seamus, clouds of iridescent lather gathering on her shoulders.

"You will have a fair way to rush, then, sweet Mavis! I bought this soap in a souk in Marrakesh. It is hand-made and milled from the finest ingredients." He continued to massage the fragrant bar into her skin. Mavis turned away, for once introspective and reflective.

"You have travelled so much. And I so little. You have seen so much, experienced so many things. And I am just Mavis Watton, provincial and repressed. What on earth can you see in me?" She frowned at her distorted reflection in the tap. He continued his ablutions, working his way around her body with tenderness and sensitivity.

"You are a beautiful woman, a woman I should have met a thousand years ago, a woman I should have loved from the dawn of time. A tiny, opinionated, feisty woman from the backwaters of Wales. But I have found you now, maybe a little late, maybe too late, but it is my wish to enjoy you, to make you as happy as is possible, given the precarious situation we find ourselves in."

Mavis threw back her head and laughed, delightedly. "Oh, you made me happy, alright!"

"Shall I make you happy again? Open your legs, you wanton woman."

Meekly, she obeyed. His hands slipped beneath the water, seeking the source of her earlier joy. Finding his goal, he gently stroked and caressed her small, firm bud of pleasure. She sat in the hot water, keeping extremely still, not wishing to move or disturb his activity.

"You are being a very naughty girl, Mrs Watton, how are you finding your punishment?" "Unbearable!" she gasped as she reached once more the dizzy heights of sheer, unspeakable ecstasy. She sank further into the depths of the bath, only to be hauled up by Seamus' strong arms.

"Please don't drown in my bath!" he laughed. "I know the old saying goes that a house isn't a home until it sees a birth, a marriage and a death! But I have no wish to witness the latter!" He wrapped her in an enormous, fluffy towel, surprisingly fresh and clean, which gratified Mavis, then picked her up once more and carried her into the bedroom.

"Now I shall make us some coffee, and you will then resume your position in my studio, as I have you for at least another hour before you have to go home." He went downstairs, leaving Mavis stretched out on the bed, unashamedly naked and replete.

Mavis walked back to the cottage, feeling joyful and relaxed. There was no sign of Ernest, so she turned around and waved at Seamus, who was loitering with intent at his front window. He smiled, waved back, then turned away.

There was going to be little opportunity to call on him again, so Mavis concentrated her thoughts on the following Thursday evening, when Seamus would host his house-warming party. Five whole days to be endured before she could legitimately see him once more. She busied herself with preparations for supper, peeling potatoes and cutting them up into chips, then putting them to soak in a yellow plastic bowl. Home made fish and chips on a Saturday night: that would be sure to put Ernest in a good mood. She took out the chip-pan from the lower cupboard and assessed it thoughtfully. Would the lard last one more use? Too tired to bother with cleaning the pan and replacing the fat, she placed it in readiness on top of the stove. She looked out of the kitchen window towards the west, and the tree covered hills; the sun was still strong. She could make out a few walkers on the track, probably with their dogs, or maybe using it as a short cut between the two villages. How lovely it would be to walk along it with Seamus, to show him hidden secrets along the way, to talk, touch, and steal a kiss or two. Changing the direction of her glance, she looked down towards Seamus' house, where she had just spent the afternoon in the most decadent and blissful way imaginable. Her skin still burned with the memory of his touch. How she longed for more, how she wished she could be with him at this moment. Slowly, she turned away from the window. Such dreams, such futile dreams.

The days lumbered by, like torpid animals just waking from hibernation, impossible to hurry and taking their own time. On Thursday morning, just as she was leaving for the shop, Mavis turned to Ernest. "Remember not to be late this afternoon, if you have to go out." Ernest looked sharply at her.

"Why? What's happening this afternoon that is so important?"

"Not this afternoon, cariad. Have you forgotten already? It's Mr O'Brien's house-warming party this evening." Mavis smiled encouragingly at her husband, who was scowling in displeasure as he pretended to read the newspaper.

"We're not going." He folded up the paper as though that was an end to the matter. He stood up, his face set. Mavis swung around to face him, desperately trying to hide her fury. "Why not?" Her voice was as sweet as honey, but she felt like throwing her bunch of keys at him.

"I have no time for the likes of him. Namby pamby artist. And I will not have you consorting with a bunch of wild bohemian people. I know all about that sort of crowd. Shameless, that's what they are. There will be drink and tobacco there to be sure. Where is your sense of decency, woman?" He glowered at her, daring her to defy him. Mavis breathed in deeply, attempting to control the anger within her.

"Ernest," she began evenly, "if you remember, Mr O'Brien said that his sister would be there, and she has something to do with the Church. So how can it be such a den of iniquity? And Eiddwen is really looking forward to going.

Ernest continued to scowl. "We'll see." And, throwing down the newspaper on to the table, he stalked out of the room, self-righteously picking up his Bible as he went.

"Well, I will be going even if you are not," Mavis muttered under her breath. Whether or not Ernest heard her remained to be seen, and Mavis didn't care. Her mind was made up. She would not be dictated to; for goodness' sake, this was the 1960s!

The shop was busy that day. The weather was warm, attracting hordes of schoolchildren at four o'clock, eager to try the new Cider Quench lollipops from Lyon's Maid. The boys and girls made Mavis laugh, as they would devour the Cider Quenches in two minutes flat, then stagger about pretending to be drunk. Harmless fun, although she doubted her austere husband would share her amusement. Finally, at five o'clock, Mavis escaped from the shop and walked briskly up the hill to the cottage. Passing Seamus' house on the way, she noticed that he had hung Chinese lanterns around the doorway, and there was music issuing forth from the open front door. "Bad to Me" by Billy Jay Kramer and the Dakotas was playing (rather loudly) and Mavis could just make out Seamus dancing with a tall, red-haired woman in the front room. They were doubled up with laughter. Mavis smiled, for she recognised the woman as Seamus' sister, Bridget, from a photograph he had shown her. She must have caught their eyes, for they both turned around and waved at her. She waved back, by which time Seamus had appeared at the doorway.

"See you later, alligator!" He grinned cheekily at her.

"Okey dokey, Mr Smokey!" Mavis felt reckless and abandoned and continued her journey home with a determined spring in her step. Ernest was not home. The cottage was silent. Dai was nowhere to be seen. Ernest must have taken him out for a walk. So be it. Mavis would not be preparing any supper, as that would be provided by Seamus' party. She would be the proverbial lady of leisure and take her time getting ready. She hadn't told Eiddwen of her husband's reticence about attending. Best to let fate take control and go with the flow, as Seamus liked to suggest, be her own woman, true to herself and no-one else.

She ran a bath and stepped into it with the window wide open, letting in the warm evening air, and the birdsong from the garden. She lay back and closed her eyes briefly, wondering what the forthcoming event would be like, allowing herself a few moments of calm relaxation. Someone along the lane had been mowing the lawn, she could smell the cut grass, and was instantly transported her back to her childhood, cucumber sandwiches and trips to Parc Hardd. Half an hour later there was still no sign of Ernest, so Mavis went into her bedroom to decide what she was going to wear. Despite Ernest's total disapproval of frivolity, Mavis had carte blanche when it came to her clothes. He wanted her to look smart, and Mavis knew very well how to manage her appearance, presenting herself as unique and attractive, with just a hint of her womanly charms emerging. Having rifled through her wardrobe, she finally selected a favourite of hers. She pulled out a red dress with an oval-shaped low back and front neck-line, and short sleeves. It had been made for her from a Vogue pattern, by Mrs Di Marco, an Italian dressmaker down in Llanelli. The fabric was lustrous acetate satin; the waist was nipped in, hugging her form tightly, accentuating her slimness. The bell-shaped skirt stopped just below her knees. A pair of plain black patent high heels would complete the outfit. Satisfied with her decision, she went downstairs. Only then did she notice a note on the kitchen table. It was from Ernest.

I have gone to visit Mr Bowen with the dog. I will endeavour not to be late.

His perfect copperplate writing was typical of his prim and proper demeanour. Mavis smiled grimly as she tore up the note and put it in the bin. Well, she thought, if he thought that would stop her from going to the party, he had another think coming.

By seven o'clock, there was still no sign of Ernest, but she was dressed and ready. Her fur coat remained in situ at Seamus' house, and anyway, the June evening was much too warm to consider wearing it. Instead, she pulled out a black mohair stole from her chest of drawers and draped it around her shoulders. She looked in the mirror, wiping away a smudge of powder from her chin. Satisfied with her appearance, she quickly back-combed the hair at the crown of her head, gave it a quick spray of lacquer, just as there was a knock at the kitchen door, and she heard a voice cry, "Hello, Mavis! Ernest! Are you both ready?" Mavis ran downstairs to find Eiddwen peering around the kitchen door. She hugged her friend.

"Eiddwen! You look lovely!" Eiddwen excitedly did a twirl. She was wearing the blue suit she had bought with Mavis.

"I know I wore this only the other day, but I doubt if anyone else there tonight will know!" Then Eiddwen's face fell as she took in Mavis. How could she possibly compete with her? She looked so svelte, polished and exotic, while she, Eiddwen, was pleasant enough, but plump and totally provincial, despite the Jackie Kennedy outfit.

"Where is Ernest? Is he still getting ready?"

"He hasn't come back from Mr Bowen's yet. I will write him a note. We won't wait much longer. The invitation said seven thirty, so if he isn't home by a quarter past, we will go on ahead." Eiddwen looked shocked. "But we can't go to a party without an escort! What will people say?"

Mavis gave Eiddwen a withering look. "People can say whatever they want, Eiddwen. And we are not living in Jane Austen's era, we do not require an escort! These are the 1960s. We are modern, liberated women." (In our dreams, she thought privately.) And with that she got out a writing pad from a kitchen drawer, and quickly scribbled a note to Ernest.

Have gone on ahead with Eiddwen. Please do not leave it very late. To hell with him, she thought. "Do you think there will be drink there, Mavis?" Eiddwen looked as though she secretly hoped there would be.

"No doubt. But you don't have to drink it, do you?" Mavis hoped that her friend wouldn't behave like an excited schoolgirl in front of Seamus' other guests.

"I had a Babycham at Aunty Vera's last Christmas." Eiddwen giggled at the memory. "I was quite tiddly!"

"Well, don't get tiddly tonight, try to be a good girl and behave yourself for once in your life, for goodness' sake," replied Mavis, acidly, her words sounding harsher than she intended. However, any sarcasm was lost on the eager Eiddwen, already intoxicated at just the thought of the evening ahead.

"Anyway Eiddwen, it's almost twenty past seven, let's go." Locking the kitchen door behind her, Mavis joined her friend and the two women made their way down the lane, Eiddwen in nervous anticipation, talking non-stop, making Mavis want to throttle her. The sun continued to peep over the hills, but the Chinese lanterns were already lit outside Seamus' house. Sounds of revelry and laughter could be heard, and music was being played. More timidly than of late, Mavis walked up the garden path, with Eiddwen's arm linked through hers. She wasn't sure how this would appear to all Seamus' sophisticated friends, but tolerated the gesture all the same. If Eiddwen was feeling as nervous as she was, then she would need all the moral support it lent.

Several smart –looking cars were parked on the drive, indicating the affluent circumstances of Seamus' other guests. Mavis wondered where they were all staying. Maybe at the house? Maybe at hotels down in Llanelli? The door was wide open; the buzz of animated conversation filled Mavis' ears, loud and opinionated English accents. She shrunk inside herself, wondering how she could manage to avoid appearing stupid and homespun. There didn't seem much point in knocking, so the two women went straight inside. A tall nun turned around and smiled at them both.

"Come in, come in! Hello, there! What'll you both be havin' now?" Mavis recognised her as Seamus' sister. Like a jack-in-the-box, up popped Seamus from nowhere, giving first Eiddwen a hug, which caused her to blush beetroot red, then Mavis, and he whispered softly in her ear,

"You look a million dollars, my sweet angel." Mavis smiled up at him, and secretly squeezed his hand, then looked up at all the other guests. They all seemed so tall, so strange, so confident and at ease with themselves. Seamus looked amazingly elegant and effortlessly glamorous in jeans and a white crinkly shirt, which Mavis later learned was made of cheesecloth.

"Where is Mr Watton? Is he coming too? Shall I get you both a glass of punch?" Seamus grinned at both of them.

"What's that?" Mavis looked blankly at him.

"Is it alcoholic?" asked Eiddwen eagerly. Mavis kicked her gently on the ankle. Please don't let Eiddwen show them up now!

"Oh, not really!" laughed the nun. "It's full of delicious fruit like peaches and oranges, and none of your tinned robbish either! And Seamus' secret ingredient as well - do you know what, he spent a whole hour making the brew this afternoon!"

"Ooh! What's the secret ingredient?" demanded Eiddwen, excitedly, her eyes like saucers as she spotted an immense black man dressed in a yellow kaftan, making his way through the throng.

"Oh, just a wee splash of tequila! I picked it up in Mexico when I was there a couple of years ago. I promise you, you won't taste it at all!" Seamus winked conspiratorially at his sister.

"Very well," agreed Mavis, happily, "We will sample your concoction – and it had better be good!" Seamus loped off to fetch the punch, leaving the women to take in their surroundings. The nun disappeared into the crowd. Candles inserted into Mateus Rose bottles glowed enticingly in every window. Thank goodness there were no curtains, thought Mavis, or they would have gone up in flames by now. Once again, Mavis could smell that same heavy, sweet scent she had encountered on her first visit to the house. She wondered what it was. Music she had never heard before was belting out of the record player. Her mind was reeling with all these strange sensations. Seamus' sister edged her way back to the women, drinking at the same time from what seemed to be a large glass of Coca-Cola. "What is that song?" asked Mavis, curiously. "I haven't heard it before. It's really aggressive, I haven't heard anything like it in my life."

"Oh, surely to God you have!" Bridget smiled in a slightly hazy way. "That's I wanna be your man by the Rolling Stones. Bloody good song!"

Mavis didn't know if she felt more shocked at a nun swearing or the fact that she was listening to the Rolling Stones. The Rolling Stones were held in abhorrence by Llannon's chapel-going community, thought to be responsible for a degenerate youthful society and a threat to all that was decent and respectable. However, she said nothing, then smiled in relief at Seamus as he reappeared with the drinks. Eiddwen almost fainted right away at the sight of the tall glasses, filled with ice cubes, golden liquid and pieces of fruit, with sugared rims and tiny pink parasols. Mavis took a tiny, cautious sip. Lifting her eyes to Seamus, she laughed quietly.

"This'll do nicely, Mr O'Brien!"

Eiddwen, on the other hand, deceived by the innocent appearance of the punch, drank a hefty mouthful. Seamus watched with interest as her eyes filled with tears, and she coughed and spluttered as the tequila hit her throat. "Powerful stuff, eh?" He beamed at the pair. "T'will kill the germs if nothing else!" Eiddwen resolved to throw it away at her earliest opportunity, and planned to ask for a glass of lemonade instead.

Mavis noticed that most people seemed to be smoking. If Ernest turned up now, he would have an apoplectic fit. Ah well, so be it. She determined to enjoy herself as long as she could. "Seam - sorry, um, Mr O'Brien," Mavis corrected herself just in time.

"Please, do call me Seamus." He chuckled, winking surreptitiously at her.

"Well, Seamus, what is that sweet smell? Is it from the cigarettes some of your guests seem to be smoking?"

"Er, well, I suppose it is." Seamus looked furtively around.

"It's the same smell that I noticed here when you showed me around last month. It's quite unusual. What brand of tobacco is it?"

"Um...it's not tobacco as such." Seamus seemed slightly embarrassed. "Are you taking the mickey, Mavis?"

"What do you mean?" She frowned in puzzlement, as he took her arm and drew her away from Eiddwen, who was no deep in conversation with a middle-aged man who had long, flowing grey hair.

"It's not tobacco," he repeated in a whisper, "and I wouldn't talk about it if I were you." Realisation dawned on her, and she whispered back, "Oh, they're smoking mari-marijuna or something?"

"Marijuana. Yes. Pot. But please keep that to yourself. We don't really want the local pigs to find out."

"Pigs?" Mavis was seriously confused now, unable to connect the smoking of drugs with the local farming community.

"Fuzz! Cops! The local fecking constabulary!" Seamus could not believe Mavis' naivety.

"I see. Do you smoke the stuff as well, Seamus?" She looked up at him, challenging him to be truthful. He looked away, for once unsure what to say. "Only occasionally. I can assure you, I am not a bloody drug addict! Now, let's go and rescue your poor friend from the lecherous clutches of Professor Drummond."

Eiddwen was actually enjoying herself immensely, and despite her earlier decision to forego the punch, had managed to down the whole glass, and was talking to the professor quite animatedly. He had her complete attention.

"We were just putting the world to rights!" The professor spoke in a refined Scottish accent. "We Celts should stick together, and rout out the Sassenachs!" He put his arm around Eiddwen's receptive shoulder.

"Well, you two seem to be getting on just fine. However, I have no time for aggressive radicals. Live and let live." Seamus laughed and turned to Mavis. "Would you care to dance?" Having consumed more than half her glass of punch, Mavis threw caution to the winds and followed him into the front room, saying to the professor as she went, "Of course. And neither Eiddwen nor I support Plaid Cymru or anything contentiously patriotic like that!"

What little furniture that had been there had been cleared away, and all the table lamps had been covered with red fabric, giving the room a warm, seductive glow. Massive cushions had been placed on the floor, and couples were relaxing on them, arms around each other. A tanned, plump woman with a bright red beehive hairstyle was in charge of the record player. Several people were dancing. Another Rolling Stones song, Come on, was now playing, and the cushion people were singing along in various degrees of disharmony.

"Dance with me Mavis!" Seamus pulled her onto the dance floor. Mavis laughed back at him.

"But I don't know how to dance to this!" Seamus was not having no for an answer and started dancing. He was a terrible dancer, shuffling randomly from foot to foot, but was enjoying himself tremendously. Mavis looked around her. Surely it couldn't be that difficult. She decided to copy what the other women were doing. They seemed to be twisting their bodies and going up and down at the same time. It didn't seem all that difficult. Mavis soon got the hang of it, to Seamus' delight. Suddenly, to her horror, Mavis spotted a blonde head bobbing up and down, and as her eyes travelled downwards, she saw a large bottom clad in the tightest of blue jeans, twisting about like a sack of potatoes.

I would know that fat backside anywhere, she thought crossly.

"What's the matter? Why the long face?" Seamus looked concerned.

"What's she doing here?" Mavis hissed back.

"Who?" Seamus looked non-plussed, desperately trying to keep time to the music.

"Her! That Gladys Williams!"

"Oh, of course! I forgot you and she were not the best of friends. She has come with Graham Rees, who did some odd jobs around the house for me. She more or less invited herself." He attempted a downwards twist but failed.

"Not surprising." Mavis could not resist another glance at Gladys, who was oblivious to her presence, and was busy shaking her pudding-like backside all over the dance floor, grinning up at her partner, Graham Rees, and fluttering her false eyelashes at him. The Rolling Stones faded away, and another, slower record dropped onto the turntable. The smooth, melodic tones of Andy Williams filled the room. Seamus pulled her close, and held her gently by the waist, just on the right side of seemliness. He breathed in her perfume. No longer the innocent Lily of the Valley for Mavis, but the spicy, heady Shalimar.

"You are not really mine, Mavis, and I suppose I will have to get used to losing you every day of my life, each time you return to your marital bliss. This song sums it all up really. I can't get used to losing you...." He said these words softly, looking down into her eyes. Their reverie was abruptly interrupted by Eiddwen, rushing towards them, panic all over her normally placid features.

"Mavis! Mavis! Ernest is here! He is looking for you! Hic!" She hiccoughed loudly. With a sigh, Mavis pulled away from Seamus.

"I'd better go and find him," she said apologetically. Seamus followed her out of the room, where they found Ernest in intense conversation with Seamus' sister, the nun.

"There you are, Ernest," Mavis greeted him, slightly nervously.

"Good evening, Mr Watton." Seamus was as smooth and relaxed as ever, extending his hand, which Ernest pointedly ignored. "May I get you a drink? We have a wide selection of mineral water and exotic fruit juices. What would you like?"

Ernest frowned. "I do not wish for a drink. I am not thirsty. I have been having a most interesting conversation with Sister Immaculata here. I have suggested she attends our prayer meeting tomorrow evening at the chapel. It will be good for her soul to be among like-minded people, instead of...." He looked around in disapproval at the high-spirited revelry taking place all about him. The nun moved silently away.

"Anyway, I have merely come to take Mavis and Eiddwen home."

"I'm not going home yet, Ernest!" Mavis retorted, crossly. "I have only been here for an hour or so."

"Indeed! I am just about to serve the food. Do stay a little while and have something to eat." Seamus was being as hospitable as he could, desperately trying to pour oil on troubled waters. Ernest drew himself up to his full height and puffed out his chest. His blue eyes were as cold as the North Sea, and his snow-white hair accentuated the high cheekbones, flushed with suppressed anger.

"Come along, Mavis. Home." Mavis glared up at him, refusing to submit to his misogynistic and dictatorial attitude.

"Yes, Ernest. I will go home. But not yet. I am having a lovely time. I will come home soon enough, when I am ready." He reached for her arm, then looked surprised when she snatched it away. "You go home, Ernest, if you wish to be anti-social. I will stay a little longer, with Eiddwen." Mavis glared meaningfully at poor Eiddwen, who felt most uncomfortable at being part of this marital discord.

"Very well. Do as you wish, Mavis. Goodnight, Mr O'Brien." Ernest turned around and stalked furiously away through the open front door, making his way through tipsy revellers who were congregated along the garden path, enjoying the fine evening. He did not look back.

"Oh, Mavis! He is so angry!" Eiddwen's earlier happiness had evaporated in a trice. "Do you think we had better go after him?"

"Certainly not!" Seamus hauled them both after him, dragging them by the hands. "Supper is served! Let him stew in his own juice! Bridget! Get these two lovely ladies some more punch!"

The kitchen was almost unrecognisable. It was clean and orderly, and vast platters of cold meats, cheeses and salads were laid out on the big, kitchen table. Mavis didn't have much of an appetite, knowing she would have to face the music when she returned home, but Eiddwen's greed knew no limit as she helped herself to an overflowing plate of coronation chicken, pickled onions and bread. "This is such a wonderful party, Mr O'Brien," she sighed, "and I have had such an interesting time with the professor. He said I remind him of Jackie Kennedy." She simpered coyly into her empty glass. Mavis smiled indulgently at her friend, who would most certainly have quite a headache in the morning.

"Well, I hope you have both enjoyed yourselves." Seamus smiled down at Mavis, who was absent-mindedly nibbling on a celery stick. She gave him a half smile.

"What's the matter? Was it something I said? Is the food disgusting?" He looked worried. Mavis glanced swiftly at Eiddwen, and was relieved to see she had helped herself to some sherry trifle, and was also starting to clear used plates away into the sink. She walked over to the kitchen door, beckoning to Seamus to follow her, which he did willingly, resembling a wolfhound following a small but irresistible terrier. Several couples were outside in the garden, leaning against trees and finding privacy in the shady corners amongst the ancient oaks which edged the grounds. Several jam jars containing candles were placed at strategic points, along the low, stone wall and upon the stone table, the small flames steady and constant as there was no breeze, creating an unreal atmosphere. Seamus and Mavis found their own secret hideaway near the back door of the garden, which actually opened out onto the track that Mavis loved so much. It was covered with ivy and wild roses, and their deep, heady perfume remained with Mavis forever. The sun had set, but there was still plenty of light in the sky, which was tinged with a peachy glow on the western hills. He placed his hands on her shoulders, looking down at her upturned face, and kissed her gently on her forehead. In the dusk, no-one was watching, nobody cared about this passionate couple who now had to say goodnight to each other.

"I must go home, Seamus." Regret filled her voice and her heart was heavy. To leave this enchanting scene, to break the magic, it made her so sad.

"Can't you stay just a little while longer?" The urgency in his voice was reassuring. Mavis sighed, then looked up at him, smiling.

"If only I could, but I'm in enough trouble as it is. Shall I pop another note in to let you know when I can come here again? Will that suit you?"

"Of course, sweet Mavis." He released her shoulders from his hands, and they returned to the house, where Eiddwen was in her element, washing dishes and chatting happily away to the professor, who wasn't listening to a word she was saying, but was enjoying the sight of her jiggling bottom as it bustled efficiently between the table and the sink.

"Time to go, Eiddwen," announced Mavis. Eiddwen looked dismayed, then remembered Ernest's icy cold anger when he had left.

"Very well, Mavis, I will get my jacket. It's upstairs on the bed." Mavis' eyes grew round with astonishment.

"On the bed? Good heavens, Eiddwen, what on earth were you doing upstairs?"

Eiddwen blushed. "Oh, the professor took me to the back bedroom to watch the sunset." Mavis was aware of Seamus grinning like a Cheshire cat behind her. Eiddwen trotted off to collect her jacket.

"Drummond is nothing but an old goat!" he chuckled. "Just as well he is off to Edinburgh on the ten o'clock train tomorrow!"

"Oh, it's nice for Eiddwen to have some male attention." Mavis was glad for her friend, who indeed seemed to have had the time of her life.

"So I shall hear from you soon, dearest heart?" Mavis looked in swift surprise at Seamus. His subtle whisper hit her like the most glorious, piercing arrow. She stared at him, her eyes shining.

"You shall."

"I'm here! I'm back!" Eiddwen's excited squeak as she bounced downstairs, breaking the emotional tension in a trice. However, her reappearance was interrupted by Seamus' sister, Bridget the nun, staggering out of one of the downstairs rooms, her veil slipping from her head, revealing a cascade of red curls, and her arms around a fair-haired man. They were giggling and kissing each other, passing a cigarette of sorts between them. A very alternative sort of sisterhood, thought Mavis. She put her stole around her shoulders, helped surreptitiously by Seamus, unnoticed by Eiddwen, and the two women walked out into the warm dusk, arm in arm, until they reached the gate, whereupon Eiddwen turned right and down to her dark, lonely house on the main road, and Mavis left, to her cottage of probable anger and uncertainty. Neither woman turned around to see the tall figure of Seamus linger longer than he need have, watching the woman he loved walk dispiritedly home to her domesticity.

Eiddwen stumbled slightly as she tottered along the lane, unable to make out the pot-holes in the moonlight. As she reached the main road, she looked up at the moon. How strange, she thought, there are two moons tonight, and the stars seemed to move about in the sky in a way she had never seen before. Rubbing her eyes in confusion, she was about to make her way across the road when she was grabbed around the waist.

"Not so fast, ma wee lassie!" The Professor spun her around to face him. "I hope you don't mind me escorting you back to your house, but I thought it would be the safest thing to do! You seem to be rather worse for wear!" He chuckled as she clung to him, giggling all the while.

"Oh, Professor! Thank you! I do think I need a bit of help!" She allowed him to put his arm around her shoulders and cuddled in to him happily.

"Call me Archie." His voice was gruff and awkward, but his intention was not. As they reached the other side of the road, just a few yards from Eiddwen's house, he pulled her to face him.

"May I kiss you goodnight, ma wee hen?" Eiddwen sighed with joy, closed her eyes and held up her cheek to be kissed.

"Not like that, like this!" And he held her face in his hands, while his eager mouth sought hers. She responded with alacrity, not quite certain what she should actually do, but allowed him to probe her prim little mouth with his tongue, then kissing him back enthusiastically. Eiddwen Lewis, Llannon's erstwhile eternal virgin, had just experienced her very first kiss.

The Watton's cottage seemed darker than any other cottage along the lane. Mavis' heart sank as she opened the kitchen door and let herself in. There was no light on downstairs. Dai whimpered softly from the corner of the kitchen. His status was now elevated, due to his good behaviour, and he was allowed to sleep inside the house.

"Sh, good boy." Mavis removed her shoes and tiptoed quietly up the stairs. The bedroom light was on, and Ernest was sitting bolt upright in bed, clad in his flannelette nightgown, his Bible open in his lap.

"So. You decided to come home." His face was impassive, but a muscle twitched in his face.

"Of course, cariad. Eiddwen and I have had a lovely time at the party. It's still going on...." Her voice trailed away as Ernest suddenly leapt out of bed, throwing the Bible at her, catching her on the shoulder.

"Ernest! What are you doing?!" Mavis shrank back in alarm. He came closer, deathly pale. "You little whore!" Flecks of spittle flew from his mouth. "How dare you, how dare you behave like a slut!" Mavis felt terror mounting within her. She had never seen Ernest so angry before. Yet something inside her refused to submit to his fury. She held her head high, defying his intimidating behaviour.

" I have done nothing wrong!" She looked him straight in the eye. Ernest gave a roar of outrage, lunged at her, hitting her hard across the face. She screamed in pain and fear, and fled from the bedroom, blood spilling from her lip. Ernest continued his tirade.

"You've been drinking! You loose, wicked whore!"

Mavis ran into the tiny boxroom, locked the door, flung herself on the bed, too shocked to do anything. She had just seen a side to her husband she had never seen before. Ernest had often been verbally harsh towards her, and was prone to sulky moods on a regular basis, but never before had he raised his hand to her. Would he hit her again? Would he do anything worse? She trembled, frightened and miserable. There was no sound from Ernest. All she could hear was the bedside clock ticking, and the faint sound of voices and laughter from Seamus' house. Oh, how she wished to be back there. Gradually, the initial shock abated, and Mavis buried her face in the pillow, and sobbed herself into a heavy, dull sleep.

At seven o'clock the following morning, Mavis heard Ernest leave the cottage with Dai. It was safe to get up. She eased her stiff body out of bed, still wearing her red dress from the previous night, and went to the bathroom to examine her face. Her lip was a little swollen and there was a small laceration, but there was no other evidence of Ernest's vicious assault. No visible evidence, she thought. She felt sick at heart. Turning the hot water tap on, she started to run a bath, thinking that the hot water would help soothe her and restore her usual resilience. Slowly, she eased herself into the warm, scented water, remembering the sensual bath she had had at the hands of Seamus. She looked down at her slim body, only just hidden by the bubbles

She looked again, quickly taking in the red spots which were dotted around her mound of Venus and her upper thighs. Oh, dear God, she thought in despair. What on earth have I caught?

Chapter Thirteen

The Ways of a Child

Mavis sat nervously in Dr Hodges' waiting room, twisting and turning a linen handkerchief in her small, sweaty hands, anxiously waiting for the impatient, white-haired receptionist to call her name. The glorious Monday morning held little joy for her that day. In fact, she hated the cheerful, fluffy clouds as they floated past the surgery window, and resented the carefree happiness of the local children as they ran shouting on their way to school.

Miss Roberts the receptionist scowled as she shuffled papers and consultation cards angrily on the reception desk, as though the patients had no consideration for her at all, had no business being there in the first place.

She strutted importantly to the doctor's consulting room, knocked quietly, then discreetly entered, emerging a few seconds later with a new set of cards, then returning to her station with even more intolerance and suspicion in her eyes.

Mavis felt sick at heart. How could this have happened to her? At her age, she should have known better. She should have realised that a bohemian character like Seamus would have had a colourful history, and would have known many women, especially in the Biblical sense. Did he even know that he had a disease? Had he made love to her in the full knowledge that he could have passed something on to her? How could she possibly explain to Ernest that she had contracted venereal disease? What on earth would happen to her?

"Mrs Watton! Doctor will see you now." Mavis jumped in terror. The receptionist glared at her, as though she could guess the nature of Mavis' symptoms. Mavis rose to her feet, and forced them to take the few short steps to Dr Hodges' room. Her heart beat uncomfortably. So loudly, she thought, that all the patients in the reception room could hear her.

Reluctantly, she knocked on the polished, wooden door, bearing the doctor's name on a brass plaque.

"Come in!" The stern, authoritative voice commanded her entry. Mavis slowly opened the door, and entered the consultation room. The smell of beeswax and antiseptic filled her senses as she made her way across the parquet floor. Dr Hodges glowered at her over his spectacles.

"Mrs Watton. And what may I do for you?"

Mavis swallowed and sat down gingerly on the austere, metal-framed chair reserved for patients, while Dr Hodges remained sternly on his large, comfortable leather one. She cleared her throat, unsure what to say, playing for time and avoiding any eye contact whatsoever.

"It's, er, rather delicate, Doctor." She looked down at the skirt of her white broderie anglaise dress. She had thought it prudent to appear as chaste and virtuous as possible.

"Well?" He regarded her discomfiture over his glasses. She wondered if he noticed the slight swelling on her lip. If he did he showed no sign of it, but continued to wait patiently for her response.

"You see, I have this rash...." Her voice trailed away miserably. Dr Hodges sighed, re-arranged some papers and got to his feet.

"I assume from your reluctance to disclose your specific symptoms that your rash is somewhere rather intimate?"

Mavis said nothing, but nodded. He sighed again. "On the couch with you, then."

As Dr Hodges examined the spots on her mons veneris and her upper thighs, Mavis examined the yellowing paintwork on the ceiling, discovering exactly how many cobwebs hung in the corners and that the light fitting was covered with dust. Her cheeks were beetroot red and she wished she was somewhere else instead, where no-one knew her. "Well," she whispered, tentatively, "what is it, Doctor? Is it serious? Can it be treated?"

Dr Hodges washed his hands at the sink then returned to his desk, leaving a highly mortified Mavis to adjust her petticoat and dress.

"Oh, yes, it's pretty serious." Dr Hodges' eyes twinkled behind his spectacles. "You should ensure that you use a new blade each time you decide to do a bit of gardening in the downstairs department!" Mavis looked blankly at him. "You have a shaving rash, my dear! That's all! A minor and superficial bacterial skin infection caused by a used razor blade. It is self-limiting and requires minimal intervention. Now run along and wash the area twice a day with coal tar soap, then apply some Vaseline to the affected area."

"Oh, thank you, Doctor!" Mavis rushed over to him and gave the surprised Dr Hodges a hug. "I am so relieved!" Then, before the doctor could start to question her about her unspoken yet obvious concern about venereal disease, she added hastily,

"I never imagined for one moment that Ernest had been up to anything!" And with a broad grin, she walked lightly away from the consultation room, leaving the perplexed doctor wondering if he would ever understand women. Especially a woman like Mavis Watton.

Mavis wandered home, her mood in total contrast to her earlier one. Now she could appreciate the beauty of the day and she smiled to herself. Turning around the corner into Bethel Lane, she waved at Eira Jones, who was pegging her whites on her washing line. Eira waved back, pegs between her teeth like two wooden fangs. Looking to the left, she glanced at Seamus' house. She hadn't seen him since the night of the party. She supposed he had had a lot of clearing up to do. It had only been a few days since the event, but how she missed him, longed to see his lop-sided grin, hear his Irish voice, always slightly mocking and teasing, sometimes soft and seductive. Frowning, she also reflected on Ernest's violence that night. Nothing had been mentioned about it within the Watton household, and a stony silence had been maintained between the couple until the following Sunday, when their attendance at chapel had finally required some sort of communication. The way he had lashed out at her had taken her completely by surprise and had shocked her to the core. She knew that the Bible taught that women should submit to their husbands, but Mavis could not possibly accept that Ernest was right to have hit her like that. She had been badly frightened, but, having had no apology from her husband, she resolved that if he ever did it again, she would go and stay with Eiddwen for a while, to think things over. Mavis wasn't sure it would happen again, yet she knew that if it did, it would be for the last time. There was no doubt, no question in her mind at all; she would never endure life as a battered wife. Satisfied with her decision, she strode confidently into the cottage. Ernest was busy in his shed, sorting out his gardening tools, she could hear him clattering about as she opened the kitchen window to let in some fresh air. Dai was capering about in the garden, pouncing on imaginary prey, then chasing his tail. Why not, she thought to herself, why not take the dog for a walk? She had completed all her chores for the morning, and it was still only ten o'clock. She picked up the lead.

"Dai!" she called, as she walked out into the sunlit garden. "Here boy! Walkies!" The dog came bounding over to her, his pink tongue lolling out of his mouth. Ernest emerged from the shed, squinting like a mole in the bright sunlight, wearing his paint-spattered dungarees over his trousers. "Are you taking Dai out? Good, as I am very busy this morning. I have to go into Llanelli to buy some things for the garden."

"What time will you be leaving?" Mavis reached for the dog's lead.

"Around half past one. And then I will call by Fred's new house. I won't be late." Relieved at her husband's good mood, Mavis fastened Dai's lead to his collar and the pair set off up the lane towards the track.

The day was full of promise now, and Mavis walked happily along, appreciating the sunshine, allowing the breeze to waft her hair in front of her eyes, and for once not minding it at all. The glorious and abundant bluebells were starting to fade; the foliage of the trees was becoming quite dense. No-one else was around. Mavis decided to let Dai off the lead, and allow him the freedom to run. Which he did, with mad abandon, scurrying around excitedly, nose to the ground, tail wagging vigorously. The young dog was reluctant to stray far, and was never more than a few yards in front or behind her. Mavis slowed her pace, and strolled along, enjoying the warm sun, glad she was wearing a cool summer frock. She was lulled into a calm, tranquil mood and felt totally relaxed. Lambs bleated after their mothers as the sheep moved from one pasture into another; bold squirrels darted to and fro along the path, in front of Dai's very eyes. They knew they were too quick for him. Mavis laughed to herself as she watched them swinging like furry trapeze artists from branch to branch, then dropping lightly onto the track and scampering away rapidly.

Without Mavis realising it, Dai gradually went further and further ahead of her, until all of a sudden she could no longer see him. She called out to him, and quickened her step. Fuelled by her anxiety, she broke into a run, thankful she was wearing sensible flat sandals. Ernest would be furious with her if she lost Dai. She rounded the corner, and there he was, trotting along happily in the distance, about a hundred yards ahead. Mavis would never have broken the Carmarthenshire record for the hundred yard sprint, but she made an excellent attempt as she continued to chase after the errant dog. Thankfully, Dai suddenly found a clump of dandelions intensely interesting, and stopped to inspect and sniff, allowing Mavis to slow down and catch her breath. She called out his name in a cheerful voice, thinking that if she sounded cross with him, he could well run off again. Dai, however, ignored her, being far too engrossed in his dandelion activity. She soon caught up with him, and resolutely put his lead back on. Puffing and panting in annoyance, Mavis continued her walk southwards, Dai keeping close to her, as though he realised he had been rather a naughty dog. Mavis' demure white frock was sleeveless, and had a low neck; she appreciated the warmth of the sun on her bare skin, which was already turning golden. She had only intended to walk as far as Felinfoel, but the day was so glorious, she decided to walk further. The blue Swiss Valley reservoirs glittered enticingly down below on her left; some truant teenagers were shrieking as they jumped into the water. Well, thought Mavis indulgently, let them enjoy themselves while they can, it won't be long before the whipper-in gets hold of them.

Very soon, Mavis found herself alongside the old cemetery at Trebuan, some of the gravestones leaning to one side, as though tired of pronouncing the identities of the long-deceased occupants whose eternal beds were now blanketed with grass and weeds. How short some of their lives had been, she thought, reading a small, grey stone which bore the inscription,

In Loving Memory of Dafydd Thomas, now safe in the arms of Jesus, born 23rd January 1899, died 24th December, 1900. So young to die, he didn't even make it to his second birthday. Probably tuberculosis or diphtheria, she thought sadly. The cemetery never failed to stimulate emotion within her. Mavis, never one to ponder on anything other than practical matters, wondered anew about the long-dead miners on their way to Cynheidre colliery, speculating whether they continued their spectral journey every night, not realising they were dead at all, passing their own graves as they travelled along in their ghost-train. She shivered, despite the pleasant warmth of the day, and shook her hair back, closing her eyes in the bright sunshine. She could smell the reassuringly familiar scent of hot grass and wild flowers, and watched with pleasure the bees busy at their work amongst the forget-me-nots and wild roses.

The scene soon changed, and Mavis found herself walking alongside the newly-built housing estate just above the track; sombre cubes of grey, the houses stood huddled together on the hillside, bleak and unprepossessing. How she should hate to have to live there. Despite her newly-discovered passion and emotional awareness, Mavis remained an incorrigible snob. She shuddered as she heard a woman screaming furiously at somebody, empty bottles smashing and then a dog barking equally furiously.....Dai pricked up his ears, and Mavis hastened her step.

A couple of hours into her walk, Mavis and Dai approached Llanelli, leaving the path at the village of Furnace, turning off into Old Road. What a wonderful place to live, she thought, turning her eyes this way and that to appreciate the big, Victorian houses which lined the street, their opulent gardens and ancient trees spilling over onto the pavement. As she made her way up the steep hill, she realised she would soon be passing the southern entrance to the park and was within striking distance of the town centre itself. She glanced at her watch, and saw to her amazement that it was almost midday. It had taken almost two hours to walk down to Llanelli. And it would take even longer to walk back up the deceptively gentle hill. But Mavis, as resourceful as ever, remembered with a smile that her husband would be coming down to Llanelli very shortly. She decided to carry on walking to Gwyneth's house, and would await Ernest's arrival, so that she could have a lift home with him in the car. He had said he would visit Fred in his new house, but surely he would call in with Gwyneth first. He usually did. Gwyneth made the most exquisite Victoria sponges; if Ernest did not call by, and the Bakers found out he had been down to Llanelli, then nothing would be right! The road turned downwards, and Mavis could see the whole of Llanelli spread out before her. The Thomas Arms Hotel was on her left, an old building, standing proudly at the junction between Felinfoel Road and Old Road. It had seen the birth of the Llanelli Freemasons in 1856. She regarded the hotel with curiosity. Ernest had no time for freemasonry, being of the opinion that the Freemasons' activities were secretive, secular and clandestine, to say the very least. On the other hand, she thought with sudden amusement, his disapproval may well lie in the fact that he had never been invited to join.

Da'Silva's School of Ballroom Dancing was held in the function room at the rear of the hotel, and Fred's young wife had won several medals there, before she had the children. Mavis sighed inwardly. Such talent....she wondered if Wendy or Julie would inherit their mother's ability. She smiled. This wasn't like her at all, feeling empathy for someone she didn't particularly like! It must be love, she thought to herself, delightedly. Dai was panting hard now, the sun was hot on his white coat.

"Not long now, boy," said Mavis reassuringly. Then she wondered suddenly if Gwyneth Baker would mind the dog in the house? Her own mother and sisters wouldn't entertain that idea for one second! Oh well, she was almost there now, too late to turn back, and she had no money for a bus home. Mavis turned right into Goring Road, walked down past the old Brynmair Clinic where she could hear babies crying and screaming. A shining battalion of empty Silver Cross prams lay in waiting outside the clinic doors, their occupants otherwise engaged in painful but necessary procedures. She felt relieved that she would never have to cope with smelly nappies, Delrosa syrup and vaccinations. Those anxious mothers were welcome to their worries and concerns.

Within ten minutes, the pair had crossed the town centre, and found themselves outside the Bakers' house. No tulips greeted their arrival this time, instead a riotous blaze of yellow pansies and early fuschias welcomed Mavis and Dai . The doorstep was as pristine as usual, and everything was bright and sparkling, ready to impress whatever visitor arrived, unexpectedly or otherwise. Mavis knocked and also rang the bell, because if Mrs Baker was outside pegging washing on the line (it being a Monday) she may not hear her. However, within a few seconds, the door was opened and Gwyneth Baker stood smiling at them.

Whatever Gwyneth thought about Mavis, she was friendly and polite, ushering her inside. "Do you mind about Dai?" Mavis was very aware of him sniffing everything in sight and panting heavily.

"Not at all," laughed Gwyneth. "We had Prince, my son's dog here only yesterday. Dogs are always welcome, although I don't think the cat would agree with that. But she has made herself scarce, so don't worry."

"I hope I am not disturbing you, Mrs Baker. I just walked down with Dai and thought I would catch Ernest here, then have a lift home with him."

"You walked all the way down from Llannon? That's such a long way!" Gwyneth looked incredulously at Mavis.

"I am quite tired, I must admit!" Mavis laughed.

"Well, the kettle has just boiled. Cup of tea?" Gwyneth led the way through into the kitchen, clean and sweet-smelling with the scent of newly baked cake.

"That would be lovely." Mavis settled down into an ancient armchair by the fireplace; the fire, owing to the warm day, was not lit. Dai curled up by her feet, having availed himself of water from the cat's bowl in the corner. Suddenly there was a shriek of delight, a flash of striped dungarees and two arms were flung around her neck, a sticky kiss planted on her cheek.

"Aunty Mavis!" Wendy finally relinquished her grip on the surprised Mavis and then climbed into her lap.

"Hello, Wendy. You seem as full of beans as usual today!"

"Can I take Aunty Mavis into the garden, Mamo?" Wendy looked pleadingly up at her grandmother. "I want to show her the fairy rose tree."

"I'm sure Mrs Watton doesn't want to get all dirty in the garden, Wendy. Now be a good girl and go and wash your face."

"No, I'd like to see this special tree," Mavis was surprised to find herself saying, and got up to follow the little girl outside. The Baker's garden was small but perfect. Ancient stone walls sheltered it from any rogue breezes which may blow in from the sea, and old apple trees at the bottom helped filter out any noise from the town centre. It was like a small, flowery oasis in the midst of urban life. Several rose bushes, Mr Baker's pride and joy, lined the walls, glowing red and yellow in the warm sunshine. In the far corner of the garden, a tiny rose bush stood alone, with a single pink rosebud starting to emerge from one of the stems.

"That's my fairy rose tree." said Wendy, suddenly shy, pulling Mavis by the hand to have a closer look. "I planted it myself."

"All by yourself?" Mavis smiled down at the little girl. Wendy looked away, grinning.

"Well, Dado helped a bit. The thorns were hurting me. But I discovered a fairy, she lives under the tree." Wendy's voice dropped to a whisper. "She tells me secrets."

"Oh, what secrets?" Mavis whispered back, joining in the game.

"Oh, she made me promise not to tell. They wouldn't be secrets anymore if I told anyone!" Wendy giggled cheekily up at Mavis. Really, she thought, this child was far too clever for her own good.

"What does the fairy look like? What's her name?" Mavis entered into the fantasy with amusement. Wendy closed her eyes in concentration. A blackbird sang a solo in one of the apple trees. A fleeting cloud cast a brief shadow over her little face.

"She is as small as a thimble. She is all pink. Her wings sparkle with silver glitter. Her name is Pink Daisy."

"But she is the fairy of the rose! How can her name be Pink Daisy?" Mavis wasn't sure how much sincerity she should attach to this continuing theme.

"She's called that because I want her to be called Pink Daisy." And that was that. A child's decision was not one Mavis could possibly argue with. She sat down on the garden bench with a sigh. Wendy stopped her dancing and prancing and eased herself onto Mavis' lap. "Can we go for a walk, Aunty Mavis? Just a short walk?"

"Of course!" Mavis was amazed to hear herself agreeing to Wendy's request. Wendy's face showed a childlike and innocent desire for her adult company, which Mavis found strangely flattering. "I have to make it quite a short one, Wendy, as your Grandpa Watton will be coming by soon, and I want him to give me a lift home!"

"Let's go, then!" Wendy took Mavis' hand and called out, "Aunty Mavis is coming for a walk with me, Mamo!"

"Don't you be taking her to the park, now, young Wendy!" Mrs Baker appeared at the kitchen door, wiping her hands in her apron. "And make sure you're back in plenty of time for your Grandpa. He will want to see you and I will be making Mavis and him some tea." Without waiting any longer, Wendy led Mavis down the garden path, leaving Dai behind, asleep on the kitchen floor. Clutching Mavis' hand, Wendy opened the back door and the pair walked down the lane, past primly clean dustbins, soon finding themselves at the Odeon cinema.

"Ooh, Aunty Mavis! Snow White is coming next week! Will you come and see it with me? We could have pop and sweets!"

Mavis laughed. "Well, you never know, Wendy!"

Wendy quickly got tired of walking sedately and began to skip and twirl about a few paces ahead of Mavis. She was, even at the tender age of six, graceful and elegant in her movement.

"Do you have dancing lessons, or go to ballet classes?" Mavis asked her thoughtfully. Wendy's happy little face became serious for a moment and she returned to Mavis' side, taking hold of her hand once more. "I have to have piano lessons, Aunty Mavis. I can't do both."

"Why not?"

"Mammy and Daddy don't have enough money. And Mammy says 'what's the point in learning to dance?' She says I should be a teacher, and teachers need to know how to play the piano. Daddy wants me to work in a bank."

"What do you want, Wendy? Would you like to learn how to dance?"

"Oh, yes!" Wendy turned to Mavis with shining eyes. "I would love to do that!"

"Well, I think I shall have a chat with your Mamo later." Mavis gripped Wendy's hand more firmly, and marched resolutely on. She was thinking to herself that her late father had left her a fair amount of money in his will, which she had hardly touched. What a shame it would be if any talent that Wendy may have was to go to waste. Not that she knew anything about dance, but it was patently obvious even to her untrained eye that the child had some sort of ability.

The Roman Catholic church loomed in the distance, tall and elegant in the summer sunshine, the huge white statue of the Virgin gazing down benevolently at the passers-by, holding the infant Jesus in her marble arms.

"That's such a pretty church, isn't it?" The little girl looked up in awe at the beatific expression on the Madonna's face. "I wish I could go there. It smells so exciting and mysterious as well! But Mamo and Dado say that I have to go to St David's church down the Dock. I go to church on Sunday morning, and Sunday School in the afternoon. Soon I will be allowed to go in the night as well!" she concluded proudly.

"Well, it is indeed a most impressive building," murmured Mavis, "but I can understand your grandparents, I suppose. The Roman Catholics have some strange ideas...." She didn't volunteer the fact that Wendy's Grandpa Watton would have had a fit if he had heard their conversation. He considered Roman Catholicism to be nothing but idolatry.

"You're very pretty, Aunty Mavis!" Wendy smiled up at her.

"Well, that's very kind of you! So are you!"

"Oh, no," Wendy shook her head, "I'm not pretty."

"That's silly! Of course you are!"

"No. I'm not. Julie is the pretty one. I heard Aunty Sheila saying so to Mamo. She said that Julie was plump and rosy and that I was a wiry, skinny little thing. But I don't mind."

But it was clear that Wendy did mind.

"Handsome is as handsome does, young Wendy! Never forget that!" Mavis conveniently forgot how important her own appearance was. "But you most certainly are a sweet-looking child, with your lovely fair hair and those blue eyes of yours. Who else in the family has blue eyes?"

"Only Grandpa Watton!" exclaimed Wendy with pleasure.

"Exactly! You are both special. Now, no more to be said about prettiness or anything like that. I think we had better be going home, now, don't you?" Wendy nodded in agreement, and they made their way back to Mrs Baker's house, crossing over the Old Castle Road, the midday sun beating down on their heads.

"I'm thirsty, Aunty Mavis. I hope Mamo has got some lemonade in the pantry." Wendy squinted up at Mavis.

"Well, I think she probably has," Mavis replied reassuringly, longing for a cup of tea herself. When they got back to the house, Ernest's car was parked outside. Perfect timing, thought Mavis.

Mavis and Ernest drove home in silence. Dai sat in regal isolation on the back seat, looking out of the windows as though he ruled the countryside, enjoying his first car journey with his white face pressed up against the glass, making slobbery smudges and causing Mavis to laugh privately at Ernest's reaction when he would see the mess. She had had a satisfactory conversation with Gwyneth Baker, resulting in the agreement that she, Mavis, would pay for Wendy to have ballet lessons with Miss Daphne at the Market Street studios for the period of two years. She would inform Ernest when she felt the time was right. But, after all, it was her money, and his granddaughter who would benefit. Gwyneth had been interested and enthusiastic, and as she was the recognised matriarch of the Baker household, it would ultimately be her decision.

The avenue of trees on the road outside Llannonwelcomed the car as it crawled its way up the hill.

"What do you want for lunch, Ernest?" Mavis wondered what there was in the kitchen which would satisfy him.

"I don't want anything. Fred and Margaret were eating theirs and I had a fry-up with them." His serious face was focussed on the road. Mavis relaxed. Maybe she could sit in the garden for an hour, close her eyes and fall asleep. He turned the car into Bethel Lane and soon was parking in the small drive.

Fifteen minutes later Mavis was sitting in her front garden, upon an ancient striped deckchair; a Barbara Cartland novel rested in her hands, falling sloppily into her lap. Her head was to one side, her mouth slightly open. She was dreaming, floating gently along on a barge, the softest of breezes caressing her face, sweet birdsong in the background. Then, suddenly, a crowd of people were pelting her with stones, calling her a witch and a harlot, and she cried out, but as is often the case in dreams, no sound would come out. She gasped for air, and opened her eyes with a struggle – to see the grinning face of Seamus peering at her over the hedge, pelting her with daisy heads.

"Wake up, sleepy head!" He threw his final missile at her, catching her neatly on the nose. Mavis sat bolt upright, horrified. Had she been snoring, or even worse, dribbling? God forbid, was there no privacy in Llannon?

"Seamus!" She hissed at him, warning him to be quiet. "What are you doing?!"

"Don't be so fecking worried!" His wicked smile twinkled at her. "Your beloved Mr Watton is down at the chapel, talking as his name would suggest, rather earnestly with the glorious Gladys! I just passed them a few minutes ago." Mavis sat up in her deckchair, squinting up at Seamus.

"Well, they are welcome to each other, I'm sure. I have been having forty winks."

"I know you have. I have been watching you for at least twenty of them!" He chuckled in delight. Mavis scowled in pretended annoyance. "But would you prefer to sit in my garden instead? It's slightly more shady."

"Well, that would be nice, but what on earth would I tell Ernest if he came home and I wasn't here?" Seamus sighed, then smiled. "My darling, sweet Mavis. He has clearly gone out (and is at this very moment fraternising with the chapel organist and part-time nude model) without informing you. So you need to come and see the finished portrait that you are having done for him, don't you?" He smiled sweetly at her.

"Very well, Seamus. Let's go!" She got to her feet and followed him down the lane to his house.

"Have you really finished the painting, Seamus?" she asked as they settled down on the stone seat in the garden. The sun flickered through the leaves of the trees, casting a dappled light onto the couple.

"Almost, but I need you to sit for me a couple more times." He took hold of her hand. "Jesus, I have missed you these past few days. How have you been? Was Ernest angry with you when you got home after the party?" Mavis looked down at her white dress, which was now slightly splattered with Ribena, which Wendy had splashed on it during her visit.

"Your silence speaks volumes." He looked at her intently, waiting patiently for her reply.

"Very well. I can have no secrets from you, Seamus." And she proceeded to tell him all about the events after the party. As her account unfolded, his face clouded and became serious. His grip on her hand tightened. When she had finished, she looked up at him, wondering what he would make of it all.

"What a fecking bastard. I want to ring his bloody neck. I want to deck the fecking brute." He looked away in anger, his jaw clenched. "And is that mark on your mouth the result of his wallop?" He gently touched her lip with his finger. She nodded. "Well, he may have given you a kiss with his fist, but I will kiss your troubles away." And he took her in his arms and kissed her gently and slowly, making her melt inside and rendering her helpless in his embrace. Pulling apart from her, he whispered,

"Shall we go inside?"

 "I thought you'd never ask." Silently the pair went back into the house, and climbed the stairs.

"I am going to undress you oh, so slowly, my angel," he murmured, closing the bedroom door.

An hour or so later, a sated Mavis was sitting up in Seamus' bed, clad only in a bright red sheet, being fed strawberries and grapes by Seamus.

"May I see my portrait?" She snuggled up closer to him, kissing strawberry juice off his chest.

"Of course you may, I am keeping it safe in the other bedroom," he replied, pulling her to her feet, and steering her towards the landing.

"Seamus!" she shrieked with laughter, "I am completely naked!"

"Just the way I like you," he said firmly, watching her perfect body as she scampered quickly into the room which housed all his work, her small, pert bottom hardly wobbling as she ran. Mavis stood in front of her portrait, amazed at what she saw. Seamus had captured her perfectly. She did indeed look quite exotic, with her dark hair cascading over her bare shoulders. There was a soft look in her eyes, a new femininity. Mavis loved it. She looked so happy in it. Another painting stood next to it, almost identical, but with Mavis wearing the fur coat, and without the expression of love that was so clearly evident in the other painting, appearing colder and more distant. Just as Ernest would prefer it, she thought to herself.

"Do you like them?" Seamus stood beside her, wearing nothing but a smile.

"Like them? I adore them, Seamus, they are wonderful! But my favourite is the one that shall never be seen...."

"I prefer that one myself. My private, secret Mavis, the real woman who has discovered her sexuality and her potential at long last!" He put his arm around her shoulder, kissing the top of her head. "But there is something else I want you to see! Let's get dressed!"

Five minutes later they were inside the musty old garage that lay alongside the house. Seamus went up to a large object which was covered with black material. He removed it with a flourish.

"Well, what do you think?" he asked proudly.

"Goodness, Seamus!" Mavis stared at the gleaming machine. "You have bought a motorbike!"

"Yes! I have been getting a bit cheesed off with having to catch fecking buses and beg lifts off kind neighbours. So I went and bought myself this little lady! And not just any motorbike, Mavis, this little darling is a Honda C92! The frame is excellent, the engine is as sweet as honey and the seat is perfect! D'you want to come for a ride?"

"Now? Oh, Seamus, I couldn't possibly!" Mavis gasped with horror at the thought of being seen hurtling through the village on the back of Seamus' bike!

"But you will, won't you? How about tomorrow? Or maybe Friday? I have to go and sort out some bank stuff on Wednesday. Do you work Fridays?" He seemed so anxious that she should accompany him on this escapade, that Mavis found herself agreeing to go for a ride.

"Friday sounds good. And where will we go?"

"I don't know, I have no idea! You shall take me somewhere pleasant, I am sure!" He smiled at her in glee.

"I know just the place!" Mavis was already planning the intricacies of her secret liaison, getting more excited as she thought about it. "Leave it with me. I won't tell you yet. Just one thing, is there any room on the bike for a picnic?"

"To be sure there is!" He rubbed his hands in pleasure.

"Very well. Meet me at the second bus stop in the village at half past eight. No-one tends to get on the bus at that time. I will think of a reason to be going into town."

"I love you, Mavis," he said, suddenly serious again.

"I love you, too, Seamus." she replied quietly. "With all my heart."

Chapter Fourteen

Dunes

At half-past eight the following Friday, the sun conveniently beating down, Mavis waited impatiently at the bus stop at the lower end of Llannon. She was a little worried about how long she would have to wait before Seamus turned up or whether anyone would see her and wonder what she was doing. It would be considered very unusual for her to be venturing into Llanelli on a Friday, as market day was on a Thursday. The basket she was carrying was heavy, containing a hurriedly prepared picnic. Mavis had had to wait until Ernest had gone over to Mr Bowen's before she could make it. She glanced at her watch anxiously. Almost twenty-five to nine. The minutes ticked by. He couldn't be coming. There was no sign of him. She looked up and down the road. The bus would be along in a moment or two, with people on it she might know. Well, she thought, she couldn't stand here all day. With a sinking feeling in the pit of her stomach, she turned around to head back up the road.

"And where do you think you are going?" Her arm was grabbed and she was tugged unceremoniously around. Seamus towered over her, grinning as usual.

"I thought you weren't coming!" she protested.

"As if I would stand a lady up! I have parked my chariot around the corner, in the lane, as I thought it would raise a few eyebrows if anyone spotted the prim and proper Mrs Watton, the deacon's wife, getting on a motorbike with a reckless and degenerate artist!"

"Oh, I see. I am sorry!" But her apologetic mood didn't last long. "Come on, then! There's no time to lose! We have got to get out of here!"

"That sounds like a good idea, sweet Mavis, and could almost be the start of a song!" He grabbed her hand and the two of them sprinted around the corner, the overgrown ferns and grasses brushing against her ankles as they ran as quickly as they could into the rarely used farm track. And there it was, Seamus' motorbike, shining and sparkling, ready to go. Seamus took the basket from Mavis and managed to put it into the top box behind the seat.

"I hope there are cheese sandwiches in there!"

"How did you guess?" Mavis smiled cheekily back at him.

"Just as well you dispensed with your customary skirt today, my darling woman, or you would have found it very difficult indeed to travel with any dignity at all." His eyes travelled appreciatively up and down her slight form, noting with approval her white pedal pushers and her red gingham shirt

"I have never been on a motorbike before. I am quite nervous." She bit her lip, regarding the vehicle with a growing sense of anxiety.

"You'll be fine. Just sit behind me, hold on tightly to my waist and off we will go. By the way, where exactly are we going?"

"Oh! Of course! I haven't told you yet!" She clambered on to the bike. "We will need to go down into Llanelli, then I will direct you. I think we shall go to Llangennith over on the Gower. It is such a beautiful day, and as the children haven't broken up from school, it should be peaceful." And off they went, the sun in their faces and the wind in their hair. Mavis had never felt such freedom, such exhilaration. She clung for dear life to Seamus' waist, praying to the good Lord that she wouldn't fall off. The bike roared down the main road, covering the hills with ease. Mavis' eyes were watering, and any artfully applied mascara was soon a memory, as it trickled down her cheeks. But it didn't matter. She was where she wanted to be, having the time of her life. They soon left Llanelli behind them, riding through Bynea, then crossing the Loughor bridge. The tide was out in the estuary, and the amber sand stretched out almost as far as the eye could see. Mavis could see the lighthouse in the distance, and felt she could walk all the way to reach it. But if anyone was to do that, they would be unable to make the return trip in time. The current around the Burry Inlet was treacherous beyond belief; many lives had been lost there over the years. The couple couldn't talk, apart from Mavis shouting directions, however both enjoyed the necessary closeness. The village of Loughor was busy, with children being taken to school, and buses holding up the traffic. The bike then turned right onto the marsh road which meandered its away along the edge of the marsh, which in turn became the sea. The marsh ponies grazed peacefully and fat sheep ambled about, competing for the tastiest grass. There was a salty tang to the air, they were entering a different world. The landscape stretched to infinity, it seemed to reach out to the end of the world. The huge rocky promontory of Whitford point resembled a primeval, predatory beast, reaching out menacingly to the sea. Beast of rock, thought Mavis with a shiver.

Before long, the bike turned right at the Gowerton junction, and they were truly on the Gower peninsula. Ignoring the signpost for Three Crosses and south Gower, they continued on their way, heading west, slowing to a crawl at Penclawdd as the road narrowed and snaked its way through the small cottages, passing Eiddwen's favourite fish and chip shop as they travelled.

"I didn't realise this would take so long!" Seamus yelled at Mavis.

"Not much further!" she shouted back. "We go through Llanmorlais next. Once we pass Llanrhidian we'll be there!" Due to the total lack of road sense of the local sheep, Seamus slowed down to a more sedate twenty miles an hour. "I don't much fancy a lamb dinner today!" he laughed loudly.

By half past nine, they had reached Llangennith, and the bike was safely stowed away against the back of the car-park attendant's shed. Mavis dismounted the bike gingerly, feeling quite stiff after the tension of gripping Seamus so fiercely.

"Well? How did you enjoy the ride?" He rubbed his hands gleefully, anticipating a positive response.

"Once I got used to it, it was wonderful! It is a very fine bike!"

Seamus beamed with delight. The blue sky and the hot sun on their faces welcomed them, beckoning and seducing the visitors; there was only a slight breeze and the sand dunes stood like golden castles, inviting exploration.

"This is a truly smashing spot!" Seamus stood with his hands on his hips, enjoying the vista.

Mavis nodded happily. "I knew you'd like it! Shall we go down to the beach? Do we have anything to sit on?"

"Under your basket of food you will discover a rug, sweet Mavis. It's quite heavy, so I will be in charge of it!" The couple strolled down across the field that served as a car park, through an ancient rusty gate and onto the grassy stretch of sand that gradually developed into the much loved sand dunes of Llangennith beach.

"We have to climb those dunes to get to the beach?" Seamus looked horrified.

"Well, yes we do! Don't be so lazy! But we should take our shoes off or we'll get sand in them, and that would be so unpleasant." Grumbling profusely, Seamus tugged at his cycle boots while Mavis slipped off her canvas loafers. Hand in hand they started their ascent of the dunes. Before long, they reached the top, and could see the whole of the beach in front of them, the tide still quite far out but twinkling in the distance. There were few people about, just a man walking his dog, but he was walking away from them, and an elderly couple sitting on deckchairs, drinking tea from a Thermos flask. Mavis and Seamus stumbled down the dune, laughing as they did so. As they faced the sea, to their left,

Rhosilli beach stood proud and majestically masculine in the morning sun, the huge, rugged cliffs imposing and forbidding. Llangennith herself was altogether softer and smoother, except for the huge waves which periodically crashed onto the shore. Where the dividing line was, Mavis didn't know. She flopped down on the sand.

"Let's set up camp here. The sand is hard enough not to be a nuisance, and we won't be too close to the sea when the tide comes in."

Seamus spread out the rug and sat down beside her. "How cold d'you reckon the water will be?"

"Hm, it'll still be quite cold this early in the summer. But we could paddle. And just as well I came prepared...!" She started to unbutton her shirt. Seamus' eyes nearly popped out of his head. Mavis giggled wickedly.

"Don't worry! I have my bathing costume on underneath!" She quickly wriggled out of her pedal pushers and stood before him in all her navy and white polka dotted glory. Seamus clapped his hands in delight.

"What a saucy wee girl you are! Fecking marvellous! Am afraid that I am not all that organised after all, and have neglected to pack my bathing costume. And I don't suppose for one second that skinny dipping is allowed on this beach!"

"I don't suppose it, either! But you can roll up your jeans and paddle. I promise not to splash you!" It took them about ten minutes walk to reach the sea and they spent the next half hour enjoying the breakers as they crashed onto the sand, leaping about like teenagers, shrieking and laughing the whole time. Exhausted, they staggered happily back to the rug and sat down, breathless and smiling. The wind picked up a bit, and whipped Mavis' hair into her eyes. Suddenly her shirt took off from the rug and she had to chase it for a good two minutes before she caught it, Seamus laughing all the while.

"Shall we retire somewhere more sheltered?" He looked at her directly, his words full of hidden suggestions.

"You mean up in the dunes?" She grinned, matching his mood perfectly.

"Let's not waste any more time, c'mon." He picked up the rug, Mavis gathered up the picnic and her clothes, and the pair made their way with almost indecent haste to the covert privacy of the dunes. They chose the highest one they could find, knowing that it would give them a safe vantage point from where they could ensure they would not be disturbed. No-one else was on the beach now. They slipped and slid down the other side, landing safely on the soft, silky sand.

"This is better." Seamus spread out the rug and the pair sat down once more.

"What shall we talk about?" Mavis smiled up at him, digging a hole in the sand with her feet, so as to have more support.

"Oh, sweet Mavis, I have no intention of talking." He turned towards her, tilting up her chin and gently kissing her mouth. She melted into his arms and kissed him back passionately, savouring his tongue in her mouth, and gently biting his lower lip as they released each other. They lay back on the rug and his hands, hungry for her body, started to stroke her bare legs, moving ever upwards, slowly edging towards their goal. Mavis sighed with pleasure as he caressed her between her legs. The tight, silky fabric of her swimming costume made his fingers slide over her most sensitive area, heightening her enjoyment and preparing her for more exciting activities. Then he got onto his knees, and, straddling her, massaged her breasts firmly, yet gently, driving her mad with desire for him.

"How does this damn thing come off?" He muttered, struggling with the halter strap.

"We shouldn't really do this!" Mavis whispered back, yet at the same time undoing her clasp quickly.

"Oh yes we should." He was breathing heavily now, as he finally managed to peel the tight costume down over her hot, pliant body. Within seconds he had also divested himself of his clothes and was lying down beside her.

"What if someone comes?" She murmured anxiously.

"Well, I will be most disappointed if they don't." He laughed quietly, licking his fingers and starting once more to stroke her mound of Venus. She moaned with ecstasy and started to writhe against his circulating hand.

"That's right, my angel, let Mr O'Brien take you to heaven." He fastened his mouth on her left breast and sucked at her nipple, all the while continuing to play with her with his hand. He inserted his fingers into her, to discover how ready she was.

"Jesus, you're wet!"

"Don't stop!" She arched her back slightly, and opened her legs wider.

"You filthy, wicked woman! Christ, you're fecking gorgeous and I am going to take you in a minute!" And with that she gasped with sudden pleasure as her orgasm swept over her in pulsating waves. He hugged her close to him for a few seconds, before plunging himself into her. His hands grabbed her buttocks and squeezed them tightly, but this only seemed to intensify Mavis' excitement, and she started to rotate her hips against his thrusting pelvis. He climaxed violently, shuddering convulsively as he did so. They lay in silence for a while, the only sound being the waves of the incoming tide and the occasional cry of a seagull. Mavis wanted the moment to last forever. She closed her eyes and snuggled up to Seamus.

"I hope you didn't get any sand in your important little places." He grinned, reaching for a cigarette in his jeans pocket, "That would be mighty uncomfortable for you!"

"I'm fine." She groped for her swimming costume, which had managed to drift further down the dune, and started to put it on. "But I think it would be wise to get dressed."

"Spoilsport!" Seamus lit his cigarette. "Here. Hold this for me." He handed her the glowing cigarette and reluctantly started to put on his clothes. Mavis held the cigarette as though it was a viper about to strike.

"I've never held one of these before," she explained, hurriedly handing it back to Seamus as soon as she could.

"I am proving to be quite an education for you, aren't I?" He zipped up his jeans, watching as Mavis adjusted the straps of her costume with one hand. "Motorbike rides, hanky-panky, cigarettes...!"

"I suppose you are, in many ways." Handing him back his cigarette, Mavis looked thoughtful. Then she smiled. "Let's have our picnic, shall we? You can be in charge and wait on me!"

"Very well, your ladyship!"

Mavis had managed to provide a delicious spread, and Seamus greedily devoured cheese sandwiches, hard-boiled eggs and tomatoes.

"You are a hungry boy." Mavis nibbled daintily on the crust of her sandwich." I didn't have time to prepare a flask of tea or anything hot, but there is a bottle of lemonade at the bottom of the basket, and two plastic cups."

"Nectar, pure nectar!" Seamus laughed. The couple enjoyed the simple pleasure of each other's company, the beauty of nature and their brief moment of solitude. All too soon, it seemed, Mavis glanced at Seamus' watch. She sighed. "It's almost half-past eleven," she said sorrowfully, "I think we should set off for home."

"Leave so soon? Surely not? Can't we stay a bit longer?" Seamus looked so crestfallen that Mavis reached out and touched him gently on his cheek.

"It would be unwise for me to be late getting back. As it is, I hope that Ernest won't be back before lunch. I would prefer to get home before him, if at all possible." Reluctantly, they got to their feet, getting dressed and clearing away the remains of the picnic . Leaving the beach and the dunes behind them, they walked slowly up the sandy path back to the car park. There were a few more cars parked there now, but none that Mavis recognised, and the occupants were ambling away to the official wooden footpath in the next field which led to the beach.

By twelve o'clock they were on their way back to Llannon and reality. Mavis had never wanted a journey to last as long as much as she did this one. Just outside Llanrhidian, they were held up by a tractor and slowed down to less than fifteen miles an hour.

"Have you enjoyed your morning, my darling woman?" He took one hand off the handlebar and touched her hand which was around his waist.

"Seamus! Keep both your hands on the handlebar! We could crash!" shrieked Mavis in horror. "But yes, Seamus, I have had the most lovely time with you. I wish it didn't have to end."

He said nothing by way of reply, but squeezed her hand in response, before replacing it on the handlebar. They reached Llannon by ten to one. The village was its usual quiet self, and Seamus was able to drop Mavis off in the lane where they had begun their expedition.

"Thank you for a wonderful morning." She smiled at him, a lump in her throat as she hauled her basket from the top box.

"When will I see you again?" His keen blue eyes met hers.

"As soon as I can manage it. May I just knock on the door when I pass?" She looked up at him, suddenly uncertain of herself, aware of the fact that to see him again was now the most important factor in her existence.

"My darling woman." He touched her lips with his fingers. "You may knock on my door any time you like. Morning, noon or night. You can call on me whenever you wish."

Mavis broke the moment with a nervous giggle. "Now who's talking musically?"

"I mean it. Seriously."

"Very well. I will take you up on that! Goodbye, then."

"Goodbye, little lady. Parting is such sweet sorrow-"

" 'That I shall say goodnight till it be morrow.'" She finished the quote for him, turned and made her way down the lane and onto the main road, heading for home. He watched her walk away, hoping she would turn around to wave. To his delight, before she reached the turning for Bethel Lane, she looked over her left shoulder, gave a big smile and raised her arm, waving madly. He waved back, equally wildly, and didn't stop until the keeper of his heart had disappeared around the corner.

Ernest still hadn't come home by the time she had returned, so Mavis had a quick bath and emptied the picnic basket. She had changed into a demure blue dress, put her hair up into a neat chignon, cleaned the kitchen and hallway, and by two o'clock was making her way down to Eiddwen's house. She hadn't seen her friend for almost a week. About time they both had a good chin wag.....but only about the usual, commonplace village things. Mavis wondered what Eiddwen would think of her erstwhile prim and proper friend if she knew the truth about recent events.

Eiddwen was scrubbing the doorstep, and looked up with a surprised smile on her face. "Why, Mavis! Where have you been? You haven't called and you weren't in Prayer Meeting last night!" Mavis smiled serenely, concealing her guilt that she had forgone the Prayer Meeting in order to wash her hair in anticipation of this morning's outing. The rainbow coloured door strips fluttered gaily in the breeze, discouraging any flies or wasps from entering the household.

"Oh, I've been busy, busy, busy! Where is everyone?" The house seemed strangely quiet for a Friday afternoon.

"Come in, Mavis, but watch the step, it's still wet. Gwyn and Meirion had their cawl early as they wanted to go down to Llanelli early. There's a match on in Stradey Park this evening, kick off at five o'clock. Of course, don't tell Ernest, but they will probably have a couple of pints in the rugby club first!"

"Don't worry, I won't!" Mavis stepped carefully over the mottled, marble step, the harsh smell of Jeye's fluid filling her nostrils.

"What about Sian and Siwan?" Mavis disliked Eiddwen's younger twin sisters. They were sharp-tongued, dark-haired and proudly conscious of the fact they were almost pretty.

"Gone down to Llanelli as well. "Dr No" is in the pictures and they wanted to see it. Sian keeps raving about that Seen Connolly chap. Don't tell Ernest that either!"

"D'you mean Sean Connery?" Mavis smiled at her friend.

"Yes, that's him, that Irish chap." Mavis gave up. Eiddwen ushered Mavis in to the back kitchen. The smell of cawl hung in the air, the aroma of leeks dominating everything. "Would you like some cawl? I can warm some up for you, and there's some Bara Gwenyth as well?"

"Not for me, Eiddwen, I have eaten already." And how lovely it had been, she thought to herself, wistfully, settling down in an armchair. Half an hour and two cups of tea later, the pair were busy gossiping about chapel life and the resulting tit-bits of juicy information.

"Gladys Williams was down at the chapel again this morning. She must be a very dedicated organist. She was there earlier this week as well, when Ernest was down there. Is there something special being organised? Were they practising?"

Mavis raised an eyebrow. "Who knows...?" she murmured. She found she really didn't care.

"And have you seen that Seamus O'Brien again?" Eiddwen leaned forward eagerly, her eyes bright with excitement.

"Oh, round and about." Mavis tried to be as non-committal as possible. "He's a very busy man."

"Gosh. he's such a wild-looking man! But there's something about him, don't you think, Mavis?"

Like all women in love, Mavis could not resist the opportunity to talk, even for a few minutes, about the man who occupied all her thoughts.

"Well, it's a bit of a secret, Eiddwen, so please keep this to yourself!" Eiddwen's eyes grew wide with excitement. "Mr O'Brien has done a painting of me wearing my fur coat, for Ernest's birthday, which is, as you know, next month. It will be a surprise, of course. So say nothing, okay?"

"My lips are sealed, Mavis!" Eiddwen clapped her hands together in glee."How wonderful! How long did it take to do? Did you have to sit still for ages? What did you talk about?"

"Goodness, Eiddwen! One question at a time! It took about a fortnight, all told, and I had to sit very still. We talked mainly about the old house back when I was a child, and the people who used to live there."

"Was it very expensive?"

Mavis was not prepared for this. She thought quickly. "He hasn't presented me with the bill yet. But he did mention that if I was prepared to sit for him again for another painting, which he wants to send to a gallery in London, he would knock fifty percent off!"

Eiddwen nearly fainted with delight. "My friend? An artist's model! How marvellous!" Mavis allowed Eiddwen time to digest this piece of fabricated information, thinking that once she had given the painting to Ernest, it would do no harm if Gladys Williams got to hear of her supposed modelling career. Gladys would be unlikely to impart this to Ernest, as by doing so, she would run the risk of Mavis also divulging Gladys' previous involvement with Seamus. The organist's track record was shady enough, without the added complication of the nude modelling.

"Tell me, what's his house like really? We saw it during the party, but there were so many people there. Has he done much to it?"

"It's a bit of a tip! But it's not too bad, and he makes wonderful coffee!"

"You had coffee there as well?"

"Yes, and why not? Posing for a couple of hours at a time is thirsty work! Speaking of which, why haven't I been offered any more tea, Eiddwen! Your standards are slipping!" Eiddwen leapt to her feet in a whirl of apologies, and set about making some more tea, all the while rabbiting on about Mavis and the painting. Mavis appeared to be listening, and murmured the appropriate responses, but her thoughts were far away, towards the south, amongst the dunes of Llangennith beach.

Ernest was home when Mavis returned to the cottage. To Mavis' relief he seemed to be in a good mood, and was mowing the lawn. Dai was tearing around after him, barking madly at the mower; it was as though he thought it was some strange new animal that had been brought to the house, about to attack him. Mavis waved at Ernest.

"Have you had lunch?" she called out. Ernest paused in his mowing, wiping the sweat from his brow.

"Yes. Mrs Bowen had some faggots and peas on the stove so I had some of that.".

"Did Dai have a share as well?" She patted the dog as he rushed up to her, wagging his plumy tail and panting.

"No. Too rich for him. I don't want him having an upset stomach. There's a letter for you on the sideboard. I haven't opened it." He turned abruptly and continued with his mowing. Mavis retreated to the coolness of the cottage, Dai following her like a small, white shadow. She put on an apron and sighed. Domesticity awaited her.

A small, white envelope lay intact on the sideboard, just as Ernest had said. Mavis sighed. He hadn't opened it. Unsurprising, really, as the author's writing was large, round and childish. Nothing for him to be concerned about. She tore it open. Then she smiled. The letter was written on lined paper, torn from an exercise book, and the author had drawn flowers and stars all down the margin. It also smelled vaguely of Apple Blossom scent, and was obviously a labour of love.

Dear Aunty Mavis, Thank you very much for sending me to ballay lesons. I have been to my first leson and it was lovly. I had to wear a pink leotard and pink ballay shoes. I may have to wear a blue leotard soon. My teacher is nice. Please come and see me again. You are nice. Wendy Watton. Xxxx

Mavis sighed contentedly. A job well done. She would have no children of her own to fuss over or spoil, not that she enjoyed their company particularly, but there was something about Wendy that appealed to her own wilful nature. Thus satisfied, Mavis continued with the dusting and then the ironing, singing softly to herself as she did so. As usual, ironing had a hypnotic effect on her, allowing her thoughts to drift and permitting rogue ideas to enter her mind. She wondered about Seamus' past, his other lovers, and his sexual activities. How did she compare with them? Was she so inexperienced that she was a mere novelty? The iron hissed and steamed as she pressed it firmly onto the crotch of Ernest's longjohns, and she breathed in the hot scent of Daz. Did Seamus regard her as a trivial dalliance? An insignificant bauble to be trifled with, then discarded when the novelty wore off? She shivered at the thought. Then, as she turned a shirt over so she could press the collar, she remembered his passion, his kisses, the effect she seemed to have on him, and relying on her own innate ability to detect any deceit or shallowness, she smiled. She knew she was a loved woman. And then, she considered again........did Ernest really love her? How could he, if he had hit her? And why did she feel so fearful of him most of the time? Was she, to him, a trophy, a prize, an accomplished housekeeper and a woman to warm his bed at night when the fancy took him, which if truth be told, was hardly ever, really. But he looked after her well enough, and she wanted for nothing.....well, nothing material, that is. She was folding the last shirt and about to put away the ironing board, when Ernest entered the kitchen. He had changed from his work clothes into a smart suit. Mavis was surprised. Where on earth could he be going at four o'clock on a Friday afternoon dressed like that?

"Going out, cariad?" She continued her folding, smiling brightly at him.

"I have to go down to the chapel. There is a wedding there tomorrow and Gladys is playing. I have to go over the hymns and the chant for the psalm with her. She also wants to discuss whether or not we should give something to the choir for their attendance. The bridal couple has given ten shillings for payment of organist and choir, but I was of the opinion that the music should be provided free of charge, and the money should go towards the chapel fund; the choir should sing gladly, and give thanks to the Lord that He is gracious enough to allow them to sing in His house." He glared at Mavis, as though challenging her to disagree. But she smiled sweetly.

"Of course the bridal couple should make a donation for the music, but I agree, the chapel should be in receipt of it. I am sure that Gladys will be delighted with that arrangement. She is paid well enough for her Sunday work, so will be more than happy to offer her services free of charge. And, having been a chorister myself, I feel certain that the choir will feel the same."

"Very well. It is indeed gratifying that you share the same opinion, Mavis. I will be back in time for supper." And he put on his hat, despite the hot weather, and walked down Bethel Lane to the chapel. She watched him go, marching briskly along, his mouth set in a straight line, a determined expression on his face. Good luck, Gladys, she thought, wondering anew about the exact nature of Gladys and Ernest's relationship. She sighed, and put the freshly-ironed laundry in the airing cupboard. A whimper at her feet drew her attention back to the present. Dai obviously wanted to go out. He hadn't had a walk today. That settled it. She put on her walking sandals, attached the lead to Dai's collar and ten minutes later she was up on the track, enjoying for the second time that day the warmth of the sun on her face. Supper could take care of itself. There was plenty of boiled ham in the pantry, and she could throw some new potatoes into a pan, add a bit of lettuce and a couple of tomatoes, and they would make do with that.

This afternoon she headed north, but avoided the exit which would take her down to her mother's house. She wondered if she should allow Dai to run off the lead, but decided against it. However, he was really no trouble at all, didn't tug or pull, trotting obediently beside her, happy to be out in the glorious weather. Hardly anyone else was around, only a couple of fishermen returning from the lake. They grunted a "Good afternoon" at her, and continued on their way, their bags heavy with illicit trout. Before long, Mavis reached the donkey field. Two grey donkeys stared curiously at her, all the while munching on hay, which was provided for them in a large container. Mavis wondered why they were eating hay during the height of summer, when there was so much grass available. But then, she remembered with a smile, the field was owned by Mad Alice. Mad Alice was an elderly lady who lived in a tumbledown cottage on the outskirts of Llannon. Like Mavis' late mother-in-law, she was fond of cats, and around twenty of them resided at the cottage. Alice's whole life had been devoted to animals; she had never married, and when she had inherited a large sum of money at the age of sixty-five, had purchased an isolated field from one of the rich farmers over at Sylen. The field was considered useless by the farmer, as it had poor drainage and was difficult to access. Alice then made it her mission to rescue donkeys, and occasionally ponies, keeping them in her field. Mavis had come across her from time to time, taking carrot tops and other vegetable scraps to her animals. She was always dressed the same; a long, flowing skirt, bright red shawl, and a large brimmed hat, from which long wisps of her grey hair escaped. Alice was friendly enough, and harmless, but would talk for hours about her donkeys. Mavis wasn't in the mood for a long conversation with Alice today, and hoped she wasn't out and about. Twenty minutes later she felt decidedly tired, and turned around. The homeward trip was easier, however, given the slight decline all the way. The sun had disappeared behind the hills, the track was shady and the light was fading. Even the birds seemed to think that night was falling, and were unusually silent. Much as she loved the track, Mavis began to feel nervous, and quickened her step. Dai walked slightly ahead of her, head down, panting slightly, but happy enough in his demeanour. Thus reassured, Mavis relaxed, and reached the turn off for Bethel Lane quite soon. She glanced at her wristwatch. Almost a quarter past six. A sly thought entered her head. Seamus had suggested, no, invited her to call by. Well, it was almost supper time, but not quite. No reason to withhold her acceptance of that invitation! Her small feet developed wings as they flew down the steps, rapidly followed by Dai, who couldn't understand what all the fuss was about, but didn't care anyway, he was going somewhere fast! There was no indication that Ernest was home, as she ran swiftly past her own cottage. She scuttled up the path to Seamus' house, rapping on the door with almost indecent haste. Mavis stood there panting, her face flushed with hurrying, willing Seamus to open the door before someone (especially Ernest) walked by and saw her.

Silence. No sound of approaching footsteps. Nothing but silence. Her heart sank rapidly. Sadly, she turned around, once more unsure of herself, feeling let down and mislead. Why the hell did he suggest she call around if he wasn't going to be there? Once the unofficial Queen Bee of Llannon, she was now as uncertain as a virgin on her first night out in Swansea, and she felt unaccustomed tears prick her eyes. As she stepped out of the garden gate, she heard a sharp hiss.

"Come back! Quick!" She spun around. "For fecking feck's sake! Come around the fecking back!" There was Seamus, peeping between the rhododendron bushes, a desperate look on his face, gesticulating at her for all he was worth. Understanding his need for immediate action, she made for the side gate, which led around to the back garden. Breathing heavily, the pair looked at each other under the apple tree, dappled light filtering through gently.

Mavis giggled. "Why all the subterfuge? Why didn't you just answer the front door?"

Dai ran around the garden, lifting his leg happily on every tree and shrub. "I couldn't! That pesky blighter Gladys Williams was here around half-past three, and I had to hide in the bedroom. When I saw it was her, I didn't answer the door, so the snooping cow even came around the side door to the fecking kitchen!"

"Goodness me! What did she want? Anyway, she was cosily ensconced with Ernest by four o'clock, and is probably still with him." But Mavis wondered privately what Gladys' agenda could possibly be....

"Shall we sneak inside?" He whispered softly in her ear. "I could murder a cup of coffee!"

"Is that all you are offering a lady?" Mavis grinned up at him, saucily.

"Well, I may be persuaded to offer her my body as well!"

"Can Dai come too? If we leave him outside, he could well run home and, as they say in the films, 'blow our cover!'"

Seamus laughed heartily. "Of course he should come in. God forbid, what if that old witch Gladys should return and abscond with him?" Man, woman and dog quietly entered the old house by the back kitchen door.

"I had a lovely morning, Mavis." Seamus leaned back in his chair. "South Wales is certainly coming up trumps. I had no idea it was so beautiful. I had imagined that it would be all heavy industry and smoke."

Mavis laughed, putting down her coffee and moving over to him, sitting on his lap. "You're a bright spark! There's more smoke in this house than in the whole of the steel works!" Seamus grinned and puffed contentedly on his cigarette, blowing the smoke away from her eyes. She cuddled up to him. Dai, curled up near the empty fireplace, looked rather suspiciously at the clouds of smoke, as they curled upwards towards the rapidly yellowing ceiling.

"It may be better if you had your cigarette after I have left. Ernest may wonder why I smell of smoke!"

"Very well, sweet woman, I will extinguish my half-smoked fag, yet will refrain from extinguishing my ardour, which is getting hotter by the minute!" And with that he smothered her face in tobacco-rich kisses, which she welcomed, returning them with a passion which equalled his own. Within seconds, the couple found themselves on the floor, cushioned from the hard, wooden floorboards by a soft, blue rug. His hand moved quickly up her leg. your stockings," he murmured into her ear, continuing with his ascent to her white, lacy panties, "and these have got to come off!" Swiftly, he removed them, and then moved downwards, his all-consuming hunger propelling him to the delights of her nether regions. He applied his tongue to her sensitive rosebud and started to send her into that private paradise where she would soar heavenwards, achieving complete and utter bliss. A sudden pressure on her outer thigh surprised her. She opened her eyes. Seamus' head was still busy in his ministrations. Puzzled, she turned her face towards her right. There sat Dai, his head on one side, paw on her leg, panting heavily, keen to join in this fun game.

"DAI!" She sat up, shooing the young dog away in astonishment.

"What's the matter?" Seamus sat up as well.

"He's been pawing my leg!"

Seamus threw back his head and roared with laughter. Dai slunk away to the other side of the room, confused as to why he was being excluded from this jolly romp, and wondering what he had done wrong. Fortunately, Mavis saw the funny side of it too, and started to chuckle. But the romance of the moment was lost, the spell broken.

"I suppose I had better get on home. It's almost seven o'clock. Ernest will be home soon, wanting his supper." Seamus sighed, disappointed. "And maybe he will be wanting more that his supper this evening." He looked miserable.

"Why do you say that? Ernest shows little interest in me these days."

"Mark my words, Mavis, you wait and see. Anyway, come here and kiss me goodbye, my gorgeous woman!" He swept her into his arms and kissed her softly, holding her close as though he never wanted to let her go.

He watched her walk away, Dai on the lead, into the warmth of a summer evening, towards the rigid coldness of her marital home. A bumble bee worked its way noisily amongst the foxgloves, a pair of blackbirds serenaded each other in one of the apple trees. The scent of lavender filled the air. Amidst this quiet beauty, he saw her walk up her garden path, and disappear silently into her cottage, not daring to turn around to wave.

Chapter Fifteen

The Ebb and Flow of Summer

June rolled on, hot summer days alternating with brisk showers and the occasional dismal, dank day. Mavis and Seamus managed to meet regularly, either in his house (in order to "complete the painting") or by fleeing Llannon altogether and escaping to the Gower for short, yet precious, private moments together.

On midsummer's eve, they were fortunate beyond all expectations when Earnest decided to drive up to Brecon in order to visit his cousin Llew, and stay overnight, in order to organise a Baptist retreat later in the year. Never before had Mavis been so grateful of the lack of telephone. She was free to do whatever she wished.

As soon as the Reliant had chugged its reliable way down the lane and out of Llannon, Mavis made her way over to Seamus. It was four o'clock. The sun blazed in the bluest of skies. He greeted her wearing nothing but a green towel, tied around his lean hips, and a smile. "Come in, oh fair one! I will dress quickly, and then we can go into the garden.

"Have you been in the bath?" Mavis quickly slipped inside the hallway, not wishing to be spotted lingering outside by the likes of Eira Jones.

"Oh, about an hour ago. I just couldn't be bothered to get dressed, that's all!"

Mavis smiled to herself. How typically Seamus. She sat in the kitchen while Seamus belted upstairs to dress.

"Shall I put the kettle on?" Her voice echoed through the cavernous hallway. His deep voice echoed back. "Yes! I will be down now!"

Five minutes later, they were sitting on the stone table, enjoying the warmth of the afternoon sipping coffee. Mavis crossed her legs, put her chin in her hands and looked up smilingly at Seamus. "So tell me, Seamus. Your sister Bridget, such a friendly, charming girl! When I saw her in your party, her behaviour seemed quite, er, liberated for a nun! Rather un-convent-ional, if you will excuse my attempt at humour! She seemed to be smoking that pot-stuff as well as drinking an awful lot of alcohol. I didn't think nuns did that sort of thing! Tell me more about her!"

"Ah, my darling sister. Now here's the thing. Bridget is the sweetest sister a man could have. I love her to bits. But she is a wild thing, like a bird. She has never been fettered within the constraints of the mundane life of an Irish woman. She has flown away……and sometimes I think, like Icarus, she has burnt her wings." His eyes had a faraway look. Mavis thought he looked sad.

"What do you mean?"

"Well, here's the story. Bridget went to the Abbey Theatre School of Ballet in Dublin, as did Carmel. It was prestigious, and both my sister and Carmel secured scholarships to go there. They would never have afforded it otherwise, as our families were of working class stock."

Mavis pondered on this. "I think I have heard of that ballet school. I read about it in the hairdresser's a few years ago, in a magazine. It's no longer a ballet school, is it? But didn't Ninette de Valois found it?"

"She did indeed. Carmel and Bridget were great friends, and both seriously talented dancers. But opportunities to perform - and get paid for it – were hard to come by, which was why Carmel started waitressing, and why Bridget, in her wisdom, left Ireland for the bright lights of London." He paused to light a cigarette. "You know what happened to Carmel, obviously. But Bridget found it equally hard to get a job in London. She was short-listed several times for West End shows and the like, but found that the fact she was taller than the average dancer disadvantaged her."

"So what did she do?" Mavis was enthralled.

"My erstwhile God-fearing sister then headed for Soho."

Mavis gasped in shock. She had heard of Soho, and its iniquities. He continued. "She became an exotic dancer, Sister Immaculata."

"An exotic dancer? What do you mean?" Mavis was puzzled, not having heard the expression before.

"Burlesque."

Mavis looked blank. "Burlesque? I don't understand…."

"She takes off her clothes. To music. In front of an audience." Mavis remained silent.

"I thought that would surprise you." he said wryly, inhaling the cigarette smoke deeply. "Mind you, she is spectacularly good at it, and she doesn't perform in sleazy clubs or anything. Her audiences tend to be rather well-heeled, and my friend the Arab sheik is also a friend of hers."

"A friend in more ways than one?" Mavis' cynical remark took him by surprise, but he did not seem at all offended.

"Who knows, who knows? But she seems happy enough, has a lovely flat and some rather grand friends."

"But surely she can't do that forever? I mean, she must be in her forties now?"

"Well, since she has never had any children (none that I am aware of, anyway) her body, like yours, my darling woman, is in remarkably good nick. But I think she is tired of the late nights, and yearns for something else. I don't think she knows what she is seeking, but she is a restless soul."

They fell silent. He reached for her hand and held it tightly. "I am so glad I have found you, Mavis." She scrutinised his face, analysing everything. "But are you yourself seeking more than I can give?" she whispered. He sighed, and stubbed out his cigarette on the ground, grinding it in with the toe of his shoe.

"Mavis, my sweet Mavis, for to me your voice is as sweet as the songbird from which your name is derived, I wish for nothing more than happiness with you. Should you suddenly become widowed, or estranged, then you will find me waiting in the wings of your life's stage, ready to play your leading man, if you wanted to be my leading lady. I set myself no goals, other than to paint, and be happy. And you most certainly make me happy, darling woman. I live each day to the full, and have no regrets for simply enjoying what life brings me. I have no desire to upset any local apple carts or rattle any Llannon cages."

The sun slipped momentarily behind an old oak tree, casting a sudden shade onto the scene. Mavis shivered, and put her coffee, which had gone cold, onto the stone table.

"Are you cold? Shall we go inside?" He put his arm around her shoulders.

"Maybe I just need to put my cardigan on." She slipped her red angora cardigan over her cotton clad shoulders. "There. Warmer now."

"I thought we could have a picnic outside in the garden this evening. Would you like that? Once the sun has sunk a little more to the west, it will warm up the garden again. Come six o'clock we will be bathed once more in glorious sunshine."

"Of course! That will be wonderful! Shall I help you prepare?"

"It is all ready, beloved woman! I have spent all afternoon in my kitchen, and squirrelled my efforts away in the pantry, hidden from your prying eyes! However, it is much too early to eat, don't you think?"

"So what are you suggesting?" She was all pretended innocence. "Do you have some hidden agenda? Have you brought me here under false pretences?"

Without saying a word, he scooped her up, put her over his shoulder and ran inside, Mavis shrieking with laughter. Not stopping to put her down, he climbed the stairs resolutely. "Welcome once more to my boudoir! Enter here freely and of your own will and leave some of the happiness you bring me!"

"You wicked man!" she squealed as he threw her on the bed. "You have been reading too much Bram Stoker!"

"And what would you know about that fine Irish writer, you wicked woman?" With alacrity he peeled off her cardigan and dress, leaving her quivering with expectation upon the bed, clad only in blue and white cotton brassiere and matching frilly knickers. He surveyed his prey with the greatest satisfaction, enjoying the sight of her, rubbing his hands, before launching himself onto her, rendering her breathless, as she pummelled his chest with her small fists.

"Get off me, you beast! You're squeezing the life out of me!" she giggled, helplessly. "And of course I know about Bram Stoker! I read "Dracula" just a few weeks ago."

"There's nothing I like better than the disrobing of a well-read woman!" The brassiere was removed with equal speed, and he buried his face between her small breasts, kissing them reverently, licking each nipple with equal attention. How well they knew each other, how in tune to each other's needs. Perfect harmony. The pace slowed, they gave themselves up to a slow, languid lovemaking. He continued to kiss her, all over, her throat, her stomach, her thighs, then he swiftly turned her over, and proceeded to the same to her shoulders and the back of her neck, making her laugh softly and arch upwards in delight. His strong hands held her hips, and his sensual mouth moved downwards, reaching her bottom, which was still clad in the pretty, frilly knickers. Using his teeth, he pulled gently at the elastic, easing it down over her smooth, pert buttocks. Within a few seconds, that garment was also dispatched to the floor, and Seamus continued his oral exploration of her trembling body. His tongue paid homage to the base of her spine, his hands massaged the cheeks of her bottom.

"Jesus, such a bloody, fecking erotic vision I have before me!" Mavis was too aroused to speak. Once again, he flipped her over, undressed himself with incredible speed, and started to take her, gently and rhythmically, all the while playing with her rosebud, driving her wild with lust. Such was his expertise, that he held back until he knew she was at the brink, and together they felt the huge wave of ecstasy crash over them. They lay back on the bed, panting, the sheets a tangled mix of purple and red beneath them.

"You are wonderful," she sighed, replete and relaxed after their lovemaking.

"You are even more so," he replied, lighting yet another cigarette. "There is something about you that keeps on turning me on, exciting me every time we see each other, and that has never happened before."

"Am I to have my bath?" She turned over onto her tummy and stretched languorously.

"But of course, oh Mistress, your every wish is my command!"

As the sun continued to shine down on the garden, Mavis and Seamus carried their picnic outside, placing laden plates and napkins onto the stone table. Mavis' eyes were round with surprise, as she took in the feast which was spread before her. Pieces of smoked salmon lay upon slices of cucumber, chunks of mayonnaise-coated chicken were speared with cocktail sticks, a delectable tomato salad, shining with oil, was sprinkled with basil; a massive bunch of black, glossy grapes, some celery, a vast, runny circle of Brie and a French baguette completed the outdoor banquet. Mavis wondered where he had bought all these exotic foods, as she had never seen half of them down in Llanelli. Swansea, probably.

"Oh, Seamus, how lovely!" she clapped her hands together in delight.

"Ah, but before you tuck in, it is my wish to corrupt you even further." He grinned wickedly at her, returning once more to the house. Five minutes later he reappeared with two glasses and a bottle of red wine. He opened it with a flourish.

"I don't care if you are a fecking Baptist, tonight you are an O'Brienist, and as such will enjoy the bounty of Mother Earth! This is a 1960 Chateau Mouton Rothschild, premier cru, classe Pauillac, and one of the most famous wines of Bordeaux. Every vintage has a label designed by an artist, and this is mine!" He was clearly very proud of his artwork, which depicted an angel blowing a trumpet, flying through the sky.

"Goodness me, you are so talented." Mavis looked admiringly at the label. "It looks almost too pretty to drink!"

"Yet drink it we will. It is a very fine claret indeed." He poured the wine into both glasses.

"I have heard of claret, Seamus, but just as a colour description."

"Well, it's another term for Bordeaux wine. It comes from the French, clairet, as it is light coloured and clear. Go on, taste it...."

She raised the glass to her lips, and sipped the wine. She smiled. "It's really quite delicious, Seamus. I didn't think I would like it, but it is heavenly! No wonder you used an angel in your design!"

"You have surely tasted wine before?" He sat opposite her, slowly savouring his own wine, enjoying every mouthful, just as he had enjoyed every mouthful of Mavis half an hour earlier.

"Well, I had a glass of Mateus Rose when I got married, and the other day I had a glass of Champagne. This is much nicer, though."

"Champagne, eh? Really? When was that? What was the occasion?"

Mavis squirmed a little uncomfortably on the grass, where she had positioned herself. "Um, when I went to London to buy the fur coat. It was the custom there that each client was offered a glass of Champagne." She looked away hurriedly. Seamus stared at her intently.

"What's the problem with that? There's no need to be all shy about a glass of Champagne!"

Mavis said nothing, but continued to look downwards, starting to pull blades of grass out of the lawn, a churning feeling in the pit of her stomach.

"Mavis." His voice sounded serious. "Is there something you aren't telling me? Do you want to tell me?" He sat down next to her, his long legs stretching out in front of him. He reached for her hand. "Please. Trust me. You can tell me anything you like. I know you too well. I know something is bothering you."

"You will hate me, Seamus, you will, I promise you, you will." She screwed up her eyes, as though trying to obliterate the memory.

"Is it really that bad? Have you murdered someone? Have you stolen money? Taken drugs?" He looked so worried, it almost broke Mavis' heart. She sighed heavily.

"Nothing like that. Do you really want to know the truth? I had a momentary lapse from the straight and narrow.... I let the fur coat salesman kiss me.... and now I regret it."

He roared with laughter. "Mavis. Dear, sweet Mavis. And who could blame him?! I am no fecking angel meself! God only knows how many transgressions I have committed. And what's in a kiss? Nothing at all! And we started this precarious path together just a number of weeks ago, so anything that happened, anything that we did, before then, is merely part of life's glorious tapestry. The best thing we can have is total honesty between us. And you have my solemn oath that your secret will be safe with me." He tried hard to look solemn, but failed as another chuckle escaped from his grinning mouth. She was so relieved he was smiling, but his eyes were unnaturally bright; he held out his arms to her and she moved towards him. Holding her close, he breathed in the scent of her newly-washed hair and a discreet hint of Shalimar. "It's nothing to me," he whispered, gently, "it is history, it pre-dates us, has nothing to do with us and never will. I am not disappointed in you, if that's what you are thinking, instead

I am amazed that you have lived your life this far without knowing how truly joyful and beautiful love can be." She pulled away from him and looked up once again.

"You have had my confession. I am thankful that you seem so accepting of it. I don't think I could have any secrets from you. You are an incredible man, Seamus. But I don't want to talk about it again." She smiled. "Now, I am getting hungry, and want to drink a little more of that wine!" Seamus sat down next to her on the warm grass and she leaned against him. Never had a moment been as precious as that. The heat of the sun enveloped them, the wine was sublime and they relaxed into the moment. Mavis closed her eyes, enjoying the tranquillity of the garden, breathing in the perfume of the overblown roses and the seductively masculine scent of Seamus' sweat. As she drained her first glass of wine, she felt the delightful warmth seep through her, as the unfamiliar alcohol found its way into her system. A tiny hiccough broke the silence. Mavis giggled. Seamus pulled her to her feet. "We had better eat before you get walloped drunk and scuttered! Come on, let me feed you, my angel!" Settling themselves down more comfortably on the grass, the pair fell upon the food, their hunger sharpened by the fresh air and their earlier, vigorous lovemaking.

"I haven't eaten cheese like this before!" Mavis spread the Brie liberally on a second stick of celery. "What's it called again?" She licked her fingers in enjoyment.

"Brie. And it's from an area near Paris. Do you like it?" He watched her enjoyment with pleasure. She nodded, her mouth full. "You certainly seem to! There's nothing better than watching a woman enjoy her food!"

"This is so decadent, Seamus." She mumbled through a mouthful of chicken and tomato. "We would never do this at home. Meals are only eaten at the table. Unless, of course, we are having a picnic -"

" –over at the Gower!" he finished for her.

"Yes. But never a picnic like this. Just ham sandwiches, Victoria sponge and tinned pineapple with evaporated milk. And, naturally, the Thermos of tea."

"Naturally." He cut another slice of Brie, as best he could, for by now it was spilling over its plate. He spread it onto a slice of bread, then handed it to her, with a couple of grapes. She accepted it hungrily.

"I'm absolutely starving! I suppose it's all that activity this afternoon!" They fell silent, enjoying the picnic until there was very little left. Mavis yawned. "I feel so sleepy, Seamus. It must be the wine."

"You only had two small glasses. But you're not used to it, are you? I will get the rug from the bike and you can have a little nap here in the garden, it's too lovely an evening to go in just yet." He rose to his feet. For once not caring about the clearing away or the washing up, Mavis lay back on the rug and closed her eyes. She soon fell asleep. Seamus sat back and watched her. Her hair was a tangled mass of dark waves, spread out on the rug, her head was turned to the side, and her red lips were slightly parted. She resembled a little girl's doll, discarded after an afternoon's play, left at an awkward angle with her legs bent sideways. Mavis murmured something in her sleep. What was she dreaming of, he wondered? Quietly, he got up and went back inside, returning with some paper and some charcoal, then set to work. As the sun slipped down behind the distant trees on the hills, the shadows lengthened, the temperature dropped and the fever of life was over, Mavis stirred and opened her eyes. "How long have I been asleep?" she asked, drowsily, stretching her arms above her head. "What time is it?

"Just past seven o'clock." He put down his papers.

"What have you been doing? Oh, Seamus! You haven't! Oh, you didn't draw me when I was sleeping? Let me see! Let me see!" She tried to grab the sketch, but he was too quick for her, leaping out of her reach with incredible agility.

"Not so fast, dear heart! It is almost finished. But this will be my own private image of you, for me to keep tucked away in my wallet, to pull out whenever I want to look at you, but cannot be with you. Now sit still just a moment longer and then I will allow you to see it." He applied the charcoal to the paper for a few more minutes, then beckoned to her to view it. She held her breath. He had caught her perfectly. What she noticed more than anything was the rapt expression on her sleeping face, revealing a woman fulfilled, a woman in her prime. Any innate and earlier sharpness in her features had been smoothed by passion and the deep love she was feeling, and this was patently evident in the small drawing.

"It's beautiful, Seamus. Really lovely. You are so clever. And you've put my middle name on it as a title!"

"I only reproduce what I see. And I see you as you are there in the drawing. My pocket Venus, my own tiny muse. And as for putting "Rhiannon" on it, well, I thought it would be a tad risky to put Mavis on it, in case it fell out of my pocket or something. But I do love that name. Rhiannon. It suits you so well!"

She threw her arms around him and held him close. He pulled her onto to his lap. "Are you in a rush to go home, or can we sit here a while?"

"I will just pop home to check on Dai, then will be back as soon as I can. Is that okay?"

"Of course! See ya later, alligator!"

"Okey dokey, Mr Smokey!" she quipped as she skipped happily out of the side gate and up the lane to her cottage.

Back home, Dai had been rather a naughty boy, although Mavis later found out that his intentions had been entirely good. Mavis had left him in the outhouse, which was perfectly adequate, being of a reasonable size and pleasantly cool, given the hot day. Mavis sighed when she saw the mess. The sack of potatoes had been ripped open, the contents rolling around all over the floor, and several half-empty paint pots had been upturned. Thankfully, they were so ancient that the lids were stuck fast, and no paint had spilled out. There was no water in his bowl as it had also been upturned. Dai was not cowering at all, though. In fact, he seemed inordinately proud of himself, his ears pricked up and his tail wagging happily. Mavis was about to scold him, when she saw the reason for the chaos. On the floor next to the mop and bucket lay an enormous, very much dead, rat. She realised in an instant what had happened. The dog must have disturbed the rat whilst it was getting at the potatoes, and had pounced on it. The resulting scuffle would have caused the mayhem she was now seeing.

"Well done, boy!" She patted him on the head, and ushered him out into the garden, refilling his water bowl from the outside tap. She wondered what to do about the rat. Although she was not squeamish where rodents were concerned, this one was a big devil, and she baulked at the thought of having to touch it. But, she thought happily to herself, that's what secret lovers were for! She remained with Dai for ten minutes, then, satisfied that he had had all his requirements met, she put him in the kitchen, and started to walk back to Seamus' house. The evening remained balmy and bright. There was no breeze to speak of. Swallows were swooping and diving overhead, feasting on midges and flies, also out in their hordes, capitalising on the fine weather. As she trotted down the lane, she could see over as far as the Brecon Beacons. Ernest was somewhere amongst those hills, forty miles away, probably deep in serious debate with Llew. Well, he wouldn't return until lunchtime tomorrow, so until then, she could do as she damned well pleased! She approached the house. To her horror and astonishment, whom should she see tapping on the side kitchen window but Gladys Williams! Mavis realised that Seamus had probably ignored her knocking on the front door, and was hiding in the kitchen. For once she was at a loss as to what to do for the best. She decided that for now the best action was no action at all. She shrank back against the old stone wall which surrounded the front garden, but which was ancient enough to allow spaces through which to peep at this trespasser into her idyll. Gladys continued her tapping at the window.

"Seamus!" Her voice had a sickly sweet edge. "Seamus! It's me! Gladys! I've got some Welshcakes for you! I know you're there! It's only me!" She was wearing a cerise mini skirt, tight around her bottom, and it made her lardy legs look like two plump sausages stuffed into a bright pink envelope. As Gladys leaned forward to get a better look through the window, Mavis could see right up her skirt. Her buttocks wobbled through the American Tan mesh of her tights, dividing her rear end like a rusty cheese wire. The little tart, thought Mavis, she may have had tights on, but was certainly wearing no knickers at all. However, she remained still and silent, waiting and watching to see what would happen next.

The front door opened, and Seamus peered out. "Is someone there?" he demanded, crossly. Gladys bustled happily around to the front door.

"It's me! Gladys! I have been knocking for ages! Surely you must have heard me? I have brought you some Welshcakes!" She brandished a white paper bag in front of him. Mavis seethed inwardly. She'd probably bought them in the Felinfoel bakery. "Can I come in?"

Seamus scowled. "No, am afraid you can't come in, Gladys. I am rather busy right now." Gladys made a silly, little girl face. "Oh, just for a minute?" she simpered up at him. "We could have a cup of coffee - you make the most divine coffee, don't you?" And she winked at him, conspiratorially. Mavis could feel the rage welling up in her, a white hot lava of fury just waiting to erupt.

"No, really ...." Seamus tried to object, but Gladys was too quick for him, and barged past him, into the house. Mavis could see Seamus desperately looking around the lane for her, but obviously he couldn't leave Gladys rampage through his house, goodness only knows where she might end up.

He darted back inside the house, but made the fatal error of closing the front door. Mavis saw red. Not pausing a moment longer, she stalked up the garden path and rapped loudly on the door. Forcing herself to regain her composure, she put a fixed smile on her face as Seamus opened the door, an agonised look on his face.

"Why! Mrs Watton! What a surprise! Do come in! Indeed, it certainly seems to be the night to go visiting! We have quite a party starting here!" He looked flushed and harassed.

"Yes," hissed Mavis through clenched teeth, "and a fine party it would be with the door shut tight!" Like Gladys a few minutes earlier, Mavis also pushed past Seamus and stormed into the kitchen, leaving him holding the door, his mouth hanging open in confused disbelief. Gladys had made herself quite at home and was busy filling the kettle.

"Well, good evening, Miss Williams." Mavis stood in the doorway, her arms folded.

Gladys swung round and nearly dropped the kettle in shock. "What are you doing here?" she demanded rather rudely.

"I may ask the same of you?" Mavis moved forward, gaining ground, hands on her hips.

"Very well, ladies!" Seamus joined them, blustering uncomfortably about the room, searching unsuccessfully for cups and spoons.

"Have you forgotten where you keep your crockery, Seamus?" Gladys winked at him teasingly, Mavis wanted to throttle her. "Your cups are here, in the top cupboard."

"Mr O'Brien." Mavis turned to address him frostily. "I haven't come here to socialise or to indulge in idle chit-chat. I need your help and I need it right now." Seamus smiled at her gratefully. "But of course! What is the problem?"

"A rat." Mavis never took her eyes off Gladys.

"But what about our coffee?" wailed Gladys in protestation.

"That will have to be cancelled, I am afraid, Gladys. This damsel is in distress and I will have to assist. Anyway, what about that nice young man who brought you to my party the other week? Graham...? My odd job man?"

"What about him?" Gladys sulkily replaced the cups in the cupboard.

"Aren't you seeing him this evening? I mean, he lives in Llannon, and you must have come up from Felinfoel on the bus?"

"Not seeing Gray until half past eight. He's taking me to a Midsummer Dance in Cross Hands. I just thought I'd pop in for old time's sake, you know?" Gladys lowered her eyes suggestively.

"Well, it's almost twenty past now. So you had better get going, hadn't you?" Mavis smiled sweetly at Gladys, who looked as though she would dearly love to scratch Mavis' eyes out. Snatching up her bag of Welshcakes, Gladys flounced out of the kitchen towards the door.

"Seems like you won't be wanting these after all. Anyway, I'm being picked up from the bottom of the lane. I may as well go now." A horn hooted outside.

"I think your chariot has arrived." Seamus pointed to the lane. Mavis stifled a snigger, for there was Graham Rees in his motorbike and sidecar, into which Gladys would no doubt have to squeeze herself.

"Why has he come up the lane, Miss Williams? Why isn't he waiting for you at the junction as you said?" She asked the questions politely enough but there was venom in Mavis' tone.

"Oh, I told him I was coming here with the Welshcakes," countered Gladys, a triumphant smile on her pale, pink lips. "There's nothing like a bit of rivalry to keep a man on his toes!"

"Well, what's the point in coming here, then, Gladys?!" laughed Seamus. Mavis shot him a grateful glance, as Gladys finally admitted defeat and stomped angrily off to her boyfriend's motorbike. Game set and match. They watched her easing herself with difficulty into the sidecar with as much dignity as was possible, given the tight skirt she was wearing. With a falsely fixed smile, she turned to them and waved, as Graham Rees transported her to whatever delights he had ready for her.

"Why did you shut the door, Seamus? I started imagining all sorts of things!" Mavis put her hand on his arm, looking up at him with a hurt expression on her face.

"Oh, sweet Mavis! I didn't realise you were there! I wouldn't just leave my front door open, would I?"

"I don't suppose you would. I just thought that you and Gladys...." Her voice trailed away miserably. Seamus placed both hands on her shoulders. "Mavis Watton. There is only one woman I care anything about, there is only one woman who occupies my heart, my mind and my every waking thought. And that woman is standing right in front of me now. As far as Gladys Williams is concerned, she is a profligate and incorrigible man-eater. She persists in her pursuit of me, seems to be getting pretty chummy with your husband, and all the while has managed to ensnare poor Graham Rees. I have no time for her, but she just doesn't seem to get the message." Mavis grinned up at him.

"You have omitted to include her seduction of the Llanelli Sunday Schoolteacher!" Seamus stared at her in surprise. "Enlighten me, oh fount of all knowledge!" She laughed, and proceeded to regale him with the scandalous account, swearing him to absolute secrecy.

"Bloody hell, Mavis, Carmarthenshire is a veritable hotbed of shameless lust and licentious immorality!"

"Lust and immorality aside, Seamus, I don't want to be standing here on your doorstep much longer. Are you going to assist me with the disposal of the rat or not?"

"To be sure, I will." He locked the front door behind them, and they set off up the lane. "Why on earth did Gladys get picked up in Llannon? She would have had to get a bus up from Felinfoel, wouldn't she? Why make all that effort to come up here when her boyfriend has his own transport?"

Mavis smiled wryly. "I suppose Miss Williams didn't want her mother to see her darling daughter gadding about on the side of a motorbike, chapel organist and all that..." She stored this fact in the recesses of her mind, aware of the fact that it could come in very handy one day.

"That's one helluva big rat!" Seamus threw it over the hedge, much to Dai's disappointment. "Supper for the foxes or breakfast for the crows! Let me just wash my hands quickly, Mavis, then we can go back to my place." She led him into the kitchen, providing him with a new bar of pink carbolic soap, a nailbrush and a clean white towel. Once he had finished, Mavis let Dai out once more, then settled him down in the kitchen, leaving the light on, as when she returned, the sun would have set behind the hills and the cottage would be dark. Seamus set off a couple of minutes before her, so as not to attract attention. Mavis locked the kitchen door and followed him down the lane, slipping as quietly as a wraith through the side gate into the back garden. Seamus was sitting on the rug, looking up at the sky, which was just turning indigo to the east, with a warm apricot glow lingering in the west. He patted the rug. "Come and sit beside me." She settled herself down next to him. "Lie down, look up at the sky. Midsummer, such a magical time, don't you think?" He put his hands behind his head. Mavis snuggled up to him but remained serious.

"There's no room in a Baptist's head for magic of any sort."

"Oh, sweet Mavis! Surely to God (not that I believe in him) you don't mean that?"

She turned to look at him, her eyebrows raised. "Oh, of course I do. It's terribly frowned upon to meddle with anything slightly sinister, and I mean anything. No old customs to be kept, and I can tell you ,Seamus, there are plenty around here. No alcohol, no smoking, nothing whatsoever which even borders on idolatry. I had a small silver crucifix which my godmother Simona gave me. I was never allowed to wear it, as it depicted Christ crucified. Plain crosses were deemed acceptable, as they implied that Christ had risen and was no longer dead."

"Simona...." Seamus looked thoughtful. "That doesn't sound like a good Welsh name. Where is she from?"

"Simona Battista. My great-aunt from Sardinia, my grandmother's sister. My grandmother was from Sardinia originally, but met my grandfather a few years after the Crimean war when she was a nurse. I am very like Simona, so it is said, although not many people can remember her now. She passed away some time ago. Of course, she was a Roman Catholic, but my grandmother had to follow the Baptist doctrines once she married my grandfather."

"So that would explain your dusky and exotic looks, my dear. But tell me, what do you think? What are your thoughts and ideas?"

She chewed thoughtfully on a blade of grass. "I have many thoughts. Many ideas. I wonder a lot about things, but never speak them aloud. Tell me your thoughts, Seamus." He sighed, then rolled over towards her, taking her gently in his arms.

" ' I know a bank where the wild thyme blows
  Where oxlips and the nodding violet grows,
  Quite over-canopied with luscious woodbine
  With sweet musk-roses and with eglantine.'"

Mavis sighed. "Oh, you are indeed my Oberon. My magical king, who brings me such wonderful joy." She relaxed into his embrace. They lay in silence for a few minutes, watching the stars emerge one by one. An owl hooted, far away in the depths of the trees. The swallows were replaced by bats, who swooped as energetically as their daytime rivals for the evening insect life. A vixen screamed harshly over in the neighbouring fields, and then all was silent. Seamus sighed heavily. "You know, we have customs in Ireland, around this time of year." Mavis turned to look at him. "At midsummer, you mean? Even though you are a Roman Catholic?"

"Sure. I was brought up a Catholic, but after life had dealt me her rubbish cards, I soon broke free of the shackles of the church. Midsummer is seen as a time when the veil between this world and the next is thin, when powerful forces are abroad. Night vigils are held in some isolated villages , and it is said that if you spent the night at a sacred site during Midsummer's Eve, you would gain the powers of a bard. But on the down side, you could also end up utterly mad, dead or even be spirited away by the fairies!"

Mavis smiled. "Well, this is not a sacred site, and you are "otterly" mad anyway! But tonight seems so special, so beautiful, that is easy to believe that there is another world, another dimension. I feel that if I wondered up onto the track right now, I might see goblins or pixies, or wander by mistake into that other mysterious country, and never return." She paused a few seconds before continuing. "But if you were treading that magical path beside me, I wouldn't want to return, anyway...." Her voice trailed away softly.

"I have some pine logs in the shed, and a small eucalyptus tree I only planted a few weeks ago. Bridget brought it down from London as a house-warming gift. I could break off a small twig, and we could have our own small bonfire right here in the garden. Shall we do that? Then maybe the Earthmother will give us her blessing!" He was smiling at her, laughing quietly, teasing her, but underneath the mirth, she knew his words hinted at the truth. "Why not?" She felt reckless and daring, wild and free. By ten o'clock they were standing beside a roaring fire, arms around each other, their faces illuminated by the leaping flames, the scent of pine filling the air, as the oil from the needles heated and caught fire.

"We could cook some potatoes on the fire!" Seamus was beaming with enthusiasm.

"Hm...! Tramps' food! That's what Ernest would say. But I am not hungry anyway!" The logs crackled away merrily, sparks shooting up into the night sky. Mavis followed their journey upwards, watching their brief flight into the darkness before they disappeared forever.

"Do you have to go home tonight?" His voice was full of longing.

"I'm afraid so." She sighed sorrowfully. " I have to see to the dog and there's a possibility, slim though it may be, that Eiddwen could call over early in the morning. And Mr Griffiths has asked to me to pop in to help him with stocktaking." She looked up at him, a sad smile on her lips.

"I understand. So what time would madam require escorting back to her residence?"

"It's almost half-past ten. I am normally asleep in bed by this time. Perhaps I should go home now." He pulled her close to him, bent down and kissed her tenderly.

Reluctantly, they left the fire, which had now settled into a pile of embers. Walking back up the lane to the cottage, keeping a respectable distance between each other, for there was still a small amount of light and they could still be seen, they regretted each footstep which brought them closer to the end of a perfect evening. Mavis paused in the doorway, and turned around.

"Goodnight, dear Seamus. I love you."

He smiled. "Sleep well, sweet Mavis, for I love you more." She slipped inside the house, and ran to the window to watch him walking slowly away towards his one house. He turned around before reaching his garden wall, and waved. She waved back, not knowing if he could see her or not.

Mavis arrived home from the stocktaking at midday. To her surprise, the Reliant was parked outside the cottage. Ernest must have left Brecon quite early, as it was a good couple of hours' drive away. She called out his name as she opened the door, but he was nowhere to be seen. Dai was sitting quietly on his bed, his tail thumping away happily when Mavis entered the kitchen. Then she saw a piece of paper on the table. In his perfect copperplate writing Ernest had written,

I have gone down to the chapel to sort a few things out for the wedding. I have not had time for anything to eat. Could you make something for me to have when I get home? Ernest.

No kisses, no endearments, no please or thank you. Ah well, so be it. Then her conscience pricked her. She knew what she would do. Hurriedly she cut some slices of bread from the Bara Gwenyth she had bought from the bakers the previous day, buttered them and made ham sandwiches. Wrapping them in some greaseproof paper, she selected a couple of ripe tomatoes from Ernest's make-shift green house at the bottom of the garden, and packed everything into an old Oxo tin.

"Love in a box," she thought. "Or not." Mavis then found an empty lemonade bottle, diluted some lemon barley water, and packed the whole lot into her wicker basket together with some bara brith. Ten minutes later she was walking briskly down the lane, casting a swift glance at Seamus' house as she went. The day was warm but cloudy, and she could see him moving around in his front room. His back was towards her, so she hastened her step and focussed her intentions on the chapel.

Bethel chapel was an austere building, having been built in 1709, then renovated in 1840, and painted a drab grey. It seemed to represent the whole Baptist effect on her life. Stern, unforgiving, repressing. She expected Ernest would be in the vestry, so she hurried around to the side of the building. Surprisingly, the door was locked. No point in knocking, she thought, as if Ernest was in the main body of the chapel, he wouldn't hear her anyway. She returned to the main entrance, the door of which was unlocked. She entered the building, which was strangely silent. Not wishing to call out, which would seem a little disrespectful in a place of worship, she walked quietly through the chapel and over to the interior door of the vestry. The door was closed, but she could hear muffled voices from inside, then a woman giggling. Opening the door, the sight which met her eyes could not have astounded her more. Ernest was sitting on a large, wooden chair, a Bible in one outstretched hand, from which he was reading aloud. Over his knee was the wriggling posterior of Gladys Williams. With his free hand, Ernest was administering sharp slaps to Gladys' plump, trousered bottom.

"You are a wicked girl, Miss Williams!" he scolded, taking a break from quoting from St Paul's epistle to the Corinthians. "Taking the Lord's name in vain! Do you repent?"

"Yes, yes!" She wriggled even more vigorously, and seemed to be enjoying herself. Ernest was red in the face and also seemed to be gaining some considerable pleasure from this activity. Mavis was dumbstruck. Silently, she put the basket down on the vestry floor. Her presence remained unnoticed. Gathering her wits about her, she endeavoured to maintain her composure. She took a deep breath and spoke clearly.

"I seem to be interrupting something."

Ernest swung around to see his diminutive wife standing in the doorway, impassive, coldly regarding the scene, like a marble statue, her face devoid of any emotion. Gladys leapt to her feet, smoothing down her shirt and pushing back her hair from her flushed face. There was an awkward silence. Mavis calmly picked up her basket and put it on the table.

"I have brought you your lunch, Ernest. I hope you enjoy it." And she turned around, leaving behind her a highly embarrassed Ernest and a smugly satisfied Gladys.

Back in the cottage, Mavis mechanically sat down with a cup of tea, her thoughts in a turmoil. She looked out of her kitchen window. Last night's hot, balmy and magical skies were gone, beyond recall. Grey, leaden clouds hung over Llannon and her entire life. Cowardly seagulls, fussing about an impending storm, screeched harshly overhead. No impression of jealousy or threat entered her mind, merely a state of confusion. Where was the strict, religious man she thought she knew? Who was he? Had she married a stranger? She wondered what the full extent of Ernest's relationship was with Gladys. She really wanted to rush over to Seamus' house and tell him everything. But in doing so she would run the risk of bumping into Ernest, who by now was probably feeling quite anxious and keen to return home. For the second time in two days, she decided that her best course of action was no action at all. She would bide her time, play her cards close to her chest, keep her powder dry. The kitchen door opened. Mavis looked up. Ernest was home.

Chapter Sixteen

The Swirling Tide of Life

Ernest cleared his throat. "It's not what it seemed." His demeanour was gruff and awkward. He closed the door behind him and sat down at the table.

"Really." Mavis didn't bother looking up from the newspaper which she was pretending to be reading. Her thoughts were reeling and she was struggling to maintain an air of cool disapproval and self-righteousness.

"Miss Williams had taken the name of our Lord in vain. She was therefore punished."

"Of course." Mavis continued to stare at the Llanelli Star's sports page, mindlessly reading about Furnace United's spectacular win over Kidwelly the previous week.

"She may be an excellent organist but her Christian values are rather suspect. I have had to chastise her about her lax attitudes on more than one occasion."

I bet you have, thought Mavis, still not looking up.

Ernest put his Bible on the table, and proceeded to search through it. Just as he opened his mouth to quote from one of the Gospels, Mavis rose to her feet abruptly

"I don't wish to be rude but I really don't want to hear you spouting forth from the scriptures. Not after seeing what I just witnessed in the vestry. I don't wish to discuss this any further." Her icy cold voice took Ernest by surprise, and he watched incredulously as she walked out of the kitchen, her head in the air. Puzzled at her lack of reaction, Ernest returned to his Bible, relieved that he appeared to have got away with things fairly lightly. However, he must remember to be more careful in future. Then his thoughts turned to events earlier, when his hand had landed heavily on Gladys' quivering bottom, and he remembered her squirming body on his lap; he felt the heat rising in his Christian soul as he also recollected the way she had not objected when his fingers accidentally brushed past her tightly-clad breasts as he reached over to pull her over his knee. What a pity she had been wearing trousers. If she had been wearing a skirt, he would also have had the satisfying pleasure of lifting it up, revealing whatever wicked underwear she had on underneath, and allowing him to view her plump buttocks, her plump, pink buttocks.... Maybe next time....

He pushed these sinful thoughts away to the back of his mind, resolving to concentrate his energies on mending the garden fence where Dai had been digging last week, in an attempt to get at some rabbits in the adjoining field.

Meanwhile, Mavis decided to spring-clean upstairs. Monotonous tasks enabled her to free her thoughts and put them in some sort of order as well. She looked through the bedroom window, watching Ernest hammering away at the fence, his face bright red with exertion. Just as she was about to start applying Windolene to the glass, there was a clatter in the front porch. Assuming it was the second post, although rather late, Mavis hurried downstairs, and picked up what appeared to be a birthday card from the doormat. Puzzled, she turned it over to examine the envelope. Ernest's birthday was another fortnight away. However, it was addressed to herself. Hurriedly, she opened it. Then, smiling with pleasure, she read the contents. It was an invitation to attend a ballet exhibition at Wendy's dancing school the following Saturday at ten o'clock. The little girl must be showing some promise already if she was to be included in the performance. Then Mavis frowned. Maybe Ernest would not be available to take her down to Llanelli. He had mentioned a possible wedding. All good intentions and thoughts of cleaning temporarily forgotten, Mavis went out into the garden, squinting in the bright daylight, the cloud cover finally breaking slightly. "Ernest! We have an invitation! It's Wendy!" Ernest glanced up from his fence mending, a frown on his face.

"What do you mean? It's not her birthday?"

"It's from her dancing school. An exhibition. Will you be able to take me down? Will you come as well?"

"That depends. When is it?" "This coming Saturday."

"Very well. The wedding is the following week. But don't expect me to stay and watch a crowd of little girls prancing around to some old lady playing the piano. I have better things to do, and your money would be put to better use, Mavis, such as sending young Wendy to Brownies, or something more practical. Far too frivolous, if you ask me!"

"I'm not." She retorted, shortly. "As long as you can drive me down to the studio in Llanelli by ten to ten at the latest, that will be fine. I can't imagine it will go on for terribly long. There will only be a certain number of dances that six year olds can do, I am sure. You can call on Mr Baker while you wait. I very much doubt if he will be going to watch." With that Ernest could not argue any further, and so returned to his work.

"I will call by Mr O'Brien's house and ask him if I can use his telephone. It looks like it might rain and it's a good ten minute walk to the kiosk in the village. I want to let the Bakers know I will be attending." And without waiting for a reply, she turned smartly and headed out of the garden, into Bethel Lane.

Mavis' full, white skirt swirled around her knees as she marched briskly down the lane towards Seamus' house, her dainty kitten heels clip-clopping quietly on the road as she hurried along. To her surprise Seamus was holding the door open for her as she drew near. "How did you know I was coming?" She smiled up at him in puzzlement. He grinned down at her, his trousers held up with string as usual, no shoes on his large feet.

"I watch your cottage for hours, just hoping for a glimpse of you. And here you are. My wish has come true. Step inside, sweet Mavis. To what do I owe the honour of your visit?"

"May I use your telephone? I have to ring my in-laws."

"But of course! Be my guest!" Mavis wasted no time, and within a few minutes she had rung the Bakers and confirmed she would be going to the ballet exhibition. Seamus wasted no time either, and as soon as Mavis was back in the hall, he scooped her up in his arms and carried her, protesting weakly, into the kitchen. "No-one can see us in here," he mumbled, covering her face with kisses, and releasing her briefly to shut the red gingham curtains at the window.

"What are you doing?!" Mavis giggled nervously.

"Taking advantage of a vulnerable female, that's what I'm doing. Exploiting the moment, for moments together are like pearls, beautiful and rare!"

"But Ernest thinks I am just making a phone call! He will wonder where I am!"

"Tell him the line was engaged, tell him you couldn't get through, tell him whatever you like, but yield to me, Mavis, let me have my wicked way with you!" He lay her down against the old kitchen table, her legs dangling over the edge. She could resist no longer, allowing Seamus' hands to find their insistent way up her legs until they reached her stocking tops. "Such delectable knickers, Mrs Watton! Did you anticipate an encounter with your secret lover this fine morning?"

"I always come prepared!" She gasped as his long fingers slid inside the frilly elastic.

"Good! Well, prepare to come!" And with that he removed the silky, white knickers and, dropping them casually on the floor, buried his face in between her legs, probing with his expert tongue, driving her wild with ecstasy and making her writhe with delight on the table.

"Not yet, my pretty one, not yet! Wait for me, here I come!" And with that he pulled at the string which held up his trousers and plunged himself into her dark wetness, availing himself of her pliant, willing body until they were both satisfied.

"That was a bit unexpected!" Mavis brushed her hair out of her eyes and searched desperately for her underwear, laughing to see that they had landed on top of a newspaper, totally and disrespectfully obliterating a photo of the Queen.

"Should you wish to avail yourself of my bathroom, which is your custom after our rumpy-pumpy, feel free to do so!" He laughed at her pretence of annoyance at his base remark, and watched her scampering away to the cloakroom. On her return, he blocked her entrance to the kitchen, taking her flushed face in his hands. "My sweet little woman. My gorgeous Mavis, made for me by a whole choir of angels!"

"Oh, such flowery compliments will get you anywhere you want, Mr O'Brien!" She dodged under his outstretched arm, and gathered up her knickers, pulling them on hurriedly.

"Really?" His hands stole up inside her skirt once more, causing her to sidestep him neatly, to head for the door. "I really must go!"

"Wait! Did I hear you say on the phone that you are going down to Llanelli next Saturday?"

"Yes. Young Wendy has a ballet exhibition. I want to go down and watch it. Ernest doesn't want to come, really....so I may have to catch the bus, and maybe get Eiddwen to come with me."

"Don't ask Eiddwen! Keep your powder dry, Mavis! Tell Ernest you will catch the bus, then I will pick you up like I did before, and whisk you down to town on my trusty steed!"

"But you won't be able to watch the display!" Mavis imagined the shocked expressions of the other mothers, and Wendy's mother as well, if she rolled up on a motorbike with the rather wild and bizarre Seamus in tow!

"Of course not! Jesus, you can be rather obtuse at times! I will drop you off within walking distance of wherever it takes place, then pick you up at a specified time. Then we can go for a jaunt!" Mavis' face lit up with pleasure.

"What a brilliant plan! Very well! I will drop a note through your letterbox on Friday, just to firm up the arrangements!" She opened the door. He grinned again.

"Oh, I am sure you will firm things up very nicely indeed, Mrs Watton!" He patted her on her bottom, laughing softly as she hurried down the garden path, heading for her cottage.

Mavis lay awake in her bed that night; Ernest, stiff as a ramrod, lay on his back, his eyes shut, his face the picture of devout and stern godliness. She lay nearest the window, and could see the clear skyscape as it turned and circled through the summer night. Venus rose late and twinkled seductively through the glass, followed by a three-quarter moon, which gazed back at her, wise and ageless.

By Friday, Mavis' longing for Seamus was becoming intolerable, so in order to distract herself, she decided to call on Eiddwen. She hadn't wanted to linger very long to chat with her after Sunday morning's service, having no wish to suffer the smirks which spread like oily margarine across Gladys' pallid face. A heatwave had started the previous day, and no breath of wind disturbed the warmth of the summer morning. Clad in a yellow slip of a dress, her slim arms brown and bare, Mavis walked briskly, passing Seamus' house, waving at him discreetly as she did, a secretive and knowing smile upon her lips. She would drop a note in later.

The hot sun beat down. The radio weather forecaster had said the temperature would reach eighty degrees by the weekend, and that the heatwave looked set to last until the first week of July. Mavis loved hot weather, she basked in the heat of the sun, hardly breaking into a sweat while other women mopped their foreheads and showed great damp patches under the arms of their blouses. Eira Jones' ancient ginger tom stretched himself out languidly on top of the family's equally ancient Morris Minor, his striped tail swishing to and fro occasionally. A skylark trilled sweetly high up in the pale blue sky, joined by a couple of blackbirds practising their duet in the nearby trees; apart from that, nothing broke the peace apart from the odd car driving along the main road.

Eiddwen's north-facing house was a cool oasis, and for once Mavis was appreciative of its rather chilly depths. She let herself in at the front door, which was wide open, the gaily-coloured plastic strips fluttering gently in the doorway, allowing any possible breeze to enter and discouraging wasps or flies. As usual Eiddwen was in her gegin fach, but not peeling root vegetables today. Cawl would be far too hot in such humid conditions.

"Ooh! What are you making, Eiddwen?" Mavis smiled at her friend, a huge pile of runner beans in front of her on the draining board. Eiddwen sighed and wiped her sweating face with a small facecloth.

"Just top and tailing these beans. It's takes forever. But they are dreadfully stringy if you don't. I am going to give everyone cold ham, new potatoes and beans for lunch."

"Well, that sounds nice." Mavis settled herself in her usual armchair, privately thinking that life was much too short to top and tail runner beans. "Any news?"

Eiddwen dropped her knife and blushed, saying nothing. Mavis looked up sharply. Silence was unusual for Eiddwen.

"Come on! Spill the beans!" Mavis laughed at her own joke. Eiddwen wiped her hands on her apron then sat down opposite Mavis.

"Promise you won't tell anyone?" she whispered nervously, leaning forwards, clasping her hands together.

"Of course I won't!" (Well, maybe she would tell Seamus, but he didn't count.)

"You remember Professor Drummond?"

"Of course! He didn't take his eyes off you in Seamus' party! What about him?" Mavis' eyes sparkled with mischief, as she guessed what was coming.

"Well, he has been writing to me. And I have been writing to him. In fact, Mavis, we have become regular correspondents!" Eiddwen looked up at her friend, anxious for her approval. She needn't have worried. Mavis was beaming with delight.

"Go on! Tell me more!" Mavis hugged her knees in excitement, curled up in a little ball in the old armchair.

"Well, he wrote to me not long after the party. He said he was a university professor in Edinburgh. He has never been married, and hasn't got any children – not that he is aware of, he said!" Eiddwen giggled coyly. "He told me that I have a body such as one would find in a Rubenesque painting, and that I am desirable beyond all thought and imagination!" Eiddwen had clearly memorised the professor's words and they were imprinted on her heart.

"So when will you see him again?" Mavis smiled encouragingly at Eiddwen.

"Oh, Mavis! In his last letter he wrote that he will be visiting Seamus in a couple of weeks, and that he is looking forward to meeting with me again! What shall I wear? Where will we meet? Oh, dear. It's all so exciting and – and you won't tell anyone, will you? I couldn't bear the gossip!" Eiddwen paused for breath. Mavis got up and hugged her friend.

"Oh, Eiddwen, yes, it is very exciting and I am so pleased that you are finally having something different, some romance in your life!"

"Oh no! It's nothing like that! It's just a friendship and letter writing!" Eiddwen blushed an even deeper shade of red.

"Of course it is." Mavis grinned conspiratorially. "Anyway, there are plenty of walks around here, you can take him to Kidwelly Castle, and there's always Parc Hardd?"

"Yes." Eiddwen sighed with happiness, and gazed through the window towards next-door's brick wall, visualising herself arm in arm with the professor, strolling through the rose gardens of Parc Howard, and of course wearing her blue suit. The two women were quiet for a few moments, then, as was her wont, Eiddwen broke the peace, unable to stop chattering for long. "So, are you doing anything nice this weekend? Does Ernest have a wedding?"

"I'm going to - " and then Mavis halted abruptly, just stopping herself in time. Keep your powder dry, girl, she told herself sternly. "Er, I'm going to do a bit of sorting out and stuff. Lots of things to keep me busy. And what about you?"

Eiddwen rose to her feet and resumed her topping and tailing. "Actually, I am going to have my hair permed at Barbara's. It will give it time to soften before the professor comes down."

"Right. That's it." Mavis also stood up and faced her friend squarely. "No more frizz from Barbara's, Eiddwen. You must go into Llanelli and try somewhere like Rikki Karas or something. Have a proper hairstyle, for goodness' sake!"

"Do you really think so?" Eiddwen patted her mousey brown curls anxiously.

"But you will need to book. Go to the phone box later on and ring for an appointment. You won't get in there tomorrow, they will be full. But maybe next week?" Mavis didn't want Eiddwen heading for Llanelli tomorrow.

"Alright, but will you ring them for me? I don't like talking on the phone."

" Very well! Once you have finished your beans we will go and phone." Eiddwen secretly noticed that Mavis made no offer to help her with her task, but merely settled down with last week's copy of Woman's Own. But she was fortunate to have such a smart woman for a friend, wasn't she?

Saturday morning dawned as hot as the day before. Ernest had not questioned Mavis' going in to town on the bus, indeed he seemed quite relieved that he did not have to go as well. Maybe he had to attend the chapel for more meetings with Gladys, she thought wryly. She got up early, too excited to stay in bed any longer. The sun was already beating down strongly and the birds, making the most of the relative coolness of the morning, sang joyfully in the garden. Ernest showed no sign of stirring, but it was only seven o'clock. Mavis went into the spare room to dress, wondering what on earth she should wear to a dance exhibition, bearing in mind that the journey into Llanelli would be on the back of a motorbike. She supposed that it would be acceptable to wear her white pedal-pushers, and a smart black shirt. Her choice made, she went downstairs, still in her nightdress, in case Dai jumped up on her or she spilled tea on her clean clothes. The kitchen, usually quite dark and cool, was still warm from the heat of the previous day. Mavis swiftly opened all the windows, fed Dai and let him out, then settled down for a quick breakfast before tiptoeing back upstairs to get ready. She regarded the contents of her make-up box with intense concentration. All her favourite brands lay waiting . Yardley, Max Factor, Rimmel.... today she must appear absolutely respectable, yet she was unable to resist the wish to appear desirable for Seamus. Quietly, she began her artistry, applying the cosmetics with subtle and clever skill, enhancing her huge brown eyes and subtly exploiting the sensual curve of her mouth. She heard Ernest get up and go downstairs. She paused. He never liked her to wear make-up, but half the time he didn't realise she was wearing any, so clever was she in its use. He merely thought it yet another weapon of the devil. Mavis sighed, and closed her powder compact. It was becoming increasingly apparent to her that her husband had incredible double standards.

By a quarter past nine, Mavis was nervously waiting near the lower bus stop on the main road. Pulling out a pair of tortoise shell sunglasses from her handbag, she put them on, imagining how mysterious and glamorous they made her look. She glanced down towards the sea, which sparkled in the distance, the Gower peninsula appearing further away than usual in the haze of the morning's heat. She noticed a shimmering above the road, the temperature already soaring. Mavis was glad she had abandoned her new-found favourite, the intense Shalimar perfume, and had instead opted for the lighter Miss Dior, which complemented both the sultry weather and her mood. The perfume of boldness, renewal and freedom. She smiled to herself, and sniffed at the inside of her wrist, closing her eyes. Her reverie was loudly interrupted by the roar of the motorbike, as Seamus swung into the lane where Mavis would get on the bike.

"Good morning, fair maid! Now I realise that you may indeed require those sunglasses whilst we hurtle down towards Llanelli, but as soon as we arrive, they have to be removed! Your eyes are your most beautiful feature, so do not, on any account, hide them from me! And I am an artist, I know about these things!"

"Very well, oh bossy one!" She grinned cheekily back at him. Within a few minutes they were racing down the main road, the sun in their faces. Fortunately, no-one was about in the village, apart from old Beryl Stephens walking her corgi; she was deaf and slightly mad, so no-one believed anything she said anyway.

Llanelli was a hive of activity that morning. The heatwave had brought out the shoppers in their scores. Families dawdled along the pavements of Stepney Street, small children devouring ice-creams out of cornets, their older siblings more sedately eating them out of little tubs, with wooden spoons. Teenagers thronged outside the cafes, tennis racquets in their hands, excitedly planning their matches in People's Park. A holiday atmosphere hung over the whole town. Following Mavis' directions, Seamus dropped her off in Prospect Place, a street close to the town centre so she wouldn't have far to walk to the dance studio in Market Street.

"When shall I pick you up?" He smiled as she obediently removed her sunglasses.

"Well, the exhibition starts at ten, so let's say we meet here at 11.30? That should be plenty of time. Where will you go in the meantime?"

"I have every intention of visiting that wonderful park we just passed. Parc Hardd, you said?"

"Excellent. Be sure to go into the mansion house, they have art exhibitions there quite often."

"Well, we will both be extremely well-exhibited by the time we meet again!" He laughed. "See you later, alligator!" And off he went, sounding his horn as he did. Mavis waved goodbye and made her way down Thomas Street, passing Buckley's Brewery on her way. No smell of hops today, thank goodness, she thought. By ten to ten she was outside Miss Daphne's dance studio, along with dozens of parents and family members, all eagerly anticipating their offsprings' chance to be the next Margot Fonteyn. The entrance was dark and gloomy, and they all had to troop up many flights of stairs before reaching the dance studio itself. The room had been prepared for the visitors, and several wooden beams were arranged at one end of the room. Mavis presented the portly woman at the door with her invitation, and searched for her daughter-in-law and Gwyneth Baker. Thankfully, they were also looking out for her, spotting her quickly. Mavis settled herself down next to them. People spoke in hushed whispers, as though they were in church. She turned to look at Margaret, her daughter-in-law. Beautiful and fragile, her pale blond hair tied back in a ponytail, Margaret sat quietly between Mavis and Gwyneth, her anxious eyes scanning the waiting pupils at the far end of the room for her daughter, Wendy. At ten o'clock on the dot, there was a ripple of excitement, and a tiny, dark woman strode authoritatively into the room. Miss Daphne, thought Mavis. Of uncertain age, what Miss Daphne lacked in stature, she surely made up for in sheer magnetism. She walked with incredible grace, her posture impeccable. Her black hair was piled up in a bun on top of her head, and she wore a black leotard with fishnet tights, a transparent black skirt wrapped around her non-existent hips. The deathly pallor of her skin was relieved by a brilliant scarlet mouth. Another fan of Max Factor, thought Mavis in amusement. The scarlet mouth then opened, and Miss Daphne began to speak.

"Welcome. The pupils of this School of Dance are eager to present you, their families, a small showcase of their skills so far. They have been taught in accordance with the Royal Academy of Dance syllabus. This morning, we will start with a short presentation by our pre-primary class, so that they may return to sit with their parents while the older pupils perform." She paused to smile briefly at all the four and five year old girls who were fidgeting and nudging each other in the front row, all dressed the same in pink leotards and tulle skirts. The plump woman had now taken her place at the old upright piano in the corner of the room. She started to play Tchaikovsky's Sleeping Beauty, gently and slowly, but it was all Mavis could do not to laugh as the infant dancers took to the floor, making hilarious mistakes and forgetting their steps, pushing each other out of the way in an attempt to see their parents, and picking their noses. After a few minutes, the small fry ended with deep curtseys, with the smallest one on the end of the line falling over altogether, causing a wave of suppressed laughter amongst the audience. Miss Daphne clapped her hands and all the little girls scampered towards their parents, to be hugged and praised.

"Our primary class will now take to the floor. You will be able to see for yourselves how these six year olds have improved and are beginning to grasp the concept of ballet." The row of blue–clad girls stood up and walked primly onto the floor. Mavis, Margaret and Gwyneth strained to see Wendy. Surely she should be in this group? She was six years old. Margaret looked anxiously at Mavis. But Wendy was not amongst the group. Mavis squeezed Margaret's hand, for once feeling empathy with the younger woman. Then they saw Wendy, also dressed in a blue leotard and tulle skirt, but with a navy blue band about her waist. She was sitting with another girl, similarly clad, and they were apart from all the other girls. Wendy was grinning from ear to ear. Margaret and Mavis sighed in unison, their worries gone.

After ten minutes of the six year olds performing plies and simple leaps to The Sugar Plum Fairy, they returned to the bench, being deemed old enough to contain themselves until the end of the demonstration. Miss Daphne got up once more, holding up her hand for silence, as the proud parents seemed to go on clapping forever.

"May I now present two of my grade 1 class. Wendy Watton and Helen Howells. Both attend the primary class, but as both pupils have shown a great deal of promise and complete dedication, they have been allowed to attend extra classes with Grade 1 pupils. Wendy in particular has only been with us a short time, but has exceeded all expectations. They will now perform a short duet, a little pas de deux, and I am sure you will enjoy it."

Margaret, Gwyneth and Mavis looked at each other in silent delight. Wendy must have been sworn to secrecy by Miss Daphne, as none of them knew anything about this. The two little girls came forward shyly, taking their places in the centre of the floor. The pianist started to play Beethoven's Moonlight Sonata. Mavis, Margaret and Gwyneth were almost too afraid to breathe as they watched Wendy start her simple dance. They need not have had any concerns. The child was born to dance, that was patently obvious. Her steps were accurate and well-executed, her posture was perfect, and judging by the ecstatic smile on her face, she was having the time of her life. The dark-haired Helen danced beautifully as well, but the three women only had eyes for Wendy. When the dance was over, Mavis clapped so hard that her hands stung, and tears filled her eyes. What a good idea it had been to arrange for Wendy to be given ballet lessons.

By eleven o'clock, the display was over, and the students disappeared to change their clothes. Margaret went along with Wendy to help her. Mavis turned to Gwyneth, her eyes shining. "She was marvellous, wasn't she, Mrs Baker?"

"I couldn't agree more, Mrs Watton. The child has talent, it must be said. Would you like to join us for a cup of tea in the market? We promised Wendy we would. She wanted faggots and peas as well, but it's a bit early for that. But she did so well, we will buy fish and chips from Chiefo's on the way home."

"Oh, thank you so much, Mrs Baker, but I have to do some shopping before I catch the bus home."

"Well, my husband will be only too happy to give you a lift to Llannon if you change your mind."

"That's terribly kind, but I have bought a return ticket. Such a shame to waste it!" Mavis squirmed inside at the speed with which all these lies came tumbling out. "Ah! Here's Wendy!" She reached out and hugged the little girl.

"Well done, Wendy! What a joy it was to watch you dance! You make sure you keep it up, and practise hard!"

"Thank you, Aunty Mavis." Wendy's tight bun was gradually escaping from its net, and the child was clearly quite tired after all the excitement. Mavis stood up, smiling at her.

"I must go, it's almost a quarter past eleven, and I don't want to miss my bus! Thank you for letting me come and see the show. And let me know when the next one is!" They said their goodbyes, then Mavis ran lightly down the stairs to the ground floor, and as she left the tall, dark building, the heat hit her like a blast from a furnace. Faggots and peas on a boiling hot day such as this? Unthinkable! Nice if it was the middle of winter, but on a scorcher like today...?

Turning right into Market Street, she passed the Cambrian Hotel, Badger's the tobacconist and West Wales Furnishers, before climbing the hill back to Prospect Place. Seamus was there, waiting for her, watching her approach in his wing mirror, revving his engine gently, ready to leave with Mavis riding pillion. She climbed aboard, putting on her sunglasses once more. As well as shielding her eyes from the glare of the sun, they also provided her with a degree of anonymity should anyone from Llannon be visiting Llanelli.

"Where shall we go today?" He bellowed out at her, turning into Thomas Street. Mavis thought rapidly. She fancied going to the beach, down at the North Dock, but that would mean driving down the main road, dangerously close to where the Bakers lived. Then she realised that they would be safely ensconced in the cafe for at least half an hour.

"We're going to the beach!" She shouted back, happily. "Follow the road down, then bear to the right, we can be there in five minutes!" The couple passed the synagogue on the corner, which that evening would be full of local Jewish people, attending their Sabbath service. Mavis could not help but be fascinated by the Jewish community in Llanelli. They all seemed such charismatic people, so hard-working and dedicated to their various businesses, whether jewellers, haberdashery, or ladies' fashions. Gwyneth Baker always swore that they would never fail to help if someone was in trouble, and she frequently mentioned the fact that Ronnie Cass, the jeweller, had even gone on to become a renowned pianist and playwright.

Llanelli beach could not be described as a tourist attraction, by any stretch of the imagination. In order to get to the beach, the pair had to drive over an iron bridge, which spanned the inlet feeding the North Dock itself. Several boats lay dormant on the muddy banks of the dock, some rusting and beyond repair. The smell of seaweed and petrol fumes filled the air, as they left the old dock behind and reached the beach itself. Llanelli beach was certainly not grand enough to merit a car park, so Seamus propped his bike against an old wooden post which they found at the bottom of one of the many sand dunes which lay along the beach.

"Oh, for feck's sake! Not more bloody dunes!" Seamus complained, shaking his head in disbelief.

"Oh, don't be such a wimp! These are half the size of the ones at Llangennith! Come on!" She kicked off her kitten heels, grabbed him by the hand and started to drag him up the hot, white sand. Indeed, these dunes were mere molehills compared to the giants over the Gower, and a few minutes later they were at the top, looking out to sea; the tide was out. The beach was busy, lots of families had pitched down on the harder sand further out, with brightly-coloured deckchairs and windbreaks decorating the coastline. Even further out, they could see men bending over, with wheelbarrows and sacks alongside them.

"What are they doing?" Seamus shielded his eyes with his hands, trying to get a better view. "Cockling. Picking cockles. Then they take them home and cook them, and sell them to the market. Have you ever tried them?" Mavis grinned wickedly up at him.

"God forbid, yes! They used to sell them back home in Ireland, disgusting little fellas they were! All rubbery and full of sand!" He made a sour face.

"Well, I won't take you out to lunch in Llanelli Market, then!" Mavis laughed.

"What's that out there, on the horizon?" Seamus gazed out to sea.

"You mean Whiteford lighthouse? You can walk to it when the tide is out, but you can't stay there very long, because you'd get cut off. The currents around here are treacherous. But I have always wanted to go there. Let's sit down for a bit, shall we?" The sand was soft and warm, making a comfortable resting place for the couple. Mavis sighed contentedly.

"This beach is scruffy, untidy and it borders on being downright dangerous.... but I love it. I look out at the lighthouse and yearn to reach it, but I will never realise that dream." She paused and scanned the beach, her eyes crinkled up against the strong sunshine. "And when the tide is out as it is today - the world stretches to infinity, miles of amber land, curly worm-tracks in the sand, razor shells to slice your feet, and the sweet sound of gulls floating on the breeze..." She fell silent. Seamus glanced down at her in surprise.

"I didn't know you wrote poetry?"

"I wouldn't describe it as such. I just think of things, impressions, atmospheres.....and I write them down. I hide them in a little box under the spare room bed. One day I may do something with them, who knows?"

"Who knows indeed?" They fell silent for a while, enjoying the sounds of summer, the shrieking seagulls and children, the laughter of youths playing cricket on the hard sand. Mavis broke the silence. "I have got news for you!"

"Pray tell, fair maid!" Seamus grinned at her, playfully.

"Your Professor Drummond and Eiddwen have been writing to each other! It's been going on since your party! And he has told her he will be returning to Llannon quite soon, and they will be able to meet up! Isn't that exciting!"

"Riveting!" Seamus laughed. "Yes, I know all about this blossoming romance. In fact I invited old Archie Drummond to stay for a couple of days, on his way to Aberystwyth University for a seminar."

"Really?" Mavis' eyes were wide with surprise. "So will he meet up with Eiddwen, d'you reckon? And what is he a professor of, exactly?"

"One question at a time, Mrs Watton! He is a professor of theology at Edinburgh University. In actual fact, he specialises in Hebrew Bible and ancient religion." In view of this, I shall be organising a little dinner party when he comes down, and shall of course orchestrate things so that Eiddwen will be invited." Mavis looked down at her red-painted toes, looking crestfallen.

Seamus laughed. "Don't worry! My other guests will also include a certain Mrs Watton and her devout husband! I am sure the professor and your husband will have a great deal to talk about! Should be quite interesting!" He grinned.

"Gladys Williams won't be there, will she?" She looked up at him, anxiously.

"Of course not. Why on earth should she be invited?" Mavis then proceeded to tell him all about the event in the chapel vestry. Seamus chewed thoughtfully on a piece of sea grass. "She's a dangerous one, that Gladys. For all our sakes, the less we have to do with her, the better. And it would seem that your saintly husband is not so virtuous after all."

Mavis laughed mirthlessly. "He said he was just chastising her."

"Chastising her, my arse! Hell will freeze over before I believe that fabrication." Seamus rolled his eyes incredulously." He drew closer to Mavis, putting his arm around her. "But enough talk about undesirable individuals like Gladys Williams. I much prefer to talk about desirable people, I quite like to touch them too, especially in naughty little places…!" Mavis snuggled up to him. They were quite isolated in this part of the beach, and she felt confident that no-one could see them. He put his hand on her knee, and started to kiss her gently. As usual, she melted and yielded to his insistent kisses, returning them with equal passion. Seamus' hand stole smoothly up her thigh, until it reached the buttons of her white trousers. In no time at all, he had undone them, and pushed his fingers inside her lacy knickers. "Christ, these jeans are fecking tight!" he complained quietly. "They must give you quite a thrill when I go over any potholes in the road!" Mavis was too aroused to object to his rather coarse joke, contenting herself with caressing his lower body with equal determination. Seamus licked his fingers, then allowed the lubricated tips to find their goal, working their magic on Mavis' swollen rosebud. Then, reaching even further, his fingers entered her, seeking the softness of her innermost parts.

"Jesus, you're so wet! It's a shame this is so public, or I would ravish you right here. But I can take you to heaven anyway……" He continued his circular movements, kissing her all the while, until she shuddered with sheer delight. Mavis flopped back on the sand, sighing with satisfaction. "That was wonderful," she gasped. "But you are a very naughty man!"

"I know I am." He grinned down at her. "By the way! I went to your Parc Hardd. The art gallery was closed! So I went and had an ice cream in the little cafe instead. I sat there for a while, then wandered around the rose gardens. Before I knew it, it was time to come back and meet you!"

"I am glad you enjoyed yourself," she smiled, buttoning up her pedal pushers, and wriggling into a sitting position on the sand.

"I am glad you did!" He kissed her cheek, running his hand through her tangled hair.

"I suppose I had better be getting home." Mavis sighed, looking at her wristwatch to check the time. "It's almost half-past twelve." Then she gasped in dismay."Oh, no! Dear Lord God! My wedding ring! I've lost it!" Mavis felt a wave of panic rush over her, her heart started beating madly. How on earth could it have happened? What would Ernest say? Where could she say she had lost it? All these illogical thoughts sped through her frightened mind like lightning. She moved quickly about the dune, wringing her hands, searching desperately for the lost ring.

"Calm down! We will find it! Stop panicking, that won't help." Seamus took her by the shoulders and held her tightly. "Take a deep breath and then we will look for it together. Come on." Meekly obeying him, Mavis managed to regain some composure and the two knelt down in the soft sand, sifting it between their fingers, hoping fervently that they would be successful."What will I tell Ernest?" Mavis could not keep the trembling out of her voice. Her mouth felt dry with anxiety and she wanted to burst into tears.

"You won't tell him anything. If we cannot find it, then when you get home, do some washing up or something that involves water, then you can relive that moment of realisation and repeat your words to your husband! Just don't let him spot it is missing until you announce it!"

"Yes, of course, that makes sense." Mavis continued her scrutiny of the sand. The minutes ticked by, and the small gold ring was still nowhere to be seen. "I suppose that's it,"Mavis said unhappily, "I suppose we had better go. No point in staying here any longer..." She turned to make her descent down the dune. Suddenly, Seamus grabbed her arm.

"Wait! There it is!" He was pointing at a clump of sea grass near their shoes. The sun had caught the gold ring, making it shine brightly. Mavis bent down to retrieve it. Still shaking, she put it on her finger. "Oh, thank you!" She flung her arms about him.

"Glad to have been of assistance! And it may be a good idea to have it made smaller!" Mavis nodded in agreement, and wasting no more time, the pair headed back to the motorbike, to return to Llannon, Seamus wondering if the loss of the ring had been in some way prophetic.

Anxious not to encounter her in-laws on the return trip, Mavis diverted Seamus around the side streets of Llanelli, driving down High Street, turning left into Paddock Street, then left again at Orsi's cafe, back into Station Road, before meandering along Robinson Street to meet the main road once more. "I have had such a lovely morning, Seamus!" cried Mavis, before the bike picked up speed on the hill leading out of Llanelli, rendering any conversation impossible.

"Likewise, dear heart!" He turned around briefly to smile at her. The bike sped along the country road, passing the junction at Sylen, then the white house in the valley where the plots for the Rebecca Riots had been hatched. All too soon, they began the ascent into Llannon. Seamus swung right into the lane to drop Mavis off.

"Well, I suppose this is where we say goodbye," she whispered softly. Seamus was just about to bend down to kiss her, when a voice made them both jump.

"Well, hello! Fancy seeing you here!" They swung around, and were horrified to see Eiddwen standing there, a plastic container in her hand, smiling brightly at them.

"Um...whatever are you doing here?" countered Mavis, playing for time, trying to gather her wits.

"Ooh, I'm picking wild strawberries! There's a lot in this lane, maybe because it faces south and the sun has been so hot! Betsan Powell told me! So here I am!" She smiled gaily at them. Once again, Seamus saved the day. He moved closer to her, putting his arm around her shoulder, in a conspiratorial manner. Lowering his voice, he whispered in her ear.

"Well, Eiddwen, we have been on a mission! I arranged to meet Mavis in town, in order to select a frame for Ernest's birthday present. She took such a long time to choose one, that she missed the half-past twelve bus home, so I brought her home myself. Now, not a word, you understand? This is top secret! It would spoil the surprise, you see!" Eiddwen, in all her naivety, swallowed every word, delighted to be included in all this secrecy. Another moment of panic averted, Mavis relaxed. "Thank you once again, Mr O'Brien for the kind lift. It was very kind of you. And I had better be getting home. Goodbye. And enjoy your strawberry picking, Eiddwen!" Mavis smiled at them both, then turned back up the lane, allowing room for Seamus to ride past her, waving as he went.

"Mum's the word!" Eiddwen giggled happily behind her. Mavis sighed in despair, and continued her walk back up through Llannon, passing the Protestant church, and the public houses. Her legs were like lead, she seemed to have no strength left in them. So many shocks in one morning! It had totally drained her. She remembered Seamus' words of warning when their relationship was in its infancy. This is a dangerous game we are playing. But, she thought as she turned into Bethel Lane, a game without which she could not imagine her life. A game where only she and Seamus knew the rules, making them up as they went along on this tumultuous journey together.

As she walked past Seamus' house, she could see him putting a cover over his bike before storing it away safely . She smiled. He looked up and gave her the tiniest of waves, which she responded to by grinning like a Cheshire cat. Reaching her cottage, there was no sign of Ernest. She wondered where he was. Then, as she entered the kitchen, she could see no sign of Dai either. Ernest must have taken the dog for a walk. She wondered what he had had for lunch, but for once she didn't care. Not feeling hungry herself, she decided to go for a lie down. She felt completely washed out. As she lay down on her bed, she thought over the morning's events. It had been so enjoyable to see Wendy dancing, so satisfying to see the positive results of her own intervention in the child's life. Then her jaunt down to the beach with Seamus. She smiled sleepily. What a wonderful hour or so they had had together, but how quickly it had gone by. Then she remembered the crisis over the lost ring, and the close shave they had had meeting Eiddwen. Mavis decided she had had quite enough excitement for one day. Her last waking thought before she drifted off to sleep was that she had forgotten to buy any potatoes in Llanelli market....

Chapter Seventeen

Altering Roles

Just as Mavis was setting a bowl of salad on the kitchen table, in readiness for Tuesday's supper, and Ernest was carefully slicing a loaf of bread with meticulous precision, there was a knock at the front door.

"Who can that be?" Mavis wiped her hands on her apron and hurried to open the door. Ernest's sigh of irritation developed into a frown when he saw the identity of the visitor. "Am I interrupting your dinner?" Seamus breezed smilingly into the kitchen. "Terribly sorry!" He didn't appear sorry in the slightest.

"Oh ,not at all, Mr O'Brien!" Mavis nervously removed her apron. "Do sit down. Won't you join us? It's only ham salad, I'm afraid, it's rather too warm for anything cooked this evening!"

"No, many thanks but I won't intrude on your hospitality a moment longer than necessary!" He plonked himself down on a chair, appreciating the sight of Mavis' slight body, tightly clad in a scarlet cotton dress, her tiny waist looking so fragile above her gently curving hips

"Good evening, Mr O'Brien." Ernest looked up from his bread slicing.

"Tea?" Mavis brandished the big, brown teapot, hopefully. If Seamus had a cup of tea, she thought, he would stay that little bit longer.

"Very well!" Seamus grinned at her. "That would be splendid! It's so terribly hot, is it not? Splash of milk and no sugar, thanks!" Mavis smiled to herself. As if she didn't know how he liked his tea.

"You seem rather anxious to share some news with us, Mr O'Brien." Ernest glowered at him from over the tops of his spectacles. Seamus took a sip of his tea before answering, infuriating Ernest even more.

"You are correct, Mr Watton. In fact, I have come here this evening in order to invite you and Mrs Watton to dinner this Friday coming."

Ernest grunted in disapproval, and put down the bread knife. Well, at least I am no longer in danger of losing my life, thought Seamus, wryly.

"Another evening of wicked debauchery and licentiousness?" Ernest challenged Seamus with his habitual icy glare.

"Not at all!" Seamus laughed dismissively. "In actual fact, Mr Watton, this will just be an intimate affair, just yourselves and your dear friend Eiddwen. There will be another guest present, a Professor Drummond. You may have heard of him, Mr Watton, he is famous for his work on ancient religion and early Christianity." Seamus had swiftly gained the upper hand now, as Ernest, devout and well-read as he was in the field of the Bible, was not inclined to broaden his horizons, and had never heard of the professor, indeed knew nothing of other religions and beliefs, preferring to exclude them from his strict Baptist mind, considering them the works of the devil.

"I see." Ernest's mouth closed in a tight line. Mavis looked anxiously from one man to the other.

"It will be a welcome night off for Mrs Watton as well! No cooking!" Seamus beamed expansively at Ernest. "I have planned the menu with great care, it will be a feast fit for a king!"

"It does seem an attractive idea..." Mavis' voice trailed away, hoping that Ernest would accept the invitation.

"I was really hoping you would be able to come, Mr Watton. With your knowledge of the Bible, and your experience as a minister, you will be able to hold a stimulating and informed discussion with the professor." Seamus looked directly at Ernest. Check mate, he thought happily. Ernest may be a pious, God-fearing man, but like any other human being, he eventually succumbed to his own vanity. Ernest cleared his throat.

"Seeing as there is no Bible study this Friday evening, I see no reason why Mrs Watton and I should not accept your invitation." Mavis breathed in sharply. How wonderful!

"What time will you be expecting us, Mr O'Brien?" Mavis' eyes were shining with excitement. "And would you like me to bring anything? A pudding, perhaps?"

"Oh, to be sure, there's no need at all! Just bring the obvious!" He winked at Ernest, who stared back, nonplussed.

"The obvious?" Mavis was also confused.

"Vino! Wine! DRINK!" Seamus knew he was really stirring things up now, but he couldn't resist the reaction of outrage and indignation he knew Ernest would display.

"We don't drink, Mr O'Brien." Ernest's arctic tone would have frozen the rivers of hell itself. "We are Baptists."

"Oh, for sure, I am terribly sorry! Of course, I should have realised! Well, maybe a bottle of lemonade, then?" Seamus rose to his feet. "And if you could come along around seven o'clock?"

"We will be there on the dot!" Mavis moved to her husband's side. "You are very kind, Mr O'Brien! We will look forward to seeing you on Friday."

"Toodle pip! Seven o'clock on the dot, then!" Seamus reached forward and took Ernest's hand, shaking it vigorously. And with that, he swirled around, leaving by the front door, shutting it slightly too loudly — for Ernest's liking. Mavis put out the plates on the table, ignoring his scowl.

"Would you like salad cream, cariad?"

On Wednesday afternoon Eiddwen stood in front of her wardrobe mirror in the tiny boxroom which served as her bedroom, the more spacious room having been appropriated years ago by her twin sisters. For the life of her she could not understand what the professor saw in her. Plain, homespun and rather plump, she did not exactly set men's hearts racing, neither did she ignite any passion whatsoever. She looked at her new hairstyle, a far more becoming coiffure than Barbara of Tumble could ever have achieved. She felt so grateful to Mavis for insisting she went into Llanelli to have it styled. The shining, brown bob softened her features, making her chin appear almost elfin-like as her hair skimmed her jaw-line. Used to dwelling in the shadow of Mavis' glamour for so long, Eiddwen failed to appreciate the warmth in her own kind, blue eyes, her sweet smile and the comfortable chubbiness which the professor found so appealing. She sighed, twisting around to check her rear view. Whichever way she turned, her bottom still looked quite substantial. Broad in the beam, she thought to herself miserably. Still, the professor had told her she was altogether delightful, and — that she should believe that. She tried on her blue suit, having already decided she would wear it on Friday evening. Heatwave or no heatwave, she was determined to give it another outing, mainly because it brought out the blue in her eyes.....or so the professor had said. He had arrived in Llannon this morning, in a taxi from Llanelli station, and had waved at her as she was walking back from the shop. She hugged herself in glorious anticipation. She would be in his company on Friday, and he had hinted in his last letter (which she had stored carefully with all the others in a cardboard box on top of the wardrobe) — that he would somehow manage to speak with her alone before Friday, and that maybe they could go on an outing! Eiddwen was too afraid to imagine anything beyond this, but how she longed to shake off the shackles of her life as a spinster and maybe make a new life for herself as a married woman.

Up at the cottage in Bethel Lane, Mavis was also regarding herself in her bedroom mirror. She had returned home from a morning shift at the shop to find the cottage empty, Ernest having taken Dai for a walk. Several dresses lay in a discarded heap on the bed, Mavis had tried them all on yet nothing satisfied her. Such tiredness overcame her, such as she had never experienced before. She yawned, sitting down on the pink satin eiderdown, supposing it was all the excitement over the forthcoming Friday night. Pull yourself together, woman, she told herself sternly, getting to her feet again with effort, and pulling yet more dresses out of the wardrobe.

The hot weather was continuing relentlessly, so there would be no need for a cardigan or a jacket of any sort. Suddenly, seized with inspiration, she selected a burnt orange dress from the depths of the ancient closet. Swiftly, she removed her skirt and blouse, and put it on. "Perfect!" She whispered to herself as she took in her reflection. Mavis hadn't worn it for years, having bought it by mail order to wear to one of the famous Richards parties - indeed she had forgotten about it completely. It was Grecian in design, made of the finest silk, sleeveless and with a deep V neck encrusted with sparkling green gems. On a more buxom woman it would have appeared rather revealing and improper, but on Mavis it appeared subtly provocative, her small golden breasts peeping coyly out of the plunging neckline. The dress flowed gracefully almost to her ankles, the fabric clinging to her slim body like a sheath. The colour, such a difficult one for most women to get away with, enhanced her tanned skin beautifully, rendering the whole effect stunningly exotic. A pair of gold leather sandals completed the look, their tiny heels hardly adding an inch to Mavis' stature. Reluctantly, she took off the dress, putting her work clothes back on and setting her mind towards the peeling of potatoes. As she started to go downstairs, she peeped out of the landing window, as was her habit of late, to catch a possible glimpse of Seamus. To her great surprise, there he was, walking down the lane with Professor Drummond, deep in conversation. Abandoning any thoughts of potato peeling, she ran down the stairs, tripping and almost falling down the bottom step. She hurried out of the cottage, not even bothering to shut the front door, so intent was she on catching them up.

"Mr O'Brien!" She called out breathlessly, hoping her hair was not too messy after all the clothes she had pulled on and off. Seamus swung round, a huge smile lighting up his face.

"Well, if it isn't the fair Mavis!" He laughed as she finally reached them, panting and flushed. "Professor Drummond, do you remember Mrs Watton from my party the other day?"

The professor peered down at Mavis from over his half-moon spectacles. He was dressed in the strangest of clothes, Mavis thought, taking in at his tweed plus-fours and his matching jacket, which seemed far too heavy for the hot weather.

"Och, aye! The little wee lassie with the big brown eyes and the mean-spirited husband!" Professor Drummond looked very pleased with himself, having remembered her so well.

"For feck's sake, Drummond! Don't be so insulting!" Seamus admonished his friend.

"I merely speak the truth!" Drummond disregarded Seamus' concern, continuing the conversation like a steam roller in full flow. "We are off to pay a visit to the delightful Eiddwen. Seamus was going to show me the house, for of course I have the address -" he winked at Mavis, conspiratorially, " but I was not certain of the way!"

"Why don't you join us, Mavis? It would seem far more proper and acceptable for you to provide some sort of chaperone service, don't you think?" Seamus seemed extremely pleased with himself for thinking of that.

"Alright! That seems a good idea," Mavis nodded. " Is Eiddwen expecting us?"

"Is she?" Seamus glanced at the professor, who looked vague.

"I don't know. I hadna thought of that."

Mavis sighed in exasperation. Why couldn't men be more organised?

"We should be okay, her sisters will be in Carmarthen shopping as it is a Wednesday and her brothers will be in work. Eiddwen should be cleaning the bedrooms today." The three made an incongruous trio as they walked down the lane, the lanky Seamus towering over the stocky professor, with the diminutive Mavis sandwiched between them. There was not much life in the sleepy village that afternoon, everyone seemed to be closeted away in their houses to stay out of the heat, or had disappeared to the seaside.

"Is it always so peaceful here?" asked the professor, enjoying the rural idyll immensely.

"To be sure! 'Tis the veritable epitome of pastoral tranquillity!" Seamus waved his arm expansively at the yellowing fields and the hazy hills on the horizon. Mavis rolled her eyes heavenwards. Maybe, she thought, they should try walking through the village earlier on a Wednesday morning, when all the farmers were taking their time in their lorries on their way to the mart in Carmarthen, and the women were queuing at the bus stop for the Llanelli bus to transport them down to the market. Bad temper would be the norm, especially when the schoolchildren added to the congestion, waiting for the school bus and generally making nuisances of themselves. They soon reached Eiddwen's house.

The men hung back, unsure what to make of the plastic strips fluttering in front of the door.

"Don't worry," said Mavis wryly, "it's only wasps and flies she wishes to discourage, not artists and professors!"

She rang the bell, then popped her head through the plastic strips and called out to Eiddwen, whose small feet could be heard hurrying down the hallway before she appeared at the doorway, her face a mixture of delight, horror and embarrassment.

"Oh my goodness!" she gasped, whisking off her pinafore as quickly as she could, self-consciously smoothing her new hairstyle into place. "Come in, come in!" The three trooped in behind her, blinking in the dim light of her gloomy house.

"You look different, Eiddwen," observed the professor, as they sat down on uncomfortable, unused chairs in the middle room, "I know! You have changed your hair!" He reached over to stroke it. Eiddwen turned bright red.

"It was Mavis' idea. I went into Llanelli to have it done."

"Well, it most certainly suits you, hen!" The professor settled back in his chair. The conversation ground to an uncomfortable halt, all four looking at each other or at the carpet, not sure who should speak next. Mavis was then seized with inspiration.

"I just remembered I left the kettle on the stove!" she gasped. "I must go!"

"Oh no!" Seamus followed her lead. "I had better come with you! The cottage could be in flames by now!" The two got up and made for the door.

"See you later, Drummond!" And with a cheeky grin, Seamus waved goodbye, following Mavis out into the sultry afternoon. The pair giggled as they strolled up the road.

"Well done, Mavis! That was quick thinking."

"I know!" Mavis sighed. "I do hope the professor will bring Eiddwen some happiness."

"He has arranged for a hired car on Friday, right at this very moment he will be asking her to go on an outing with him."

"Really?" Mavis smiled coyly up at him, as they passed Eira's cottage. "Ernest has to go into Llanelli on Friday by eleven o'clock, he has an appointment with a bereaved family who wish their grandmother to be interred in our graveyard at Bethel."

"Now how would that be to my advantage, sweet Mavis?" murmured Seamus softly, a wicked smile on his lips. Mavis said nothing, but continued looking straight ahead, an equally wicked smile playing around her mouth as well.

"May I therefore expect a visit on Friday morning? After the departure of certain individuals?"

"You may indeed." Mavis flashed her eyes at him, saucily. "In fact, you can count on it, Mr O'Brien! I shall look forward to my visit!" They reached Seamus' house, but did not pause to say goodbye, unwilling to draw unnecessary attention to themselves. Mavis returned to her cottage joyfully, with a spring in her step. So much to look forward to, such a promising weekend..

Friday morning dawned, the sky a relentless blue and the sun showing no sign of releasing its hold on South Wales. Both Eiddwen and Mavis woke up with a feeling of delicious excitement and anticipation, although for slightly different reasons. Mavis hurried through her chores, taking Dai for one of the briefest walks he had ever had and rattling through the washing up like an express train. Ernest left for Llanelli at half-past ten, leaving Mavis half an hour to prepare for her liaison with Seamus. It had been a number of weeks since she had worn her satin waspie, so she thought she would give it another outing. Despite the heat of the day, Seamus' house would be cool, and although the undergarment was tight and restricting, Mavis doubted it would be worn for very long, anyway. She put it on, admiring herself in the mirror. The hot sunshine had turned her skin an even deeper brown, and her breasts peeped out enticingly above the bodice. Mavis shifted the straps. It seemed slightly tight, and her bosom seemed to spill over the top a little more than usual. Ah well, she thought to herself, the heat was probably making anything tight feel rather uncomfortable. After fastening her stockings to the suspenders, she pulled a loose, cotton shift over her head. Mavis didn't possess a single item which did not flatter her, and this was no exception. Despite the unstructured cut of the dress, instead of swamping Mavis' tiny frame, it merely complemented her waif-like body, and the pale cream colour enhanced her Mediterranean glow. Satisfied with her appearance, she left the cottage by the kitchen door, glancing swiftly up and down the lane to check for passers-by. She paused. Eira Jones' husband was just pulling away in his car. Poor Denzil Jones, perpetually known in the village as Mr Eira Jones.

As soon as the car had turned left at the junction, Mavis continued her way towards Seamus' house, walking as quickly as she could, without actually breaking into a run. He had left the door ajar, so she pushed it open and let herself in.

"Boo!"

Mavis shrieked in fright, then laughed as Seamus appeared from behind the door, wearing absolutely nothing. He slammed the door shut behind her, allowing no attempt at conversation, and covering her face with kisses before picking her up in his arms and carrying her upstairs. The cream shift had been on her body less than twenty minutes before Seamus relieved Mavis of it, and he gazed at her in lustful appreciation as he put her gently down on the bed.

"I want to paint you all over again, I want to capture that slightly wanton look in your eyes, that slumbering desire within your soul and your fecking gorgeous body! But, sweet Mavis, my Cupid's arrow wants you far, far more!" Mavis gasped as she looked at his swollen member, standing proud and erect before her.

"Such a monstrous weapon of seduction, Mr O'Brien," she giggled, "is it heading my way?"

"If you are a good girl and do everything I say." He swiftly lay down next to her. "Open." Obediently, she parted her legs. He put out his hand and started to stroke her satin-clad mound of Venus until she writhed with sheer pleasure. As he caressed her, he watched her intently, moving his eyes from her face to her satin panties and back again.

"Undress for me." Mavis looked at him in surprise. He had never asked her to do that before. "Strip. Go on. Obey me, Mavis." He leaned over and flipped the switch of the record player he had hidden under the bed. From the depths of the purple blanket which was dangling on the floorboards, came the sad yet sexy voice of Ben E King...asking her to stand by him. Mavis rose to her feet, and did something she had never done before. She danced, she swayed, to such sensual and throbbing music as she had never heard before. Mavis had never danced like this in her life, let alone wearing only frivolous underwear and in front of a man. Yet she let the music move her, yielding to the rhythm, allowing her body to follow its instincts, submitting to innate forces which had been dormant all her life. She caressed her own body as she danced, stroking her arms, her breasts, which were still held captive in the satin waspie. Slowly, she reached around and swiftly undid the hooks which held it together. Turning her back to him, she let the pretty garment fall to the floor, flirtatiously looking back at Seamus over her shoulder. Clad only in her panties and stockings, she gradually rotated herself until she was once more facing him, but holding her hands over her breasts, concealing their delights from him until she was ready to display herself fully.

"You fecking tease," Seamus murmured softly, "you must have graduated from Holland's Leaguer itself! Come here at once!" And with that he leapt to his feet, grabbing hold of her undulating body. Within a few seconds he had removed her panties, and had pinioned her upon the bed, straddling her hips, looking down at her with such ferocious desire it took her breath away.

"Make love to me, Seamus," she begged, filled with lust and longing.

"Ah-ah...not yet, my darling woman!" He reached down once more underneath the bed, and produced a bottle of baby oil. "Now no more talking.

Just lie back and enjoy what Mr O'Brien is going to do to you." So Mavis did as she was told, and lay back on the crumpled bedcover, still only in her stockings and suspenders. Within seconds he had undone the top of the bottle, sprinkling some of the oil onto his hands, rubbing them together to warm it up. Sighing deeply, he started to massage her body, working his magic from her shoulders and chest, deliberately avoiding her heaving breasts , gently caressing her abdomen, descending towards her hips and legs, diverting his journey around her forbidden triangle, using his thumbs to press deeply into the softness of her inner thighs, but not touching her most sensitive, receptive areas. Mavis felt as though she was at screaming point, and unable to contain herself any longer. Why didn't he touch her where she wanted him to? As if he had heard her thoughts, his hand roamed up her body and started to caress her breasts. She winced slightly.

"What's wrong?" He stopped his stroking abruptly.

"You were a little rough just then!" She smiled up at him apologetically.

"Oh, to be sure, that was remiss of me! I will be much more gentle from now on.!" He added more oil to his fingertips, then proceeded to rub them delicately on her yearning rosebud. Using three fingers, he circumnavigated and stimulated her most feminine area, making tiny circles, then bigger ones, generating such immense feelings of pleasure that Mavis thought she could not bear it any longer. Unable to stop herself, she reached out boldly and seized Seamus' hard member.

"In me!" She begged him. "Now!"

She gasped as he entered her, forcefully yet easily, as she was more than ready for him. But he had not forgotten her needs, and continued to stroke her as he took her rhythmically, bringing her to the most breathtaking climax she had ever had. Within seconds he had joined her in that private paradise that only lovers share. They lay together on the crumpled sheets, exhausted and replete.

"You have worn me out once more, you wicked woman!" Seamus sighed contentedly, lighting a cigarette, and idly watching the clouds of smoke swirl up towards the ceiling.

"I have just got time for a bath, Seamus, if you would like to run one for me." Mavis grinned up at him impishly, drawing her knees up and hugging them close

"Your wish is my command, oh mistress mine." He hauled himself out of bed, and padded out in his loose-limbed fashion onto the landing and into the bathroom, where Mavis could hear him turning on the taps, swishing the water about. She lay back, closed her eyes and wished she could just fall asleep. How wonderful it would be to remain here all day, all night, all the time.

"What's it to be today? A deeply aromatic bath oil by Aqua Manda? Or pure essence of rose oil, from my travels in Turkey?" His voice echoed above the sound of the running water and brought her back to earth.

"I will take your recommendation! Whatever you say, boss!" Mavis looked up as Seamus re-entered the room.

"I have used the Aqua Manda," he announced, "because it is more suitable. It is spicy, exotic and totally unforgettable. Just like you."

"Flatterer. Now carry me to my bath, and see to my needs!" Mavis threw back the sheet and stood up. Seamus stood back, admiring the view.

"Turn around, sweet Mavis, let me look at you naked, fresh from lovemaking and full of my seed! Turn around." She obeyed him, and slowly turned around until her back faced him. There was silence. She twisted her head to see what he was doing.

"Be still," he murmured softly, his eyes narrowed, taking her in, appreciating the bow-like curves of her thighs, her high, pert bottom, the hour-glass waist and the gentle slope of her shoulders, over which her glossy, dark hair spilled most gloriously. He sighed.

"Let's get you bathed, then!" He scooped her up easily, and carried her into the bathroom. Mavis immersed herself in the perfumed water. Seamus started to soap her, gently lathering her neck and shoulders, and working his hands down her spine. Suddenly she turned towards him, looking up at him with an incredibly sad expression on her face. She gazed into his blue eyes, her own brown ones dark with unspoken emotion.

"What will become of us, Seamus?" she whispered. A wave of melancholia swept over him. He stopped what he was doing and put his arm around her wet back, hugging her tightly.

"I have no idea. But I do know, my darling woman, that I love you as I have never loved a woman before. I was young when I was with Carmel, and have since travelled through life's journey, treated women casually and experienced many joys and sorrows. Then I met you. You have made my life complete, and whatever happens, my heart will be yours until my dying day." Mavis looked down at her soapy knees, saying nothing, but holding his hand tightly as though she would never let it go. Then she raised it to her lips and kissed it softly. Looking up at him again, she sighed. "And mine is yours likewise." How she meant those words.

He frowned. "But Mavis......why don't you leave him? I can support you. I will look after you! Leave him! Tell him you can't live with his unkindness any longer! I am not exerting any pressure, but you live your life in such stifling unhappiness! You are like a wild flower cut back because it does not conform within the orderly garden. Surely you cannot live like this any longer?" Mavis raised her eyes sorrowfully. Her heart felt like lead. How she longed to accept his offer.

"You don't understand......my life is restricted, and I have to accept the fact that life in this village as the wife of the minister is my destiny. I cannot dream of doing as you suggest. I would be ostracised, excluded from this society, ridiculed and reviled. A scarlet woman bringing shame and dishonour upon Ernest's family. I could never do that..." Her voice trailed away, miserably. The remaining bubbles reflected the despair in her face, distorted and alien , like her life, and tinged with bright pink and green. Seamus squeezed the bath sponge so hard it started to crumble. His face was rigid with grief. Swiftly, he composed his features.

"Of course, dear heart. I always promised not to upset the local apple cart. But I want to bloody well tip it right on its prim-arsed fecking side! But I understand." He dropped a kiss on her wet shoulder. "And I do love you very much."

She smiled again. "Now I had better remove myself from this bath before I become like a wrinkled prune!"

Twenty minutes later, Mavis was back at the cottage, having promised not to be late that evening, and to try and get to Seamus' house a little early if at all possible. He had advised her that she should present Ernest with his portrait that evening, as it was framed and ready for the occasion. Professor Drummond had decided he would call on Eiddwen to escort her to the dinner party. Mavis was just happily thinking how much that would infuriate Eiddwen's sisters, when Ernest arrived home. Thankfully, he was in a good mood, having secured a fairly acceptable financial arrangement about the burial plot.

"I hope Mr O'Brien can cook, Mavis. I can see you have only laid out some bread and cheese for lunch, hardly enough to sustain a hard-working man!" He glowered down at the white cottage loaf and the mature Cheddar Mavis had placed on the table, along with some tomatoes from the greenhouse and beetroot chutney Eiddwen had made a few weeks ago. Mavis refused to rise to his sarcasm and with her head in the air, floated out of the kitchen. "I am sure he can, Ernest."

By half-past six, Mavis was ready. Ernest was struggling with his starched collar, so Mavis had to help him fasten it. "You must have put on weight, cariad." Mavis smiled inwardly, knowing full well that when the button had fallen off the collar a couple of weeks ago, she had sewn it on in a different place so that the collar would be smaller. Ernest had been particularly unkind to her that day, and she hadn't been able to resist it.

"Perhaps you had better put a different one on." Mavis sighed as Ernest stomped off upstairs to change his shirt. He was always complaining that she kept him waiting when they were about to go out, now he was the one under pressure to hurry up. It felt good. Ten minutes later Ernest re-appeared in the kitchen, putting his pocket watch safely in the top pocket of his jacket. He regarded his wife with his customary disapproval.

"Where did you get that dress? I haven't seen it before."

"I bought this before we were married, cariad. Don't you like it?" Mavis twirled around so the dress swirled about her legs.

"Humph. It is rather revealing." Mavis continued in her twirling, but said nothing. Ernest scowled. Was she being deliberately provocative?

"Well, come on then, Mavis. It is a quarter to seven. Let's go." He watched her as she flounced out into the hallway to fetch a flimsy piece of pale yellow silk from the banister, which she draped artistically over her tanned shoulders. His diminutive wife was an enigma to him. She was attractive, he could not dispute that, and on the face of it was an upstanding member of the chapel congregation. But he could not fathom her, could not understand her way of thinking, could not reason why she did not conform, or comply with his expectations of how the wife of a man of God should behave. Why wasn't she like other women around Llannon? Why didn't she know her place, behave obediently, and not challenge him with her flamboyance and assertiveness? His first two wives had been sweet-natured and docile, meek and respectful. Why couldn't Mavis be like them? And why couldn't she be more bonny, have more meat on her, like Gladys Williams.....He shook his head and banished lustful thoughts from his mind. He took Mavis' arm and, placing it through his, lead the way down the lane to the big, pale house, the solitary bottle of Llan lemonade swaying about in a brown leather bucket bag. The garden was wilder than ever, but at least the hot, dry weather had inhibited the growth of weeds slightly, allowing for a reasonably straightforward journey up the path to the front door. Seamus was waiting for them, dressed in a formal, yet ancient, black suit, looking incredibly glamorous, as only a tall man can, despite the fact his clothes may have seen better days.

"Welcome! Enter!" He threw out his arms in greeting. "Isn't it a fine evening? I have mown the lawn at the back of the house, and have put some chairs there. Such a shame to sit indoors in such glorious weather! Follow me!" They trooped through the hall, and entered the kitchen, where the most enticing aromas were wafting about. A massive pot was simmering away on the Rayburn, crockery and napkins were stacked neatly on the table. The table of illicit passion, thought Mavis nostalgically. The house was spick and span; Seamus was clearly set on making a good impression. Mavis wondered how he could have found the time to do all this, as it certainly hadn't been in this pristine condition when she had left at lunch-time. He led them out into the garden. Mavis caught her breath. It had been transformed. Seamus had hung mirrored ornaments from the branches of the trees, and they sparkled in the early evening sunlight. Elgar's Nimrod spilled forth from the hidden record player, which Seamus had placed as close to the open French doors as he could. Two sofas were placed at right angles to each other, and they had been generously draped with white, gauzy fabric, which had been tied at each corner with green satin ribbon. A faint hint of musky rose filled the air, and Mavis could see that a couple of incense burners lurked secretly underneath the stone table. She could only attempt to imagine what Ernest would think of those! Instruments of the devil, no doubt. However, Seamus would probably explain them away by saying they were keeping wasps at bay. Ernest looked on in amazement as he took in the giant, plastic toadstools which lined the cobbled path to the kitchen, unable to believe his eyes as he regarded the glittering ornamental fairies Seamus had placed on each one. Mavis could almost read his thoughts – were they having dinner with a complete lunatic? She wanted to burst out laughing.

"Have we wandered by mistake into fairyland, Mr O'Brien?" She smiled mischievously at him.

"You have indeed! My elves have been very busy! Take a seat! May I get you something to drink?" Seamus beamed happily at the Wattons, as they sat down on one of the sofas, Ernest rather gingerly and suspiciously.

"We have brought some lemonade with us," Mavis offered him the bag. "I think Ernest and I would like a glass of that. I have kept it as cool as I could, it's been in the pantry all day."

They could hear him clinking glasses inside the kitchen, and five minutes later he returned with two tumblers, which were frosted with sugar and had ice cubes in them, a novelty for the Wattons, who had no refrigerator.

"Chin chin!" Mavis raised her glass, pleased with her cosmopolitan knowledge of drinking terminology, took a sip, and her eyes opened wide with surprise.

"Bottoms up!" Seamus grinned wickedly, watching her reaction, raising his own glass of whisky in return. Ernest glowered at him, such unacceptable language. Bottoms up, indeed. Then, as he tasted his drink, his thoughts turned to Gladys' plump, quivering buttocks. He started to sweat heavily, pulling at his collar, wishing he could remove his tie. Hastily, he pushed away all immoral memories, and in order to divert his attention, he downed his lemonade in one mouthful. He coughed and spluttered. Seamus watched him with great interest.

"You must be incredibly thirsty, Mr Watton! Shall I refill your glass?" Wiping his mouth on his handkerchief, Ernest handed him the tumbler.

"Very well. It is certainly hot today. Thank you."

"May I use your bathroom, Mr O'Brien?" Mavis stood up, putting her drink down. "I am so hot I wish to run my wrists under the cold water."

"Follow me, Mrs Watton." Seamus led the way into the house, leaving a bemused Ernest sitting on the sofa.

"What was in that lemonade?!" Mavis hissed at a chuckling Seamus.

"Oh, only the tiniest splash of poteen!"

"Poteen? What's that?"

"Similar to vodka. My mother makes it, my sister makes it, every fecking buggar makes it in Ireland and I had a drop left from my party! Ernest can do with a bit of loosening up!"

"Well don't give him anymore!" Mavis rushed off to the cloakroom, allowing Ernest to slip another small shot of poteen into Ernest's tumbler. They were all seated on the sofas, when there was a loud rap at the front door, then a booming Scottish voice called out,

"We're here! Coming through!" The professor wearing a Scottish kilt, and Eiddwen, appeared at the kitchen door. She was resplendent, if rather too hot, in her blue suit, and looked as though she had died and gone to heaven, and not a straight laced Baptist one at that; her eyes were sparking and her cheeks were flushed at the thought of her first ever dinner date. The professor looked like a kilt-wearing cat who had got the cream, putting his arm around Eiddwen proprietorially.

"At last! 'Tis my helper elf and his pixie friend, a vision in blue, if I may say so!" Seamus got up and kissed Eiddwen on the cheek, which made her blush even more furiously.

"Your garden is so pretty, Mr O'Brien," gushed Eiddwen, feeling awkward and unsure of herself, "you are so incredibly artistic!"

"Well, he is an artist, after all, Eiddwen." Mavis couldn't help her sarcasm, ashamed at how jealous she'd felt when Seamus pecked Eiddwen on the cheek.

"Drinks, anyone?" Seamus looked at the couple.

"A wee dram for me! You know my poison! Old Bushmills, no ice!" The professor grinned from ear to ear.

"And you are happy to forsake the liquor of your own nation, you old fossil?"

Professor Drummond laughed heartily, slapping his hands on his plump and hairy knees. "Indeed I am! Now hurry up and get on with it!"

Seamus turned to Eiddwen, who sat on the edge of the sofa, not quite wanting to be seen being too close to the professor. "And yourself?"

Eiddwen felt indecisive. She could feel Ernest's disapproval aiming straight at her, even though she wasn't looking at him. Suddenly, feeling the slight pressure of the professor's leg against hers, she felt bold. "I will have a Babycham, if you have any!" Mavis groaned inwardly. In a minute Eiddwen would be asking for glace cherries....

"But of course, fair maid, I have bought some in especially, as the drinks fairy told me that Babycham was your favourite tipple." Seamus winked at her.

Eiddwen giggled. "And do you have any glace cherries? I am so fond of them!"

Mavis wished Seamus wouldn't flirt so obviously with Eiddwen. Even though she realised it was just a decoy, to ensure Ernest did not suspect anything untoward, it still grated on her nerves. Then, with impeccable timing, Seamus' eyes met hers across the garden. Such a blaze of desire was evident there. Any insecurities she may have harboured dwindled away in the heat of his glance. She allowed herself a small smile, directed at him, and him alone. The next half-hour was spent in idle chit-chat. The sun continued to beat down, relentless in its intensity, despite the late hour. Seamus had placed several bowls of cheese and onion crisps on small picnic tables beside the sofas, and the professor wolfed them by the handful, Eiddwen picking at them more discreetly. Ernest shunned them completely, feeling rather suspicious of these new-fangled flavoured crisps. Mavis didn't feel particularly hungry, however and didn't bother. After his second glass of doctored lemonade, Ernest appeared to be relaxed, and actually seemed to be enjoying himself, discussing the founding minister of the Welsh Baptists, Hugh Evans, with the professor. The time is right, thought Seamus. Beckoning Mavis with his hand, he disappeared into the house, Mavis following discreetly. "Wait here," he said, "I won't be a second. You look stunning, I must say!" True to his word, he was back almost immediately, carrying the portrait of Mavis wearing the fur coat, which he had wrapped in blue tissue paper.

"Hold it steady for me." She giggled at the double entendre, but managed to keep hold of the painting, Seamus carried out an easel into the garden. "Ladies and gentlemen!" He bowed theatrically. "It is with great pleasure that I inform you that one of our guests celebrates a birthday next week." Eiddwen looked at Ernest excitedly. Ernest looked rather suspicious. Seamus continued his speech. "Many happy returns for next week, Mr Watton! May I now present......Mrs Mavis WATTON!" Mavis staggered in with the painting, which was almost as tall as she was. Placing it on the easel, with a lot of assistance from Seamus, she then walked over to her husband, giving his a kiss on the cheek.

"Penblwydd hapus, cariad! Happy birthday for next Wednesday! Go on, unwrap it! I had it done for you." Ernest got to his feet, a little unsteadily. He assumed, however, it was the heat of the evening. Tentatively, he tore off the paper, and stood back. Everyone gasped in amazement. There was Mavis, in her fur coat, looking haughtily over her shoulder, cool and aloof. And immensely beautiful.

"Bravo! Bravo!" Professor Drummond stood up, applauding loudly. "A masterpiece! You must be so proud, Mr Watton, to have such an attractive wife!" Ernest was dumbfounded. He cleared his throat, searching for words. But he knew when to be gracious.

"What can I say? Yes, indeed! It is a magnificent piece of work. I shall be proud to have it above the fireplace, for all to appreciate. Thank you, Mr O'Brien. Diolch, Mavis."

Seamus, looking very pleased with himself, picked up the portrait. "I will put it in the hall until you are ready to leave, Mr Watton. Then, once I have put the finishing touches to the dinner, we can all be seated in the dining room."

It was now almost eight o'clock, and the sun slipped behind the trees at the edge of the garden, allowing a brief respite from its searing heat. Eiddwen was busily fanning herself with her hands, Ernest was sweating profusely and the professor looked like a well-grilled rasher of bacon. Only Mavis appeared cool and serene as she sat composed and self-possessed on the gauze-covered sofa. Just as the conversation was petering out, Seamus reappeared at the door.

"Dinner, my friends, is served!" There was a murmur of appreciation, and the guests rose, following Seamus back into the house. Mavis had never really been inside the dining room before, not even on the night of Seamus' infamous party. It was quite cosy by the house's general standards, although both the kitchen and parlour of the Wattons' ground floor could have easily fitted inside it.

Red velvet curtains, albeit rather worn and slightly dusty, hung in voluptuous folds around the bay window, and the parquet floor was welcomingly cool. An ancient chandelier hung from the ceiling, but remained unlit, hiding the copious cobwebs which decorated the crystals. The table was laid for the five of them; several tall candles in empty wine bottles flickered upon a snowy white tablecloth, and an enormous vase of wild roses, foxgloves and ferns had been placed in the centre. The general effect was of shabby, faded bohemian splendour. Once they were all seated comfortably, Seamus disappeared once more into the kitchen, returning with steaming plates of food.

"Am a complete philistine when it comes to dinner party etiquette, so sorry, folks, no serving dishes! Hope you enjoy!"

Ernest looked down in horror at the plate in front of him. It looked like a mass of white worms, covered in a reddish sauce. He looked up at Seamus in puzzlement. Eiddwen, feeling equally confused, but emboldened by the Babycham, came to his rescue and piped up,

"What is this, Mr O'Brien? I don't think I have ever eaten anything like this before." As he placed a basket of bread on the table, alongside the enormous bowl of salad, Seamus smiled. "Spaghetti bolognese! My own secret recipe! Well, if truth be told, it isn't really mine at all, as it was given to me by an old Italian nonnina, in a tiny village in Emilia-Romagna. But it is extremely unlikely she will discover my plagiarism, so bon appetit!"

"What's that?" Mavis pointed to a small bowl of cream-coloured shavings.

"Parmesan cheese! Or smelly socks, or even baby sick, as my less enlightened friends have named it in the past! Help yourself!" After one sniff at the pungent cheese, Mavis decided her food was good enough without it. A temporary silence followed, as everyone attacked their dinner, only interrupted by a few slurps from the professor and some irritated sighs from Ernest, who was having some difficulty mastering the art of spaghetti-eating. Mavis picked listlessly at her food, puzzled as to why her usual healthy appetite had deserted her. However, she made a valiant effort, as the food was truly delicious. Neither she nor Ernest had tasted anything like this before, European cuisine had yet to infiltrate the depths of rural Wales. Eiddwen was having particular difficulty in keeping the pasta twisted around her fork. Inevitably it would slip off just before it would reach her mouth, resulting in a considerable amount of the sauce being splattered over the tablecloth. Suddenly, Mavis felt incredibly hot, and a wave of nausea overcame her. She got up suddenly.

"Excuse me, I don't feel well!" She ran from the room, and only just made it to the cloakroom in time, where she vomited whatever food she had eaten into the toilet bowl. Wiping her mouth with her hand, she looked at her reflection in the mirror. The horrific truth suddenly hit her like a punch in the stomach.

What on earth would become of her?

Chapter Eighteen

Subtle strategies

Mavis' face was flushed with the effort of being sick. She looked at her reflection in the mirror. A stranger gazed back, whose eyes were huge and haunted. A stupid, irresponsible stranger. Of course. She should have guessed. It was in early May that she had last had a period; she had assumed that at forty-three things could get a little irregular, so hadn't been worried about it. She had also failed to notice the other tell-tale signs, the inexplicable tiredness, her full and tender breasts. Then, the frightening reality of her situation took hold of her. She hadn't slept with Ernest since January. He hadn't seemed all that interested in that side of things, and hadn't made any advances towards her. The fact remained that she was pregnant with Seamus' child. What on earth was she going to do? She could be about six weeks gone. Hastily she splashed some cold water on her face and rinsed her mouth out, dabbing at her smudged mascara with a piece of tissue paper. Holding on to the wash basin for dear life, she felt the cold hand of fear grip her heart. Any concerns about her future with Seamus paled into temporary insignificance — what was going to become of her, respectable Mavis Watton, pregnant with her lover's child? What would Seamus think? Would he abandon her? It was one thing being his secret lover, but another landing him with an unwanted child. No, she had to think fast, self-preservation high on her list of priorities.

There was a knock at the door. "Are you alright in there?" Seamus sounded concerned.

"Just coming!" Mavis took a deep breath, checked her appearance once more, and unlocked the cloakroom door. Seamus took her by the arm as she emerged.

"Are you sure you're okay?"

Mavis smiled up him, desperate to reassure him. "Positive," she whispered, "but I will need to have a little talk with you tomorrow. Is that possible?"

"Of course! Pop down whenever you want! The professor is taking Eiddwen out in the morning and intends being out all day." Anxiously, he followed her back into the dining room.

"Are you feeling better, Mavis?" Eiddwen asked, dutifully, however her focus remained doggedly upon the professor.

"Yes, just a touch of indigestion." Mavis sat back down in her chair, amazed at how hungry she now felt. Ernest had not reacted to her hasty exit at all, and was still ploughing his way through the mountain of spaghetti Seamus had placed in front of him. She resumed eating her dinner, aware of the relief and pleasure on Seamus' face as she ate it enthusiastically. As Seamus cleared away the empty plates, Mavis' mind was working furiously. She was in an incredibly difficult situation, and it was up to her to come up with a solution. The pudding arrived just as Mavis was formulating her plan. "Tiramisu!" Seamus placed a bowl of what appeared to be a trifle-like concoction on the table, and encouraged his guests to help themselves.

"What a seductively sweet dessert!" The professor smacked his lips greedily as he filled his dish to the brim. Yes, thought Mavis, seduction. That's what I will have to do. And the sooner the better. She turned to Ernest and smiled. "Such lovely food, cariad, don't you think?"

"Very nice indeed," Ernest replied, wiping some cream from his mouth with his napkin. At least he seemed to be in a good mood, which would make her task all the easier to accomplish later on. After they had finished eating, Seamus produced a bottle of port, which of course Ernest and Mavis politely declined, requesting some coffee instead. Eiddwen, feeling reckless and defiant, accepted a small measure of the sweet, potent wine. The conversation turned to the subject of Roman Catholicism and its doctrines. Mavis could hear the droning talk between her husband and the professor, but absorbed none of it. She remained detached from the others, her thoughts remaining solely on her predicament. How could she be pregnant? Married to Ernest for three years, and having known him in the Biblical sense at least half a dozen times, there had been no inkling that she had "caught," as her women friends liked to put it. She was so unprepared for this, it was totally unexpected, like a bolt out of the blue. Assuming she was past the age of childbearing, Mavis had forgotten about the possibility of this ever happening. And now it had happened. No, there was no official evidence, no test to prove without a doubt she was expecting a baby, yet all the signs pointed to the fact that she, Mavis Watton, at the ripe old age of forty-three, was going to have a child. What would she tell Ernest? And Seamus? She stared through the tall windows at the darkening sky, which was becoming increasingly covered with threatening, grey clouds. She was unaware of Seamus watching her intently, a puzzled expression on his face.

"And I assume you were brought up a Roman Catholic, Mr O'Brien?" Seamus was oblivious to Ernest's question, and continued to gaze in Mavis' direction, trying to fathom what seemed to be troubling her. "Mr O'Brien?"

"What?" Seamus roused himself from his concerns. "Sorry. I was daydreaming. What did you say?"

"I asked you if you were brought up as a Roman Catholic?" Ernest waited for a response.

"Um, to be sure I was, but I suppose you could say that I am rather lapsed right now!" Seamus laughed heartily, as though he had made a great joke, but in reality he was terribly concerned about Mavis' strange behaviour. She was simply staring out of the window, a small smile on her lips and her eyes slightly glazed.

The clock in the hallway struck ten.

"I am so tired, Ernest, I think it is time we were going." Mavis feigned a yawn. Ernest looked sharply at his wife, quite surprised. He had thought he would have had to prise her away from the evening's festivities.

"As you wish. But the professor and I have only just begun our discussion!" Ernest looked dismayed. Seamus seized the opportunity.

"Well, maybe you can both call over tomorrow evening to continue! If Mavis and Eiddwen won't be too bored, that is?" Mavis looked at him gratefully.

"Ooh! Am I invited as well, Seamus?" Eiddwen gave a tiny hiccough, which thankfully went unnoticed by Ernest.

"But of course! There's so much food left over, we can have it heated up! Do we have another date, chaps?"

"That's very kind, Mr O'Brien. We shall look forward to it." Mavis smiled encouragingly up at him. "I shall just collect my shawl from the garden, I think I left it there." She hurried out into the garden, which in the dark looked like a scene from a Walt Disney film, all the fairy lights twinkling in the trees.

"Are you sure you left it there?" Seamus followed her quickly, glad of an excuse to get her on her own. Outside, they turned to face each other. "What on earth's the matter with you? Are you angry with me? Have I done something to upset you? Why are you leaving so soon?" He looked so distraught that Mavis wanted to reach out and touch his face to reassure him, but as they could be seen from the house, she merely spoke to him quietly. "One question at a time, Seamus. You have done nothing wrong, cariad, not at all. And I am really feeling incredibly washed out, I must go home to bed. I have had a lovely evening here tonight. And clever you, asking us back again! That was a brilliant idea! I do love you so much....." Her voice trailed away into a whisper. "And I will see you in the morning, alone."

He put his hand on her shoulder briefly. "Until tomorrow, then."

Back in the house, Ernest was preparing to leave, picking up the painting with some difficulty. Mavis looked at Eiddwen and Professor Drummond, wrapped up in their mutual adoration, looking up briefly to wave goodbye. Despite her own predicament, she smiled indulgently.

"Do you need a hand with the portrait?" Seamus held the door open for them.

"Not at all," Ernest grunted as he shifted it awkwardly through the doorway.

"Thank you for a wonderful dinner, Mr O'Brien. Goodnight." Mavis smiled up at him as she and Ernest turned and made their way back up the lane to their cottage. Seamus watched them walk away into the stifling gloom, the tiny woman he loved so desperately walking away with her husband, and back to her domestic reality. As the couple entered the cottage and shut the door, the first rumble of thunder echoed ominously through the valley.

Mavis and Ernest lay rigidly side by side in their bed, not speaking or touching, the eiderdown folded neatly at their feet due to the sultry night. Well, it's now or never, Mavis thought to herself, steeling herself for the task ahead. Assistance came in the form of a violent flash of lightning, followed immediately by a deafening clap of thunder. She threw her arms around her husband. "Ernest! I am so frightened! Cuddle up to me!" Mavis had never been afraid of storms in her life, but her ploy seemed to work and Ernest rolled over on to his side, putting his arms around her. She wiggled her bottom against his hips suggestively. "Closer, cariad, closer!" As Ernest complied with her request, she could feel his manhood stiffening and twitching into life. Without saying anything, he pulled her onto her back, lifting her cotton nightdress and silently removing her white, broderie anglaise knickers. Mavis only had to lie there and think of tomorrow's ironing . He made no attempt to kiss or caress her, and the whole thing was over in about five minutes. He grunted in satisfaction, then turned his back to her and fell asleep almost immediately, leaving her staring up at the ceiling, listening to the thunder, and watching the brilliance of the lightning as it flashed, illuminating the room as brightly as though it was daytime. She closed her eyes, longing for sleep, but the storm continued its ferocious assault on Llannon, eventually bringing with it a tattoo of heavy rain, flattening flowers and washing away the dust of the past few weeks. If only it could wash away her problems as well.

By dawn, the searing heat was a thing of the past. Fluffy, white clouds scudded across a bright blue sky. The smell of wet grass and foliage filled the air and a brisk summer breeze wafted its way through the trees. The heatwave was finally over. The calm brought sleep, and a dreamless slumber.

Eventually, Mavis opened one sleepy eye, then the other. The alarm clock said eight o'clock. Ernest was nowhere to be seen. She had slept so late! Hurriedly, she got up, had a quick bath and dressed. Ernest had probably gone over to the Bowen's farm to collect the eggs. The knowledge of her likely condition made her less inclined to have any breakfast, so by nine o'clock she was on her way down the lane towards Seamus' house, rehearsing the words she would use to tell him the news. She wondered how he would take it, how he would react. Part of her was excited and delighted, yet she was also worried as to what he would say when he knew what she had done about the situation last night. They had never discussed Mavis' personal life, so she assumed he must think her intimate relationship with Ernest was quite normal, whatever that was. Maybe there was no need to worry on that count. Tentatively, she made her way down the path which led to his front door, and knocked, confident that he would be alone, and the Professor away with his new paramour, Eiddwen.

Silence.

She waited patiently for a couple of minutes. Maybe he was in the bath? Still no sound came from within the depths of the house. With a mounting feeling of anxiety, she knocked again, louder this time. Nothing. A wave of irrational panic possessed her and she ran quickly around the side of the house to the kitchen door. Throwing caution and good manners to the wind, she tried the handle. It opened. Pushing it wider, she stepped inside. Her heart was pounding so loudly, she thought it would burst. "Seamus! Are you upstairs?!" Her voice sounded alien, strained and frightened. No friendly, Irish voice replied. The silence remained. She looked around her. Last night's dirty dishes lay on the kitchen table, and the sink was full of used glasses. Mavis hesitated no longer, and raced upstairs, two steps at a time. Flinging open his bedroom door, she could see that the bed had either been made (unlikely) or hadn't been slept in at all. Where could he be? Forlornly, she sat down on the top of the stairs, her head in her hands, wondering what she should do next. Reluctantly, she got to her feet again, making her way back down, and out through the kitchen door. Tears filled her eyes as she forced herself to leave the house; her feet felt as though they were made of lead as she dragged herself back outside. She was trying desperately to compose herself when someone came running up the lane, shouting her name.

"Mavis! Mavis! Wait!" She swung around properly to see Eiddwen scampering as fast as her sturdy, little legs could carry her. She was holding an envelope.

"It's for you!" She gasped, panting for breath as she held it out to Mavis.

"What do you mean? Who gave it to you?" Mavis took the letter, examining it, trying to establish who had sent it.

"Archie! Professor Drummond! He said I must give it to you as soon as I saw you!" Eiddwen watched curiously because Mavis' expression was one of sheer despair and she had never seen her so distressed before.

"Thank you. Thank you, Eiddwen. Now I must rush home! I think I have left the kettle on the stove again!" Mavis turned abruptly and walked briskly up the lane.

"Shall we have a cup of tea, Mavis?" Eiddwen started to trot after her.

"Not now!" Mavis couldn't keep the exasperation out of her voice, leaving her friend confused and a little hurt. Eiddwen turned around slowly, and made her way home, wondering what on earth she had done.

Back in her bedroom, lying on the bed, Mavis opened the letter with shaking hands. The envelope had been addressed to Mrs Mavis Watton, and sealed. It was from Seamus.

My dear, darling woman,

I have asked Archie to give this letter to Eiddwen, so she could give it to you. When you read this, please remember that at this precise time, you should have been lying in my arms. However, events have overtaken us. My brother Patrick telephoned me from Ireland last night, after you had gone. My mother, who is now well into her eighties, has had a heart attack. It is not certain if she will survive. Archie kindly offered to drive me to Fishguard to catch the ferry to take me home. We left at seven o'clock this morning, to catch the mid-day sailing. I am so sorry that this has happened. I have to return home, I may never see my mother again. I hope you can understand that.

I realise that you are a hot-headed, passionate woman, and that your initial response will be that of anger, and maybe disappointment (sure enough that is rather conceited of me) but I hope that when you have had time to ponder upon my situation, you will be sympathetic. You must remember this, you must... I love you dearly. Whatever it is that you wished to tell me this morning, well, I am sure it is something we can sort out when I return. When that will be I am uncertain. But I will keep in touch. I will write to you once I get home, and I will write my Ireland address at the end of this letter. My letters to you will be sent to my house in Llannon. You will find that I may have left my kitchen door unlocked. There is a key hidden behind the potted lilac outside the kitchen door and I would be eternally grateful if you could pop over and lock it for me. We left in rather a hurry. You can let yourself in and check for my letters this way. This may be inconvenient for you, but it will be far safer. My dear Mavis, my sweet woman, take care of yourself and keep me in your heart, for you are in mine always.

Seamus.

71, Lyons Road

Newcastle, Co. Dublin. Ireland.

With trembling hands, she folded the letter up into a small square, placing it safely in her box of poems under the bed, underneath all the pieces of paper she had scribbled her thoughts on, and took care to throw the envelope into the stove to burn once she went downstairs. She sat down at the table, too stunned to think properly. Her first reaction had not been anger at all, just a sense of relief. However, she felt so alone, there was nobody to talk to about what was happening to her. Seamus was the only person she could have confided in. Should she tell him now? By letter? Or should she wait until he had returned from Ireland.....but who knew when that would be? She closed her eyes in frustration, but then, with her typical stoicism, she started to think logically. Seamus would have to be told, that was a certainty. However, he would be with his sick mother in Ireland, under considerable stress himself. It would be unfair of her to burden him with this emotional baggage right now. No, she would reply to his letter after a few days, allowing him time to settle into whatever situation awaited him, but she would not divulge anything just yet. For the first time in her life, Mavis was considering the feelings of another person instead of thinking of herself. Satisfied with her decision, she got up to make herself some breakfast. It was now half-past nine, and she was starting to feel quite light-headed. Just as she was buttering a piece of bread, and thinking of opening a tin of sardines to make a sandwich (she assumed her condition was to blame for this unusual choice of food) there was a timid knock at the door and Eiddwen tiptoed in, looking nervous. "Er....Mavis? Are you alright?" She sat down at the table. "I hope the letter didn't contain bad news?"

"Oh, not really, Eiddwen." Mavis was quickly regaining her composure. "It was just a letter of apology from Mr O'Brien, cancelling this evening's dinner because of his mother's illness. I feel a bit washed out, that's all. I'm sorry I was a bit rude just now. I was a little distracted as I had overslept and thought it was Sunday not Saturday. There was no sign of Ernest, so I was up and dressed to go to chapel!" Mavis wasn't sure if Eiddwen believed this lame excuse but her friend nodded amicably.

"It was a lovely evening, wasn't it? Such a beautiful garden, such wonderful food!" Eiddwen sighed with pleasure at the memory of it.

"But poor Mr O'Brien! Fancy having to drop everything and rush back home to Ireland? Archie was knocking my door at a quarter to seven this morning, just before they left. He said that he will carry on from Fishguard with his journey to Aberystwyth, for his conference, then leave the car there, and return to Scotland by train." She looked so forlorn that Mavis almost reached out to comfort her, but stopped herself. She and Eiddwen were not often given to hugging each other, and no doubt her friend would have been quite surprised if she had done so. Maybe her heightened emotional state had allowed her to let her guard down. With great effort she forced a smile on her face. "Cup of tea, Eiddwen?"

Later that day, Mavis took Dai out for a walk. After the recent heatwave, the temperature now felt quite cool, and she shivered slightly as she made her way back down to Seamus' house to lock the door, making sure there was no-one to watch her going in. Inside, the strange silence hit her once more. She wandered around downstairs, going from room to room, picking up a discarded sweater belonging to Seamus, breathing in the scent of her absent lover, the scent of tobacco and his personal, special aroma, inhaling deeply, with her eyes shut tight, remembering his embrace and his passionate kisses. Despite the unfamiliar silence, she felt happy and calm in the house, filled as it was with Seamus' personal belongings, his habitual mess and his artistry. He had only been gone half a day, but already she missed him terribly. Reluctantly, she went back out into the garden, locking the door behind her and replacing the key where she had found it, but making a mental note to return at her earliest opportunity to give the place a spring-clean.

Within a few minutes she was making her way along the track. Once in the shelter of the hill and the trees, the sun beat down as pleasantly as ever. Dai trotted happily alongside her, panting with his pink tongue hanging out of his mouth. As they settled into their stride, heading north, she began to gather her tumultuous thoughts together, trying to make sense of the situation. Inside her body, a new life was developing, a tiny speck of life, a mix of Irish and Welsh, an unexpected newcomer to wreak havoc upon her already complicated existence. But, a welcome newcomer, a child begotten of love and passion. The thought comforted her. As she walked along, she looked down at her stomach, as flat as ever, nothing to suggest for one moment that she cradled a little baby within her. But even now she was aware of the dramatic changes taking place within her. She fast-tracked a few months into the future in her mind......how would Seamus react when he saw her swollen tummy, no longer enticing and desirable? Would he want her anymore? Would he cast her aside, find another lover – God forbid – what if he turned his attentions towards the vile Gladys Williams?! Irrational ideas raced through her mind, banishing any common sense. And what should she do next? What did a woman do if she suspected she was pregnant? Her muddled thoughts flew to and fro. There was no-one else around, and Dai was slack on the lead, so she allowed her hands to steal up towards her breasts. She caressed them gently, but even her soft touch felt harsh. She winced as the tenderness of her flesh caused her pain. If this was the discomfort of pregnancy, she thought, how would she cope with the agony of labour? But on such a balmy July day, fresh with the south westerly wind, and the sun on her face, she couldn't feel dismal for long. By half-past eleven, she had reached the turn-off for her mother's house. She stopped walking and deliberated. Could she face her sisters' vitriolic and sour remarks this morning? She sighed. Family obligations would have to wait until another day. Anyway, she had asked Ernest to take her shopping in Llanelli that afternoon, so it was time to turn back. He hadn't said much when she had told him about this evening's cancellation. He had merely grunted by way of response and demanded what they would have for their supper instead. "Bacon and eggs," she had said, "bacon and eggs...."

The market was a seething mass of weekend shoppers; old ladies wearing heavy coats despite the mild weather, jostled each other for the pick of the tomatoes at the greengrocer stalls; small boys begged for Matchbox cars at the toy stall; but what caught Mavis' eye was the array of knitted bonnets on the baby-clothes stall. She shuddered. What monstrosities, she thought. If the baby was a girl, she would never allow her to wear one of those huge, frothy concoctions.

"Mavis!" Ernest nudged her arm. "How much bacon did you want?" Mavis turned around, absent-mindedly. The butcher looked at her expectantly.

"Um...give me a shilling's worth. That should see us through until next week." She forced a smile on her face, looking at the piles of sausages, chops and faggots piled up on the counter. Once again, a wave of nausea surged up within her, making her clench her teeth in an attempt to stop it. She took slow, deep breaths, having read somewhere in her medical directory that this was supposed to be helpful. Surprisingly, it was. Taking hold of her husband's arm, she announced firmly,

"Let's go and have an ice cream in the Gardenia!" Ernest looked at her in astonishment. The Gardenia cafe was at the top of Station Road, rather too close for comfort to the New Dock area, which Mavis despised so much.

"The Gardenia?"

"Yes. I want to have a knickerbocker glory there. With raspberry sauce and nuts on the top. And then, maybe we could go and visit Mrs Baker? It's not too far to walk, and we can leave the car in Stepney Street." Mavis felt a sudden need to see her step-granddaughter again. "Very well, if that is what you wish." He took her arm and the couple walked out of the market and down Stepney Street, making their way through the throngs of Saturday shoppers, mostly women with children in tow, elderly couples walking arm in arm, and mothers pushing

Silver Cross prams. That will be me soon enough, thought Mavis, trying to imagine herself proudly walking through Llannon, with her baby in a beautiful, shining carriage. As well as wishing to see Wendy, Mavis felt overcome with the desire to be within a family setting, to be included as part of the group. They passed the cinema with its crocodile queue of excited, chattering people outside. It was now showing "Cleopatra." How pertinent, Mavis thought to herself. A tangled web of passionate love, schemes and a child born out of wedlock.

They settled down into their seats. The Gardenia was a fairly basic Italian cafe, with a restaurant upstairs. However, its ice creams were considered the best in Llanelli, and for once Mavis was happy to endure the rather austere environment in order to indulge her craving. The sardine sandwiches seemed an age away, and, having been unable to eat any lunch subsequently, Mavis fell upon her knickerbocker glory with relish. Ernest contented himself with a cup of tea, not seeing why he should line the pockets of those money-grabbing Italians with his hard-earned cash. He watched Mavis in amazement as she wolfed her ice cream within five minutes; she was usually so restrained and fastidious, and here she was, wiping away some cream from her lips with her fingers and then licking them clean! He was pretty certain that if they hadn't been in a public place, she would have licked the empty glass as well.

By half-past two, they were knocking on Gwyneth Baker's front door. No-one answered. "Maybe they have gone to town as well?" offered Mavis, disappointed. Ernest knocked the door again, and after a few minutes, the couple turned to walk away. Just as they were turning the corner of the street, along came the Bakers in their new car, with Wendy waving madly at them in the back seat. Retracing their steps, Mavis and Ernest hurried back to the house.

"We nearly missed you!" Gwyneth Baker struggled to find her door key as Wendy launched herself at Mavis.

"Is it inconvenient? Shall we leave it for another time?" Mavis asked anxiously, at the same time trying to disentangle herself from Wendy's exuberant embrace. Gwyneth looked at her in surprise. Mavis never usually demonstrated any social sensitivity.

"Of course not! Come in! I'll just put the kettle on. We just went to pick up Wendy as she is sleeping at our house tonight, because Mr Baker is working nights."

Sitting around the big, kitchen table, the conversation soon turned to Wendy's progress with her ballet.

"So how is she doing, Mrs Baker?" Mavis daintily sipped her tea from the bone china cup.

"Really well." Gwyneth looked as proud as punch. "She has been entered for her first ballet examination — grade one, I think it is called — and her mother has been told she will not have to do the pre-primary examination, as she would be far too good for it. Oh, Mrs Watton, the child lives and breathes ballet. It was the best thing anyone could have done for her. Margaret is so grateful."

"Well done, Wendy!" Mavis smiled benevolently at the little girl, who was showing off, practising her ballet positions and plies in the corner of the room, using the dado rail as a barre, all the while grinning cheekily at the grown-ups. The two men, having had quite enough of such women's talk, retired to the shed, Mr Baker being very keen to show Ernest his new lathe.

"It's Wendy's birthday in a few weeks' time," whispered Gwyneth confidentially, "and I am thinking of buying her some new ballet shoes, and a pink bag to put them in, like all the other little girls seem to have."

Mavis sighed happily. "She has such obvious talent. I am so pleased I can help fund her classes. You know, I like to think of her as my little protegee!"

Gwyneth nodded in agreement. "It must be hard for you, Mrs Watton, having no child of your own. I suppose the next best thing is to have grandchildren, even though they are not actually your own flesh and blood." Normally, Mavis would have responded with a sharp tongue to this clumsy remark, but not even Gwyneth's insensitivity could upset her, not now that she had the most beautiful secret hidden within her. She merely smiled serenely at the other woman. "Yes, you are quite right. I consider myself very lucky indeed." And in more ways than one, she thought to herself.

The afternoon passed pleasantly enough, with Gwyneth Baker for once actually enjoying the company of the erstwhile prickly and snobbish Mavis, who in turn appreciated Gwyneth's natural warmth and genuine friendliness.

That evening, after supper, Ernest retired to the parlour to perfect his sermon for the following day, leaving Mavis to her own devices. Her portrait lay propped up against the dresser, waiting for Ernest to put it up properly in the hallway, which is where they had agreed it should go. Mechanically, she washed the dishes and tidied the kitchen, her thoughts constantly straying to Seamus and what he may be doing, so many miles away across the sea in Ireland. Once her chores were finished, she took off her apron and quietly climbed the stairs to the spare bedroom. As she passed the landing window, she looked down towards Seamus' house, standing empty and silent across the lane. The sun was setting behind the hills, casting a rosy glow over the walls of the house, making them appear pink and magical. A fairy castle, thought Mavis wistfully, and my prince has gone far, far away. Trying hard to dispel the melancholic feelings which were threatening to overcome her, she settled down to write Seamus a letter.

My dear Seamus,

I received your letter this morning. It was a shock and a disappointment, yes, but I hope you had a safe journey and are now with your family.

Is your mother recovering? She is a great age, and I remember only too well the situation with Ernest's mother recently. Not, of course, that your mother will necessarily suffer similarly, but I do understand.

Oh, my darling Seamus, I miss you terribly, more than you can imagine. You have only been gone one day, yet it seems like a lifetime. We had such a wonderful time in your house last night, the food, the way you decorated the garden, it was so lovely.

I have found the key and have locked the kitchen door. The house has been left in a mess, I must say, so I will pop over and have a little tidy-up as soon as I can. Is your sister able to join you in Ireland? It would be a comfort to you if she is able to be with you.

I wonder what your mother would think if she knew me....... hastily she scribbled out that sentence and started again.... I think it would be so nice to have met your mother. Maybe one day I will, you never know. You haven't said much about her. Is she much like you? Is she as funny, as creative, as loveable as you?" Mavis paused, her eyes filling up with tears. How she longed for that funny, creative, loveable man. Pulling herself together, she resumed her writing.

All is well here in Llannon" (liar, she thought to herself) but I think poor Eiddwen is pining terribly for the professor. I hope they will be able to meet again soon, they seem perfectly matched.

It is now almost nine o'clock and the sun has set behind the hills which overlook us. The same sun will soon set behind your house, wherever it is, and I wonder what you are doing....I think of you all the time, my darling man, write back to me soon. My next letter will have more news for you, I am sure.

Your own

"sweet Mavis!" Xxxx

She dabbed a few precious drops of her Shalimar perfume onto the paper, folded it into four, then hastily popped it into an envelope. Once she had addressed it, she hid it in her underwear drawer, underneath a pile of brand new satin petticoats. It would have to lie there until she went down to Llanelli the following week. She couldn't risk posting it from Llannon post office, that would set tongues wagging for sure. She lay down on the spare bed, closed her eyes and allowed herself the indulgence of day-dreaming. In the perfect existence, she would be living with Seamus, and this evening she would be preparing the most delicious dinner for him, when she would break the news of her condition. She imagined the delight on his face, the sparkle in his eyes, and the proud way he would put his arms around her - or would he be disappointed? Maybe he would consider her less appealing, her glamour would be dimmed with the inevitable changes that pregnancy would shortly bring. Would he think that he was too old for fatherhood, nappies and sleepless nights? Would the new arrival prove too trying at his age? He was only a little younger than her husband. She wondered when she would tell Ernest? When should she go and see the doctor? All these thoughts crowded her tired mind, until she could not make sense of anything.......and she drifted off to sleep, fully clothed.

"Mavis?! What on earth are you doing? It's ten o'clock!" She awoke with a start. The room was in darkness now, and she felt confused, not knowing where she was or even what day it was. She sat up, rubbing her eyes. Ernest stood in the doorway, a mug of cocoa in his hand. "I must have drifted off!" She rose to her feet unsteadily, Ernest just catching her in time as she stumbled over her slippers which she had place near the bed, almost spilling his cocoa in the process.

"Really, Mavis! If this sort of behaviour is a result of the late night you had last night, you had better not have any more of them! Come on, it's time for bed!" Filled anew with resentment at her husband's stern and sarcastic manner, she followed him back to their bedroom, but it was a long time before she was able to fall asleep.

It seemed she had only been asleep a few minutes when she had to get up again to pass urine. How annoying, she thought to herself as she staggered sleepily along the landing in the darkness, groping for the light in the bathroom. As she slipped back into bed, Ernest turned over irritably.

"What a racket you were making," he grumbled, "it was like hearing a horse passing water!" Mavis was too tired to retaliate, and fell back to sleep almost immediately. Her slumber was plagued with dreams of babies (who all had mops of untidy hair, just like Seamus) crawling through Bethel chapel, all clamouring for their daddy, searching for Seamus, while the congregation looked on in horror.

There were no babies in chapel the following morning, just the usual crowd of devout Baptists, some reluctant children straggling in behind their parents and the vapid Gladys Williams thumping out the hymns on the organ. How Mavis managed to last the whole service, she never knew, but she made it through to the end without having to rush outside to be sick. Sitting next to Eiddwen in the front pew, she wondered if her friend could guess that she was pregnant. Did she look any different? Maybe she was paler than usual? She tried to concentrate on the service. Ernest's sermon was based on the wedding at Cana. Wryly, she considered his narrow-minded views about alcohol. Would he have refused to drink the best wine that Jesus was supposed to have conjured up when the wedding ran dry? Suddenly, her tummy gave a loud rumble, just as Ernest pausing for dramatic effect. Eiddwen looked at her and stifled a giggle. Mavis tried to hide a smile. She hadn't eaten anything yet, being unable to face breakfast. After the sermon was over, and the organ started up again for the final hymn, Eiddwen whispered discreetly, "Would you be able to come over for a little chat before you make the dinner, Mavis? I would be so grateful if you could?" Eiddwen looked beseechingly at her friend, her little face full of hope.

"Yes, of course." Mavis spoke quietly, keeping her eyes straight ahead, watching her husband descend ceremoniously from the pulpit. "I'll come with you straight away, once we've finished here." And Ernest can sort out the potatoes, she thought crossly. She was becoming increasingly irritated by his surliness; he didn't really intimidate her, apart from when he had slapped her that day, but his dour manner was beginning to wear her down and she constantly felt as though she was in a state of alert. He was mildly surprised when she told him she was going to Eiddwen's, but did not make a fuss.

The two women were settled down in Eiddwen's kitchen, drinking tea. Her twin sisters had stayed behind in chapel to help count the collection, and her brothers were away in Haverfordwest, visiting relatives. Mavis' tummy gave another loud rumble.

"Any biscuits, Eiddwen? I'm starving!" Eiddwen looked at her in shock. Mavis never ate biscuits, cakes or anything like that.

"Um....yes, I'll have a look. Hopefully the twins will have left a few Garibaldi's behind after they raided the pantry yesterday evening." Eiddwen watched in fascination as Mavis ploughed her way through the remaining biscuits in the tin box, shovelling them in one after another, hardly chewing them properly in her haste to eat them.

"So, Eiddwen, what do you want to tell me?" Mavis dampened her finger in order to pick up the remaining crumbs. Eiddwen looked down at her hands, neatly folded in her lap, and sighed.

"Oh, Mavis. Is it possible to be really happy, yet sad at the same time? Please don't breathe a word of this to anyone, not even Ernest - especially not Ernest - but the professor has asked me to become engaged to him." She paused, and looked up to see Mavis' reaction.

"But that's wonderful news!" Mavis protested. "Why should it be a secret? And why are you so unhappy?"

"Well, the professor – Archie, I should say – he is an atheist, and would not consider for one moment getting married in a church or chapel. And there's the promise I made to mam when she died."

"What d'you mean?" Mavis glanced up, sharply.

"I promised to live here and look after the others, being as they are so much younger than me...." Her voice trailed away, lamely.

"For heaven's sake, Eiddwen! The twins are thirty-three years old! And your brothers are out more than they are in! You should do what you want!"

"Maybe." Eiddwen sighed. "I am so happy that he has asked me, and, oh, Mavis, it is so wonderful to be in love! But, of course, you know what that is like, having been married to Ernest for three years!"

"Yes, of course." Mavis said nothing else, but allowed her friend the time to talk at length. Eiddwen rambled on, sometimes laughing and smiling with joy, then breaking down in tears as she faced the potential difficulties she would have to overcome.

"And he has bought me a ring as well," she said finally, drying her eyes with a handkerchief. "He brought it down from Scotland for me, it's a bit big, actually and I can't let anyone see it, so I wear it around my neck on a chain. Look." She pulled out a necklace from inside her sweater, and showed Mavis a beautiful sapphire ring, which twinkled and sparkled on the silver chain. The stone was large, and was surrounded with tiny diamonds. The delight and pride in Eiddwen's eyes was touching to say the least, and Mavis had difficulty swallowing, due to the lump in her throat. She reached forwards and took Eiddwen's hands in hers. "Eiddwen Lewis. You are a fortunate woman to have found love at your time in life. Don't let it go. Keep hold, be brave and to hell with your bloody sisters!" Eiddwen stared in disbelief. Mavis swearing?!

Unable to bear it any longer, Mavis reluctantly got up. "I have to go back, Ernest will burn the potatoes! But I will see you tomorrow!" Eiddwen stood at the front door, watching her friend hurrying away. She replaced the ring underneath her sweater, and retreated to the gegin fach to put her vegetables on to boil and to consider her future.

Mavis walked home briskly. How she envied her friend, how lucky she was to have found a man who adored her, and whom she was free to marry. Mavis was certain she could persuade Eiddwen to stand up to her family and do what was best for her. As she passed Seamus' house, she thought it was ironic that his arrival in Llannon had been resulted in so many tumultuous events and upheaval in their lives: feeling passion and true love for the first time in her own life, her best friend discovering her soul-mate and of course, most significantly, becoming pregnant with Seamus' child. Arriving at her cottage, she opened the door. The smell of burning potatoes hit her, and she rushed upstairs to be sick.

Chapter Nineteen

The Elevation of Status

The next few weeks proved a trial for Mavis. Her proud and wilful nature did not bend easily to the demands and changes that the small life within her dictated. It was hard for her to disguise her nausea, and eat normally. Even though her stomach remained as flat as ever, she had difficulty in doing up her brassieres, and her breasts, whilst still firm and pert, felt like a couple of large, bruised apples. Ernest seemed to notice nothing unusual, and was his usual, dour self. When she visited her mother and her sisters, they were so absorbed in their own petty squabbles, any change in Mavis completely passed them by.

She had gone down to Llanelli as planned, and had posted her letter to Seamus. There had been no reply from him when she had last gone to check his house, but she had refused to allow this to dishearten her, instead she decided to channel her energy into tidying the place, cleaning it within an inch of its scruffy existence. However, things came to a head sooner than she would have liked. One Tuesday morning, she had gone in to work at the shop as usual. Mr Griffiths had decided to carry out a stock-take, and wanted Mavis to help him. It was not heavy work, but involved her having to climb up the step-ladder to fetch boxes down from the top shelves, a job which Mr Griffiths found difficult, being rather plump and far less sprightly than the nimble Mavis. The day was humid, she hadn't been able to eat any breakfast. As she climbed up the steps for what seemed to be the hundredth time, she could hear Eva singing to herself in the back room, enjoying her precious day off. Reaching up for the final box of cigarettes, she started to feel faint, only just managing to climb down in time before collapsing in a heap on the shop floor.

"Eva! Quick! It's Mavis!" Mr Griffiths was in such a state of panic that he didn't know what to do. His wife bustled in, wondering what on earth had happened. She took one look at the prostrate Mavis, and was immediately back on duty once more. Swiftly, she placed Mavis on her side, asking her urgently, "Are you alright? Can you hear me, Mavis?"

Mavis started to come round, lifting her head groggily off the floor.

"Keep quite still. I think you fainted. I just want to make sure that's all it was before you get up. Fetch a glass of water for Mrs Watton, and my nurse's bag as well." Her husband scuttled off to do as he was told, glad to be of some use in a situation which terrified him.

"Oh, I'm so sorry, Eva, I didn't want to make a fuss. I don't know what came over me." Mavis struggled to sit up, but Eva made her lie back down again.

"What are you doing?" Mavis watched in puzzlement as Eva fastened a tight cuff around her arm. She winced slightly.

"I'm just checking your blood pressure. Don't worry, it will feel quite tight." Mavis winced as the cuff tightened on her upper arm.

"It is a little low, but perfectly normal." Eva let the pressure down, and offered Mavis some water. "Have a little sip, no more. Did you hurt yourself when you fell?" Mavis shook her head. "Are you ill or something?" She looked at Mavis intently.

"No, not unwell or ill, Eva....." Mavis sought for the right response, but failed. Eva glanced up sharply, a knowing look upon her face. "Are you pregnant?" There was no point denying it. Mavis nodded mutely, twisting the material of her skirt anxiously, feeling vulnerable under this scrutiny. "How far gone?"

"Er, I'm not exactly sure. Maybe about a couple of months? Maybe more? I don't know."

"When was your last period? Any idea at all?"

"Um....March? May? I honestly can't remember."

"Does Ernest know?" Mavis shook her head. "No-one knows. I guessed I may be expecting a couple of weeks ago, but wasn't sure.....I am forty-three after all. I didn't know what to do." Eva rolled her eyes in exasperation, very much the professional.

"Honestly! For someone who is usually assertive and in control, you have changed into a dithering shadow of your former self. But then, that's what pregnancy tends to do to women! Your colour is better now, can you get up?" She helped Mavis to her feet, taking her in to the back room where she made her sit down in a comfortable armchair. She frowned down at Mavis. "So. We can't keep this a secret much longer, can we?"

Mavis smiled to herself as Eva stood with her hands on her hips, treating her like a patient already. But she didn't want anyone to know, not just yet. Despite the fact that he was hundreds of miles away across the Irish Sea, Mavis thought that she should write and tell Seamus first, as he was the father of her baby.

"Before I tell Ernest anything, what should I do, Eva? Do I see the doctor or what?"

Eva laughed gently. "No need for that. Dr Hodges and I have an excellent working relationship, and I will inform him about the situation. Leave everything with me, and I will organise a test to be done at Llanelli Hospital. Then we can sort out the following appointments with the doctor."

Mavis looked up in horror. "A test? What sort of test?"

"A urine test. Don't worry, Mavis, it's all very discreet. You provide a specimen of your early morning urine, then take it down to Llanelli General Hospital. This will confirm your pregnancy. But, cariad, you had better get used to some mildly unpleasant or uncomfortable tests being carried out over the next few months, and put your dignity away in a drawer, not to be brought out again until you have had the baby!" She smiled reassuringly at Mavis, who did not feel reassured at all. Eva was right. She felt totally out of control, she was having to submit to the will of others, and she didn't like it one bit. Then she thought of Seamus, and what he would say. He would laugh at her worries, tease her until she laughed too, and he would make her see sense. Well, he wasn't here, so she would have to pretend he was, and compose herself. "Thank you, Eva. You are very kind. But if you wouldn't mind, please say nothing to Ernest until everything is confirmed. I don't want any false alarms." And buy myself time, she thought to herself.

"You have my word. I cannot breach confidentiality, anyway!" Eva returned to her bag, and pulled out a form. As she rapidly filled it out, she added, "Pass some urine first thing in the morning, into a small, washed jam jar or something, then take it down to the path lab in the General the same day. It must be the first time you pass water that day, or the results won't be accurate." She handed the completed form to Mavis. "Now you go home and have some rest. I will tell Mr Griffiths you have a stomach upset, and won't be in work until you feel a bit better. But, honestly, Mavis, once you have passed the first three months, you won't feel so sick and you will have adjusted."

"How can a urine test show that I am pregnant?" Mavis was curious, wanting to know more, despite her reluctance to accept any interventions in her pregnancy.

"When you are pregnant, your body produces a hormone, a tiny, natural chemical." Eva was on a roll, now, enjoying her teaching role. "The hormone is called human chorionic gonadotrophin - we call it HCG as it is a bit of a mouthful - and the lab will be able to detect it in your urine. That will confirm your pregnancy."

Mavis got up to leave.

"And you make sure you have something to eat once you get home." Mavis nodded obediently. She supposed she would have to get used to obeying instructions from now on, but felt her natural stoicism would see her through. She walked home slowly, having hidden the form in her handbag. Tomorrow, she would take the sample down to Llanelli, and at the same time would post her letter to Seamus. But first, it had to be written.

Mavis merely told Ernest that she had a stomach upset so had been told to go home. Once she was certain that he was busy in the garden, mowing the lawn, then planting potatoes, hoping for a second crop in a few months, she slipped upstairs to write to Seamus.

My dear Seamus,

I know I am writing out of turn, but I have to tell you something important. This is a very difficult time for me, as you will realise once you have read the letter. I had planned to let you know my news the morning you left for Ireland, but fate took a hand and the opportunity was lost.

I have kept my little secret safe until this morning, when it became a secret no longer.

My darling man, I am having a baby, and the baby is yours. There can be no doubt about it. I realised I was pregnant the night of your dinner party, and since I had not been intimate with Ernest for several months before that, the child is certainly yours. The only other person who knows is Eva Griffiths (the midwife, whose husband I work for.) I fainted when in work this morning, and she guessed at once. She has to keep it confidential, from a professional perspective. I have no idea what thoughts will be going through your mind as you read this, all I can hope is that they are not bad ones. I never thought for a million years that I would have a baby at forty-three. (There. That's another secret disclosed! You always said you would find out!) I feel excited, terrified and joyful all at the same time - is that possible? Excited that I am to be a mother, and will join that exclusive, elite group. Terrified at what lies ahead of me, will everything go well? Will it hurt unbearably? Joyful that, whatever becomes of us, I will always have a little part of you in my life – forever. I make no demands on you, my love. This has happened, so be it. But it was important that you should know - and (apart from Eva) be the first to know. With regards to Ernest's reaction, given my earlier information about my marital relationship, well, my dearest love, in order to protect myself (and you) I took measures to ensure that he will think the child is his, as soon as I found out. I think you know what I imply. Please forgive me for this deceit, but it was necessary. You transformed my life from the moment you arrived in Llannon, and now you have transformed my life in the most wonderful way imaginable. I hope you will reply. I hope you will not be angry or disappointed. I love you so very much, and I always will.

Mavis. Xxx

She sighed, then sealed the letter, hiding it once more before returning downstairs to the kitchen, where she hastily made herself some scrambled eggs and toast, devouring it in five minutes, before reproducing her late breakfast soon after in the bathroom.

The half-past nine bus rumbled down towards Llanelli, with an anxious Mavis on board. Thankfully, it was quite empty and the journey passed in a haze. It was all Mavis could do to keep down her meagre breakfast of a single piece of toast, as the bus lurched its way along the country road. At least the sun shone, which helped to lift her spirits. She needn't have worn the white angora shrug, it was warm enough to have gone without. Her cream shift wafted gently about her knees in the breeze from the open window, and Mavis started to feel better. The letter to Seamus was tucked safely inside her handbag, along with her urine specimen which she had wrapped in a brown paper bag, appropriated from the shop before she had left the previous day. She hoped she would remember the way to the hospital, as she had only been there once before. Young Wendy had managed to jam her finger in the door one day whilst Mavis and Ernest had been visiting the Bakers, and as Mr Baker had been in work, Ernest had driven everyone to Casualty, where Wendy's finger had been found to be unharmed. Alighting from the bus in a quiet Stepney Street, Mavis made her way to the General Post Office, a rather grand building across the road from the cinema. She pulled the letter from her bag, and before handing it to the assistant for overseas posting, first class, she discreetly kissed it. Back outside, in the pleasant sunshine, she turned left up Murray Street. Maybe she should see if she could catch a bus - but she didn't know where to find one. Or a taxi? That would be an unnecessary expense, she thought. Resolutely, she continued on her way. She knew that if she headed for the the Nonconformnist chapel, Capel Als, at the bottom of Marble Hall Road, the hospital would be found at the top of the hill. She only had to stop to ask the way once, and was soon climbing up the steep Marble Hall Road. It was hard going in the sunshine, and she wondered how difficult it would be when she was heavily pregnant. She considered what it would be like to live in one of the terraced houses which lined the street. How strange to live on such a steep hill, and have to climb up and down it every day. Even stranger, what must it be like to have neighbours on each side of you, so they could hear everything that went on in your house, unless the walls were particularly thick. Mavis noted with approval that each house was immaculately presented, with sparkling windows, net curtains and scrubbed doorsteps. She supposed it was necessary to have net curtains at one's windows when passers-by could peer in and see into one's front room. Her legs ached with the unaccustomed effort, and she was relieved to arrive at the hospital. As she entered the main entrance, which was also the out-patients entrance, she watched admiringly as the nurses bustled to and fro, wearing their smart, striped uniforms, their starched white caps perfectly positioned on their heads and their aprons tightly belted around their neat waists. They appeared so competent and efficient. Then the smell of disinfectant hit her nostrils and she felt a wave of anxiety wash over her. Why did hospitals have to smell so, well, hospital-like? She looked in vain for a sign which would direct her to the path lab, and felt her frustration mounting as she walked along corridor after corridor, unable to find it. It was bad enough having to be in the hospital anyway, without wandering about, increasing the risk of bumping into someone she knew. Finally, she came across a hospital porter, pushing a trolley full of linen towards the casualty department. "Excuse me," she began, imperiously, "where is the path lab?" She hoped he couldn't guess the reason for her visit.

"Back there." The porter grunted his reply, and started on his way again

"What do you mean?" Mavis asked, annoyed at his rudeness. "I just walked through that corridor and there were no signs for the path lab!" The porter sighed tiredly. "It's right there. In front of you, if you turn around." He pointed at the wall. Mavis frowned.

"But that says "Pathology." I am looking for the path lab......" Her voice trailed away in embarrassment. The porter ambled away, shaking his head. Thus informed, Mavis hurried down yet another corridor until she arrived at the elusive path lab. It was actually just outside the main body of the hospital, in a pre-fabricated building. A small, owl-like woman in a white overall was sitting behind the counter. She scowled at Mavis.

"Yes?" she snapped.

"Er....I was told to hand this in." She fumbled around in her handbag for the form and sample. The woman snatched the form from her and held out her hand for the pickled onion jar, which was all Mavis had been able to find.

"First urine of the day?" The owl woman glared at Mavis through her thick-lensed glasses. Mavis nodded, starting to blush.

"Good. You'd only have to repeat it if it wasn't." Turning around to some hidden colleague behind a hatch in the wall, she called out. "Another pregnancy test, Dafydd! You can go to break then." Mortified, Mavis turned and rushed from the building as fast she decently could.

The next few days were uneventful. Eva had said it would be about a week before any results would come through, but had reassured Mavis that she would personally telephone the hospital to ask for the results by the end of the week. However, there was no doubt whatsoever in Mavis' mind. The changes taking place within her were becoming more obvious, and she didn't think she would be able to keep her secret from Ernest for much longer. Her appetite was atrocious, it was hard to keep food down in the morning and she kept getting up in the night to pass water. Also, her breasts strained painfully against the rigid scaffolding of her brassieres, spilling out over the top, and blue veins now completed the maternal look. She hadn't bothered going back to the shop, either, as Eva had advised her not to. Ernest did not trouble himself to broach this with her, he didn't really approve of her going out to work. Mavis' place was at home, looking after him.

On Friday morning, she woke at dawn. Pulling on her favourite red cotton dress, she brushed her hair and soon after crept out of the house taking Dai with her, leaving Ernest snoring gently in bed. The morning was cool, the sky was overcast and the whole world seemed to be still asleep. She started to make for the track, then, unable to resist the temptation, knowing full well that she was setting herself up for disappointment, she turned back and went towards Seamus' house. She tied Dai up to the leg of a chair which had been left outside after the party, and quietly opened the door. Her heart was in her mouth as she made her way to the front porch. A few letters lay on the doormat. Quickly, she sifted through them. One electricity bill, two letters from London and a folded up note, which had obviously been hand-delivered. Nothing for her. With shaking hands she opened the note, thinking with a sinking heart that it may be from Gladys Williams. But no, it was merely an invoice from the Co-operative store in Felinfoel. She lowered herself onto the bottom step of the staircase. Nothing for her. Maybe Seamus had forgotten all about her. Maybe life was so hectic and demanding over in Ireland that she had become of secondary importance. Perhaps he had even met a far more suitable Irish woman, who was free to marry him. These tortured thoughts crowded her head as she locked the door behind her, before departing once more for the track. At six o'clock, there was no-one else about, which pleased her. She craved peace and solitude in order to wallow in her self-pity and despair. Only birdsong broke the silence, and the gentlest of summer breezes caressed her sad face. Dai kept pace with her, stopping occasionally to sniff at a clump of dandelions or to lift his leg. A succession of scents wafted in the air – buddleia, heavy with promise and almost cloying in its sweetness ; then the smell of hops from the brewery a few miles down the road; finally, new mown hay, cut by the farmers the night before, ready to be rolled into neat bundles. Maybe it was her pregnancy, but all her senses seemed more acute than usual. However, as much as she loved the countryside, and appreciated its early morning beauty, her mood could not be lifted. Her thoughts swung relentlessly across the Irish Sea. How would she continue to live her life, knowing that the father of her child may no longer love her? How fragile their supposed love was, then, if it could be destroyed as quickly as that. Had she been nothing but a gullible little fool, allowing herself to be seduced by an opportunist philanderer .....but it hadn't seemed like that at all. How could she exist in her claustrophobic marriage, never again to see her baby's father? Was she going to be able to cope with the turmoil of emotion she was experiencing? After ten minutes of walking, she sat down on a large boulder which was situated at the side of the track. When she had been a child, it had been called the "Thinking Stone" and had been the agreed meeting place for many secret escapades and games. She put her head on her knees and closed her eyes, remembering a time when her life was straightforward and uncomplicated. The minutes ticked by and the climbing sun warmed her cotton-clad shoulders. Dai pulled slightly on his lead.

"Quiet, boy," Mavis soothed the dog. But he strained even harder. Squirrels, thought Mavis. She tightened her hold on the lead, then looked up in alarm as she heard someone running quickly towards her. Someone calling out her name. Someone with the dearest face in the world.

"Seamus!" She jumped to her feet and, forgetting Dai, ran towards him, her arms outstretched. He pulled her into his arms, and hugged her as though he would never let her go.

"Oh, my darling, beautiful, otterly stupid woman!" He breathed in the perfume of her hair as he murmured into her ear, before kissing her as softly, and as passionately as he had done the very first time. As they pulled apart, he looked down at her, concern etched into his features. "You shouldn't be running like that! Anything could happen!" She looked up at him, her eyes wide and full of uncertainty.

"You know? About the baby?"

"Of course I fecking know! That's why I came rushing back as quickly as I could!"

"But I just left your house. There was no letter there for me! I thought it would take a while for my last letter to reach you."

"Both your letters arrived together, yesterday. Typical of the bloody Irish postal system, all or nothing. As soon as I had the letter informing me about the baby, I jumped on the next ferry, the eight o'clock sailing last night, and I didn't stop travelling until I was here in your arms again."

Mavis shook her head in delighted disbelief. "How did you know I was here? I left your house ages ago. You couldn't have seen me."

"I know. But I just dumped my bags in the house and made my own way up here. It was so early I thought you would still be asleep. I know it sounds crazy, but I knew you liked walking up here, so I came anyway, hoping all the time that you would soon be up and about." Mavis smiled, for what seemed like the first time in weeks. "You are a crazy man, Seamus! But it is so wonderful to have you back. Pinch me! Am I dreaming?"

"Not dreaming, my sweet Mavis!" He scooped her up in his arms and carried her to where she had been sitting, so despondently, a few moments ago. "This stone is big enough for two, and you have such a delectably tiny bottom! Shall we sit here a while?" The couple sat down on the boulder, entwined in each other's arms, saying nothing at all for the next few minutes, relishing the fact that they could touch each other, satisfied with the moment. Eventually, he pulled away from her slightly, and caressed her stomach, gently. "My baby," he murmured in wonder, "how big is it now? There doesn't seem much room for it in there! You don't look pregnant at all!"

"The baby is due around February, I think. I am waiting for the test results, but that is just a formality. How can you say I don't look pregnant?! I feel so different."

"Have you told Ernest?"

Mavis shook her head. "I would have had to quite soon, though. Oh, Seamus - you aren't angry about what I had to do? In order to make sure he would think he was the father?" She looked up at him anxiously. But he hugged her closer.

"No, my sweet woman." He sighed heavily. "But I so wish things could have been different. I wish you lived in a more liberated community, where you could just pack your bags and tell Ernest you were leaving him. And then we could be together, and be happy." Mavis remained silent, hating herself for lacking the courage to do as he suggested, despising herself for causing him pain. She lay her head on his shoulder and closed her eyes. Two blackbirds provided the perfect background harmony, with the occasional bleating sheep joining in. Dai interrupted them by deciding he had had enough of staying still and being ignored. He nuzzled into Mavis' knees, and started to paw at Seamus' shabby grey trousers. In turn, they patted his white head absent mindedly.

"How long are you back for?" Mavis was almost afraid to ask the question, let alone hear the answer. She fiddled with the buttons on his shirt, twisting and turning them in her anxiety, then allowed her small fingers to burrow into the hairs on his chest, winding them painfully into tendrils, as was her wont. He seemed oblivious to the discomfort; he sighed, closing his eyes in extreme tiredness.

"Only until Sunday evening. Then I have to catch the boat train, and return home." He opened his eyes again and looked at her. "My mother is stable at the moment, and all the family are with her. But my sister returns to London on Tuesday, my uncle Dermot is a total alcoholic and everyone else concerned is running about like headless chickens. I am sorry."

Mavis hugged him so hard that it made him catch his breath.

"Don't say sorry! I am so pleased you are here! I am so God damned happy you are here! You have no idea how delighted and amazed I am!" She burst into tears, and wept without restraint.

"Oh, to be so happy and yet sad in one single moment." He smiled wryly, and held her tightly, for what seemed like a lifetime, cherishing the closeness, suspended in time and oblivious to their surroundings.

Seamus pulled away eventually. "I don't suppose for one moment you can meet me this afternoon?" The hope in his voice was almost painful to hear.

"Well, I expect I can arrange something!" The old sparkle returned to her eyes. "I have to pop down to the shop at two o'clock to have my results from Eva, and Ernest is supposed to be down at Felinfoel by half-past to sort out a family baptism with the deacon at Adulam. So yes, my love, I can be with you this afternoon." She smiled up at him, her world so different from the one only half an hour earlier. "I suppose we had better set off now. It's almost half past six, and the brewery workers will start using the path, or even Mad Alice! We shouldn't really be seen together!"

Seamus looked at her incredulously. "Mad Alice?"

"I'll tell you later!" Mavis laughed. "You go on ahead, then I will follow at a respectable distance." Reluctantly, he started to walk away.

"See you later, alligator." His smile crinkled his eyes.

"Okey dokey, Mr Smokey!" She giggled in response. She watched him amble along the track, his easy gait so familiar to her, and she wondered anew what would become of them. He walked away, getting smaller and further from her.....then she started to follow him home.

Ernest seemed in an irritable mood when Mavis returned. He was in the kitchen, polishing his shoes. She wished he wouldn't do that so close to the table.

"You were out early." He scowled at her. Her heart sank. How on earth could she break the news to him when he was always in such a difficult mood?

"Yes. I couldn't sleep."

He looked up at her sharply. "Well, see the doctor, then, if you can't sleep." Now's my chance, she thought, but he stalked past her into the hallway, returning with his briefcase, which he used for all his chapel documents. The opportunity faded away.

"I thought you didn't have to be in Adulam chapel until half-past two," Mavis remarked, "why are you getting ready now?"

"I have to go earlier. The deacon in Felinfoel wants to bring the meeting forward to ten o'clock, as the family are travelling back to Cardiff this afternoon." Mavis' heart sank. Her chance of being with Seamus seemed unlikely now.

"So you'll be wanting a late lunch, then?" She asked, forlornly. To her surprise, he shook his head.

"No. I have arranged to meet with Miss Gladys Williams to discuss the Harvest anthems. She cannot get transport herself, so I will be collecting her from her mother's house at two o'clock. We will be at Bethel for quite some time, I suppose. And Mrs Williams has unfortunately offered to make me lunch." Mavis nodded understandingly. Mrs Williams was probably the worst cook in Llanelli. But she found it hard to conceal her delight. Her plans could go ahead after all.

"Very well, I won't bother making anything special for lunch. Instead, we will have a fine supper." And I will make it a good time to tell him the news, she thought, fill his tummy and his mood should be better. She set about planning the meal, rummaging through the well-stocked pantry, remembering she had boiled some ham earlier in the week. Some new potatoes, peas from the garden and parsley sauce should do the trick. Ernest left the house soon after half-past nine, leaving Mavis scrubbing the tiny potatoes at the sink. She didn't dare peel them, that would have been considered extravagant. As soon as she had finished, she went up to the bedroom to have a lie down. Tiredness such as this she had never experienced before. Within a few minutes she was snoring gently, relaxing into a dreamless sleep, and not waking until eleven o'clock.

Mavis enjoyed the luxury of a long soak in the bath, then massaged some Vaseline into her breasts and abdomen, having first mixed it with a few drops of L'Interdit perfume. She hoped she wouldn't have stretch marks; maybe if she kept her skin smooth and supple she wouldn't. Mavis vowed to moisturise her skin every single day. How dreadful it would be if her skin became marked and unsightly. She had never seen stretch marks, but they sounded terrible. The few married friends she had had remarked that once the babies had been born, their bodies were never the same again, with flabby tummies, bladders that had become unreliable and of course, the dreaded stretch marks. But those had been brief, covert conversations, ones that Mavis had just caught the end of, being of that alien race, a childless woman. She could not bear the thought of becoming undesirable to Seamus. But it was all out of her control. All she could do was hope.

By midday she emerged from her bedroom, fresh as a daisy, dressed in an old pink gingham dress, which clung enticingly to her hourglass figure, accentuating her still-small waist and womanly hips, and flirting below her tanned knees like a flag on a dainty ship. She peeped out of the kitchen window, up at the hills. Only six hours had passed since she had been up on the track with Seamus, yet it felt like days.

The track, the scene of so many emotional highs and lows for her, and it drew her like a magnet so frequently. She sighed. Time for something to eat, she thought, and wandered over to the pantry. What should she have, she wondered, casting her eyes over the cheddar cheese, cold beef and the bara Gwenyth from Jenkins' baker shop down near the station. Ernest had gone into town shopping with her yesterday, and had popped down to buy the bread, as they both enjoyed it so much, leaving her to browse in Marks and Spencers.

A few minutes later she was tucking in to cheese on toast, with sliced tomatoes on the side. She could never bear the taste of tomatoes actually with the cheese, she didn't know why, but it turned her stomach, and even more so now that she was pregnant. With a bit of luck, the meal would stay put and give her much-needed energy.

The shop was empty of customers when Mavis arrived at two o'clock as agreed with Eva. "Prynhawn da, Mr Griffiths." He looked up from reading the paper.

"Oh, hello, Mrs Watton. Eva is in the back. Go through. Are you feeling better?"

"Much better, thank you." And smiling at him over her shoulder, she went through to the Griffiths' living room. Eva Griffiths was in her uniform, writing up some case notes. "Well, Mavis. Your test confirms that you are indeed going to be a mammy." She smiled broadly. "Better late than never!"

"Well, I suppose so." Mavis smiled nervously back, not sure what to expect next.

"I'll just make us a cup of tea and then I'll go through what we need to do."
Mavis sat down anxiously, her heart beating quickly. Over the tea, which was much too strong for Mavis' liking, Eva shuffled some important looking papers and wrote down Mavis' date of birth, address and other required details. "So, Mavis, you are forty-three. Now that is what we would call an elderly primip." Mavis nearly choked on her tea.

"Me? Elderly?!" She spluttered furiously. "That is so insulting!"

Eva grinned wickedly. "I realise it does sound rather strange, but it is purely a midwifery term. As this is your first child, you are a primipara, but as you are over the age of thirty, you are considered elderly, purely from an obstetric perspective. So don't go having a tantrum when you hear yourself described as such!"

Mavis said nothing, but glowered into her tea, which she no longer felt able to drink. Eva took no notice of her mood, and carried on regardless. "I will book you in for Brynglas Maternity Home, and your ante-natal care will be carried out by me, possibly the obstetrician and your GP. If all goes well, and your blood pressure remains normal, there is no reason why you should have to travel to Carmarthen or Swansea for more specialised care."

Mavis looked horrified. "Eva, this sounds terrible. I am not ill! I am having a baby!"

Eva looked up sharply, suddenly looking serious. "I agree, Mavis. However, things are changing for women, and increasingly, doctors are taking over the care of women in childbirth. As a midwife, with many years of experience, I know full well that I am far better equipped to supervise a woman's pregnancy than any doctor who has been qualified just a few years. Rest assured, you will have the best care, you and your little baby will want for nothing, not while I have any say in the matter!"

Mavis looked at her in astonishment. Never before had she seen Eva so passionate; her normally pale face was flushed with annoyance, and her green eyes were bright with anger.

"Why, thank you, Eva." Mavis got up to leave. "I suppose I will be telling Ernest my news this evening. He is out at the moment, down in Felinfoel, then he said he had to meet up with our delightful organist Gladys to sort hymns out."

Eva glanced at her. "You watch that one, Mavis. She is poisonous."

"Don't worry, I will." Mavis smiled wryly and made her way back through the shop, bidding Mr Griffiths farewell as she went.

The world was her friend as she tripped lightly up the lane to Seamus' house; the sun had never shone so brightly, neither had the birds sung more sweetly and even the wild flowers seemed to nod greetings at her as they waved about in the summer breeze. She was going to meet the man whose very existence dominated her life, with whom she was passionately in love, and who was the father of her unborn child. Eira Jones waved at her as she passed by, pausing in her carpet beating to call out, "Lovely day, Mrs Watton!" Mavis waved back, smiling in return, hoping her neighbour would resume her activity and not notice where she was going. Fortunately for her, Eira's husband shouted out to his wife that he couldn't find his slippers, which sent her scuttling into her cottage. Mavis quickened her step, anxious to get to Seamus before anyone else appeared on the scene. The house stood tall and imposing as she pushed open the gate; she glanced up at it, thinking to herself how what a major part it had played in her life. The track and the house, she thought, chief players in her small world.

The garden was as wild and overgrown as ever, and the path could hardly be seen for all the daisies, dandelions and grass which had sprung up over the past few weeks. She smiled at the note which had been stuck on the front door – "I must not be disturbed. So if you don't have an appointment, (and if you do please come around the back,) kindly bugger off!" Following Seamus' advice, she made her way around the side of the house, and let herself in at the kitchen door.

And there he was, his back to her, busy putting the finishing touches to the frame of a painting which lay on the table. She paused for a moment, taking him in, enjoying the very sight of him. Even wearing his scruffy old trousers and a baggy grey shirt, his unusual height and his wild, long hair made him the stuff of a romantic novel. How could she not have noticed that when they first met? She cleared her throat. "Hello?"

He swung around, the widest of smiles lighting up his face. "She has come! The Queen of my Heart has come!" He scooped her up in his arms and hugged her tightly. "So? What news with the midwife? Are you indeed with child? My child...." he added softly, once again caressing her stomach. She buried her face in his chest, enjoying the familiar scent of his sweat and tobacco.

"I am indeed," she murmured.

"You must eat!" he exclaimed, releasing her and rushing to the pantry. "I must fatten you up! You have lost weight, sure to God you have! What'll you have? Pickled onions? Pregnant women always like pickled onions, don't they? But I draw the line at coal! I'll not be giving you any coal to eat!" Mavis burst out laughing. "I have already had some lunch! And yes, I have been quite poorly, with the morning sickness. But it does seem to be getting a bit better now. I am sure I will start blooming very soon!"

"Thanks be to God!" He looked relieved. "And I must say, sweet Mavis, that you have done a grand job of tidying the place up! Spick and span!" He took her hand and led her to the bottom of the stairs. She hung back, suddenly uncertain. "What's the matter?" He paused with one foot on the bottom step. "Is something wrong?"

For once Mavis was lost for words.

"I-er, um....d'you think we should? With the baby and everything?"

"Ah, I see. Don't worry, I have no unbridled and lustful designs on your body! Well – I may have! But I do want to undress you, to look at you, to stroke your skin, to hold you close..." He looked deep into her eyes. She melted. The familiar and irresistible sensations of desire and lust filled her soul. She lowered her eyes and smiled coyly.

"Lead the way, Mr O'Brien. I am sure I can trust you!"

She stood before him, her gingham dress a thing of the past, lying in a crumpled heap on his bedroom floor. He sat on his bed, observing her closely as she waited for his next move, quivering in her white cotton brassiere and knickers, her smooth brown legs as perfect and bow-like as ever. His eager hands reached up to fondle her breasts, straining as they were against the constraints of her underwear. "Jesus, you are so fecking gorgeous! You were adorable before, but now – oh, my fecking God, what a sight for a desperate man!" He stretched around her back and with one swift move undid her brassiere, flinging it dismissively into the corner of the room. With eyes full of wonder, he slowly massaged her full breasts, gently stroking them, then lifting each one worshipfully, before fastening his lips over each nipple in turn, softly sucking and licking them until they stood proud and erect. Any embarrassment or concern Mavis felt about her changed body disappeared in a moment, as she watched in fascination at the reverence Seamus was awarding it. He buried his face in her abdomen, carrying on his kissing and licking of her skin. She moaned in ecstasy. Carefully, he lay her down on the bed, then slowly removed her knickers. She opened her mouth to object, but he quietened her, putting his hand lightly over her mouth. "Ssh... Not a word. Relax and enjoy. There can be no harm in that, can there?" She closed her eyes obediently, and allowed him free reign over her body. He lay next to her on the bed, having first taken off his shirt. Nuzzling into her neck, he whispered endearments to her, then his mouth sought hers. Such tender, prolonged kisses followed, his tongue probing easily into her willing mouth, and all the while his hands moved further south, gliding easily over her moisturised skin, down to her thighs, then, oh bliss – between her legs. She was so ripe and ready for him, that she opened them almost involuntarily, letting his fingers begin their magic on her swollen rosebud. Within a few minutes, she had reached that pinnacle of enjoyment, and gasped in pleasure, shuddering in delight.

"Oh, you wanton, glorious woman," he murmured into her ear, "Christ, I want you so much."

"Then take me," she whispered back, her hands reaching down to undo his trousers, seeking his hardness with equal alacrity.

"Only if you're sure...?" He hesitated a moment, unwilling to make any wrong move.

"I'm sure. As sure as anything. All will be well. So take me, Seamus, take me right now!" Once undressed, he lowered himself on to her, propping himself up on his forearms, before entering her slowly and gently. He sighed with satisfaction and began rotating his hips without putting any pressure on her body.

"You are so hot, Mrs Watton, so very hot indeed! I am in grave danger of burning my member for Cockshire!" Mavis giggled, and responded to his circular movements by mirroring them herself.

"I like this new way of making love." She reached down to caress him between his legs. "I can reach other naughty parts of you! Ooh! Seamus! I can be your luggage handler!" She cupped his gonads in her hand. He laughed slyly. "Oh, wicked lady, that feels nice, to be sure! D'you like playing with my family jewels?" She slapped his buttocks playfully with her free hand. "Yes. I do. It feels nice."

Seamus continued his pelvic gyrations, then suddenly withdrew.

"What's the matter? Is something wrong?" Mavis sat up, concerned.

"Nothing at all, my wicked woman!" And he pulled her up and placed her on top of him. "I'm not as young as I was, and am so afraid of crushing you! Ride me, Mavis, ride me and make me a happy man!"

Mavis sat astride him, controlling things easily, and watching the expressions on his face. She ran her fingers through her hair, then caressed her own breasts, before reaching down and kissing him once more. "You little tease!" He convulsed as he climaxed, holding her close as the orgasmic spasms shot through him, again and again.

They lay there a while, not speaking, just holding each other. Mavis turned to him. "I love you, Seamus."

He stroked her hair. "I love you more. More than you can ever imagine." Then he reached down for his cigarettes by the side of the bed.

"D'you mind awfully if you don't smoke right now?" Mavis asked anxiously.

"Of course not! Why?" He looked puzzled.

"Cigarette smoke makes me feel sick!"

Seamus laughed and hugged her. "Well in that case, let's have a coffee!"

"I have to be thinking about going back soon. Ernest could come home, and I have no idea when that could be. But a quick coffee would be lovely."

They sat on the bed, Mavis wrapped in a sheet, and Seamus just wearing his trousers. "When do I see you next?" His question was direct and to the point. She sipped her coffee thoughtfully, concentrating, her brown eyes narrowed.

"Well, you only have tomorrow and the day after. So we shall have to exploit every single moment available. On Sunday you will be gone away again.... I had said to Ernest that I wanted to go into Llanelli tomorrow, to have a look around. He isn't particularly happy about that, so I could tell him that I want to go alone. He won't mind. He may well offer to take me down in the car, and fetch me, but I could meet you somewhere, like before? When we went out on your motorbike?"

Seamus looked at her in horror. "On my bike?! My dear woman, there is no way on this earth that I would allow you, the mother of my unborn child, to take a perilous ride on my bike! Have you taken leave of your senses? Anything could happen!" Mavis stared at him in wonder. Her new status as a pregnant woman seemed to be arousing quite a few passionate responses – she wondered what sort of response she would get from Ernest! "What do you mean?"

"It's far too dangerous! I will ride down to Llanelli, that's not a problem, but you, my sweet darling, will not be riding pillion! Can we get a train somewhere?"

"I know! Let's go to Kidwelly castle! The train station is only a short walk from the castle itself, and you would love it, I know you would!"

Seamus grinned in agreement. "That's a much better idea. What time shall I meet you in Llanelli, and where?"

Mavis thought quickly. "Meet me at Llanelli railway station at half-past ten. You will be able to leave your bike there quite safely. We will have to sit separately on the train, in case anyone sees us!"

Seamus frowned. "But what if you are seen anyway? What on earth would you be doing on a train and getting off at Kidwelly?"

"I have an aunt who lives on the road out of the village. I can always say I decided to visit her on a whim."

"And if she sees you? Sees us?"

Mavis chuckled. "Don't worry, she won't. She is bedbound and as mad a hatter anyway!"

He smirked. "Anyway...Kidwelly isn't a village! It's a town!"

"Are you sure?" Mavis glared at him in mock annoyance.

"As sure as you're alive! I know my stuff, before I came to South Wales, I did my homework!"

"Smart-Aleck!" Mavis punched him playfully in the chest, as he fended her off, laughing.

"Did you see what I was doing when you came in?" He drew her closer.

"Yes, well you were working on a frame or something?" She glanced up at him, quizzically. "I was. Your portrait. The unofficial one! I have completed it. I want to send it away, either to London or Paris, I haven't quite decided, for an exhibition. Are you willing?"

"Why shouldn't I be? I don't know anyone in Paris!" Mavis snuggled down into his arms. "I hope we will have a good day tomorrow!" Seamus smiled at her naivety, but said no more. He held her close, cherishing the moment.

"See you at half-past ten, then." He bent down to drop a kiss on her bare shoulder, before laying her down again, to start kissing her properly.

At four o'clock, Mavis said goodbye to Seamus and returned to her cottage. Ernest's car was parked neatly outside, but the kitchen door was closed. They usually kept it open except in the most inclement of weather. Maybe he had gone out with the dog, she thought. Even more surprising was that it was locked. Nobody locked their doors in Llannon, there was really no need. As she used her key to enter, she heard voices coming from the parlour. A woman's laughter filtered through into the kitchen. Mavis had no doubt whose it was. Silently, she tiptoed into the parlour. Gladys was sitting on Ernest's lap, her arms around his neck, giggling. Her tight red mini-skirt had ridden up her plump legs, showing acres of white, dimpled flesh. A pile of music manuscripts lay scattered on the carpet, disregarded and unimportant. Mavis stood like a statue, saying nothing, transfixed by the scene she was witnessing. She felt no emotion, but despised her supposedly pious and God-fearing husband, wondering anew at his double-standards, wondering how many times this sort of thing had happened before. Maybe there had been other women like Gladys, only too willing to befriend and entertain the strict Ernest Watton. She watched in lurid fascination as Ernest's hand crept up inside Gladys' skirt – where did he want his hand to go? she asked herself. She looked on in disbelief as Gladys wriggled in enjoyment, making no attempt to curtail his advances, instead opening her legs wider to invite his attentions, revealing a scarlet V of tight knickers. Ernest's fingers soon found their goal, burrowing inside the cheap, shiny fabric of Gladys' underwear. He grunted in satisfaction, and started to rub his hand between her chubby legs. Like a woman in a dream, Mavis was speechless and powerless to intervene. She would have remained there, paralysed, but Gladys started to moan and writhe, twisting and turning until she was facing Ernest, starting to unbutton her blouse. Brought back to reality with a snap, Mavis shook herself and stalked haughtily into the room.

"I really don't think that this is appropriate behaviour, Ernest." The freezing blast of her icy voice forced the pair to spring apart. "It is certainly not the way that any father of an unborn child should be acting, especially if he is a man of God."

Ernest jumped to his feet, causing Gladys to tumble to the floor in a most undignified fashion, her legs in the air, showing great tufts of black hair around her knicker legs, reminding Mavis of her portrait in Seamus' studio. She glanced down at Gladys.

"I think you'd better leave." Her tone was sharp and authoritative. Gladys didn't argue, but scrambled to her feet, gathered her manuscripts and hastily left the cottage without another word.

"It isn't what it seemed - I didn't mean to - she encouraged me, I - I......." Ernest's voice faltered. He had the grace to appear shamefaced.

"How long has this been going on?" Mavis turned her back on him and stalked out of the room into the kitchen, Ernest following her like a little puppy.

"Nothing has been going on, not really, she is a temptress, a loose woman! It wasn't my fault!"

Mavis swung around to face him, her eyes blazing. "Say what you like, Ernest! But at least have the decency to be more discreet! That woman is wicked indeed, and not in the way you think. She destroys people, and you seem to be her latest victim! Mark my words, you had better think twice before being alone in her company again."

Ernest rushed towards her, about to hug her, but she turned away from him. "Don't touch me. You pretend you are such a devout man, Ernest, yet you are deceitful and your whole life is a lie!" To her astonishment, Ernest went down on his knees, and held up his hands to her.

"Forgive me, Mavis! If you are expecting a baby, and I am to be a father once more, then please forgive me, for the sake of the child?" Mavis looked down at him in contempt, deploring his weakness.

"I'll think about it." she snapped. "Now leave me alone. I need to have a lie down. We will discuss this later." She ran upstairs to the spare room, gathering her thoughts rapidly. She really didn't care one jot what Ernest got up to, but she did know that Gladys could stir up serious trouble for all concerned. However, Mavis now had the upper hand, and Ernest would be every inch the contrite husband, in order to protect his reputation and maintain his status in the eyes of the local community. Gladys would have to be dismissed with immediate effect, that was certain. Thankfully, she lived far enough away in Felinfoel not to cause too many problems. Mavis was totally confident that Ernest would do exactly as she wished. Then she thought to herself, maybe here was her golden opportunity to leave Ernest, and start a new life with Seamus. But to stay in Llannon? With all the tongues wagging? And so near to Ernest? She needed to consider things very carefully indeed, play her cards close to her chest and keep her powder dry, as Seamus would say. Yes, she would be discreet, yet keep all her options open. Seamus would be returning to Ireland very soon, and would not be in a position to help or support her, so she must be patient. She closed her eyes, the only sound was the ticking of the clock as she drifted off to sleep, a half smile on her lips as she looked forward to making Ernest squirm at supper time....

She was roused from her nap by a hammering on the front door. Not a neighbour, then. She wondered where Ernest was, why he hadn't answered it.

Smoothing down her crumpled dress, she ran downstairs, seeing that Ernest was out chopping firewood and probably hadn't heard anything. Her head felt muzzy and she was still half-asleep as she slid back the heavy bolt of the door. To her astonishment, two angry young women stood there, identical twins, anger written all over their faces. Like a couple of vengeful furies, Eiddwen's sisters stood before her.

"What do you know about this?" squawked the taller one, waving an envelope in the air, her black ringlets shaking as she did so.

"You know our sister! You're her best friend! What's been going on?!" The shorter of the two scowled accusingly at Mavis. Gingerly, Mavis took the envelope from the first twin. It was addressed to no-one, and had been opened. Pulling out the letter, she read the following words.

Dear everyone,

I have run away with my fiancé, Professor Drummond. We will be married soon. Please don't be worried about me, I am very well. I will come home at some point. Please tell Mavis. Eiddwen.

To the twins' horror, Mavis threw the letter up in the air, laughing. "Well done, Eiddwen, well done!"

Chapter Twenty

The Serpentine Way of Things

The twins stood with their mouths hanging open for a minute, then turned around and marched away furiously, hissing at each other like a couple of angry vipers, looking over their shoulder, as they hurried down Bethel Lane. Mavis smiled in satisfaction as she watched them depart, her hands on her hips. Who would have thought it of Eiddwen? Mavis envied her, all the while feeling glad for her mouse-like friend. No doubt she'd get in touch once the furore had died down, and the chapel tongues no longer wagged, although that could take a few months......

Mavis closed the door.

Supper was a strained affair, Mavis for once behaving in an aloof and distant manner, with Ernest making several attempts to engage her in conversation. She knew full well that she was even more guilty than Ernest, but she was incensed at his blatant hypocrisy and total indiscretion. She toyed with her supper; Ernest's appetite seemed unaffected, and he wolfed down his ham and vegetables, having smothered them with parsley sauce. How genuine was his contrition, she wondered, pushing her peas aimlessly around the willow-patterned plate. She put her knife and fork to one side and watched him mopping up the last traces of sauce with a piece of bread.

"Very nice, Mavis, very nice indeed! I hope that if our baby is a girl, she will grow up to be as good a cook as her mother." He beamed at her. She cringed inwardly at his words, "our baby."

"When is the baby due?" He looked over at her, wiping his mouth on his handkerchief.

"February, I think." Mavis got up to clear away the dishes.

"When did you find out? Have you seen the doctor? I suppose you had better start looking for a pram. Nothing but the best for my child! " There was no actual concern in his voice — as to how she was feeling, he was absorbed in opening a packet of biscuits to eat with his tea. "And if you have to buy the most expensive milk for the baby, so be it!" With a self-satisfied grunt, he started to munch away on a Rich Tea biscuit. Mavis glanced over at him, momentarily surprised.

"Oh, but I won't be needing baby milk, Ernest. I will feed the baby myself." He looked up sharply, his eyes hardening in disapproval.

"I'll not have you exposing yourself! No wife of mine will be allowed to do that!"

"Really?" There was a steely edge to Mavis' voice. "I disagree with you, Ernest, and the baby will be breastfed. Eva has advised me how important it is for the baby, and as she is the midwife, I think I should heed that advice, don't you?" She stared at him defiantly, daring him to dispute Eva's opinion. He spluttered on his tea, acknowledging defeat, changing the subject quickly in order to save face.

"When shall we tell Fred and Audrey?"

"Enough questions, Ernest, I'm tired of them." Abruptly, she left the kitchen and escaped to the garden with a magazine, taking refuge under the apple tree, where she sat, hidden from sight. Let Ernest wash the dishes, she thought, let him sort everything out. She leaned back against the trunk. Dai trotted up to her for some fuss and petting. She smiled and stroked his white head. He was getting quite big, now, and had an appetite to match. No doubt he would enjoy all her left-overs from supper. She closed her eyes, trying to escape into her own private world. The late summer breeze played a soft tune amongst the drying leaves on the branches of the tree, soothing her soul and caressing her face. Wearily she attempted to make some sense of her situation. How long had Ernest, the most straight-laced and God-fearing man she had ever met, been behaving in such a duplicitous way? Did all ostensibly honourable men act this way? Had she, and many of the other women she knew, been duped? Maybe she shouldn't feel any guilt on her own part at all. But tomorrow, she would see Seamus again, she would touch him, feel his arms around her, they would laugh together, and for a few brief hours would forget the reality of their situation.

Eiddwen stared up in amazement through the window at the imposing Edinburgh Castle which overlooked her hotel. She could hardly believe she was here. She was finding it difficult to assimilate the fact that she was now a married woman, about to spend her wedding night in one of the most opulent hotels in Scotland. The Caledonian Hotel was grander than anywhere else she had ever been. The breathtaking decor and sparkling chandeliers made Eiddwen feel she had wandered onto a Hollywood film set. Any moment now, Cary Grant would come running down the magnificent staircase to keep his secret appointment with Audrey Hepburn....

Sitting nervously on the enormous bed, Eiddwen fingered the exquisite lace which edged her white silk nightdress, a gift from her new husband, as she remembered the events of the last twenty-four hours. The overnight train journey from South Wales to Scotland had been exciting, and they had travelled first class, enjoying a champagne dinner as they departed. Eiddwen hadn't really liked the champagne, Babycham was more to her taste, but the glamour of the event helped it slip down easily. For the first time, Eiddwen was able to wear her engagement ring openly and with pride. The couple did not sleep much in their couchettes that night, but talked endlessly about their future together. The discreet registry office wedding in Edinburgh earlier that day had made her happier than she had ever thought possible, and now, at the age of thirty-nine, she would be able to shake off the shackle of spinsterhood and welcome her new role as a married woman. She tried not to imagine what her family was thinking, in particular her younger sisters. Putting them determinedly out of her mind, she focussed her thoughts on her immediate situation, and the night to come. The steak with peppercorn sauce she had eaten for dinner mingled uneasily with the chocolate mousse she had enjoyed for pudding. She prayed she wouldn't be sick. On her wedding night of all nights! The bathroom door opened, and the paisley-pyjama clad form of her new husband emerged. He walked towards her, his arms outstretched, smelling of Colgate and Old Spice aftershave. She fell into his embrace like a refugee finding love and comfort at last.

The bed was already turned down, and on each pillow a gold-wrapped chocolate had been placed. Ordinarily, Eiddwen would have demolished these in excitement, entranced by their novelty, but tonight her attentions were on things other than her appetite for food. She clung to her husband, uncertain and fearful as to what to do next. Eiddwen need not have worried. He eased her down onto the satin quilted cover, holding her in his arms all the while, then pushed her gently onto her back, kissing her tenderly, constantly. His determined hands pulled down the lacy straps of her nightdress, exposing her splendid, freckled cleavage. Eiddwen became aware of a deep yearning, a longing for him to go further. Fear was a mere memory.....she submitted to his caresses, her pink nipples stiffening in response to his hands. Nobody had ever touched her breasts before, other than herself, and that had been cursory, when she had washed or undressed. Her late mother had always warned her never to let a man touch her there. But how wonderful it felt, how strange it made her feel. Why was she becoming so damp between her legs? Nobody had ever told her about this. His hands lifted the silk which concealed her luscious, chubby thighs, and he feasted his eyes on her plump mound, the sensible white cotton knickers concealing his island of fantasy; a few stray blond hairs escaped the restraining elastic, and a tell-tale wet patch betrayed her intense desire. In desperation she clamped her legs together, resisting her natural urges. The Professor had no such inhibitions.

"Take your knickers off, Eiddwen! Let me take them off!" His voice was thick with desire. In a trice he removed his pyjamas, and swiftly knelt down on the floor beside the bed, so Eiddwen wouldn't be able to see his rather large tummy and other wobbly bits. There was nothing wobbly about his manhood, however, which stood proudly to attention as he raised himself up slightly in order to ease Eiddwen's knickers down over her quivering legs. She suddenly sat bolt upright.

"Archie!" The horror and fear in her voice startled him.

"Whatever's the matter, hen?" He forgot his bashfulness about his corpulent body and sat down next to her on the bed.

"I've never seen one of them before!" She pointed down at his member, which was gradually losing any of the pride it had had a few moments earlier. "What are you going to do with it?!" All the while, she kept her eyes riveted on it, as though it would suddenly spring back into life and attack her.

"Oh, Eiddwen, dearest Eiddwen. I suspected you may be a wee virgin, and your innocence confirms my theory! Oh, come here, hen, and I will make your deflowering as delightful and enjoyable as possible. All you have to do is relax, and let Archie Bear get to work on you. Trust me. I promise you, I am about to take you to heaven.... But before you do anything else, don't be afraid of Mr Snakey! He only wants you to be nice to him, because he wants to be nice to you, very nice indeed!. Go on. Touch him." Gingerly, as though she was about to touch an unexploded bomb, Eiddwen reached out and cradled the professor's semifreddo appendage in her nervous hand. Within seconds, it had resumed its hardness. Fascinated, Eiddwen started to stroke it, gently and tentatively. Amazed at the effect her actions were having on her new husband, she grew bolder by the second, using both hands and also kissing him as she performed her ministrations.

"Lie back, hen, lie back and let me pleasure you...." His voice was loaded with intense desire. Eiddwen complied, and did her best to relax. Within a couple of minutes, he had divested her of her nightdress, casting it in an expensive heap on the floor. Eiddwen wished the bedside lamp had been turned off, so that it could be dark. She felt so ashamed of her full-figured body. Why, oh why hadn't she managed to stick to her reducing diet, as advised in Woman's Own magazine? Then she would have been slim and lithe like Mavis. However, her husband seemed to relish in her curves, and was making little grunts of pleasure as he moved his hands up and down her trembling form, satisfying his need to touch her pale, voluptuous flesh. Oh, goodness! Now his hands had moved from her breasts and were heading downwards. But she didn't really want to stop him. Eiddwen's breathing quickened, as he started to rub his hand between her legs. This was so naughty! So deliciously naughty! Without stopping the movement of his fingers, he whispered in her ear, "You do realise I have a PhD, Eiddwen? I am a doctor, yes? And as a doctor I am honour bound, professionally, to prepare your secret place for further activity. Open your legs wider for Doctor, there's a good wee lass...." Obediently, Eiddwen did as she was told, and sighed with rapture as he inserted his fingers into her. "Excellent. Coming along nicely. Very moist indeed. Now I am going to inspect this area more closely. Keep very still..." Eiddwen had no idea what he intended to do, but closed her eyes and remained motionless. An intense wave of pleasure washed over her as she felt the heat of his mouth on her Mons Veneris. His tongue started to lick her sensitive spot, sending a thrill of delight through her body. She felt she should really have stopped him, but she didn't. The room was silent and all that could be heard was the sound of late night traffic running along Princes Street. Eiddwen gave herself up to Archie's attentions, experiencing sexual enjoyment for the first time in her life. Suddenly, there was a loud, gurgling rumble. Eiddwen gasped with embarrassment and slapped her tummy in shameful panic. Archie looked up in surprise.

"What the hell was that?"

"Um...my supper going down! Am so sorry! It was so terribly loud!" How devastatingly unromantic, she thought, wishing the bed would swallow her up. Archie laughed. "Naughty, wee tummy!" And he patted her tummy playfully, before returning to his previous activity. Further rumbles went unnoticed, as Archie's clever tongue worked its magic, and Eiddwen achieved her nuptial orgasm within a few minutes.

"Nice?" Archie smiled at his wife in satisfaction. Eiddwen lay panting on the bed, dazed and quite uncertain as to what had just happened to her. She felt like a rag doll, incapable of movement or speech; every muscle in her body was relaxed, and she was aware of a deep throbbing sensation between her legs. Heaven it certainly was.

"Now, my bonny wee doll! Prepare to bid farewell to thy virginity! Archie Bear is coming to get you...!" And roaring as he did, he climbed on top of her,

Eiddwen squealing and laughing in excitement, taking her with him on this new adventure.

Mavis climbed out of the Reliant just outside Llanelli Town Hall on Saturday morning, having told Ernest she would be having lunch in town and would require collecting at four o'clock. She hadn't mentioned Eiddwen's elopement to him, as she was unable to face his diatribes and condemnation of her friend when she had enough worries of her own to deal with.

"Bye- bye, Ernest. Remember to pick me up here at four." She waved him goodbye, and walked in the general direction of the town centre. Once she was certain he had driven away back in the direction of Llannon, she turned around, and made her way down towards Station Road. Late summer had brought with it weather of a more unsettled nature. The sky was grey, the temperature was falling and Mavis was glad she had worn her red angora cardigan over her cream linen shift dress. Her tight skirts still fitted her – just – but were becoming rather snug around the waist. She sighed. However, Seamus seemed to delight in her new voluptuous body, almost appearing to venerate it. She relished in her secret news. To be a mother, to bring a new life into the world, and to be the mother of a child begotten of the deepest love, she was indeed fortunate.

Mavis had dispensed with her kitten heels that morning, as they would be downright dangerous when climbing around Kidwelly Castle. Her beige leather sandals were flat and comfortable, so it didn't her long to walk down the road to reach the railway station . She turned right down Gathen Terrace, and there on the corner was Seamus, busy parking and securing his motor-bike. Breaking into a slight run, she hurried up to him."Hello!" She tapped him on the shoulder. He turned around, a broad grin on his face. "Well, hello, sweet Mavis! I thought we weren't meeting until we were on the train? Or at Kidwelly?"

"We aren't! See you on the train! Sit near me if you can, but not next to me!" And with that she continued on her way, Seamus chuckling behind her, muttering words about spies and intrigue. The twenty-to-ten train to Milford Haven was almost empty when they got on, so they picked a compartment near the rear end, with Seamus sitting near the door and Mavis near the window. The surly guard popped his head around the door, and inspected their tickets with a scowl."Kidwelly is a request stop, you realise that? Good job I checked your tickets, isn't it?" And with that he stomped away crossly. The pair burst out laughing once he had gone, and settled back to enjoy the brief journey downline.

"It was still dark the last time I travelled along this track," said Seamus thoughtfully. "It was getting on for five o'clock in the morning, and I couldn't get to you quickly enough. How worried I was about you, how I was longing to see you." Mavis remained silent, looking out at the sea, churning and grey, as unsettled as a Roman Catholic nun at a Presbyterian prayer meeting. Seamus watched her intently.

"Say something." His voice seemed demanding. She turned to look at him.

"What do I say?" Her voice was a mere whisper. "Shall I say the truth? That I am overjoyed to love and be loved as I am now? That I am distraught at the situation I find myself in? That I fret for the future?" Her voice dropped even further. "That I rage against the unfairness of my life that I have found you too late?" Tears filled her eyes and she found it hard to continue. "But I love you, Seamus, as I have never loved before in my life." She turned away once more to watch the bleak waves, so he wouldn't see the sadness in her face. The train rolled on, passing the village of Pwll on the right, which stretched itself out lazily along the main road, clinging to the Graig hillside. Soon, the train reached Burry Port. A crowd of young couples got on, their destination Carmarthen and hopeful of an exciting day out. Seamus and Mavis watched them enviously as they held hands and giggled, teasing each other, laughing and joking.

Mavis decided to change the subject. "So. What do you think about Eiddwen and the professor? Fancy them eloping! The news will be breaking all around Llannon by now, and tongues will be wagging nineteen to the dozen!"

Seamus grinned in delight. "So the old bugger has gone and done it! He told me he was thinking about eloping with Eiddwen. I knew he was absolutely besotted with her, but I didn't realise he was that serious!"

"I am so pleased for Eiddwen. She has had a miserable life, if you think about it, hen-pecked by her dreadful sisters, acting as a housemaid to all her family, afraid of her own shadow. I hope they will be happy together. I hope I see her again...." Mavis suddenly thought of all the implications of Eiddwen's elopement. "But I know I will see her, of course I will!"

Seamus reached over and touched her hand. "Both your lives have changed immeasurably since I arrived on the scene, haven't they? All our lives, I suppose. Yours, Eiddwen's, Drummond's and mine. Most definitely mine. Run away with me, Mavis! I'll look after you! Come back to Ireland with me! Let's stay on this train until the end of the line and catch the first boat to Ireland!"

Mavis looked at him sadly. She smiled and shook her head. "My heart would go with you this very moment, but I lack courage, my dear Seamus. Forgive me..."

A bitter smile touched his face and he turned his gaze away.

Kidwelly station was deserted apart from a trio of seagulls, who were busy pecking away at a discarded sandwich. The couple crossed the bridge and made their way up Station Road, before turning into Water Street, where all the shops were. Within a few minutes they were within sight of the castle.

Kidwelly Castle. Ancient and full of dramatic history, it was in remarkably good condition, despite having been built in the twelfth century. Seamus took Mavis' cold fingers into his big hand, and they continued walking until they arrived at the castle gates. He turned to look at her. "Have you been here before?"

Mavis smiled, sadly. "When I was little. Everyone came here at some time or other. My Sunday School teacher brought us all here." Her face softened. "She was lovely, Miss Davies. She made Sunday School fun, and she laughed a lot. Would you believe it, she hired a bus, and brought twenty of us here on a trip!" Her face clouded. "She died. About five years ago. She was so beautiful. She died, only fifty-eight, no husband, no children, just a disabled mother to look after and a head full of dreams..." Then, smiling, she turned to him. "Shall I tell you the history of the castle?"

Seamus threw back his head and laughed. "My darling woman! I have researched it well enough! I was asked a few weeks ago to accept another commission, to paint it, from an ex-pat who lives in South Africa. I haven't accepted it because of all the problems I have, back home in Ireland." Crestfallen, Mavis retorted, "So you don't want me to tell you all about Princess Gwenllian, then!" Seamus grinned down at her. "Go on, then, you tell me about her, I can see you are absolutely dying to do so!"

"Well, all right." Mavis was slightly mollified. "Shall we sit down here?" She paused on the grassy slope which lay in front of the gates.

"May be wiser to settle ourselves around the back, d'you reckon?" He grabbed her hand and pulled her with him, seeking a more discreet position towards the rear of the castle. "So. Fire away!" He pulled a stern and serious face. "I'm all ears!" Mavis gave him an old-fashioned look, but could not resist telling him.

"She was so brave, Gwenllian, as well as being beautiful. She helped her husband Grufydd against the Normans, fought alongside him even. But it got her nowhere. She was captured and beheaded. It is said that she died on a field nearby, and a spring suddenly welled up on the spot where she fell. Can you imagine that? I could never have been as brave as her."

Seamus ruffled her hair. "But you are brave, you take such risks to be with me, brave to put up with that miserable husband of yours."

"Yes, but the risks I take to be with you are easy! I want to be with you so much, I don't even think about them!"

"Exactly. As did Gwenllian when she fought with her husband. Life was cheap then."

"I see. I suppose you're right." Mavis looked thoughtful. "And, interestingly, the scholar Andrew Breeze has hypothesised that Gwenllian could well have been the author of "The Four Branches of the Mabinogi." She was certainly an interesting character. And of course, she was supposedly the great-great (I forget how many greats) granddaughter of Brian, High King of Ireland! How's that for an Irish-Welsh connection?"

He was taken aback by Mavis' arms, thrown about his waist in a tight, sudden embrace. "Our Irish-Welsh connection made itself felt most keenly this morning, just around half-past seven!" She grinned up at him. "This little one certainly cannot tolerate honey on toast!"

"Oh, you poor thing! Not sick again? When will it end?" Seamus' concerned face was almost comical. Mavis laughed softly. "Eva says that it is a sign of a well-established pregnancy. Plenty of the right sort of hormone surging through me! But it is getting better. Soon I will be tucking into a fry-up every morning!" He held her close, his hand gently caressing the small swelling where the new life was developing.

"I wish I didn't have to go back to Ireland tomorrow. I have no idea when I can come back, and I will be anxious about you and the little one, sweet Mavis. But, what the hell! Today is ours for the taking, so let's tramp around the castle then go and have some tea!" They got up and followed the castle wall around to the entrance. The lazy Gwendraeth river meandered its way along the edge of the castle. How many secrets it kept, how many tragedies it must have witnessed, how much blood it must have washed away.... The couple entered the castle, looking up in awe at the soaring twin-towered gatehouse reaching up towards the grey sky, and started exploring one of the best-preserved Norman castles in the British Isles, hand in illicit hand, forgetting for a short while their impossible situation.

By one o'clock they were sitting down in the Central Cafe in the middle of Kidwelly, Seamus trying to suppress his longing for a cigarette while Mavis scanned the plastic-bound menu. The coffee machine hissed and spat, filling the air with its evocative aroma, mingling seductively with the scent of vanilla and tobacco.

"What'll you be having, oh sweet lady-in-waiting?" He grinned at her.

"Ssh!" Mavis looked around her anxiously, but apart from an elderly couple taking their time over a pot of tea, they were the only customers. "I think I'll have cheese on toast! Heavenly host, I like to call it! My mother would never allow us to have it, too much mess, she would say. And brown sauce as well!"

They caught the eye of the proprietress, a short, plump Italian woman with rosy cheeks and her black hair tied back in a bun. "Whadda you want?" She licked the end of her pencil, her little note book at the ready.

"We'll have two cappuccinos , one cheese on toast, and one sausage and chips." Seamus beamed at her. She scribbled it all down, peering at Mavis over her spectacles.

"You needa feeding up, piccolo mama!" She tapped Mavis' cheek playfully, then turned to Seamus. "Your wife, you must look after her well, now, with da bambino on the way!"

Mavis gasped in horror. "How did you know?"

"Ah, I know these things! I can tell a breeding mother by the glow on her skin and the sparkle in her eyes, eh?!" And with that, she returned to the counter, shouting the order in Italian to some invisible person behind the curtain.

"How could she possibly know? I am so glad she doesn't live in Llannon!" Mavis was mortified.

"Well, we must surely look like a married couple!" Seamus laughed and squeezed her hand under the table. "I quite like that!"

"But, I mean, I'm not showing or anything!" Mavis hadn't realised that her voice had increased in volume, and the elderly woman on the table opposite turned to her.

"Oh, Mama Giulia is a clever one, siwr o fod. Congratulations to you both! Llongyfarchiadau!" The old couple raised their empty cups to her and smiled. Seamus and Mavis collapsed into giggles, relaxing and feeling bold enough to hold hands on top of the table. Within a quarter of an hour their order had arrived, with a flourish and a knowing smile from Giulia. Mavis could hardly wait to sink her teeth into the melting, savoury cheese, but not before she had emptied half a bottle of brown sauce over it. Seamus smiled indulgently as he watched her devour the generous helping of Welsh rarebit, mopping up every scrap with the crusts of toast, making short work of his own sausage and chips in no time at all.

"I am surely glad to see you eating up your crusts, my darling woman! At home, it would be a fecking crime to leave anything behind!" He grinned at her, putting his knife and fork together on his empty plate. She dabbed at her mouth with the paper napkin.

"What shall we do now? We've seen the castle, and there isn't a lot more to do in Kidwelly. If we had come on your bike, we could have gone down to St Ishmael's, down to the sea. The lighthouse seems so close down there, you could almost reach out and touch it...." Her brown eyes took on a wistful expression.

"Sometimes, I just want to run away, Seamus, run away and be on my own." She looked up at him, surprised to see that his eyes had misted over.

"Don't do that, sweet Mavis, never run away from me, will you?"

"Oh, Seamus, it was just a manner of speaking, you know that. You mean the world to me and I wish things could be different. I'm just a prisoner in my own home, an unhappy captive, with no means of a proper escape. All I can ever hope for is a day release, when I am with you, for you hold the key to my secret escape route. But as from tomorrow, even that desperate pleasure will be denied me."

"But I will be with you in my thoughts, I will dream of you every night, and I will long to take you in my arms every minute of the day." He took both her hands in his and squeezed them. "C'mon! Let's go. Where shall it be?" Mavis thought long and hard for a few minutes, spooning up the remains of her frothy coffee as she did.

"I know! It's only a quarter to two. Let's get the next train back to Llanelli. I know you don't want to take me on your bike, but what I have in mind will only take about five minutes, it should be perfectly safe!"

"Do tell, I am all agog!" He smiled down at her, relieved at her change of mood.

"When we get off the train, we can go on your bike down to Machynys. It's wild and desolate, and we can be alone, with only the reeds and the seagulls for company. Fred, my stepson, and his wife Margaret, live in a street we must pass, but it will still be close to lunchtime, and they won't be out and about." She grinned at him cheekily as he searched in his pocket for money to pay the bill.

Twenty minutes later they were back on the train, heading east for Llanelli, the old sparkle back in Mavis' eyes and a determined expression on her face.

Eiddwen lay perfectly still in the enormous bed, afraid to move. The morning sun's beams struggled to find their way through the gap in the heavy, brocade curtains, and the hotel room remained in semi-darkness. Slowly, she sat up slightly. She could just about make out the ornate mirror opposite. Was that her own pale face staring back? Was that really Eiddwen from Llannon? She didn't look all that much different from the shy virgin who had gone so willingly into her husband's arms the night before. Eiddwen looked at her sleeping husband, who was lying on his back, snoring gently. She smiled indulgently, then returned to her worried thoughts. She'd never realised that sex would be so messy....she was too scared to shift her body from the position it had been in last night, when they had finally fallen asleep. Everything felt sticky and wet, and when she had plucked up enough courage to go to the bathroom for a much needed wee before the final marathon, she had been horrified to find out that she had bled. Archie had reassured her, calmed her down, when she had almost burst into tears with horror. It was his honour and delight, he had said, to have deflowered the most beautiful blossom in Wales. He told her it was to be expected, after her chaste and virginal life. She sat up in bed slowly, clutching the sheets to her chest, in order to hide her breasts, slightly tender after a night's lovemaking. The bottom sheet stuck to her thighs, and she had to prise them away. How embarrassing! And that funny smell! As though someone had emptied a bottle of bleach over the sheets! Or was it like fish? Was it her fault? Had she done something wrong? What on earth would Archie think of her? She had better go and have a bath before he woke up. She stretched out a white leg, and started to hoist herself over the edge of the bed. Not quick enough, alas, for a strong arm snaked its way around her waist.

"And where do you think you are going, my gorgeous wee lassie?" Archie's voice was still hoarse with sleep, his face crumpled and creased after the long and vigorous night.

"Um….I think I should have a bath?" Eiddwen could have died with embarrassment.

"Now why is that?" His voice deepened suggestively. "Are you denying the bounty of Mother Nature, or the goddess of love herself, the fair Aphrodite, the venerable Venus? Do you for one second wish to rid yourself of the base perfume of sex? Yes, sex, Eiddwen! It is a normal, healthy activity! Our birthright! And the result is the stench of lust, and the celebration of our bodily secretions, both yours and mine! Mingling in the swamp of seduction and ecstasy! Enjoy it, Eiddwen! Relish in it! Do not be afraid of it!"

Laughing huskily, he drew her back into his embrace, smothering her face with enthusiastic kisses. She squealed and pulled away in alarm. "Archie! I haven't brushed my teeth!" He ignored her protests and continued to kiss her thoroughly, pushing his tongue into her mouth, and easing her down once more onto the bed.

"Do you want Archie Bear to be nice to you again?" He nuzzled her neck, whilst his eager hands roamed gleefully over her full breasts. "Does ma wee lassie want to be taken to heaven once more? Would she like that?" Eiddwen could only gasp her assent, allowing Archie's determined hands to work their magic once more, leaving her panting with delight, as he charmed her thighs into a welcoming forty-five degree angle of invitation. One and a half hours and two orgasms later, Eiddwen had her bath, enjoying the luxury of the huge, free-standing bath, and the extravagant scent of Penhaligon's Bluebell in the water. She emerged warm and flushed, wrapped in the complimentary white, towelling robe which completely drowned her, and trailed behind her like the train of the wedding dress she had never worn. Archie was already sitting in a velvet-upholstered chair, also wearing a similar dressing gown, reading the Times, which had been delivered outside their room earlier. There was a knock at the door.

"Ah! That'll be room service! Enter!" Eiddwen admired the authority in his voice. The door opened and a smartly dressed waiter wheeled in a trolley laden with cereals, exotic fruits, and several hot dishes. It smelled delicious. "You may leave us now!" Archie handed the man half-a crown, and took charge of the trolley. The door shut behind the waiter. Archie whipped off his dressing gown and swaggered over towards Eiddwen. "Cumberland sausage, darling?"

Eiddwen simpered. "Ooh, Archie! You are so naughty...!"

"Are you sure you will be okay?" Seamus anxiously helped Mavis onto the pillion seat.

She withered him with a look. "Let's get a move on! I want to get down to the Bulwarks so we can enjoy what little time we have left!" They were soon on their way down New Dock Road, heading south towards the coast, passing a baker's shop, two hairdressers, three butchers and some newsagents, which were all, thankfully, closed for lunch. As they reached the end of the road, Seamus felt surprised at Mavis' choice of destination. All he could make out was a maze of industrial premises, a saw-mill, railway tracks which seemed to run all over the place, in a confusing and haphazard fashion, and trucks filled with shiny heaps of tin. Why on earth would Mavis want to bring him here?

"Are you sure of the way? Is this where you want to go?" Mavis laughed and clung on to him tightly. "Yes! You'll see!" Now they were passing a row of terraced houses, and the landscape was changing, becoming wild and desolate in appearance. A couple of farms relieved the severity of the place, but it was dominated by grassland, reeds and rubble. The wind picked up, whipping Mavis' hair around her face, making her eyes sting and water. The road became rough and irregular, and the bike came to a halt where it began to fork.

"So. Which way? Left or right? East or west?" Seamus was starting to feel decidedly uncomfortable. However, Mavis seemed perfectly happy, despite the less-than-salubrious surroundings, which seemed so much at odds with her fastidious nature.

"Turn right. We really do not want to be going left. If you take a look over there -" she pointed at a group of caravans huddled together, about half a mile away – "that's the gypsy camp. Travellers. They own dangerous dogs. Irish..." she stopped herself just in time, having been about to say "Irish tinkers." Seamus guessed as much and smiled to himself, as he turned the bike and steered it to the right, driving along until they reached a steep embankment. "Here we are." Mavis alighted from the bike, and, pulling Seamus' after her, clambered up the concrete slope. At the top, she stopped, and looked up at Seamus to see his reaction. He whistled slowly. "Fantastic." He stood very still, taking in the view, appreciating it with an artist's eye. The verdant, undulant hills of the Gower peninsular curved gently westwards, eventually becoming craggy, sculpted and rocky as they stretched out towards the ocean. The tide was out, and he felt he could easily have walked across the estuary over the sand to Penclawdd, through which they had travelled a few months previously. To his left he could see the urban sprawl of Swansea in the distance, as the estuary dwindled and became the river Loughor. Several marsh ponies grazed contentedly on the amber mudflats of the saltmarsh. To the right, the sea could be seen in the distance, a thin sliver line, illuminated briefly by the sun, which was struggling to emerge from behind the gloomy, grey clouds. A skylark hovered high above them, and apart from the cry of wild ducks, there was peace and quiet.

"What do you think?" Mavis whispered, afraid to spoil the moment, holding his hand.

"It's amazing. So wild and – and- inspirational, I suppose." Seamus continued gazing out towards the horizon. "I would so love to paint this. Maybe one day I will, who knows?" Mavis closed her eyes, murmuring softly,

"Sea grass waving, languishing over the lonely shore,
reaching out to Atlantis, Lyonesse and Ys, hidden lands from aeons ago,
seen by the few who care to stare
long enough at the deep, dark sea.
I see them.
I stare in wonder at the ocean mountains, hazy and cloudy.
Monster lizards lounge at the end of the world, hungry and sly,
edging out to the brink of beyond, but forever still and silent.
Beasts of rock.
I look up at the sea, for that's where it is;
cupped in the hand of Donn, safe for now,
but when the west wind howls and rages, whips itself to a frenzy,
and the moon is full and white....
....the thin silver line is breached, and the water reclaims the earth."

Seamus looked surprised. "Such pertinent words. Who wrote that? Was it a Welsh poet?" "In a manner of speaking," she replied. "I am Welsh, but not really a poet!"

"You wrote that?" He looked incredulously at her. Mavis continued to gaze out over the estuary. "Yes. I love this place. I only discovered it a few years ago, not long after I got married. Ernest wanted to bring Wendy down here, so I came along too. It's only a fifteen minute drive from Llannon, but it feels like a million miles away. Wild and free, so different from my orderly, predictable life…"

"So you wrote about it?" Mavis nodded. "Along with other poems. Still in a box under the bed in the spare room!" He hugged her affectionately. They sat down on the concrete slope, simply enjoying each other's company, their closeness, and the solitude. The sun succeeded in making a belated but welcome entrance, warming them up as they talked and held each other. "We have had some very naughty moments by the sea, haven't we?" Mavis snuggled closer into Seamus' arms. "Deliciously naughty moments!" "Are you propositioning me, you wicked woman?" His hand moved instinctively to her full breast, starting to caress it gently.

"Not at all! This is not the most comfortable place to be wicked in!" She laughed and allowed her own hand to stray between his legs. "But I wish we could have some more shenanigans before you leave…" Seamus roared with laughter, startling a young seagull who had ventured rather close to them in the hope of rich pickings. "Shenanigans, eh? That's a nice way of describing our beautiful moments of passion! But I will forgive you, seeing as I love you! But for punishment, you will have to come by once more, so we can shenanig again!"

She looked crestfallen. "How can I? You go back tomorrow!" "Ah, but I have a cunning plan….. I know it will be nigh on impossible for you to see me tonight, but what about early tomorrow morning? My taxi arrives at a quarter past eight. Could you slip out before then? We could have an hour or so, maybe?" Mavis considered this carefully, her forehead furrowed in concentration. "That, dear Seamus, is entirely possible. Ernest always sleeps until eight o'clock on a Sunday, but I could escape very early to see you." She paused, her mind working quickly as she made plans. "I will be back at the cottage before he awakes, hopefully, but even if he is up when I return, I will have taken a bucket and a cloth with me, and will just say I have been to wash his late mother's headstone so it will be clean before Sunday's services. That will certainly put me in his good books, even though we are not supposed to do any work on the Sabbath. I actually cleaned the grave two days ago, so he won't notice!" Buoyed up by their new arrangement, they returned to the bike.

"You can drop me off at the bottom of New Dock Road, in the back lane so I won't be seen, and I'll walk into town from there," she decided. "I want to buy some wool from Iris' wool shop. About time I started knitting!" Seamus looked blankly at her. "Booties! For the baby!" She rolled her eyes in mock exasperation. "Oh, of course! Women's stuff!" He started the engine.

"By the way," she added, as she put her arms about his waist, "Do you mind if I breastfeed your baby?"

Sunday morning dawned, as grey and sombre as any self-respecting Baptist would wish. Mavis had slept fitfully, having put up with Ernest's practising of his sermons for the following day and swallowed the pork chops with mashed potatoes for supper as best she could. She longed for the morning, and was eternally grateful that Ernest decided to sleep in the spare room, accusing Mavis of keeping him awake with her frequent trips to the bathroom and fidgeting.

Sunday morning. All was silent in the lane as Mavis crept from the cottage at six o'clock. Dai had merely thumped his tail sleepily on the kitchen floor as she closed the door behind her, the alibi bucket on her arm. Good dog.

This silent, grey world was a different one to the previous day, a stranger, almost alien; not unfriendly but respectful. Mavis hurried down the lane to Seamus' house, having dressed quickly in her red, cotton dress and cardigan, desperate to meet once more the lover she craved. He answered her knock immediately, hauling her inside with almost indecent haste. Their kisses could have set the whole of Llannon alight. By the time Mavis had reached the bottom of the stairs, the red dress was a thing of the past, and she was clad only in her white, cotton brassiere and knickers. Scooping her up in his arms, he carried her into his bedroom, laying her down reverently on his bed.

"You are mine for the hour." He removed her clothes, and threw them dismissively onto the floor. "Mine. And I will make sure you know it!"

An hour later they were drinking tea at the kitchen table, both keenly aware of the speed at which the minutes ticked by.

"Promise me you will write regularly." He clasped her hands in his. "I want to know how my darling woman and my little one are getting on. Every single detail. Leave nothing out!"

Mavis smiled, despite her despondent mood. "Even how many times I have to get up in the night to go to the bathroom? Even how many pounds I gain each month?"

He laughed. "Yes. Even all that. But especially when the baby moves for the first time, quickening, isn't that what it's called? You will let me know, won't you?"

"Yes, of course. Eva says that a first-time mother may not feel that until about half-way through the pregnancy, but a slim woman like me could possibly experience it earlier, so maybe in a month or two?" She drained her tea and replaced the cup in its saucer, for Seamus to refill it. His large hands fascinated her as he poured the tea from the big, brown teapot, before handing her the milk jug. Such strong hands, such artistic fingers, in more ways than one...

Sitting down again, his expression became serious. "We must try and write every week. I will send my letters here as I did before, and I will address them to myself... but as they will be from Ireland you will know they are from me. I won't address them to you, as our friendly, neighbourhood postman will wonder why the fair Mrs Watton is having her mail delivered to my house! And you can let yourself in to collect them. I will of course include a telephone number which you can use in case of an emergency. And maybe we can prearrange a time when you can ring me, anyway, from my house? You will you write back, won't you?"

She looked up in surprise, taken aback at the misery in his voice. "Of course! Wild horses wouldn't stop me! What I may have to do is to keep a diary of sorts, and then post the whole lot off to you each time I go down into Llanelli to the main post office. Oh, Seamus, I will miss you so much..." The second cups of tea went cold, remained full, as the couple clung to each other, gathering as much comfort as was possible as they faced Seamus' departure and their subsequent separation. By ten-to-eight they stood in the hallway to say their final farewell. Holding hands, they looked into each other's eyes.

"Goodbye, sweet Mavis. Keep safe. I love you."

"Goodbye, my darling man. I love you." Her voice was just a whisper, as she fought back the tears which threatened to pour down her face. The cheerful birdsong in the lane seemed to mock the dismal sadness of the moment. So many opposites.

She walked quickly back to her cottage, not looking back, not until she reached her gate, when she turned around to wave at the frantically waving Seamus, and then she was gone.

Chapter Twenty-one

The Sacking of Jezebel.

"Congratulations!"
"When is the baby due?"
"Oh, you do look well, Mrs Watton!"

Mavis glanced around at the sea of smiling faces outside the chapel doors. Ernest certainly hadn't lost any time in publicising the news about her pregnancy. He had walked down the lane with her to the chapel, his chest puffed out and a smirk on his face, knowing full well that by the time they reached Bethel, the congregation would have been regaled via the loose tongue of Eira Jones, in whom he had deliberately "confided" the previous afternoon, just before he set off to fetch Mavis from Llanelli. It may have been late summer, but the day was chilly, and Mavis wore her fur coat over a light, cotton dress. At least it would hide her tiny bump from the prying eyes and intense scrutiny of the chapel women. There was no sign of Eiddwen's twin sisters, so unless they had availed themselves of the Llannon broadcasting service (Eira Jones) their scandalous news would remain unshared. Her own sisters were also absent, so no doubt they would be furious to be the last to know about her condition. So be it. That was entirely their problem!

The service would start in five minutes, and Mavis took her usual place in the pew towards the middle of the chapel, next to Eva Griffiths and her husband.

"Seems like your secret's out!" Eva whispered, smilingly. Mavis nodded discreetly, whispering in return, "Yes. It's all official now. Ernest is very pleased. I hope to return to the shop this week."

"Only if you are feeling better, mind." Eva turned to her hymn book as Ernest solemnly climbed up to the pulpit and the service began. Gladys Williams laboriously played her way through the hymns and psalms, but as her back was to the congregation, Mavis could not see the expression on her face. As she watched Gladys' plump shoulders move up and down as she played, a plan was forming in Mavis' mind. Yes, this morning would provide her with the perfect opportunity to oust Gladys once and for all. Now that she had Ernest eating out of her hand, it would be child's play to bend him to her wishes.

The austere layout of the chapel seemed to reflect the strict ethos of Baptist beliefs. Rigid, inflexible and stern. There were no delicate lines to relieve the architecture, and even the arch of the ceiling seemed to warn of dire consequences. The smell of old prayer books was overpowering today, and the whole event seemed to reek of ancient and musty ceremony. Why had Ernest chosen such lengthy hymns? She wished she didn't have to stand so long, it would be embarrassing if she fainted in the middle of the service.

After the service, the usual crowd gathered at the doorway, exchanging pleasantries, as superficial as ever, the men talking about the price of petrol and the women gossiping like fussy starlings, all the while eyeing each other up and down, trying to determine if their rivals' clothes were newer, or more expensive than their own.

"Eiddwen is so lucky to be shot of this lot," Mavis thought to herself, catching Sioned Thomas looking at her fur coat with undisguised envy written all over her Max Factor powdered face. "But then I used to be just like them, before..." Her trail of thought broke off as she was reminded once more that Seamus had gone back to Ireland.

Ernest was deep in conversation with Eira Jones' husband, when the group was joined by Gladys Williams, a bundle of manuscripts under her arm.

"Bore da, ladies," she simpered, casting a sideways glance at Ernest, a pouting smile on her lips.

Before anyone else could respond, Mavis moved closer to her. Brazen hussy, she thought.

"Bore da, Miss Williams. I must say that you played very well this morning, didn't she, Ernest?" Ernest nodded dumbly, wondering what on earth was coming next. "It's such a shame though, isn't it?" Mavis continued, "Such a shame that you have to leave us for a new position in Llanelli! How will we manage without you? But Ernest says that our choirmaster will be able to cope with a few services until we find a replacement, won't he, Ernest?" Mavis smiled sweetly up at her husband. Ernest could do nothing more than nod his assent.

"Er, um, yes, Miss Williams, we are indeed regretful that you are leaving. I hope you will be very happy in your new position."

Gladys glared at Mavis in disbelief, her pale face becoming even whiter with anger. Eira looked surprised at this news, wondering why Ernest hadn't mentioned anything yesterday. Sioned Thomas perked up instantly, here was a juicy bit of gossip! Hastily regaining her composure, Gladys stared back at Mavis with a fixed smile.

"Yes, thank you. I will be starting at the Parish Church next week." There were several "oohs" and "ahs" as to be the organist of the Parish Church would certainly be prodigious. Mavis laughed to herself, wondering how long it would be before Gladys' hasty lie would be detected.

"What a shame!" Eira put her gloved hand on Gladys' arm. "We haven't had time to buy you a leaving present!"

"Oh, don't you go worrying about that!" Mavis chuckled. "Our Miss Williams would never accept it anyway! She is far too modest and God-fearing for that! No, our best wishes will be all that Miss Williams needs to see her on her way, isn't that so, Miss Williams?" It was all Mavis could do to stop herself from bursting out laughing at the agonised expression on Gladys' face. Check mate, she thought with satisfaction.

The next few days passed in a whirl of congratulations and astonished reactions. Mavis' mother and her sisters were stunned into unusual silence at her news, and, as her sisters lacked any sort of knowledge of motherhood, for once kept their own counsel, including her mother. Fred and Margaret seemed surprised but pleased, when the Wattons paid a visit to their new house the following week. It had been difficult to conceal the news from Wendy, who had hopped and skipped about the place when they arrived. The little girl seemed to hold Mavis in some kind of reverence, and refused to leave her side when they sat in the half-decorated parlour, the step-ladder still in place in the centre of the room. However, Wendy seemed thrilled that her fairy godmother was soon to have a baby, and plagued her with questions, most of which Mavis found difficult to answer. Wendy expressed her sincere wish it would be a girl for her to play with, as Julie, her own sister was deemed "so boring."

"Will the baby come and see me dance, Aunty Mavis?" Wendy pirouetted about the room on tiptoes, a confident smile on her face.

"Well, I will certainly bring the baby to watch you perform, Wendy. You must be sure to practise every day to be ready for it!" Fred looked at his stepmother quizzically. What had happened to the cold, sharp-tongued woman he knew? What had happened to thaw her brittle facade? He returned to his painting, leaving his wife Margaret to carry on the conversation with his father and Mavis.

The scandal about Eiddwen gradually seeped through to the gossip-hungry residents of Llannon, the actual source unknown, although Mavis realised it must have been the twins. They had painted a rather dramatic picture of what had taken place, describing the professor as a person of immense importance, who had taken advantage of their "poor sister" and led her astray. Mavis wondered when Eiddwen would contact her, and whether she would be brave enough to write a letter, in case Ernest opened it. She missed her friend, although she would not have been able to confide, even in Eiddwen, the truth about her current condition. Mavis was lonely in her knowledge, isolated in the facts, desperately longing for the one person she could talk to. Seamus.

The days that followed his departure also heralded a dramatic change in the weather. The temperature plummeted, and schoolchildren heading out early in the morning pulled on their thick winter jumpers and even coats as the first frosts decorated the fields of Llannon. Mavis consulted Eva after her shifts at the shop, and was told that all was well, that the baby was growing properly and her blood pressure was that of a twenty year old. The terrible morning sickness gradually eased, and Mavis started to feel much better.

The sudden cold weather came to an end, and summer reasserted itself, warming the land and the residents of Llannon. Mavis let herself in to Seamus' house a few days after he had left, but there was no letter there as yet. Now that she realised the erratic nature of the Irish postal service, she didn't even worry too much when nothing had arrived after a week of his absence.

Ernest was solicitous and less stern with her, which made life a lot easier. He started offering to wash the dishes after supper, telling her to put her feet up, fussing over her and plying her with endless cups of tea, which didn't help her nocturnal visits to the bathroom. However, not even this positive change in Ernest's attitude could help to fill the aching void in her heart, or salve the gaping wound in her soul which she sustained when Seamus departed.

Chapter Twenty-two

A Month of Missives.

The first letter to arrive was from Eiddwen. It was delivered to the Griffiths' shop, postmarked Edinburgh, and addressed to Mavis. Clearly, Eiddwen was exercising caution and didn't want Ernest to open it, or maybe she was acting on the sound advice of the Professor. Mavis waited until she was on her way home before reading the letter, settling down on the bench at the bus stop to open it.

Arden House, Roslin, nr Edinburgh. 15ThSeptember
Dear Mavis,

I hope you are keeping well. By now you will have been made aware what I have done. I hope you don't think too badly of me, that I hadn't told you anything, but Archie my husband (oh, how strange it seems to be writing that!) said it was best to tell no-one at all, not even you. He didn't even tell Seamus!

I have had a wonderful honeymoon in Edinburgh. We stayed in the Caledonian Hotel, right by the castle. Oh, Mavis, it was like a fairytale. I wish you could have seen it.

I am now living with Archie at his house in a little village outside Edinburgh called Roslin. It is quite small, but not as small as Llannon. Our house is big and old, full of books and ancient things. The garden has many apple trees and beautiful flowers, not a vegetable patch in sight! I am so happy, Mavis, please be happy for me. I have written to my family, of course. I wonder if they will reply? They are probably furious with me, especially the twins. I cannot wait to visit Llannon, to show off my new husband, and to have a good chat with you. There's so much to talk about, things that I couldn't possibly write down here, if you know what I mean! I hope you will find a moment or two to reply.

Yours truly, Eiddwen, xx

Mavis smiled and folded the letter up, placing it in her handbag. She would reply later, when Ernest was busy writing his sermon. Before she returned to her cottage, she let herself in at Seamus' house, and was delighted to discover a letter addressed to Seamus, but in his own handwriting. Not wishing to arouse suspicion by being unusually late, she put it in her bag with Eiddwen's, and could hardly wait for evening to come so that she could devour it at her leisure.

My dearest Mavis,

As I write this, dawn is breaking over the sea which separates us. The sun shines upon the water, and I wonder if you are watching the same sunrise as well. It may be a fine day, but my heart is heavy, for I have left behind something so precious and I fear for its safety and security. I hope you are well, and that the little one is not causing you too much discomfort. My mother is, as the district nurse says, "stable," but she seems to be fading on a daily basis. My family have managed to establish some sort of order, and things are calmer. They are all plaguing me with questions about my hurried departure for Wales; of course, I won't be telling them anything. Not yet. But, who knows…? I will be able to confide in my sister, but she is back in London, and a terrible letter-writer, so I will leave that until I see her next. On the boat, during the crossing, I kept seeing families, parents with small children, and I thought to myself, "I am going to be a Da soon!" A little bit of me to carry on the line! And yet….. I have only been back in Ireland a short while, but I miss you dreadfully. I yearn for the sound of your sweet voice, the softness of your skin and the perfume in your hair. You have totally bewitched me with your womanly wiles! I am addicted to you and need you desperately!

Write back to me as soon as you can, my darling woman. I love you.

Seamus.

Thankfully, Ernest's sermon was demanding his full attention, leaving Mavis with ample opportunity to reply to both letters. As Seamus' reply required the utmost secrecy, she wrote his first, before answering Eiddwen's

September 20th

My darling Seamus,

How are you? I miss you so much and want to be with you. It's only a couple of weeks since you left, yet it feels as though you have been gone for months. All is well with the pregnancy. Eva is pleased with everything, and I am, as everyone seems to be telling me, blooming! My bump is quite obvious now; it feels like a tennis ball very low down in my tummy. I don't feel sick anymore. Ernest is as pleased as Punch about it all. I hope that doesn't upset you when I tell you that. It's easier for me if he is in a good mood, anyway, for if he wasn't then I don't know how I would be able to cope.

I hope your mother isn't in any pain or discomfort. As Eva would say, I hope she is "comfortable." Do you have district nurses like ours in Ireland? Ireland seems so very far away, hundreds and hundreds of miles away. I have been into your house a few times (and tidied up!) and I just sit there, remembering everything we shared there, imagining you being there with me, pretending I am yours officially and waiting for you to come home from an ordinary job... I have suddenly started fancying smoked mackerel. Isn't that strange? I hated smoked fish up until now! And beetroot as well! Eva says it's my body craving essential nutrients, or something. I have been "booked" to have the baby at Brynglas Maternity Home, in Llanelli. There was a bit of concern as to whether this could be possible, due to my advanced age! But as I am so well, there's nothing really to prevent this. The baby will be due around February. I hope you will reply soon, and don't forget the telephone number so we can actually talk before too long! I love you, my gorgeous secret lover, my absent other half of me.

Mavis xxx

Securing the letter in its envelope and hiding it in her underwear drawer, she then started on Eiddwen's letter.

Dear Eiddwen,

Congratulations! I am so pleased for you! The twins turned up on my doorstep the other day, demanding if I was privy to your escape! I was so delighted when they showed me the note you had left. You deserve happiness, and it is wonderful that you have found it before time ran out. Seamus told me that the professor was besotted with you, and of course, he wasn't told about your elopement either.

I have some news too. Brace yourself, Eiddwen — I am going to have a baby, and he or she will arrive around February. I cannot believe that this has happened to me at my age! I have been feeling a bit sick, but am better now. The whole village knows, and Ernest is extremely proud; as usual he is planning on buying the best of everything, a Silver Cross pram etc.. I am going to have the baby in Brynglas. Every time I go past there now I feel this quiver of fear and excitement rush though me. Will I be able to cope with the pain and lack of dignity?

There's no need to write to me at the shop anymore, because I will stand up for you where Ernest is concerned. Unless, of course, you have to write something highly confidential, in which case it may be prudent to write to me there.

Write back soon.

Mavis xxx

p.s – Gladys Williams has left! And good riddance!

Mavis took the opportunity the following evening to broach the subject of Eiddwen with Ernest. He snorted with disapproval as she began the conversation, looking at her frostily with his cold, blue eyes. Mavis, however, was having none of his sulking, and carried on like a steam roller, expressing her joy that Eiddwen had found wedded bliss and was now a respectable married woman. In the end, she wore him down, and he found himself nodding in agreement.

However, it was with mounting disappointment that she waited and waited for Seamus to reply to her letter. Even Eiddwen's gushing response did little to lift her spirits.

Dear Mavis,

How wonderful! You are going to be a mammy! I wonder if you will have a boy or a girl? It will be lovely for Ernest if it's a boy, and he can do all those boy things with him! But a little baby girl would be so nice, and you could dress her up so beautifully, with frills and lace. (Mavis shuddered.) How big are you now? Are you wearing a smock yet? And what about work? Is Eva letting you carry on working? Oh, Mavis, I am so looking forward to seeing you again. We will have so much to discuss. Whatever happened to Gladys Williams? My life with Archie is quite different from my old life in Llannon. We don't go to chapel on Sundays (he is a Protestant, anyway) but we just laze about the place, eating when we feel like it, going for strolls in the park and watching television. Archie works a lot at home, but now that it is the end of September, he has to go to the University during the week. I went with him once or twice. Edinburgh is such a big city, and has so many shops. And the castle – well, it dwarfs poor Kidwelly! Some of the days I stay in the village and have been wandering around, getting to know the place. Mind you, it's quite hard to understand the accent here, and the locals (especially in Edinburgh) seem to find it hard to understand me, so I have to speak slowly. The trouble is, when I do this, my voice gets louder, and I end up almost shouting at people, as though they were deaf! I have taken some photographs of my house with Archie's Instamatic camera. He always has to have the latest gadget! Over the next few weeks, I will get them developed and send them to you, along with some of our wedding photos. We only have about five or six, and these were taken by our witness, who happened to be the owner of a bookshop near the registry office! I am going to make cawl for our dinner, now, so must say

Bye for now.

Eiddwen xx

By the end of September, there was still no word from Seamus. Mavis had written a few letters in diary format, but had not sent them. By the thirtieth of the month, she decided to swallow her stubborn pride and sent them anyway.

September 26th

I despair. I have heard nothing from you. Is something wrong? I can only hope that nothing has happened to your letter, or, worse, that you have had no time to consider us, or have no thought to do so....

I apologise for my outburst. Somehow, it makes it easier for me if I can write my thoughts down here. Sometimes it feels as though I will explode with the anxiety I feel when there is no contact. I promised I would keep a diary, and so I have.

I swear I felt a little kick this afternoon. I was just lying on my bed, watching the clouds scudding across the sky, thinking that they had been sent on their way from you in Ireland, when I felt this tiny "hiccup" in my stomach, as though a large butterfly had fluttered its wings inside me! Maybe it was our baby? It is now so real.... a little baby is alive inside me. Your child kicks its way into my reality! But maybe I was mistaken?

Life goes on as usual in Llannon. The gossip-mongers have become bored with the subject of my pregnancy, Eiddwen's elopement and Gladys' so-called "new job." Have I mentioned that? If not, when we speak on the phone I will tell you. I hope we will speak soon.

September 28th

Still no news from you. It is so hard to bear, yet bear it I must. The weather here has turned warm again, which I prefer. How is your mother doing? When will your sister return to Ireland? These are such polite, superficial questions, but ones I must ask, I suppose. But all I really want to write is to tell you that I miss you terribly and long for you. Ernest is solicitous, and not nearly as crotchety as he has been. All is well with the pregnancy. I told Eva about the baby moving - the quickening, it is known as. She said that from the time I am about seven months pregnant, I have to count at least ten kicks a day. I wish I could lie in bed with you, with my stomach against your back, so you could feel your little one playing havoc as you attempt sleep!

September 29th

I went for a walk this evening, around six o'clock. We are having an Indian summer and it is blissfully warm. Such a beautiful evening should not be wasted, and as I had spent the whole day stuck in the shop, I knew I needed to escape to the track. Ernest went down to see Fred his son in Llanelli, so I slipped out with Dai, up onto the track, then headed south. The sun was setting and the sky was a magnificent shade of deep apricot. There wasn't a breath of wind and the birds were still singing. It all made me think of you, such bitter-sweet memories of us in that same place. I allowed my imagination to run riot and pretended that any moment you would come stealing up behind me and surprise me. I am allowed to pretend, aren't I? I have never before experienced such intense longing and melancholia. The beauty of the evening made it possible to bear these intense emotions. As the sun set completely, and dusk fell, I stopped walking and let the shadows of twilight surround me. Dusk is such a wonderful word, isn't it? It actually sounds purple and soft. Don't worry, I returned home before it was completely dark. I wish you would write.

September 30th

Still nothing from you. I can hardly eat or sleep for my despondent mood prevents both, yet I know I must make an effort for the sake of the baby. It is seven o'clock in the morning and the weather is changing. Showers are forecast this afternoon, so I will catch the bus down into Llanelli at half-past nine and post all these diary recordings to you. I hope all is well with you, my darling man. Please write.

Mavis xxx

The first week of October brought gale force winds and heavy rain to Llannon, and Mavis' spirits sank as she battled her way to the shop. Just as well there was no Seamus to see her right now, with her mascara running down her face and her hair like rats' tails clinging to her neck. So intent was she in reaching the shop with no further damage to her appearance, her head buried in her umbrella, that she failed to notice the postman battling his way up Bethel Lane in the opposite direction, stopping finally at Seamus' house.

The day dragged interminably, with not one single customer calling in to relieve the boredom. Mavis re-stocked the shelves, dusted and swept until she could do no more, and eventually passed the time knitting tiny white booties ready for her baby. Eva and her husband wouldn't mind; Mavis was an industrious and thorough worker, and if a quiet spell occurred, she was welcome to do as she wished. Her thoughts plagued her, however, and as she knitted and counted stitches, she kept thinking "He loves me, he loves me not." Irrational ideas formed in her troubled mind, she started thinking that if she managed to knit another four rows before needing to start another ball of wool, then all would be well. She ran out of wool after three rows, and her heart plummeted. Gloom and despondency reigned supreme. Finally, it was five o'clock, and she could go home. The heavy rain had slackened to a slight drizzle, and the wind had dropped considerably. When she reached the top of Bethel Lane she could see that Ernest's car wasn't in its usual place outside the cottage, so she retraced her steps, deciding to check for post at Seamus' house. She almost wept with sheer relief when, amongst the piles of brown envelopes and other assorted mail, she found the letter she had been longing for. With shaking hands she opened it.

My darling woman,

I hope you are well and that the little one is starting to kick the hell out of you! I have missed you terribly, and am also guilty of not writing before now, but such a lot has happened. My poor mother died two weeks' ago, and we buried her last week. It has been chaotic over here, and as the oldest of her children, it was all left to me to sort stuff out. She didn't suffer, just slipped away quietly during her sleep. We should all hope for a peaceful ending like that, I suppose.

I actually wrote you a letter, then I put it down, meaning to post it, but couldn't find it, so had to write another. But then Ma passed away, so I never managed to post that one either. It was all such a crazy rush. I am not the most organised of people, as you well know, but the family were depending on me so much I just had to pull my finger out and take charge. Now I want to organise a phone conversation with you. It shouldn't be too difficult, but it will be necessary that I will be pretty much alone in the house when I ring. I am staying with my brother Niall and his wife, as my mother's small house will soon be cleared out and sold. The vultures await the rich pickings...... The new address is on the back of this page. But back to the telephone; Niall and Kate go to Mass on a Saturday evening, around six o'clock, and I will be alone for sure, then. The rest of the family usually go too, but as I am the heathen lapsed Catholic, my presence will not be expected. So, my darling woman, if you can arrange to be in my house three weeks from now on Saturday October 16th (for God only knows how long this letter will take to get to you!) at a quarter past six, I will ring you there. I hope you will be there, and I will be able to hear your sweet voice again.

I love you dearly.

Seamus.

Mavis folded the letter and kissed it gently, before putting it safely away in her handbag. Suddenly, all was right in her little world once more, and she returned home to her cottage with a lighter step, grateful that Ernest was still not home, and she could savour the letter once more, at her leisure, before writing a brief reply.

My dear Seamus,

Yes, I will make sure I will be standing right next to your phone when you ring me at precisely a quarter past six on Saturday the 16th of October! I am very sorry to hear about your mother, it must be such a sad time for you, but as you say, she went peacefully, and that is a blessing.

By now you should have received quite a collection of my thoughts and fears! Please forgive me, but it helped to write them down. Take care of yourself, and I will take care of our little one, I love you.

Mavis. Xxx

She couldn't wait for Thursday to come when she could go down into Llanelli on the pretext of visiting the market and post the letter. How she longed for the days to pass quickly, and for the sixteenth to arrive. The autumn storms abated, and Llannon settled into October. Mavis continued to take Dai out onto the track and enjoyed long walks with him, appreciating the spectacular browns and oranges of the trees, savouring that special quality that autumn brings to the air. When she went out early in the morning, the dewdrops glistened like diamonds on the intricate, lacy webs which hung delicately on the hedges, and the very air seemed to sparkle.

The baby was certainly making its presence felt now, and to Mavis it felt as though it was turning tiny somersaults inside her. She felt happy and positive, hugging herself in anticipation of being able to talk to Seamus very soon. Fate, however, threw a spanner in the works the morning of the sixteenth, with Ernest deciding to visit Fred and Margaret in the afternoon. "What time will we be back, Ernest?" Mavis demanded anxiously that morning.

"Well, I don't know, do I? They may ask us to stay to tea." He was oblivious to Mavis' concern.

"Invite us to tea? Oh, surely not!" Mavis' mind was racing, desperately trying to find a reason why tea at her stepson's house would be totally out of the question.

"What's the matter with you?" Ernest looked at her in exasperation. "Did you have some grand supper planned for us or something?"

"Yes! Yes I did!" Mavis crossed her fingers behind her back, hoping he wouldn't pursue it further. But he did. "What are you making, then? I don't want the mother of my child exerting herself too much." Ernest smiled at his saintly consideration.

"Um...a surprise." Oh, God, she thought, what on earth could she make? Then, inspiration seized her, and she continued, "I want to leave for Llanelli a bit earlier, so I can call in the Co-op in Felinfoel on the way and get what I need for tonight." There, she thought, all sorted. I'll buy some faggots in the co-op, I've got plenty of potatoes and there's dried peas in the pantry. He loves faggots and peas. She sighed with relief.

Ernest acquiesced, gruffly. "Very well. We will leave at two o'clock."

It was almost impossible for Mavis to relax and enjoy the afternoon out visiting. Margaret was quite chatty, for once, eager to tell Mavis all about her protegee's continuing success with ballet. It was with all her power that Mavis tried to pay attention to Margaret's account of Wendy's progress; her mind was elsewhere, longing for the moment when she would be able to speak with Seamus.

"Wendy won't be home until about four o'clock. Will you wait to see her when she comes back? She has had a ballet exam this afternoon, and Fred has to go up to town to fetch her when it finishes at half-past three."

"Yes, of course!" Mavis felt relieved that it would be no later. "I can't wait to see her. She is doing incredibly well, and so young too!"

"We have you to thank for that, Mrs Watton, you have been so generous."

Mavis smiled. "Please stop calling me Mrs Watton! You make me sound so old! And as I am going to be a mother before very long, I can't afford to appear old! From now on, you must call me Mavis!"

Margaret laughed. "I will. And I haven't asked you how you are doing? How far gone are you now?"

"Well, there's a bit of uncertainty about the exact dates." Mavis thought it prudent to stick to this "fact" just in case the baby put in an early appearance with a healthy weight. "But I am due around February. I dare say it will come when it's cooked. It kicks quite a lot now, and I have a little bump. Look!" She proudly smoothed the folds of her shift dress over the small swelling.

Margaret smiled. "Oh, I hope it all goes well with you. I had such an easy time with Wendy, all over in a few hours, and I came out of Brynglas wearing a pencil skirt! Mind you, with Julie it was another matter. She was the wrong way around and got stuck. I had to be transferred in an ambulance to Swansea, in the middle of labour! They had to use forceps to deliver her..." Margaret prattled on, as is the wont of mothers when they are talking to women pregnant for the first time. Mavis let her carry on, having learned by now not to believe all the horror stories and scaremongering so beloved of women who have been through the experience of childbirth. It couldn't be all that bad, they kept on having babies...

Fred arrived back with Wendy promptly at four o'clock, and she treated Mavis and Ernest to an impromptu performance of her exam pieces, humming the music as she danced. By five o'clock, Ernest got up to leave. There had been no offer of a meal, and the Wattons were able to depart punctually. As they drove home, Mavis was racking her brains as to the excuse she could come up with in order to escape at a quarter past six.

As they opened the back door, Dai rushed up to them, whining in pleasure at their return.

"I'll just take him out for a walk, then." Ernest reached for the dog's lead which was hanging on a hook by the door.

"No! I'll do it later, after I've peeled the potatoes! I need some fresh air, Eva told me that fresh air and exercise is vital for the health of the baby." Mavis wondered if all these fabrications would ever be uncovered.

"Oh, all right, then. I'm going to the shed to sort out the seeds for next year." And off he stomped, in his usual irritable way. The potatoes were peeled with lightning speed, and placed in the saucepan ready for boiling. Mavis had put the faggots in the oven, to be heated up later on, and the dried peas were soaking . At a quarter to six, Ernest returned from the shed.

"I thought you were taking Dai out? Seeing as you are still here, can you give me a neck shave, please?" Mavis wanted to scream with frustration. All the odds seemed stacked against this phone conversation with Seamus. There was no reason for her to refuse Ernest, however, so she got the brush and razor out ready. Poor Ernest was given the quickest neck shave of his life, and how Mavis didn't manage to slice his skin to ribbons or even cut through his carotid will remain forever a mystery. By ten past six, she was putting Dai's lead on him and heading for the door. "Don't be long, will you? I'm hungry!" Ernest settled down into his armchair, and unfolded the Llanelli Star, scanning the obituaries.

"I won't!" Before he could engage her in any further conversation she escaped and was walking briskly down the lane, Dai trotting along beside her.

It was a disappointed dog who followed her reluctantly into Seamus' house. He'd thought a nice long walk was on the cards, yet here they were in this house again. He would never understand humans...

Mavis sat down on the bottom step of the staircase and looked at her watch. Almost a quarter past. What if he didn't ring? How long should she wait? She was trembling with anticipation when she jumped out of her skin as the phone rang shrilly through the silence of the house. She snatched up the receiver.

"Hello?" Her voice sounded shaky and uncertain.

"Ah, 'tis wonderful to hear your voice, sweet Mavis!"

"Oh, Seamus, it's so good to hear you too! I have been so looking forward to this moment!"

"And how is the little one? How are you both faring?"

"We are both fine, Seamus, all is going well. I am so sorry about your mother. Such a sad time for you and your family."

"Yes, it's been a bloody nightmare. But as I said in my letter, my mother didn't die in pain and she wasn't distressed in any way. It is the end of an era, though. She was the linchpin of our family, everything revolved around her, we all turned to her in difficult times. We will all miss her terribly. But my family is fecking useless in a crisis, they couldn't organise a piss up in a brewery, and they are leaving it all to yours truly. And returning to the subject of letters.....such nonsense seems to fill your head, Mavis! Never doubt for one second that I love you – ever. Is that clear?" He sounded so stern, that for a moment, Mavis thought he was being serious. Then she heard his soft chuckle at the other end of the line.

"I'm sorry. It must be the pregnancy making me so neurotic."

"No need to apologise, my darling woman, just have faith, and remember that although we are apart, I think of you all the time, and can't wait until I see you again."

"And – and when do you think that will be?" There. She'd asked the crucial question. Seamus sighed heavily. "Oh, God only knows. There's so much to sort out, financial stuff, selling the property and so on. It's pointless me coming back to Wales until everything is done, I'll only get called back to sign some fecking document otherwise. But as soon as it's all completed, I'll be back! And I'll tell you what, Mavis, I won't stop nagging you to leave that miserable husband of yours! I'll get my woman in the end, you mark my words!"

Mavis smiled at his vehemence. "I do love you, Seamus."

"Ah, but I love you more..." They managed a few more minutes conversation, before Seamus said, reluctantly, "I have to go now, Mavis, this is an overseas call I am making, and it will be very easy to incur a hefty bill! But, I tell you what, if you can be here in a fortnight, the same time, we can have another little chat. Is that okay with you?"

"Of course, Seamus. Not much happens in Llannon on a Saturday night! I think I will be able to manage it!"

"That's grand! We have another date, then! Take care, my gorgeous woman, I love you." "Goodbye, Seamus. I love you too...." She waited until she heard the click as he put the phone down, then she gently replaced the receiver. Mavis looked down at the dog, patiently waiting for her at her feet. "C'mon, Dai, let's go for our walk now."

Chapter Twenty-three

A season of change.

October may have started balmy, but it shivered its way into an unusually frosty November. Mavis had been fortunate enough to enjoy quite a few phone conversations with Seamus, and even though she left his house longing for him, it made her feel so much happier and secure. Indeed, it had become fairly routine that they should speak once a fortnight. However, it was never merely routine in Mavis' mind, she always felt her heart thumping wildly as she opened the door to Seamus' house.

It was during a quiet moment in chapel that Mavis felt the baby move really vigorously. Everyone's heads were bowed in deepest prayer, when she suddenly felt a flickering in her lower abdomen. She clasped her hand to her tummy with a sharp intake of breath. Eira Jones looked up at her in astonishment, but Mavis was grinning like a Cheshire cat, her eyes sparkling in delight. She wanted to laugh out loud and announce it to the whole congregation, but she didn't think it would go down too well amongst the dour, stern chapel members. Instead, she consoled herself by planning how she would tell Seamus when they spoke on the phone in a couple of weeks.

"Are you coming to the Sisterhood meeting on Tuesday evening?" Old Flossie Pugh caught her as she was leaving after the service. Mavis groaned inwardly. She couldn't think of anything more boring than sitting with a crowd of middle-aged and elderly women, listening to a visiting speaker on subjects like collecting butterflies or the real meaning of Christmas. But she supposed as the deacon's wife she should really make an effort.

"Yes, of course," she replied, suppressing a sigh. "I shall look forward to it. Who is the guest speaker?"

"Oh, we are having a special guest, indeed!" Flossie Pugh's false teeth were almost rattling in her excitement. "Mr Peter Brown from Ynys Fach farm is coming to speak to us about his recent holiday to Ireland."

Mavis smiled, thinking she may even learn something about Seamus' native land. "I shall certainly look forward to it."

Her appetite had returned, thankfully, and Mavis was able to enjoy her Sunday dinner with Ernest. His initial solicitous manner had diminished somewhat, but he still insisted she put her feet up on Saturday afternoon while he peeled the vegetables for the following day. Always the same, she thought, as she poured gravy over her food. Roast lamb (or chicken if she had been over the Bowen's farm) mashed potatoes, (roast potatoes were reserved for Christmas dinner) mashed carrots and parsnips and Leo dried peas. But it was so lovely to feel hungry again, although she certainly didn't feel like eating for two.

"What's for pudding?" Ernest looked up expectantly as he scooped up the last drops of mint sauce and gravy with his knife, before popping it into his mouth. Mavis wished he wouldn't do that. She got up to clear the plates away.

"I haven't made anything special. I could open a tin of peaches and there's a can of sterilised cream in the pantry as well."

Ernest grunted his disapproval. "We always have that for Sunday tea, not pudding. Never mind. I suppose it's due to your condition that you seem to be neglecting your housekeeping!" Mavis said nothing, but pursed her lips and got on with the washing up. It just wasn't worth starting an argument. Lying down on her bed for an afternoon nap (she was excused Sunday School duties on account of the pregnancy) she ran her hand over her tummy. Her bump was getting quite pronounced now, although when she positioned the mirrors to check her appearance from behind, she still had a neat waist and didn't look pregnant at all. She had quite forgotten to tell Ernest about the baby kicking her. All her excitement had been focussed on Seamus' reaction when she would tell him. Oh, well, she would tell him over the despised tinned peaches and cream later on. She drifted off to sleep, her fingers lying protectively over her tummy.

It may have been the relaxing effect of the pregnancy hormones, but her sleep these past few days had been calm, her dreams pleasant and she felt at peace regarding her long-distance relationship with Seamus.

Tuesday evening was bitterly cold, and Mavis longed to be able to wear her fur coat to attend the Sisterhood meeting, but felt it would be rather ostentatious, so opted for her camel hair coat instead. Passing her portrait in the hallway, she glanced up at it, remembering the happiness she had felt during its production, and her longing for Seamus cut through her like a knife. The softness of the fur coat seemed at odds with the cool expression on her face. If anyone could ever guess at the heat of that moment, when she and Seamus.... She pulled a red woolly hat on her head, and set off down the lane towards the Sunday School Hall, where the meeting was taking place. The sky was inky blue, with no moon to light the way, but the stars sparkled with an intense wintry brilliance, not being overshadowed by their lunar sister this evening. Just as well it was a short walk, as she had forgotten her gloves and her fingers would soon be frozen. The members of the Sisterhood were already seated when she opened the door to the main room, mostly dressed in drab shades of dark brown and navy, like a bunch of disapproving prison wardens. Removing her warm coat, Mavis took her seat, once again standing out like a beautiful red rose against a stony wall, as she sat down in her scarlet corduroy pinafore dress, which was loose and hid the bump quite nicely. The guest speaker had already arrived and was busy setting up a table, placing numerous postcards and photographs on it. He was clearly nervous, as he kept having to have a drink of water from the carafe thoughtfully provided for him by the Chairwoman, Mrs Thomas-Y-Llaeth, the milkman's wife. Mavis watched in lurid fascination as his Adam's apple bobbed up and down vigorously when he swallowed mouthful after mouthful of water. Any hopes she'd had of an interesting insight into Seamus' heritage were soon dashed, as Mr Brown's voice droned on and on, lulling her into a soporific state. Just as she was slipping into a delightful dream about rowing across the sea to Ireland in a gigantic pink shell, she suddenly became aware of someone waving frantically at the glass panel of the door. It was Eiddwen! "Er, excuse me, I don't feel terribly well, I have to go," she whispered to Flossie Pugh on her right, "please give my apologies to Mr Brown. It's the baby, you know." Mrs Pugh nodded understandingly, and looked pleased at having been taken into the confidence of the deacon's wife. Mavis left the room as discreetly as she could, and found Eiddwen, wearing a chic tweed suit, almost hopping with excitement in the porch.

"Oh, Mavis! I'm back!"

"I can see that!" laughed Mavis. "Let's not wait around here! Shall we go somewhere else? Your house? Where's the Professor?"

"Oh, we can't go back to my house! I went there when we arrived, and the twins wouldn't let the Professor in!" Eiddwen looked agitated.

"Where on earth are you going to stay tonight?" Surely, thought Mavis anxiously, they wouldn't stay at Seamus' house?

"Oh, Archie booked us in to the Thomas Arms Hotel. He's outside in the hired car, he could take us there now and we could have a lovely chat!" Mavis looked dubious. If Ernest discovered she had left the Sisterhood meeting and gone gallivanting down to Llanelli with Eiddwen and her husband, he would have something to say about it.

"Oh, please, Mavis." Eiddwen looked at her with beseeching eyes.

"Oh, very well. But I will have to be back by half-past eight. You know how fussy Ernest is." They linked arms and headed for the Professor and the hired car, which to Mavis' astonishment turned out to be a huge, black Humber Super Snipe, brand new and shining under the yellow light of the Sunday School Hall lantern. She settled down in the back seat, and the car purred its way back on to the main road, and down towards Llanelli. Over two glasses of lemonade and a packet of crisps, Mavis and Eiddwen sat in the snug of the Thomas Arms Hotel and exchanged news, hardly able to get their words out, such was their eagerness to talk. The Professor had made himself scarce and retired to the hotel room, aware of the friends' need to gossip and indulge in womanly talk. There was nobody else around. Tuesday evenings in November were not the busiest in Llanelli. A few portly gentlemen were propping up the bar in the front lounge, but the snug lived up to its name and provided a cosy venue for Mavis and Eiddwen. They spent the first half hour looking at Eiddwen's wedding photos. Mavis ooh-ed and ahh-ed in all the right places, and she had to admit that even the mousey little Eiddwen looked like a film star at her wedding, so radiant was she with sheer joy.

"How are you feeling? What's it like being pregnant?" Eiddwen's eyes were nearly popping out if her head as she took in the little bump just visible under Mavis' dress. She reached out a hand to touch it, tentatively.

"It does feel strange sometimes, as though my body isn't my own anymore!" Mavis laughed. "But it's lovely at the same time. How long are you back home for?"

Eiddwen became serious. "I don't think I can call Llannon "home" anymore. I have become the black sheep of the family. Scotland is my home, now, Mavis. We are going to stay a few days, and go back in the hired car as far as Cardiff, then catch a train. I have to collect my clothes and sort out financial things. Archie will help me do that. Since I have known him, it's made me realise how empty my life was before, how much I was taken for granted, and that nobody really cared about what I felt or what I wanted. Now my life is so different. Archie is a wonderful husband."

"I am really happy for you, Eiddwen." Mavis gently squeezed her friend's hand then grinned broadly. "Now! What's all this you wanted to tell me about, er, married life?"

Eiddwen blushed and tittered behind her hands. She took a deep breath. "Well, Mavis, it's like this…"

By twenty-five past eight, Mavis was walking up the lane to her cottage, having made arrangements to meet Eiddwen in Llanelli on Thursday, as she would be working in the shop the following day. Mavis would catch the bus down, and get off at the Thomas Arms, which lay on the main road in to the town. As she passed Seamus' house, she glanced at the dark, empty windows, and wondered anew at the dramatic changes she had experienced over the last six months. Was the shadow of their love lingering within the house's darkened rooms…? Before pushing open the garden gate, she turned around, looking over at the twinkling lights of Swansea in the distance, and saw an enormous golden moon peep over the eastern horizon. Moonrise in Wales, she thought, may the same moon look down on my love, so far away. Sighing with longing, she walked up the path and went into the cottage.

Ernest was sitting facing away from her, reading the paper.

"Hello, I'm back," she announced, removing her coat.

"Are you indeed?" His back with rigid with displeasure, his voice loaded with sarcasm. "And how did the meeting go?" In an instant, Mavis realised that he had found out she had left the meeting. Her heart beat faster, and she felt a wave of panic threaten to wash away her normal composure.

"Wh-what do you mean?" She played for time, dreading his next words.

"You know perfectly well what I mean." He turned around, glaring at her from above his glasses. "I went down to the hall to check on the boiler as it was so cold, and lo and behold – no sign of the virtuous Mrs Watton! She was unwell, I was unreliably informed by Flossie Pugh! So – where in God's name have you been? And at this time of night, in the dark?" Mavis felt trapped. There was no way around it, she had to tell him where she had been. She took a deep breath and swallowed. "Eiddwen turned up at the Hall, she is down in Llannon for a short visit. It was inappropriate that we should gossip during the meeting, so her husband drove us down into Llanelli so we could have a nice chat. And anyway, if you had been told I wasn't well, why are you sitting here reading a newspaper?! Why aren't you searching the ditches and roadsides for me? I could have been seriously ill! No, you had already decided I was committing some transgression or other! " But despite her vigorous attempt at turning the tables, she felt her stomach churning, knowing what the next question would be.

"And where exactly did you go in Llanelli? And what was wrong with Eiddwen's house? And why didn't you ask me first?" The questions were being fired at her rapidly, one after the other, as though from a machine gun. She clenched her fists together in her intense anxiety. However, Mavis refused to be intimidated by him. She looked up at him defiantly, her head in the air. "I don't need your permission to go anywhere, Ernest." Her tone was icy and far from apologetic. "But since you feel I owe you an explanation, Eiddwen and her husband took me to their hotel, the Thomas Arms. We had a lovely hour together."

"The Thomas Arms?!" He spluttered in disbelief, his face contorted in anger. "My wife, the mother of my unborn child was cavorting in a pub? How dare you behave like that!"

"I did no cavorting. I drank lemonade. I had a conversation with a female friend. In a hotel." It was all Mavis could do to prevent herself bursting into tears, for she knew in her heart of hearts that Ernest would see that as a sign of weakness and an admission of guilt.

White with fury, he stood up and walked a few steps towards her. Dai whimpered and went to hide under the kitchen table. The kitchen clock ticked loudly and audaciously during the brief silence that followed. "Don't you answer me back, you brazen woman! Don't you dare!" He started to raise his hand as though to slap her.

"Stop!" Mavis shouted instinctively, holding her hands out as if to fend off an attack. "Don't come any closer. There is a defenceless little baby in my body, Ernest. If you lay so much as a finger on me you will never see me again. Do you understand?"

Ernest remained speechless, his hand still held up. Mavis continued, her eyes blazing. "I know full well that you seem to take pleasure in inflicting punishment on certain disreputable women, but I am not one of them. You need to control your temper, Ernest, or it will be your downfall." She didn't wait to see his reaction, but left the room swiftly, slamming the kitchen door behind her.

"Attack is the best form of defence," she murmured to herself as she ran upstairs, before locking herself in the spare bedroom for the night. She heard no more from him that night.

"Whatever's the matter, Mavis?" Mavis did not look up, but carried on stacking the bottom shelf with liquorice sticks. Eva's concern was almost too much for her to bear, and she had to bite the inside of her lip to stop the tears filling her eyes.

"Nothing, I'm fine." Mavis forced a bright smile on her face.

"You know, if coming in to work here is getting too much for you, then you can always give up early." Eva looked kindly down at Mavis' pale face.

"Oh no!" Mavis' protest came out with almost indecent speed. "I enjoy my work here in the shop. It isn't heavy work, and it keeps me occupied!" The thought of being stuck at home with Ernest an extra two days a week filled her with dread. Breakfast had been silent and strained; Ernest had then stormed off down to the Sunday School Hall, to mend the boiler, which had indeed been faulty the previous evening.

"Very well. But the moment it becomes difficult, you must let me know, yes?"

Mavis smiled weakly. "Of course." Then, filled with inspiration, she added, "Does Mr Griffiths want me to take the coins down to the bank for him tomorrow? I was thinking of going in to town?" That would give her the perfect excuse to go into Llanelli and meet up with Eiddwen, as she would have no way of letting her friend know that she wouldn't be coming. Eiddwen would be terribly disappointed and worried.

"Well, that would be most helpful, Mavis! If you're sure…?"

"No problem at all, Eva! My pleasure!" Mavis continued tidying up the shelves with a more cheerful expression on her face. Eva turned away, thoughtful. That woman is hiding something, she pondered, as she left the shop to start on her rounds, I only hope it is nothing serious.

When she left the shop at five o'clock, it was almost dark. Bethel Lane had no street lights, but the road was so familiar to her that she didn't stumble or trip on the rough ground. As she passed Eira Jones' cottage, Mavis could see the warm glow of the fire through the window, and Eira bustling about in her kitchen, the picture of domestic happiness. Mavis sighed, despondently. Any warmth she felt these days came long-distance, over the sea from Ireland. Her own home was like the North Pole. Entering the cottage, Mavis found a letter addressed to both her and Ernest on the doormat. It was postmarked Llanelli and had tiny pictures of Christmas trees dotted all the way around the envelope. It must have arrived with the second post around mid-day, or Ernest would have opened it. It was an invitation forwarded by Fred and Margaret, to watch Wendy's ballet school in their Christmas performance. Two tickets had been enclosed.

Miss Daphne cordially invites you to attend this year's Christmas ballet at the Parish Hall. The primary classes will perform a selection of short dances with a Christmas theme, and the senior school will perform "The Nutcracker." We would like to introduce one of the primary students during this performance. Wendy Watton, just seven years old, will dance a solo as a snowflake during the Land of Snow scene.

We look forward to your company on December 10th at six o'clock. Curtains up at half past six.

Now that's just what I need to cheer me up, Mavis thought with pleasure as she put the invitations back in the envelope. She wondered if Ernest would come with her. If he didn't want to go, maybe she could ask Eva to join her, if she wasn't on-call. And there he was, taking off his muddy boots at the kitchen door, back from helping Mr Bowen over at the farm.

"What's for supper?" He searched for his house shoes. Mavis picked them up from under the settle and handed them to him.

"I thought I'd make a shepherd's pie." Honestly, she thought, once again he behaves as though nothing is wrong, as though nothing at all happened last night. Dutifully, she showed him the invitations.

"Hmph!" He scanned the writing through his half-rimmed spectacles. "Namby-pamby fancy stuff! You go if you want, Mavis, but I won't be going. It's close to Christmas and there's too much going on at the chapel."

"I will be going." she replied, archly. "Wendy is your grand-daughter, and a very talented little girl. Do you realise how much of an honour it is to have been chosen to dance a solo at the age of seven?" Ernest looked at her blankly.

"No, I have no idea and have no interest in such frivolity. Have you boiled the potatoes yet?" Mavis gave up any hope of generating any interest, and carried on making the supper. As she mashed the potatoes for the topping, she turned to Ernest and said,

"I will be going into Llanelli tomorrow morning, I will be taking the petty cash down to the bank for Mr Griffiths." He looked up from the Llanelli Star.

"I will take you down if you like."

"Oh, that's not necessary." Damn, she thought, what excuse can I make to catch the bus. Then, her usual resourcefulness came to the rescue. "No, there's no need for you to do that. I'll have to call in the shop to collect the money on the way, and Eva said she may give me a quick check-up. She thought I looked a bit peaky this morning." Phew, she thought, only a little fib.

"As you wish." He continued his reading. "I hope supper won't be long. I'm hungry."

Mavis spent a delightful couple of hours with Eiddwen the following day. They didn't stay at the Thomas Arms, but headed into town, settling down in the Blue Orchid for coffee as soon as the money had been deposited at Lloyds' Bank. Mavis felt there was nothing wrong in being seen with Eiddwen in a cafe, although she suspected Ernest strongly disapproved of Eiddwen's dramatic elopement with Professor Drummond. The last time they had sat in this cafe, Seamus had been with them. How she missed him, what wouldn't she give for him to saunter in through the door, with that roguish grin on his face and irrepressible twinkle in his eyes.

"I said, what are you having, Mavis?" Eiddwen looked at her quizzically into her reverie.

"Oh, sorry! I was just daydreaming then. I think, as it's so cold, I'll have some soup and a roll. Yes, that'll do me."

"Ooh, I'll have a custard slice and an éclair!" Eiddwen giggled naughtily. "Archie likes me nice and rounded!" Mavis smiled indulgently at her friend. Long gone were the days when she would chide Eiddwen for being greedy.

"You enjoy yourself, Eiddwen. Life is too short to deprive yourself." Mavis turned to the window while Eiddwen attracted the waiter to take their order, and watched the passers-by, all muffled up against the frosty weather, their noses red from the cold and their breath hanging like clouds in front of their faces. It would be December in a couple of weeks, and time to start preparing for Christmas. What a pity Eiddwen wouldn't be in Llannon for much longer, she could have come to see Wendy's performance with her. They spent the rest of the morning wandering around the market, then popped in to Marks and Spencers because Eiddwen wanted to buy some new underwear. Just as Eiddwen picked up a pair of sensible white cotton knickers, Mavis put her hand on her arm, saying quietly, "Eiddwen. You are a married woman, your husband is well off, you should consider buying your lingerie from Renee Gwylim. Something silky and pretty!"

"Do you think I should?" Eiddwen looked doubtfully at the size 14 knickers and reluctantly put them back on the counter. Mavis smiled triumphantly. "Most definitely. Come on, let's pay my favourite shop a visit!" Arm in arm, they retraced their steps down Vaughan Street, turning left into Stepney Street. Eiddwen was quite pink with excitement when they finally emerged from the shop, weighed down with bags of frothy "bits of nonsense," as the discreet shop assistant put it.

"I wonder what Archie will say when I put them on!"

"Do you let him see you in your underwear?" Mavis teased.

"Actually, yes, of course I do!" Eiddwen giggled, conveniently forgetting how timid and shy she had been on her wedding night. They walked slowly back up the hill to the Thomas Arms, the sun warming them nicely, any early morning frost having long disappeared.

The Town Hall clock struck the hour. "It's one o'clock, Eiddwen, I had better be getting home," Mavis said, reluctantly.

"So soon? We leave tomorrow. You will keep in touch, won't you? I'll send you a Christmas card!"

"Yes, of course!" They hugged each other, and Eiddwen stood on the steps of the hotel, waving goodbye to Mavis as she headed for the bus stop. As she sat on the bus, looking out of the window at the small houses which lined the main road, then enjoying the beauty of Parc Hardd, she turned to her right, to Brynglas Maternity Hospital. She shivered, wondering anew what childbirth would be like for her. So far, all was going well with the pregnancy. Her blood pressure remained normal, and her weight gain was announced "perfect" by old Sister Leeman, a midwife in her late sixties, who didn't go out on call on but ran the Llannon ante-natal clinic. Mavis was fortunate in that no varicose veins had developed, no stretch marks had appeared and she felt incredibly healthy. Best of all, the baby seemed to be growing nicely.

Mavis had thoroughly enjoyed her morning out, and resolved to return to Llanelli before Christmas in order to indulge in a little Christmas shopping. Maybe she should start buying clothes for the baby? And what about a secret gift for Seamus, one she could post easily over to Ireland? She would go alone into town, and make a day of it, maybe next week.

The weather, however, decided otherwise. By Saturday, snow clouds from the Arctic circle had descended upon South Wales, covering Llannon in a soft, white blanket, effectively cutting it off from the rest of the world. Ernest forbade Mavis from trudging down to the shop through the ten inches of snow which lay on the ground, so she was confined to the cottage, while Ernest joined the other men of the village in clearing the main road as best they could. Local children, excited beyond belief, spent hours making snowmen, and having snowball fights. Several bumps and bruises were sustained whilst tobogganing down the many hills on makeshift sledges made from pieces of cardboard and tin trays. How beautiful everything looked, thought Mavis, as she sat at her bedroom window, looking out at the countryside. After the heavy snow which had fallen overnight, the sky had cleared and was now a brilliant blue. The ground was dazzling in its whiteness; everything sparkled and looked as clean as Eira Jones' Monday wash. She longed to go outside and walk up to the track, but her desire to protect her baby was uppermost in her mind. One little slip and goodness only knows what could happen. Although Eva had told her that once a pregnancy was well-established, it was extremely difficult to lose the baby, Mavis didn't want to take any chances. She wondered how long the snow would last, and whether the postman would be able to get to Bethel Lane. She was due a letter from Seamus, and he would be telephoning in a week's time. The whole world seemed a different place, as though Llannon had been uprooted and transplanted far away in Switzerland. There was a strange silence over the whole village, only shattered by the occasional shriek of children playing in the snow. No cars travelled up from Llanelli, and nothing came the other way, from Tumble. Mavis was jolted out of her reverie as some snow fell off the roof, having melted in the midday sun, landing with a thump on the front garden. She got up and went downstairs, and let Dai out into the back garden. He had already been out earlier, when it was still dark. Now he revelled in this wonderful and strange environment, as excited as any Llannon child, leaping about, scattering pawfuls of snow as he went, trying to eat it, before deciding it was time he started digging. It was anyone's guess where the digging was actually taking place – it might even be just above Ernest's prize-winning carrots! As she sat and knitted mittens, her mind wandered aimlessly from the pregnancy, to Seamus, to Christmas. With a gasp of horror she realised she hadn't responded to the ballet invitation. It was only two weeks away, Margaret would think her terribly rude if she didn't reply. But she didn't have a telephone, and goodness only knew when the post would start running again. The forecast on the radio had announced that there would be little chance of any more snow, but that it would remain extremely cold. I know, she thought, I'll ring from Seamus' house. Fred and Margaret don't know that Seamus is away and that I let myself in, and Ernest won't be back until after three, as he is going to check all is well at the chapel. Pulling on a thick jacket and her wellington boots, she cautiously made her way across the lane. Only Ernest's footprints could be seen, as their cottage was the last one before the lane came to an end and the hills began. The cold air and bright sunshine made her eyes water, making her sneeze and sniff. How unromantic, she thought to herself, just as well nobody can see me! The big, old house stood empty and lonely, with cruel-looking icicles hanging from the eaves. Un-lived in and bereft. As Mavis opened the kitchen door, she noticed how terribly cold the house was. She hoped the pipes hadn't frozen. Poor Seamus, imagine coming back to a flooded house! She went straight to the phone without checking the porch for any letters, and rang the Bakers immediately. Gwyneth answered, sounding as pleased as punch when Mavis said she would be attending the show. The phone call wasn't a long one, as she told Gwyneth she was ringing from a neighbour's house.

Taking a cursory glance at the porch, she was surprised to see that a small package had been posted through the letterbox, along with some other post, mostly in brown envelopes. She bent down to pick it up. It was addressed to Seamus, but then she recognised Seamus' own sprawling writing immediately, as well as the Irish postmark, so was obviously meant for her. It must have arrived yesterday, as it hadn't been there when she had checked a couple of days ago. The little parcel took ages to open, as it had been secured over and over again with Sellotape. Cursing as she broke a nail in her struggle to tear open the thick, brown paper, she found that there were in fact two separate, tiny parcels inside, along with a covering letter.

My darling Mavis,

I hope you are blooming! I have enclosed your Christmas presents, one you may open now, because I know how insatiably curious you are, but keep the other until the Big Day! I have labelled them number 1 and number 2, so open them in that order. You may be puzzled at the first one - but just remember the meaning of your name, and all will become clear. I hope you like them. I am so looking forward to talking again very soon, my darling woman.

I love you, Seamus.

The packet with the number 1 on it was covered in red tissue paper, which Mavis opened as carefully as her quivering fingers would allow. Her eyes lit up with pleasure as she uncovered a tiny golden brooch in the shape of a little bird. My name, she thought to herself, "Mavis" means "songbird." On closer examination, she could see that the bird's eye was formed by a minute blue stone – a sapphire, maybe? – and the wings were tipped with even smaller red stones, which sparkled prettily in the sun as it shone through the fanlight above the door. She pinned it to the inside of her jacket. Later she would think of a way to wear it. Putting the letter and packet number 2 into her pocket, she returned to her cottage with her spirits renewed and a steely determination to go down to Llanelli as soon as she could, to choose her gift for Seamus.

The temperature continued to hover just below freezing, and Mavis began to think a thaw would never come, that she would be confined to the cottage for ever. The soft snow froze overnight, becoming deadly once morning came. Dai, the greedy dog, would rush out, slipping and sliding everywhere, gobbling up all the breadcrumbs Mavis had put out in the garden for the birds, so she resorted to placing them on the window-sill. She smiled at herself. The old Mavis would never have done that, for fear of the birds messing on her windows. On the clothes-line, Ernest's white shirts were rigid with ice. Just like Ernest, Mavis thought, ruefully. She was grateful that they had plenty of food in the pantry, and there was always powdered milk if they ran out. Bread and milk, she thought, why did everyone panic about bread and milk each time it snowed? Anyone would think they were all a nation of hedgehogs! But the thaw did come eventually, with sombre rain-clouds scudding in from the west overnight on the Wednesday, washing away the snow and ice into a grey and grimy slush. Good, Mavis thought, she would venture into town on the weekend, or maybe the weekend after, and have a good look around for Seamus' present.

A curtain of fog welcomed Mavis when she woke on the first Saturday morning in December. It was still quite dark at eight o'clock, and she had to put the kitchen light on to see what she was doing. Maybe should wait until the afternoon before going in to Llanelli, she thought, as she put a saucepan on the stove to boil water for her egg. If she left it late enough, the Christmas lights would be turned on in the town centre, the shops would be brightly lit and prettily decorated. She hoped Ernest would cut a decent tree down for them this year. Mr Bowen the Farm did a roaring trade this time of year, as he had a small field dedicated to growing conifers. Ernest took whichever one he fancied, as he helped the Bowens so frequently on the farm. However, he tended to choose a small tree, making it easier to load into the back of the Reliant.

The baby gave an almighty kick just as she was finishing the piece of cheese she was eating alongside the egg. It always amused her that whenever she had a meal, the baby would kick in excitement (or so it seemed to her) as though enjoying the food as well. She had no real idea as to how advanced the pregnancy was, she just hoped and prayed that it wouldn't arrive too early. None of her normal clothes would fit her anymore, and she'd had to resort to loose-fitting tunics – but she refused to consider smocks.

Ernest had gone down to the chapel to turn the boiler down; now that the cold spell had broken, there was no need to waste precious funds on overheating the place. Mavis shivered into her mackintosh as she waited for the two o'clock bus into Llanelli. The fog was cold and damp, penetrating even the three layers of clothing she was wearing. But she had her long-distance love to keep her warm, and she reminisced about the phone call she had had with Seamus the previous week. He had been delighted the parcel had arrived safely and wanted to know how she was managing to wear the little brooch. Mavis had told Ernest that Eiddwen had given it to her as an early Christmas present before leaving for Scotland. There was little chance he would be in contact with Eiddwen, as she wouldn't be returning to south Wales for a while, and the two had never been close friends anyway. With numb fingers, she caressed the tiny bird, which she had pinned to the lapel of her mackintosh. Such a beautiful gift, and she still had the other one to open on Christmas Day! But she had better find a present for Seamus this afternoon, as the days were racing by, and she would have to wrap it, address it and post it by the end of next week at the latest.

As the bus passed Brynglas maternity home, she saw a young couple emerging , then getting into a waiting taxi. The woman was holding a white bundle as though it was the rarest piece of Dresden china. How wonderful to be taking a baby home, just in time for Christmas. Once again, she felt a wave of trepidation, as she considered her relentlessly approaching labour. The town centre was bustling, with crowds of people thronging the streets. Although the snow had gone over a week ago, it was still cold, with dwindling piles of dirty slush gradually melting on the pavements and street corners. The Salvation Army was gathered around the entrance of Boots the Chemist, and was busy tuning up before embarking on their Christmas repertoire. Mavis needed to buy a few things in Woolworth's, namely tree lights and presents for Wendy and Julie, but first she needed to pay a visit to the jewellery shops, as she now had a more definite idea of what she would buy for Seamus. She didn't want to be weighed down with shopping and have to carry heavy bags from shop to shop.

Saul Cass, Thomas' and Samuel's had nothing to tempt her, so she made her way back through the market, heading for Station Road. The spicy smell of faggots hung in the air, making her feel suddenly hungry. But she had no time to spare. The walk down Station Road in the winter seemed so much more prolonged and arduous than in the warm days of summer, and it took her a good ten minutes to reach her destination. Mavis had almost forgotten about the small jewellery shop at the bottom of the road, but then had suddenly remembered passing it in the car with Ernest only recently. Alan Evans' jewellery shop stood tucked away between the dark, red brick houses of lower Station Road. As she pushed open the glass door, the bell rang and a small, bald man peered at her from over his thick-lensed spectacles. "Good afternoon, Madam. How may I help you?"

"Do you have any cigarette boxes? I wish to buy a special one." The man removed his glasses and sighed heavily, shuffling the papers on the glass counter.

"Let me see.....I think I have one or two left. Not that popular anymore, not here in Llanelli, anyway." He disappeared behind a bead curtain, returning with two packages and placing them on the counter. Mavis took little time in selecting the box for Seamus. She thought the alligator skin case rather ostentatious and common, so opted for the sterling silver box. The shopkeeper beamed in approval. "Excellent choice, Madam, if I may say so. This is made by Joseph Gloster – see? There's the hallmark and the maker's mark. Mind you, it is rather expensive."

"How much?" Mavis felt inside her handbag for her purse.

"Three pounds and ten shillings." He looked up at her anxiously, as if afraid she would change her mind, but she was smiling at him.

"Will you wrap it up for me please?" She placed a five pound note on the counter, delighted with her purchase. Perfect.

Retracing her steps back up Station Road, Mavis noticed with pleasure that the fog was beginning to lift rapidly. A watery sun was reddening and starting to sink down behind the steeple of St Peter's church in Paddock Street, casting a rosy glow upon the shops and houses which lined the right side of the road. The most beautiful apricot sunset was developing, with candy-floss clouds stretching across the western sky. The eastern sky was already a dusky purple, night was fast approaching. As Mavis hurried along the pavement, she noticed a few Christmas trees in front windows, cheerfully lit with multi-coloured fairy lights. She wondered about the families who lived inside, whether they had children, what it would be like for them on Christmas Day. What would her life be like once the baby arrived? Would she ever experience that cosy, secure home life? Maybe Ernest would finally thaw when the baby arrived – but then, what about Seamus? It was all so confusing. Mavis turned up Murray Street to return to the main shops, trying valiantly to keep her mind on the present, and not to worry about her uncertain future.

"Aunty Mavis! Aunty Mavis!" She was almost knocked off her feet as a small pair of arms threw themselves around her hips.

"Be careful, Wendy! You must be more gentle with Aunty Mavis!" Margaret Watton fussed apologetically. "We have been to see Father Christmas in the Co-op." Margaret looked harassed but happy.

"He gave me a baby doll! Look!" Wendy was hopping up and down in excitement, her scarlet coat lending a glow to her usually pale cheeks.

"Well, aren't you lucky! I am sure you must have been very good indeed for him to have been so generous! And what did Julie have?" Julie stared solemnly up at Mavis from the depths of her black pushchair, her dark eyes watchful and serious.

"Oh, she just went to cry when she saw him, so Mammy has her present safe in her bag," replied Wendy dismissively.

"Would you like to come over to my mother's for tea, Mavis? We are on our way there now, Fred is working until six o'clock." Margaret suggested tentatively. "My father could give you a lift home then, if you want?"

"Oh, that would be really lovely, Margaret, but I have to go to Woolworth's to buy a few more things first. Could I call by after that?"

"Yes! It will lovely to see you, won't it, Wendy?" Wendy nodded in agreement, a beaming smile on her face. Julie sucked determinedly on her thumb.

Enjoying her second cup of tea cocooned in Gwyneth Baker's warm kitchen, Mavis was heartily glad she had bumped into Margaret and the children. Her feet were aching, and her back felt stiff as well. The joys of motherhood, she thought to herself ,wryly. Woolworth's had been packed full of busy shoppers and noisy children, so she had bought a few things then hurried over to Gwyneth's house. The stars had been peeping out as she'd made her way along the street, and only a faint pink blush had remained in the west. The two little girls were snuggled up together in an ancient armchair, sleepily looking through an equally ancient copy of a Bunty comic, their mouths covered with breadcrumbs and their cheeks smeared with butter.

"I am so looking forward to the show next Saturday." Mavis replaced her teacup. "Shall I ask Ernest to drop me off here and we can all go over to the hall together? Or shall I meet you there?"

"I have to take Wendy over early, about four o'clock," Margaret replied, "Mothers aren't allowed backstage! So, yes, come here around half past five and we can walk over in plenty of time. Mind you, we want to make sure we get good seats!"

"Yes, indeed!" Gwyneth Baker bustled about her kitchen efficiently. "I want to have a good view of my grand-daughter in her debut performance!" Mavis smiled. How she had enjoyed the women's company this afternoon. She should do it more often.

Seamus' present was duly packed and dispatched to Ireland, which Mavis felt bold enough to do from the local post office. After all, it was the time of year when everyone was sending cards and presents all over the world, so her little parcel shouldn't raise any eyebrows.

The days were bright and clear, the nights frosty and cold, but the weather held and there was no more snow. Saturday arrived, colder than ever, which gave Mavis the perfect excuse to wear her fur coat.

"Oh, that is such a beautiful coat, Mavis." Margaret gently stroked one of the sleeves. "It looks so glamorous!"

"It's nice and warm, anyway!" Mavis settled down onto the hard, wooden seat in the hall. Once more, she was surprised at how much she had changed. Just eight months ago she would have boasted about going up to London to buy it, and how expensive it had been. Modesty was a hat that she was starting to wear more easily. The hall was packed, the audience murmuring and busily reading the programmes. An important looking man behind them was puffing away on a pipe, sending clouds of aromatic smoke into the air. Mavis wished he would stop, or move further away, it made her feel quite unwell. The mayor and his sweet little wife were seated as guests of honour in the front row and Mavis was surprised to see that the school even had a small orchestra at the foot of the stage, with teenagers from local schools at the ready with violins and clarinets. A bespectacled, spotty youth was sat in front of the timpani and an elderly gentleman was ready with a trumpet. How professional! As she scanned the programme, she was gratified to spot Wendy's name listed amongst the soloists, as well as in the primary class group names.

"Wendy Watton." she read. "Snowflake." Her heart swelled with pride.

"Miss Daphne has had a new stage curtain put up," Gwyneth Baker whispered, passing round a paper bag of rum and butter sweets. "It doesn't rattle back, but rises up. Fancy that!" Just at that moment, the orchestra started to play, and the dark green curtains quietly lifted up with a subtle swish, revealing all the little dancers dressed in party clothes, ready and waiting to start the performance.

The general coughing and sweet-paper rustling soon stopped, and the ballet began.

Mavis was unfamiliar with The Nutcracker, so watched and listened intently, enjoying the music, which she seemed to remember from somewhere. The "babies" were soon on stage, as they had to leave early, and the audience had to try hard to hold back their laughter as several four year olds forgot to dance at all, preferring to seek out their parents in the crowd in order to wave at them.

"Good heavens," whispered Mrs Baker, in amusement, "I'm sure the little redhead on the end is still wearing a nappy! She must be younger than four, surely!" Margaret leaned over, giggling quietly. "That's Miss Daphne's little niece, Lynwen! She had a tantrum when she was told she couldn't be in the show, so they have allowed her this one scene. She's only two and a half!" The tiny Lynwen only lasted a few seconds on the stage, however, being totally overwhelmed by the lights and the sight of so many people. She scampered off into the wings, wailing and asking for her mother. The show was twenty minutes into the first half when Wendy ran lightly on to the empty stage to start her solo. Mavis and Margaret held their breath. Wendy stood in the centre of the stage, her head held high, with a beaming smile on her face. Mavis was sure she caught her eye, and that Wendy even gave her a cheeky wink! As she started to dance, the audience could tell they were watching a child with dance in her very soul. Each step was executed perfectly, and Wendy sailed through the air during her leaps. She appeared weightless, carried along by some invisible force, her white, tulle skirt floating along, glittering with hundreds of sequins, sewn on by her patient mother. The solo lasted just a couple of minutes, then the other "snowflakes" joined Wendy on the stage, but not before there was a deafening roar of applause. Wendy grinned happily at the audience, and even dipped into a quick reverence.

"Oh my dear Lord, I think I'm going to cry!" Margaret sniffed into her handkerchief. "Am I just a proud Mammy or was she as good as I thought?"

"Oh, yes. She was good, Margaret. She was superb." Mavis hastily brushed a tear away from her own cheek. The ballet continued, which Mavis found herself enjoying immensely. Much of the music did sound familiar, and it was wonderful to see it brought to life by the dancers and their colourful costumes.

The Sugar Plum Fairy was played by a tall, pretty girl of about fifteen.

"That's Jayne Howard." Margaret said quietly, as the soloist pirouetted and danced daintily across the stage. "She auditioned for the Sadler's Wells. She didn't get in, though."

I wonder if Wendy will audition for something like that one day, thought Mavis. She knew nothing about ballet or dance, but surely anyone could see the raw talent that Wendy possessed.

After the show, Miss Daphne beckoned Margaret over to talk to her backstage, while Gwyneth Baker and Mavis were left to calm a thoroughly over-excited Wendy, who was bouncing about still wearing her stage make up and ballet shoes. When she returned to join them, Margaret looked flustered, but was smiling.

"Miss Daphne wants Wendy to start having extra lessons! She said her performance this evening was astonishing, and that she has proven that she has tremendous promise. I am so thrilled, but I don't know how much it will cost! She mentioned some grants we could apply for, but maybe they wouldn't cover the cost anyway! And she was talking about auditioning for a place called Tring, or something!"

Mavis suddenly hugged Margaret. "Don't worry, she shall have the extra lessons. I will arrange the payment. This is a wonderful opportunity for her, Margaret. Don't let it slip away." Margaret looked at her step-mother in sheer gratitude. "How can we ever thank you, Mavis?"

Mavis smiled wickedly. "By helping me cope when my baby arrives!"

As they left the hall, all three women arm in arm, with Wendy skipping along in front of them, they heard the excited shrieks of the young dancers. "It's snowing again!"

Indeed it was. Tiny flakes of snow were whirling about in the air, settling on the pavements and casting a sugar frosting on the cars parked nearby. Maybe we'll have a white Christmas after all, thought Mavis happily.

Chapter Twenty-four

Noel

The Christmas tree lights shone brightly in the Wattons' rarely used parlour, and through its window the tree could be seen by any passers-by. But not many passed by these days, thought Mavis wistfully, as their cottage was the last in the lane, and there was no Seamus to walk by on his way up to the track. Outside, a light dusting of snow from earlier in the day provided a sugar-frosting on the grass, and a shy, crescent moon shone down upon Llannon. The room was otherwise in darkness, the multi-coloured lights casting a magical glow over the austere walls and furniture. In the dim light, the ancient paper chains on the walls looked grey. A sprig of holly had fallen off the mirror, awaiting the unwary to step on it. It was almost midnight on Christmas Eve, and Ernest had already gone to bed, leaving Mavis alone downstairs. She hardly ever stayed up so late, but she had decided to wait up until after twelve o'clock in order to open Seamus' remaining present. Reaching into her dressing gown pocket, she pulled out the small packet. After tearing open the white tissue paper, she could see that a note had been enclosed as well.

"I'll read that in a minute," she thought, hastily unwrapping the gift completely. It was a beautiful square of white linen, edged with delicate, intricate lace, with white satin bows at each corner. Slightly puzzled, she unfolded the note.

Happy Christmas, my darling woman,

I expect you are wondering why I have bought you a handkerchief. Well, it is a special one. It is a magic hanky, which would be given to you on our marriage, and then saved for our first born, to be made into a christening hat for the baby. I do not have you as my wife, but your first-born child is mine, so please accept this Christmas gift from me, on behalf of our little baby as well. Try and be at my house on Boxing Day morning at eleven o'clock if you can, as the family go to watch a rugby match around that time. I will ring you. I love you, sweet Mavis. Seamus.

Tears filled Mavis' eyes as she clutched the square of linen to her chest. What a beautiful gesture. Regretfully, she switched off the fairy lights, and crumpled up the note, kissing it briefly before throwing it in to the Rayburn fire. She could wake Ernest at this hour if she went scuffling about in the spare bedroom, and it would be far too dangerous to leave the note anywhere else until the morning. The hanky would attract no attention. Quietly, she climbed the stairs and slipped into her bedroom, where a lightly snoring Ernest had his back to her. Turning back the blankets, she got into bed and closed her eyes, trying to bury her own heartache and her longing for Seamus.

More than a light dusting of snow lay on the garden belonging to Eiddwen and the professor. The village had been snow-bound all week, with no cars or buses able to get through. Luckily, the professor had been prudent enough to ensure the larder was well-stocked and there was plenty of coal in the cellar to last them weeks. A huge leg of ham and a couple of pheasants had been procured from the wealthy landowner on the edge of the village, so while their Christmas dinner would be unusual, there would be plenty of it. The blizzard continued outside, making the bedroom unnaturally bright for half past eight in the morning. Eiddwen happily cuddled up to her husband. "Happy Christmas, Archie, cariad," she whispered, "are you awake?" She was answered by his hand creeping up inside her pink satin nightdress.

"Awake and ready, my angel!" He chuckled wickedly, then rolled her over on to her back. "Oh, Archie! You naughty boy! On Christmas morning as well?" Eiddwen giggled in delight as he nuzzled into her neck, working his eager mouth down towards her voluptuous breasts.

"Don't make me answer with my mouth full," he mumbled, his tongue licking her erect nipples.

"Don't you want your presents?" She wriggled away from him, teasingly.

"Don't you want to check what I have got for you?" he demanded, huskily. Eiddwen decided it was time to play the strumpet and nodded eagerly. She flung back the covers and screamed aloud with laughter, for there was Archie's proud member, beautifully decorated with silver tinsel. He grinned. "Happy Christmas, hen! You can unwrap it for me if you want!" Eiddwen started to undo the tinsel with her fingers, but he stopped her.

"Unwrap it with your teeth, Eiddwen." She looked at him in astonishment. "What d'you mean?" However, she was beginning to guess at what he was asking of her.

"Go on. Do it." He feigned a stern expression. "That's an order."

"But – but I..." She looked up at him in panic. "I don't know what to do." Her voice trailed away lamely, her cheeks aflame with embarrassment.

"Do what feels right," he whispered, kindly, "do anything you like - but don't bite me for heaven's sake!" To save her further distress, he quickly removed the tinsel himself, then lay back in the still-warm bed, to see what she would do.

"It smells of Lifebuoy soap," she observed, as she held it in her trembling hands.

"Of course it does!" He roared with laughter. "I got up while you were still asleep and gave it a good scrub!" Eiddwen brought it closer to her lips and breathed on it. "I am hotting it, that's what my mother used to do when I was small, and hurt myself."

He smiled, indulgently. "Well, hot it some more, and nearer as well!"

Obediently, she placed her lips over the tip, but without touching it, and breathed hard over it once more. Archie sighed in pleasure and anticipation. Looking up at the effect her actions had on him, she decided to take the plunge, and delicately licked it with her tongue, gently at first, like a kitten lapping milk, then more boldly. It's not so bad after all, she thought. In fact, it was quite exciting to do something as daring and wicked as this! Archie wisely interrupted her ministrations after a few minutes. One step at a time, laddie, he told himself, one step at a time.

"Roll onto your tummy, my plump little pudding! I want to play with your bum!"

The alarm clock rudely shattered Mavis' slumber at seven o'clock on Christmas morning. Groaning inwardly, she rolled over on to her side. However, Ernest threw back the blankets, creating an unwelcome draught. "Hurry up, Mavis! Don't be lazy, we can't be late for morning service!"

And a Merry Christmas to you, too, she thought irritably, reluctantly getting up and rubbing her stiff back. The baby gave a vigorous kick in sympathy. It was still dark, so Mavis put on the bedside lamp. "Happy Christmas, Ernest." She turned her face towards him and he dutifully pecked her on the cheek.

"Happy Christmas, Mavis. Shall I give you your present after breakfast? And then we'll have to get a move on to be in chapel by eight o'clock."

"Yes, of course." Mavis found it hard to shake off the melancholic feeling which was descending upon her. "Will we have time afterwards to visit my mother? Before we go to the Bowens', mind, because they are expecting us at half-past twelve." It was their custom to have Christmas dinner over at the farm each year, as the Bowens' children had long grown up and flown the nest. Mavis quite looked forward to Mrs Bowen's company, as she was jolly, talkative, and even more importantly, an excellent cook.

"If we must," he sighed, leading the way down the stairs, a look of martyrdom on his face.

"Thank you very much, Mavis." Ernest held up the maroon jumper in front of him. "It is indeed a lovely sweater. I will wear it today. And the socks are just what I needed. Diolch. Now open yours."

Mavis carefully unwrapped the square-shaped parcel on the table. A plain cardboard box was revealed, requiring more work for her small fingers. "Pass me a knife, Ernest, it's stapled down." What could it be, she wondered, as she struggled to open it. She made a valiant effort to force a smile on her face as she pulled out a shiny new saucepan.

"How lovely," she murmured through gritted teeth. "Just what I wanted. Thank you."

"Yes." Ernest looked immensely pleased with himself. "You were saying only the other day how much you needed a new saucepan!"

"Well, I am sure it'll come in very handy." Mavis put in the cupboard. "Now we had better get ready." At least it's fur coat weather today, she thought to herself.

Only a dozen or so people sat shivering in the pews that Christmas morning, which did not please Ernest at all. Backsliding, that's what his congregation was doing; he must put a stop to it at all costs. Mavis snuggled down into the depths of her coat, her hands tucked firmly into the pockets. Despite wearing woollen gloves, her fingers were almost numb with cold. The little brooch twinkled discreetly on the red scarf which she had wound around her neck, and the linen handkerchief was folded into a small square in her handbag. There was no organist to accompany the congregation, so no carols were sung. Ernest was having some difficulty in appointing a new organist, but didn't dare suggest inviting Gladys Williams to return.

The music-less service was over within half an hour, and the chapel rapidly emptied with almost indecent haste, the not-so-devout flock anxious to hurry home to their warm houses, the prospect of a hot Christmas dinner foremost on their minds.

"Shall we walk over to my mother's?" Mavis waited while Ernest locked the big wooden door of the chapel. "It's dry, and if we walk quickly we'll keep warm."

"As you wish, Mavis. But let's not stay long, I find your sisters quite tiresome, and they haven't been to chapel for many a Sunday." He took her arm, and they made their way through the quiet village. A few excited children were out and about, tentatively trying to ride shiny new bikes and scooters along the frosty pavements. Chimney smoke rose silently above the roofs, unchallenged by any breeze, and the smell of roast meat floated out from every slightly open, steamed up window. Ernest snorted in disapproval as they passed by the pubs, the landlords greeting each other across the road, getting ready for the expected revellers later on. The brightness of the sunshine made Mavis' eyes water, and she sneezed suddenly. To her horror, she felt a warm dampness between her legs. Surely she couldn't have wet herself? How dreadful! "We must go home, Ernest!" she cried in alarm.

"Why? Whatever is the matter now?" There was no concern in his voice, just irritation about the sudden change in plans.

"I, er, I think I am going to be sick! Quick, let's go home!" Without waiting for his assent, she turned around and practically ran back to Bethel Lane, Ernest storming after her in exasperation. Once inside the cottage, Mavis flung open the door of the bathroom and removed her clothing. How embarrassing! She had indeed involuntarily wet herself; with a burning face she hastily washed herself and dressed once more. Eva had told her this could happen, but was avoidable if she did her pelvic floor exercises. So far, she hadn't bothered, but made up her mind to practise them every single day from now on.

She returned to the kitchen, where Ernest sat irritably drumming his fingers on the table. "Are you finally ready?" He got up, pulling on his coat. Mavis stared at him incredulously. Ernest's insensitivity seemed to be reaching new heights, these days.

"Yes, I'm ready," she murmured, "but perhaps we had better drive over to my mother's."

After a tense and depressing visit to her mother's house, Mavis was able to relax in the friendly warmth of the Bowen's farmhouse kitchen. The log fire crackled in the grate, the smoky perfume of peat seeped comfortably into the room and the scent of cinnamon and nutmeg filled the air, as the Christmas pudding steamed away happily on the hotplate next to the fire. "A small sherry, Mr Watton?" Mrs Bowen's face beamed rosy and smiling as she held the bottle of Harvey's above four crystal glasses on the dresser.

"Oh, no, not for me," Ernest shook his head vigorously, " too many good Christian people have fallen from the wayside on account of the demon drink." He glanced meaningfully at Mavis, who artfully ignored his look and continued to smile happily at Mrs Bowen.

"Oh, cariad, if it wasn't for the little one I am carrying, I would join you in a festive celebration!" She looked sideways at the scowl on her husband's face. "If truth be told, alcohol has turned on me now, not that I was any big drinker anyway! But once my baby has safely arrived, I will most certainly be happy to celebrate his safe arrival!"

"It's a BOY?" Mrs Bowen looked at her incredulously, ignoring Ernest's glare of disapproval. "How can you possibly know?!"

Mavis laughed. "I don't know at all! It was a slip of the tongue! In fact, I keep imagining the baby in a froth of pink frills and as a mop of yellow curls!" In fact, she thought to herself, the opposite was true. The unborn baby seemed to enter her dreams with gangly, long limbs, clear blue eyes and a mop of untidy, straw-like hair. Mrs Bowen certainly did not disappoint her guests. Mavis, determined to enjoy her dinner for once, pushed all negative thoughts to the back of her mind, and sighed with pleasure at the loaded plate in front of her. Succulent slices of tender chicken, creamy mashed potatoes, crisp roast potatoes and a variety of vegetables from the farm garden lay in a pool of the tastiest gravy, and Mrs Bowen's secret recipe stuffing was absolutely sublime. The baby also showed its appreciation and give a walloping kick as Mavis forked up her last buttery carrot.

"Ready for pudding yet?" Mr Bowen beamed cheerfully at Mavis and Ernest, draining his glass of home-made beer, his cheeks shiny and pink.

"Oh, goodness me, not yet!" Mavis laughed, patting her tummy. " I think I need a bit of a rest!"

"Shall we play Consequences?" Mrs Bowen giggled over her glass of Snowball. "We can have pudding later!"

"What's that?" Ernest frowned across the table. He hoped it wasn't a frivolous game involving alcohol.

"Oh, it's a silly schoolgirl game, Mr Watton!" Mr Bowen busied himself handing around pieces of paper and pencils. "We'll explain as we go along...."

Twenty minutes later, Mavis was unfolding her sheet of paper, starting to giggle even before she had finished. "May I go first?" She snorted in laughter.

"Go ahead, go ahead, cariad!" Mrs Bowen chuckled in delight. "We'd better not keep the expectant mother waiting and laughing like that, she might wee herself!" Ernest scowled at this impropriety, while Mavis blushed and looked away, this morning's incident all too fresh in her mind.

Composing herself, she cleared her throat.

"Here goes. The Queen met Muffin the Mule at midnight outside the men's toilets. She said, "Happy Christmas." He said "I want a carrot." She bent over backwards to help him. They had twenty children!" Mavis roared with laughter, until the tears were running down her cheeks.

"Mr Watton! You're next!" Mrs Bowen was clutching her sides, even more so at the sight of the staid Ernest Watton, self-consciously opening his piece of paper. Putting on his most pompous, pulpit voice, he began reading. "Enid Blyton met the lavatory attendant at Buckingham Palace at midnight. She said "Lashings of ginger beer!" He said "I've scrubbed all the toilets!" He had difficulty in reaching his water trough. They fell in love. Honestly! Such rubbish!" Angrily, he crumpled up his paper. "Come on, Mr Bowen, I think we need to go down to the bottom field to pump up the water. Mavis will give a hand with the washing up. We can have pudding after that." He stormed out, with a slightly inebriated Mr Bowen trotting meekly in his wake. Mavis and Mrs Bowen stared at each other in astonishment for a few seconds, then burst out laughing once more.

Seamus sat on the wooden bench on the harbour, overlooking the Irish Sea. At three o'clock the sun had already sunk quite low behind him, but the sky was still clear and blue. Howth was quietly making merry; the harbour was deserted, even the seagulls seemed to be taking a holiday – no rich pickings for them today – and the whole place was strangely silent. No ships could be seen to the south in Dublin Bay, and the rest of the world seemed far away. The sea lapped gently against the harbour wall, and Seamus watched with interest as a little Turnstone hopped along with a mussel shell in its beak. Closing his eyes, Seamus breathed in the sharp, salty tang of the air, going back in time to the summer, when he and Mavis had visited the beaches in Llanelli, over the Gower, and down at Machynys. Such blissful, happy days. He took out the silver cigarette case Mavis had sent him, stroking it gently, while his thoughts meandered unhappily through the aching void inside him. His family was still celebrating, carrying on drinking and playing party games. His cousin Gregory was drunkenly playing Christmas carols on the piano as he had slipped away, unnoticed, to make his way down to the sea, just a few minutes walk down the road. Seamus wondered what Mavis was doing. What had she thought of the Magic Hanky, he wondered. He would know soon enough, he supposed, if she managed to get over to his house tomorrow to talk on the phone. Maybe she would pluck up courage to leave Ernest and come to Ireland with him. After all, her friend Eiddwen had done much the same with Archie. But then, Eiddwen hadn't been married.

Taking out a cigarette, he put it to his lips and lit it with little difficulty. The sea breeze was also taking a rest, it seemed. Imagine being a father at my age, he marvelled, inhaling deeply. He longed to announce it to the family, but even in this enlightened age, they would disapprove of his situation, which he was finding increasingly unbearable. It would be about another six weeks before he would be able to return to Wales, he considered, but then he would stay there permanently. The temperature dropped as the sun disappeared completely, and the sky deepened to a velvety indigo in the east. Time to go back, he thought.

What a difference in two days, thought Mavis miserably as she peered through the kitchen window at the deluge outside. Thankfully, Ernest had gone down to the chapel to conduct a short service due to begin at eleven o'clock (for the very devout, no doubt), to celebrate St Stephen's day, leaving the coast clear for her to go to Seamus' house. Pulling an old raincoat on, she hurried over to the house, taking care not step in the puddles as she ran.

The old house seemed even more dismal and empty than ever on such a depressing day. She sat down on the bottom step of the stairs, waiting for Seamus to ring. Somehow, the bottom step seemed the right place to sit, she always sat there, it had become a habit for her, so to sit anywhere else would now be unlucky, she thought, irrationally. Eleven o'clock came and went, and the phone remained silent. Sadly, she got up and wandered about the hallway, a sick feeling in her stomach and a horrible dryness in her mouth. She glanced at the grandfather clock on the wall, then again at her wristwatch, comparing the times. Both said the same, just gone quarter past eleven. He had obviously forgotten. Anxiously, she realised she would have to leave in a few minutes, as the chapel service would only take half an hour or so, and she dared not risk Ernest catching her leaving Seamus' house on his return. Just as she was about to leave through the kitchen door, the phone rang shrilly in the hallway, making her jump. She rushed to answer it, almost tripping over the runner in her haste. "Seamus?" She was breathless in her excitement.

"Who else?!" His voice sounded reassuringly happy to hear her voice. "Sorry I am so late, but I got the times wrong for the rugby match, and the others only left a few minutes ago. Ring me back on this number, my angel, as quick as you can! You'll find it written on a piece of paper on the wee table the phone is on." They were soon chatting away, both relieved to hear the other's voice.

"Did you like the hanky? I haven't overstepped the mark, have I?" She could hear the uncertainty in his words.

"Oh, not at all. It made my day, it really did! I understand what you meant by it, and appreciate it so much, my darling. Thank you!"

"And thank you for the cigarette case. It is beautiful, and I will cherish it forever. So how is the wee one behaving? How much longer to go now?"

Mavis sighed. "Oh, I wish we all knew, Seamus! There's complete confusion about my dates, and I am small anyway, but Eva has told me she is confident all is well, and the baby will come when it's cooked. She seems to think I could be about six or seven months gone, possibly more."

"Well, not so long to wait now! And I hope to be over by mid-February, or March at the latest, so I will see my little woman radiantly blooming and great with child!" Mavis cringed as she thought of her rapidly growing tummy, and what it would look like to Seamus.

"Hm, yes!" She laughed. Reluctantly, they said their goodbyes, as the clock had just struck half-past eleven, and made plans to talk again on New Year's Day.

To her horror, Ernest was already home when she opened to kitchen door.

"You've been out? In this weather?" He looked at her incredulously, his eyes narrowed in suspicion.

"Oh, I felt so claustrophobic indoors, I felt I simply had to go out for a walk!" Mavis took off her raincoat, shaking the raindrops onto the porch tiles.

"You're not very wet. Where did you go?"

"Only as far as the thinking stone on the track. But I was under the trees most of the time." She hoped he hadn't noticed the slow flush which was rising up her face.

"Well, you could have taken Dai with you. I'll have to go out with him now." He stomped away, in search of the dog's lead. Relieved to have got away so easily, Mavis shouted after him, "I'll be making a few sandwiches for lunch. Remember, we have to go down to Llanelli to have tea with Fred and Margaret this afternoon." Ernest snorted by way of reply, slamming the kitchen door behind him.

Boxing Night tea at Fred and Margaret's house was quite a riotous affair, as Margaret's wicked Uncle Ronald had arrived unannounced, and was regaling the family with uproarious tales of his escapades as a young man. Ernest looked on stonily, saying very little. Uncle Ronald had a sharp wit, but some of his stories and jokes were rather close to the mark, and Mavis had to bite her lip in an effort not to laugh too much. Wendy and Julie were hopelessly over-excited, running around shrieking. Uncle Ronald bent over and whispered something in Wendy's ear. "What are you telling that child, now, Uncle Ronald?" Margaret frowned. Wendy giggled loudly.

"He told me he would give me sixpence for every glass of Babycham I drank! What's Babycham, Mammy? Is it pop?"

"Really! Enough of that nonsense, now, Uncle Ronald! Wendy, go and eat your tea! Mavis, you haven't put half enough on your plate. Go on, have another mince pie, or at least some more trifle. It'll go to waste if it's not eaten up." Mavis sighed, and went over to the table. Honestly, she could hardly face another morsel. If she ate another sausage roll, she would begin to look like one. Besides, she was having the most annoying heartburn. Reluctantly, she put a couple of cheese and pineapple on sticks onto her paper plate. She watched quietly as Margaret and Fred played games with the children. That'll be me soon, she thought. Everything was ready for the baby, the pram had been bought, and the cot stood ready in what was still the spare bedroom. Only white baby clothes had been purchased, along with two dozen Harrington nappies. Mavis had never even held a newborn baby in her entire life; she wondered if she would cope. Eva had promised her that she would be shown how to bath the baby and change nappies while she was in hospital, so maybe there was no need to worry. As if reading her thoughts, Margaret smiled at her. "Won't be long now, Mavis. Are you excited?"

"Nervous is the word I would choose," Mavis laughed in reply. "The trouble is, the baby could arrive anytime! There is such confusion about my dates." As an afterthought, she added, "And it's possible I may go into labour quite early, so I've been told." Best to pave the way for a surprisingly early birth, she thought.

"Will you be going out to wet the baby's head?" Uncle Ronald winked cheekily at Ernest, who turned a delicate shade of magenta. "I'll organise it for you, if you like!"

"I most certainly will not!" Ernest's mouth clamped shut tightly. "There is far too much drunken and licentious behaviour, if you ask me!" Pot-kettle situation, thought Mavis to herself. She sat back and enjoyed the remainder of the visit, envying Margaret and Fred as she watched their domestic happiness. They didn't have much in the way of money, and the little house was just about adequate to accommodate them all. But that didn't matter, it didn't matter at all, really. What good was money, high quality furniture and expensive clothes, if you were unhappy?

Mavis and Ernest drove home in silence, the windscreen wipers squeaking as they went to and fro, the earlier rain having dwindled to a fine mist. The streets were empty, only a few cars passed by. The roads looked greasy and unfriendly; golden puddles reflected the yellow street lights, the only festive thing to be viewed amidst this sad, sombre scene.

As she closed the kitchen door behind them, Mavis felt incredibly lonely.

Chapter Twenty-five

Parturition

On the last day of February, Mavis went into labour. She did not realise it at first, assuming the pains in her tummy were as a result of having eaten too much apple pie the previous day. Awaking at five o'clock in the morning, she paced up and down the landing, wondering what she should do. Her abdomen tightened every ten minutes or so, but not very painfully. She felt generally restless, and started to clean the kitchen for want of anything else to do. Ernest called down to her at around seven o'clock, demanding that she should keep quiet. However, Mavis ignored him, and carried on washing the floor, her mind preoccupied. Whilst the tiles were drying, Mavis bustled into the outhouse, and started sorting through all the lotions and potions which had accumulated there over the years. Tut-tutting with annoyance, she rummaged through the ancient packets of detergent. Fancy even thinking of buying Omo! Why on earth had she ever done that? Clearly, it hadn't lived up to expectations, as it had hardly been used. No wonder she had reverted to Daz. And Eiddwen had mentioned something quite unsavoury about Omo - apparently, bored women on one of the new estates down in Llanelli would place an Omo packet in their window so their "fancy men" would be able to see that their Old Man was Out! Several almost empty bottles of Zal soon joined the redundant Omo, by which time the kitchen floor was dry, whereupon Mavis started cleaning the Rayburn. At eight o'clock, Ernest strode sulkily into the kitchen. "Where's my breakfast, Mavis?"

"I don't know, Ernest," Mavis replied irritably, "maybe it's in the parlour." Ernest looked at her in surprise. "And mind your feet, the floor has just been washed." Frowning, she hurried from the Rayburn to the sink, holding on to her back and wincing in discomfort.

"What's the matter?" For once, Ernest was jolted out of his usual impatience.

"I don't know, I just feel uncomfortable, and my tummy hurts." She sighed, then caught her breath as her abdomen tightened once more. The penny dropped. She was in labour.

Ernest suddenly became concerned. "What could it be? Shall I go down to the village and call the doctor? Maybe you are sickening for something?"

Mavis smiled wryly. "Oh, Ernest, I don't think it's the doctor that I need, but Eva!"

Grabbing his coat, shoving a startled Dai out of the way, Ernest made for the door. "Stay here! I'll go and get Eva and I'll be as quick as I can!"

"Oh, I'm not going anywhere, Ernest, don't you worry!" As he slammed the door behind him, Mavis felt another contraction start, and instinctively breathed in deeply, as she had been advised by Eva, exhaling slowly, as though blowing out a candle. She moved over to the kitchen table and leaned over it. The pains were coming every three minutes now, and they seemed to be getting stronger each time. Dai whimpered and looked up at her anxiously. "Don't worry, boy," she whispered, "I'll be alright." Remembering Eva's instructions from her clinic visit last week, Mavis walked around the kitchen resolutely, only pausing when she had a contraction. After the next five pains, they gathered momentum, taking Mavis' breath away with their intensity. She felt as though she was being pulled into a dark vortex, swirling downwards into some unknown place, with each contraction.

"So! Who's in labour, then?" Eva hurried efficiently into the room, placing her bag on the table.

"Well, it's certainly not the dog!" Mavis grimaced as another contraction started.

"How often?" Eva took Mavis' pulse.

"Two minutes apart!" Mavis gasped.

"Right. Out you go, Ernest, get the car ready. I hope there's plenty of petrol in it. Can you make it upstairs, Mavis? I need to check you over." Eva took off her coat and went over to the kitchen sink to wash her hands.

"No...no, it's impossible! I don't think I can!"

Ernest scuttled out, and just in time, for at that moment, there was a silent gush, and the kitchen floor was once again soaking wet. Eva wiped her hands dry.

"Well, your membranes have just ruptured, Mavis! Let's go into the parlour, and I'll fetch a couple of towels from your airing cupboard."

"Well? Am I in labour?" Mavis got up from the sofa.

"Oh, most definitely." Eva smiled, removing her gloves. "Now don't stand up, your waters have gone, and your cervix is more than half way dilated. I'll just check the baby's heartbeat...." She took out a silver trumpet-like object from her bag, and placed it on Mavis' abdomen, putting her ear against it for a whole minute. "Yes, a good steady rate, a hundred and twenty two beats a minute. Perfect. Now! Ernest must drive you to Brynglas immediately. I will follow you in my car, just in case."

"What d'you mean? In case? In case of what?" Mavis' voice quivered with fear.

"Just in case." Eva replied firmly. "Now let's get you packed and ready to go. You can come back in, now, Ernest!"

Ten minutes later, Mavis was huddled in the passenger seat of the Reliant, Ernest grimly gripping the wheel for dear life. Eira Jones, once again pegging out her washing, looked on with interest as the old car rumbled past.

"I feel sick," Mavis moaned, faintly, "and please don't drive too fast, Ernest! Every bump in the road hurts so much!"

"We have to get there quickly! Eva said you won't have long to go! Yet that very same woman told you that first babies take a long time to come!" He said all this without taking his eyes off the road for one second, his jaw rigid with tension.

"You're not in chapel now, Ernest, so don't give me a sermon for Pete's sake!" Mavis hissed. Ernest decided it was wise to ignore this. For once, the beauty of the late winter morning was lost on Mavis, as she crouched down into her seat, clinging on to it, oblivious to the bright sunshine and the sparkling sea in the distance.

"Cattle ramp coming up!" Ernest changed into a lower gear in readiness.

"Oh, Jesus have mercy!" Mavis screwed up her eyes in agony as they bumped jerkily over the offending grid. Ernest frowned slightly, but seeing as his wife was in pain, he made allowances. After a record-breaking fifteen minute drive to Brynglas, Ernest finally pulled up outside in the car park, Eva arriving a minute later, bristling with professional efficiency. "Stay there, I'll get the midwife in charge, and a wheelchair."

Within a short space of time, Mavis found herself being wheeled into a large room, which had a strange black bed in the middle of it, Ernest having been ushered into the fathers' room down the corridor. The smell of disinfectant filled her with trepidation, and she felt frightened, even more so of the stern-faced midwife who stood glaring at her, her hands on her ample hips.

"She won't be long, Sister Taylor," Eva helped Mavis remove her coat, "she was six fingers dilated when I examined her half an hour ago." Sister

Taylor peered disbelievingly over her thick-rimmed spectacles, her navy uniform stretching with difficulty over her immense bosom.

"Really? An elderly primip? I hope your assessment is correct, Sister Griffiths, and we are not wasting our time here." Bitch, thought Mavis, gritting her teeth as her abdomen tightened like a vice once more.

"I'll administer the S.B.E., Sister Griffiths, or will the student be doing the honours?" Sister Taylor heaved Mavis unceremoniously onto the couch.

"I think you can leave Mrs Watton in my hands, Sister." Eva smiled down at Mavis. "I can manage from here."

"But it's your day off. Shouldn't you be getting along home?" The other midwife scowled suspiciously at Eva, annoyed at being thwarted in her duty of inflicting embarrassing, humiliating procedures on another woman.

"No, Sister Taylor. I decided to work an extra day this week so I can have next Tuesday off for a funeral," Eva smiled sweetly at her colleague. Sister Taylor glared at Eva challengingly, however she had no option but to retreat with as much dignity as she could. "What's an S.B.E.?" Mavis looked anxiously up at Eva, who was busy organising a trolley full of sheets and equipment.

"Don't worry, you're too far gone for that!" Eva smiled reassuringly at her. "It stands for shave, bath, enema. But young Master Watton here has ideas of his own! He is well on his way!"

"Is it a boy? How do you know?" Mavis gasped again as yet another contraction swept though her body, causing her to see an explosion of stars before her eyes.

"I don't! But it's going to be one or the other! Now lie back and let me check how things are progressing again. Ah! Here is pupil midwife Toft. And just in time!" A short, pleasant-faced young woman came hurrying into the delivery room, beaming from ear to ear.

"Only just came on duty, Sister Griffiths," she panted, "and the ward clerk from ante-natal said you'd asked for me."

"Yes indeed," Eva replied, "I know you've reached your target of fifty deliveries, but Sister Tutor informs me you are in need of more experience in taking the baby?"

"That's correct, Sister." The pupil busied herself donning a white gown and a mask.

Mavis looked horrified. "She's only a pupil? Does she know what she's doing? She won't drop the baby, will she?!"

Eva sighed impatiently. "Pupil midwife Janys Toft is one of the best pupils we've had this year. And what's more, she even has three children of her own! Now relax, Mavis, and everything will be fine!"

Suddenly, Mavis grabbed Eva's arm. "I have to go to the toilet, Eva! Now! Oh, my God, but I can't get off the bed!"

"Is she fully dilated, Sister?" The pupil midwife looked enquiringly at Eva.

"Seems highly likely." Eva pulled back the sheet. "Pop your legs up on my hips and let's have a look, Mavis." Mavis groaned as she complied.

"The head's crowning. Open the delivery pack for me quickly!" Eva rushed to the sink and started scrubbing her hands. "Pant, now Mavis, no pushing yet!" Pupil midwife Toft squeezed her hand, kindly. "You can do it, Mrs Watton, baby will be here very soon." Mavis held back as long as she could, but very soon, an overwhelming, primeval urge to bear down proved too much for her. She was drenched in sweat, her hair clung in wet tendrils to her head. She felt as though she was being torn apart, and her bottom end felt as though it would split. What was happening to her? Would it ever end?

"Episiotomy?" The pupil's eyes met Eva's over their masks.

"I don't think she will need one. Our little Mavis is stretching out quite nicely! Good girl, Mavis, you're doing so well. Keep it coming, keep it coming, just another little push - now PANT! No pushing now, Mavis, do as I say, pant for me!" Mavis panted obediently, her eyes huge, staring at Eva, who at this point was her sole source of support and focus. Suddenly there was an incredible stinging sensation then a blessed relief from the pressure.

"The baby's head is out, Mrs Watton," the pupil said encouragingly, "won't be long now! Sister Griffiths is just checking that the cord isn't around the baby's neck. Do you have a name ready?" Mavis shook her head rapidly, just as another contraction seized her abdomen, and the baby slithered out onto the bed, giving a loud wail at the same time.

"A baby boy!" Eva announced triumphantly. "Look, Mavis, here's your little son!"

The pupil held the yelling baby up for her to see. His face was screwed up in indignation at his speedy arrival, and he was covered in blood and vernix, but to Mavis he was the most beautiful creature she had ever seen.

"Little James!" Mavis started to weep with joy. The pupil looked at her in surprise.

"So you did have a name ready," she laughed, her kind eyes twinkling in amusement.

"Yes, I did," sobbed Mavis, smiling at the same time, "but I wanted to keep it a secret. When can I hold him?"

"Nurse Toft will clean him up and weigh him, then we'll dress him in a nice little gown, and he'll be yours to cuddle, my dear. Congratulations and well done!" Eva smiled kindly down at Mavis, her own eyes misting over and a lump in her throat. Turning to the pupil, she continued. "I will supervise the third stage and the placental examination, Nurse Williams, if you could carry out the first toilet of the baby, and don't forget to make sure the length and head circumference are recorded on the cot card, as well as the weight. Some of the pupils have been forgetting to do that recently."

Mavis flopped back on the bed, exhausted but incredibly happy. She was a mother at last.

Several hours later, up on the post-natal ward, Mavis cuddled her little son. He weighed just five pounds ten ounces, but was perfect in every way. Ernest had been allowed to see Mavis and the baby, and was then sent on his way, beaming with middle-aged pride.

Who could have ever predicted the tumultuous emotions surging through her right now, Mavis pondered. She'd never imagined that such love was possible. Gazing out through the window, she watched the sun starting to set behind the trees in Parc Hardd, the tall pines casting long shadows over the lawns. The old mansion house stood silhouetted in the fading light, and some youths kicked a football about on the grass, ignoring the warnings shouted out by the park-keeper that it was closing time. A young couple ran hand in hand through the park gate, heading down towards the town. They made her think of Seamus, and her heart ached for him. What was he doing now? Was he thinking of her? Did he have any sense or impression that he was now a father? The baby whimpered, and she looked down at him. His downy head was turning from side to side, and his tiny mouth was busy searching for his fist. "Nurse!" Mavis called out, tentatively, "I think the baby is hungry!"

Pupil Midwife Janys Toft proved invaluable to Mavis over the next few days, shielding her from the acerbic tongue of Sister Taylor, and protecting her desire to breastfeed the little baby. "Don't you worry about that old harpy!" She whispered to Mavis as she was helping her fix little James to feed. "She's a bitter old spinster and we will not mind her at all!"

"Oh, you are so kind to spend so much time helping me." Mavis looked up gratefully, trying to stop herself from wincing as the baby launched himself once more at her tender nipple. "Sister Taylor keeps telling me it's now the modern way that all babies should be put on the bottle. But I don't want to! I don't want to!" Her voice rose tremulously as she raised worried eyes to Janys, who smiled reassuringly at her.

"Don't then."

There was silence, as the baby finally latched on properly, the quiet only broken by the satisfying sound of deep swallowing and the feeling of relief as her milk was removed by the ravenous James.

"You've got away quite lightly, haven't you?" Janys settled down on the chair next to the bed.

"Lightly?" Mavis smiled up at her, puzzled.

"Yes, such a quick labour — so unusual in a small woman who is having her first baby - and no tears or stitches. And what's more, no stretch marks either!" Jeanne helped her move the baby to her other breast. "I had lacerations with each of my little ones, and you should see my tummy! It's like a map of the London Underground!"

"Yes, I suppose I have been very lucky." Mavis looked down at James, who had nodded off, full to the brim with his mother's milk. "Nurse, when will I be able to go home?"

Janys thought for a moment. "Well, you are five days post-natal now, so in another five days, if all is well. And everything is progressing perfectly normally, so there's no reason why you shouldn't be discharged early next week."

Mavis pondered on this. Once she got home there would be no chance of getting a letter to Seamus. She would be confined to the cottage, and probably only start going out and about once the baby was a few weeks old. And she couldn't leave him! She couldn't just hop on a bus and pop down to Llanelli! But Janys seemed a friendly person. Perhaps.....an idea was forming itself in her head. "Nurse, I need to write a letter to my family in Ireland. Mr Watton is terribly absent-minded and would forget to post anything I gave to him. Could you get me some paper and an envelope? And if I gave you the money, would you post it for me as well?"

"Yes, of course, Mrs Watton, that'll be no problem at all!" Janys removed James from Mavis' arms and placed him gently in the cot. "Leave it with me."

Mavis lay back on the pillows and closed her eyes, planning what she would write.

My darling man, You are now a father. Young James was born at twenty-past nine in the morning on February 28th, and he weighed five pounds ten ounces. He is tiny, but perfect. I can't say he looks like anyone as yet, but he has blue eyes and no hair at all! He is feeding well, and has started to put on some weight.

I am fine, the labour was quite dramatic and speedy, and I only just made it to the hospital in time. I am still here in the maternity hospital, and a very nice young nurse called Janys will be posting this for me. I hope to return home next week, as I am recovering quickly, and there have been no complications at all.

Once I am home, I will try at some point to pop over to your house to see if there is a reply to this letter. I will have to bring the baby with me. I wonder what he will make of his Daddy's house? I will also make the Magic Hanky into a little hat for him, at some point, although we don't have Christenings, and I am not the best needlewoman! Oh, Seamus, James is so sweet, and I love him so much!

Please reply soon, my love, I am missing you dreadfully.

Mavis xxxx

On the Monday morning of the following week, Mavis returned home, holding the baby closely as she sat in the back seat, while Ernest carefully drove at a snail's pace back to Llannon. Such a difference to the mad dash when she went into labour, thought Mavis. It had been sad to say goodbye to Janys, who had been so kind, going beyond the normal duties of a pupil midwife, and duly posting Mavis' letter for her.

Her legs felt strange and weak, as she had spent the past ten days in bed, and yet, here she was, longing to get home and go for a lie down! Looking down at James, she wondered anew at his perfection, his tiny fingers, his rosebud mouth, and a feeling of trepidation washed over her. What if she didn't look after him properly? What if she dropped him? It was all down to her now, all her responsibility. The thought almost overwhelmed her. The baby opened his eyes and looked up at her, and all her worries melted away. He was her baby, she was his mother, and she would protect him with every fibre of her being.

The car trundled up Bethel Lane. Eira Jones stood on her doorstep, waving. Ernest must have told everyone she and the baby were coming out of Brynglas. Even the trees edging the lane seemed to be in a congratulatory mood, as they bowed and swayed in the breeze, paying homage and welcoming home the mother and child. The car pulled up outside their cottage and Ernest opened the passenger door for her.

Mavis and little James had come home.

Chapter Twenty-six

Introductions

Mavis and little James settled into their new life at home with surprising ease. Ernest made himself scarce most days, being disinclined to involve himself in women's affairs. He helped out with the more "manly" chores such as cleaning the windows and putting the rubbish out, and doing whatever was asked of him by a recovering Mavis. Eva visited regularly and announced that she was more than happy with progress. The days were balmy and unusually mild for March, so Mavis was able to venture out, showing off her baby in his shining Silver Cross pram, exulting in the praise and adoration of her neighbours, like the Bowens and Eira Jones.

Her first visit to see her mother and sisters had been difficult, as expected. They had decided not to call down to see the baby, as they were "too busy," so Mavis trudged up the hill to visit them instead, to be presented with a vile orange cardigan, knitted by Enid and a silver cup from her mother. She left after just half an hour, seething with fury at the criticisms and snide comments hurled at her by her jealous sisters, and frustrated by her feeble mother. "Well, that's the last time I'll be going there for a good while," she muttered to James, who, blissfully unaware of his extended family's rudeness, was fast asleep in the pram.

As she walked slowly down the hill towards Bethel Lane, she lifted her face to the sun, enjoying its gentle warmth on her skin. Daffodils were nodding their heads in the slight breeze, like a group of gossipy young women at a dance and there was a distinct spring-like feel to the world. Mavis sometimes felt as though the seasons ran in her blood, and today she could feel a tangible newness to the world, a feeling of hope and freshness.

Ernest was down at the chapel, carrying out some renovations, so the cottage would be empty. Mavis had had no opportunity to go to Seamus' house since she had come home from hospital, and she was burning with curiosity. Would there be a reply from Seamus? Now, it seemed, was her chance. Glancing backwards she ensured that Eira Jones was nowhere to be seen, then pushed the pram around to the back of the house, entering through the kitchen door, only just managing to squeeze the pram inside. James stirred slightly, then settled down once more into his infant slumber. Parking the pram by the pantry, Mavis hurried into the hallway. She caught her breath in excitement, as there on the porch floor lay an envelope addressed with the familiar writing. Her fingers trembled in her haste to open it, and she scanned the letter quickly, before sitting down on the staircase to read it properly.

March 10th

My darling woman, mother of my child! How happy I am! I wish I was with you now to hug you and kiss you! This is a very short letter as I have a great deal to accomplish in a short space of time and I want to catch the last post this afternoon! The sorting out of my mother's affairs has not quite finished, but what the hell! My brother can take over. I have done quite enough, and my own personal needs now take priority. And that priority includes you, and of course, the baby. My family cannot for the life of them understand why I am striding about like a cat with two tails. And I cannot tell them, not yet anyway.

I will be sailing at midnight on the 2nd April, then getting the train from Fishguard to Llanelli. Allowing for the erratic nature of Irish ferries and the vagaries of Welsh trains, I hope I will be in Llannon by the evening of the 3rd. Watch for the light going on in the front bedroom, that'll mean I am home. Come over to see me as soon as you can, regardless of the hour. I cannot wait to see you and wee James.

I love you.

Seamus

Mavis kissed the letter in relief. Today was the 26th March, only a week before she would see Seamus once more. She looked up and caught sight of her reflection in the hall mirror. Did she look any different, she wondered? Did she still resemble the secret lover who had stolen Seamus' heart? Was Mavis Watton now a dowdy mother, whose energies were wholly focussed on her new baby? But she didn't look much different, she decided, just a little dark under the eyes and slightly pale, maybe. And with an impressive cleavage, she giggled to herself.

James had his moments, he certainly knew how to bellow if he was hungry, but on the whole he was a contented little chap and as long as his tummy was full, he didn't cause her too much trouble. Ernest had moved out of their bedroom into the spare room, as he didn't wish to be disturbed by the night feeds. Along with Mavis' family, he was keen to have her "put the baby on the bottle" as he thought it would make the baby more settled and may even make him sleep through the night. More pertinently, he was of the opinion that Mavis would no longer need to expose herself if she was bottle feeding. However, Eva's word was law, and not even the rigid Ernest would dare challenge it. So baby James carried on having his mother's milk, was thriving beautifully on it, and Mavis was saved the stress of causing Ernest broken sleep.

As James was still sleeping in his pram by the pantry door, Mavis decided to have a quick tidy up before returning to the cottage. She whisked from room to room, opening windows a fraction and plumping cushions. At least the house wouldn't smell stale and stuffy when Seamus returned the following week.

The following day brought a small parcel in the second post. Eiddwen had sent an exquisite white romper suit for James, and had enclosed a short note.

Dear Mavis,

How wonderful! A little baby boy! I rang my niece last week and she told me the news! I am so pleased for you! How are you feeling, was the birth really terrible? I bought this little outfit in Edinburgh, in a very exclusive shop – no other baby in Llannon or even Llanelli will have one like it. So it is a special romper suit for a very special baby. Archie and I hope to come down to Llannon in a few weeks' time, so I'll get to have a cuddle then, I can't wait!

Yours with love,
Eiddwen.

Mavis folded up the letter with a sad smile on her face. She missed her friend. With her recently acquired sensitivity, she realised that she had frequently spoken sharply to Eiddwen, and taken her for granted. And now she was gone. But at least they would be able to see each other soon.

The third of April dawned bright and sunny. Mavis could hardly contain herself in her excited anticipation. By nine o'clock in the morning she had fed and changed James, cleaned the kitchen and was just thinking about starting the laundry before settling him in the crib once more, when Ernest returned from walking Dai.

"Do you need any help, Mavis?" Ernest walked over to the sink and started washing his hands. "I was just going to go over the Bowens' to help with the muck-spreading." The dog rushed over to her, sniffing happily at James' rear end.

"Off you go, naughty boy!" Mavis shooed him away, laughing. "No, it's fine, Ernest. Everything is under control. But thank you for asking."

Ernest looked over at his wife. "You are certainly managing motherhood better than I expected." He actually looked proud for a few seconds.

Mavis glanced up at him, a wry smile on her lips. "Well, that's kind of you, Ernest. I do my best." Any irony was completely lost on Ernest, as he opened the door and marched out, Dai trotting happily at his heels, only to be thwarted at the garden gate, whereby he returned sadly to the kitchen. The baby hiccupped slightly in her arms, so Mavis put him over her shoulder, placing his soft, downy cheek next to her own. He smelled so sweet, she thought. Then, as she cuddled him gently, she reconsidered this. Maybe not so sweet after all, she thought, as she looked down at the yellow mess escaping from his nappy!

"Bath time, you little rascal," she announced firmly, replacing the gurgling James in his crib, before reaching for the blue baby bath from behind the armchair.

By seven o'clock that evening, there was still no sign of Seamus, and the sun was setting rapidly behind the hills. There was no way she could escape from the cottage now, as James would need to be settled for the night, and there would be no reason whatsoever for her to go out. By half past nine, she decided to go to bed, and snuggled down under the blankets, James already sleeping peacefully next to her in his cot. The cottage was silent, and it was dark outside. Mavis heard Ernest coming upstairs around ten o'clock, going into the spare room and saying his prayers. What a pity she was in the main bedroom, as it overlooked the garden and the countryside to the north west, and the spare room allowed a pretty good view of Seamus' house. Never mind, she thought, all good things come to those who wait. She was feeling sleepy, she couldn't keep her eyes open....

....and then she was woken up by James restlessly stirring, wanting his night feed. She looked at the clock in surprise, as it was already starting to get light. Ten past six! Heavens! He had slept all night! She suddenly became aware of a heavy ache in her breasts, and to her dismay realised that her nightdress was completely soaked in milk. Hastily, she lifted the baby into her arms, and settled down to feed him,

appreciating the swift relief as he removed her milk with his eager little mouth.

Once James was back in his crib, she tiptoed out onto the landing, and peeped through the window at the top of the stairs. And there it was. The light was on in the bedroom window at Seamus' house! He was home!

By seven o'clock, she was dressed and ready to go out, James tucked up beneath the white quilt in his pram. Ernest, thankfully, was still asleep. She had left a note on the kitchen table, stating that James had been fretful and she was taking him out for a walk. Deciding what to wear had proved tricky, as although Mavis had more or less lost all the pregnancy weight, her chest was now quite splendid! She settled for a black pencil skirt and a white shirt, only just managing to do up its buttons. Hastily she pulled on her mohair cardigan. As she slipped quietly through the kitchen door, she cursed silently as the pram noisily bumped into the door frame. Pausing briefly, she held her breath in case she had disturbed Ernest. But all was still.

The morning air was clear and rather chilly, the sun was starting its slow ascent above the Swansea landscape in the distance, and not a cloud marred the bright blue sky. To her intense annoyance, Evans the Milk was loitering down at the end of the lane, chatting to Eira Jones. Why on earth was Eira up and about so early?!

Mavis dared not leave until he had gone. Thankfully, she didn't have to wait much longer, and the old milk float rattled away back into the village. She walked as swiftly and discreetly as she could, once more navigating the pram around to the back of Seamus' house, her heart beating quickly. The kitchen door was open, and she pushed the pram inside. She stopped and held her breath, taking in the scene and praying her eyes were not being deceived.

Seamus was sitting with his head lying on the kitchen table, snoring gently. His tangled mop of hair looked as though it hadn't been combed for days. Several empty coffee cups lay alongside him, and the ashtray was overflowing. He looked so vulnerable sitting there, so Mavis just stood and stared at him for a few minutes. He's back, he's really back, she thought. She walked softly over to him and put her arms about him.

"Seamus. Welcome home." Mavis bent over and kissed his head. Sleepily he lifted his head and looked up at her in wonder, a huge grin lighting his face.

"My darling woman! My darling fecking woman!" And with that he grabbed hold of her properly and kissed her passionately, as though he would never stop. He tasted of tobacco and caffeine, but to Mavis there had never been a sweeter taste, and she melted into his embrace with a passion that matched his.

"Oh, Jesus, I've so longed for this, my darling woman! I waited up all night just in case you were able to come over!" He pulled away from her. "Let's have a good look at you! Why, you look exactly the same! I thought all new mothers were supposed to look as though they had all the cares of the world on their shoulders and were all fat and harassed! But you look as beautiful as ever!"

Mavis laughed delightedly. "It's so good to have you back, my love. Now sit down...."

She walked over to the pram and picked up the sleeping baby. Shyly, she returned to Seamus and tenderly handed James to him. "This is your son. This is James." Seamus stared down at the baby in wonder.

"My son," he whispered, "my little boy! And thank you, sweet Mavis for having him for me. He is truly a child of love." Seamus stroked the infant's tiny fingers, marvelling at their perfection, smiling with joy when James caught hold of his own finger and held it tightly. Mavis smiled down at them, tears filling her eyes. This was the most beautiful moment in her life. Whatever happened from now on, she would always remember it, and would know that Seamus loved her dearly, and welcomed their child with all his heart.

"I don't have very long, Seamus," Mavis explained, "I'll have to go back soon."

He looked crestfallen. "Already? Can you come back later? I'll be here all day, and all night, but please come as soon as you can?"

Mavis smiled. "Of course I will. If Ernest goes out for any length of time, and it's safe, I'll be right back."

Seamus put little James back into the pram and drew her into his arms. "And how is he treating you? Is he kind?" The concern in his voice moved her.

"Everything's alright. He's as proud as Punch about the baby, and he hasn't been cruel or anything. But...." Her voice trailed away sadly.

"But what? Tell me!"

"I have been so miserable without you, Seamus. And now you're back, I realise just how unhappy my life is without you in it. I have lived in an emotional wasteland all these months, and now you're back, it's brought that home to me."

"So what are you saying?" The hope in his eyes was painfully obvious. Mavis buried her face in his chest, not quite daring to speak her mind.

"I'm saying that maybe I need to be brave, and to change my life for the better."

He tilted her chin so he could see her face. "So will you leave him?"

She took a deep breath. "Yes, Seamus, I think I'll have to. Not yet, I'm still getting over the birth, and I need time to plan things properly. But I can't live the rest of my life unloved, being scolded and hauled over the coals for stupid misdemeanours, and I can't live the rest of my life without being with you." There. She'd said it.

Seamus hugged her as though he would squeeze all the breath out of her. "My darling woman. Thank you. And take as much time as you need. I'll be ready for you always." The he pulled away suddenly. "By jaysus! Me shirt's all fecking wet!"

Mavis burst out laughing. "Oh, it's my milk! There's lots of it!"

"But why is it leaking everywhere? Doesn't the wee boy drink it all?" Seamus looked bemused.

"Oh, he does that, don't you worry! But Eva did warn me that sometimes the slightest stimulation can set the milk flowing!"

His eyes narrowed. "Did she, now then? And how much, er, stimulation d'you reckon you can handle, sweet Mavis?" His hand crept around to her breasts, fondling them gently, and kissing her parted lips at the same time. "And, er, when d'you think we can, er, you know...?"

Mavis giggled. "Another couple of weeks, I think. If you can wait that long... And Eva has reminded me to take care, or I could fall pregnant again."

James let out an indignant wail. "My little alarm clock just went off!" Mavis looked at Seamus apologetically, disentangling herself from his embrace. "I'll be back as soon as I can."

He sighed. "It can't be soon enough, sweet Mavis."

Seamus stood watching through the front window, as she pushed the pram back to her cottage, furtively looking up and down the lane in case she was seen, then disappearing once more through her kitchen door. He turned away, lighting a cigarette and pondering over the possibility she might finally be his.

The next few weeks seemed to fly by. Mavis and Seamus managed to see each other almost every day, even if only for a few minutes. Mavis had her post-natal check with Dr Hodges, and was pronounced fit and healthy. Eva had broached the subject of contraception with her during her first visit to baby clinic on a sunny, Tuesday afternoon.

"Don't think it can't happen again, Mavis." she whispered, with a twinkle in her eye. "You could conceive again now! The fact you are feeding the baby yourself will reduce your fertility, but accidents can happen!"

"I'll be careful!" Mavis grinned back. "Little James is the best form of family planning for me!" However, she thought privately that she and Seamus would certainly need to take care.

Ernest had been called to officiate at a wedding in neighbouring Cross Hands the following Saturday and would be away most of the day. Mavis and Seamus had planned to spend the whole day together, and she was fervently hoping that nothing would happen to spoil things for them. James was now almost two months old, and becoming more regular in his routine. He would sleep around five or more hours each night, usually from eleven thirty until five a.m, and his wakeful period tended to be first thing in the morning, with a longer nap towards midday. All Mavis' care and attention to him was now regularly rewarded with a beaming smile. Mavis had briefly considered asking Eira Jones to babysit for her on the Saturday, or even Eva. But the more she thought about it, the more she realised she could no more hand him over to anyone else than she could cut off her own hand. And they would ask awkward questions, which she had no wish to answer.

Saturday morning dawned, cloudy and dull, which reflected Mavis' mood. She felt tired and irritable, her eyes prickled with fatigue. James had broken his routine, feeding every hour during the night, and each time she had started to drift back to sleep, Ernest's elephantine snores woke her up from the spare bedroom. Motherhood, she muttered to herself, as she changed James' nappy for the umpteenth time, wearily smearing his bottom with Vaseline, will it ever get better? Eva had warned her about growth spurts, but surely at this rate, James would be the size of a hippopotamus by the time he was six months old.

Ernest set off for the wedding at half past ten, Mavis waving goodbye through the kitchen window. James was now unconscious to the world, asleep in his crib. Little devil, she thought, affectionately, as she tucked the sheet over him.

Seamus was bustling about in the kitchen when she pushed open the back door, the smell of garlic and herbs hanging pungently in the air. "Just preparing some goodies for us!" He grinned wickedly at her, wiping his hands on the back of his jeans, ignoring Mavis' disapproval.

"For breakfast?" Mavis looked puzzled, as she parked the pram with its slumbering occupant next to the pantry. Seamus practically skipped in glee as he went over to lock the door.

"No! We'll have a leisurely lunch, after we've er...."

"After we've er, what?" Mavis moved closer to him, swaying her hips teasingly. As he took her in his arms, she sensed his urgency, his mouth bruising her lips with fierce passion.

"I am taking you captive, my gorgeous woman," he murmured before scooping her up in his arms and striding into his studio, which had been transformed into delectable boudoir, with huge pink plump, cushions on the couch and pink satin drapes at the windows, shutting out the rest of the world. He put her down gently onto a fluffy white rug, and started to unbutton her blouse.

"Be gentle, Seamus?" she whispered anxiously. "And did you remember to buy the er...?"

"Of course, my darling woman, as if I'd be anything else. And as for the er, well I won't be a joker, I'll wrap the old poker!" He nuzzled into the soft hollow of her neck, whilst his hands busied themselves in releasing her bra. He stood back to admire her. "You are truly a fallen Madonna, look at these pneumatic beauties!" He caressed her breasts until she could bear it no longer. Moaning with pleasure, she hastily unbuckled his belt.

"Wait." It was a quietly spoken command, but one that had to be obeyed. Mavis looked up at him, suddenly apprehensive. He smiled down at her. "I want to look at you properly. Undressed. Totally naked. Bare. Brazen." Within seconds she had wriggled out of her skirt and the rest of her clothes, and lay before him, as self-conscious as she had been on their first intimate encounter.

"And any evidence of childbirth cannot be seen." There was wonder and amazement in his voice, as he stroked her limbs, then her tummy, which she immediately sucked in. He laughed. "Don't do that. It's not necessary, sweet Mavis. I love you just as you are."

"But it's still a bit wobbly, isn't it?" The uncertainty in her voice touched him.

"You're a mammy, now." He brushed her cheek with his fingertips. "The mother of my child. I wouldn't have it any other way." He lowered his mouth to her navel, and grabbed her backside firmly with both hands, kissing his way inch by inch down her tummy. When he finally reached his goal, his tongue worked its magic, sending wave after wave of ecstasy through her. As she climaxed, a fountain of milk shot into the air, hitting Seamus squarely in the eye as he lifted his head in order to look at her flushed, post-orgasmic face.

"Fecking hell! Is this a new form of titillating foreplay?" He wiped his eye with the back of his hand, chuckling as he did. Mavis burst out laughing. "I have a very powerful let down," she giggled, helplessly, "I do the same thing to poor James on a regular basis!"

Seamus feigned a stern expression. "Well, you may rest assured that I am not hell bent on vengeance, and I won't go spraying you in return! Part your legs, you wicked woman, I mean to enjoy myself now, and you can cover my funnel so I can enter your tunnel, nice and easy..." He handed her the wrapped condom, and told her how to put it on him, laughing at her caution.

Seamus was true to his word, entering her gently and adopting a slow, sensual rhythm, which made her moan with pleasure. She placed her legs around his hips and gave herself up to the measured momentum of his lovemaking, until he exploded inside her, shuddering violently as he did. However, their post-coital glow was rudely interrupted by a wail from the kitchen. James was hungry.

"Welcome to parenthood." Mavis smiled wryly, getting to her feet, and hastily pulling on her clothes.

Ten minutes later they were sitting in the kitchen, Mavis feeding James, and Seamus watching them with besotted admiration. "How often do you have to do that?" He stood behind her now, trying to get a better look at what was going on, smiling at the sound of James noisily gulping milk. "He's a hungry wee lad!"

Mavis chuckled. "How often? As often as he wants it, I suppose! Eva said not to read too many books or manuals, and to follow my instinct. James is a lovely baby, but also has a good pair of lungs if I keep him waiting too long." Once James had enjoyed his early lunch, Seamus and Mavis settled down to theirs.

"What is this, Seamus?" Mavis forked up a piece of chicken. "It's wonderful!"

"Chicken Chasseur. I learned how to make it in Montpellier a few years ago. Glad you like it!" He smiled at her, approving of the way she was demolishing her plate of food. "Good God, you've finished already! Do you want some more?"

"Mm, yes please, and some more tatws as well!" She wiped her lips with the pink napkin Seamus had provided.

"I take it that by that you mean you want some more spuds? Well, you shall have them, my queen! And what's with this enormous appetite?"

"Oh, that's the baby! I'm hungry all the time." She continued to wolf down her second helping. "Not terribly romantic, is it?"

Seamus grinned happily. "Nothing more stimulating than a woman with a healthy appetite, in all respects!" He winked at her, mischievously. "Shall we go to bed?"

Two hours, two breastfeeds and one more condom later, Seamus and Mavis were curled up on the sofa drinking coffee, enjoying the closeness and the silence. The clock ticked away loudly, reminding Mavis that her day of joy that she had looked forward to for so long was soon coming to an end. How natural and right it felt to be here with Seamus. How relaxed, happy and contented she felt. And yet, there was a heaviness in her heart when she thought of returning to the cottage and Ernest. She couldn't decide if she was now living in a dream, and would soon return to her reality, or if she was actually in her reality and would return to her nightmare of coldness and stifling religion. The sun shone through a small gap in the curtains, casting a beam of light onto her face, making her squint.

"A penny for them?" Seamus stroked her hair absent-mindedly.

"Oh, I was just thinking I don't want to go home, yet I have to." She sighed, and slowly got to her feet.

"Don't, then." He regarded her seriously, his searching blue eyes meeting her sorrowful brown ones.

"Please don't tempt me, Seamus." She put on her cardigan and started to push the pram to the kitchen door. "I really do have to go now. Ernest will be home soon. I've had one of the best days of my life, and I want it to go on and on, but ..."

"One last kiss, then!" He got up and crushed her into his arms, kissing her hard. Pulling apart, he patted her on the bottom. "Off you go then, sweet Mavis. Until tomorrow."

A few days later, Mavis decided to walk down to the shop to see if Eva was about. She wanted to ask her about teething. James was always shoving his fists into his little mouth, these days, and dribbling. She had been lucky enough to have seen Seamus a couple of times since their reunion, although the meetings had been brief. Short, but very sweet. As she walked past Seamus' house, she noticed that his motorbike was parked up outside his gate. He must be off somewhere, she thought. Luckily for her, Eva was a day off, bustling around the shop, trying to explain to the new girl, Mavis' replacement, how to check the stock and place an order. She burst into laughter as Mavis explained why she had come down. "Oh, you new mothers," she smiled, "it's always teething! Mavis, James is a couple of months old, now. It isn't impossible for him to cut a tooth, but unlikely. The chewing of fists and dribbling is completely normal for his age! It's his expected development and nothing to worry about."

"Oh, sorry, Eva, I didn't realise!" Mavis murmured in embarrassment.

"No need to apologise, you new mothers always ask the same question! And now that you're here, perhaps you'll let me have a quick cuddle of the baby while you explain to young Val here how to stock take? She's wearing me out!" Young Val turned crimson, which clashed horribly with her ginger mop of hair, and she hastily rushed into the back room.

"Useless," Eva whispered, "I have to tell her to do everything, she can't see for herself. And she wants to go in for nursing! She's a long way to go before she can even consider that!"

Half an hour later, having assisted the unfortunate Val, Mavis was making her way home along the main road. She allowed herself to daydream. Wouldn't it be lovely if she was going back to Seamus' house now, instead of the cottage? How happy she would be if she was truly his wife, and didn't have to behave in such a furtive manner.

Suddenly, her reverie was rudely interrupted by the sound of a motorbike roaring up behind her. Mavis swung around, to see Seamus riding towards her. But he was leaning too far over as he took the bend, much too far - what was he doing? Mavis held her breath in horror, unable to believe her eyes. And then the bike keeled right over, throwing its rider into the hedge.

"Seamus!" She screamed and screamed.

Chapter Twenty-seven

Cruel Tricks

Seamus lay motionless on the grass verge, his eyes closed. Mavis' legs felt as though they had turned to lead as she tried to run as quickly as she could, pushing the pram all the while, to where he was lying. Eira Jones' husband got there before her, however, and was trying to move Seamus.

"Leave him! Don't move him!" Her voice sounded shrill, causing the baby to wake and start crying. She'd remembered something Eva had told her years ago, about making sure no further damage was done after someone had an accident.

"I'm only trying to help!" Mr Jones was clearly put out. Putting the brake securely on the pram, Mavis knelt down at Seamus' side.

"Go and call 999!" she snapped, "Go to the shop, tell Eva what has happened! I'll stay here with him. Are you okay, Seamus?" Her voice was quivering with panic, which was sweeping over her in waves. Seamus slowly opened his eyes.

"I'll not be needing any fecking ambulance. I'm fine. Is my bike damaged at all?" It was all Mavis could do to stop herself hugging him in front of Mr Jones.

"For goodness' sake!" Her voice sounded sharper than she'd intended. "We thought you were dead, or seriously hurt! And you're worried about your bloody bike?"

Seamus squinted his eyes up at her, as if trying to make out who she was. Then his face creased into his familiar grin, and he sat up, rubbing his left shoulder gingerly.

"There'll be no need for an ambulance, Mr Jones." Seamus gradually got to his feet. "I'm fine. All good. Nothing dented apart from my pride and a few scratches on my bike." Mr Jones appeared quite disappointed at having to forsake his role as an emergency service, and helped pull the bike into an upright position.

"Well, if your absolutely sure. I'll help you wheel it back to your house, just in case." Mr Jones puffed out his chest and tried to look important. Not wishing to cause offence, Seamus allowed his good Samaritan to assist, and the three of them made their way slowly up the road, young James settling down again with the momentum of the pram.

Outside the old house, the bike was stowed away in the garage and Mr Jones returned to his own cottage.

"I'd better make you a cup of tea, Mr O'Brien." Mavis spoke loudly enough for Mr Jones to hear, as she watched his retreating figure walking down Bethel Lane.

"Yes, that would be a grand idea." Seamus swiftly closed the door behind them, a smile on his face.

Tears rolling down her face, despite wearing the illicit sunglasses so disliked by Seamus, Mavis pondered over the days' events as she chopped the onions for the casserole she was making for supper. He had said that his sister would be coming down from London to visit him, and that he had had a phone call from Drummond as well, also asking to stay for a few days. How wonderful it would be to see Eiddwen again! Seamus had also decided to throw another dinner party, the excuse being that the previous one had been cancelled due to his rapid departure for Ireland. The best part of a whole year ago! Mavis would have dearly loved to have been able to go into Llanelli to buy a new dress for the occasion, but she didn't want to leave James with anyone, and she couldn't get the Silver Cross chariot on the bus! No, she would simply have to rummage through her wardrobe and make do.

She was still shaken after Seamus' accident earlier on. Motorbikes seemed so dangerous. It had, however, provided them with an unexpected opportunity to see each other again. But what if he hadn't been so lucky? What if the unthinkable had happened? What if Seamus had....died? She shuddered. There were some things her mind simply could not deal with.

Another couple of weeks, she thought, another couple of weeks and I will leave Ernest. His initial good mood after the birth of James had fizzled out, and the deacon was back to his usual dour self. He spent more and more time over at the Bowen's farm, or down at the chapel, only troubling himself to talk to her when he wanted to know what was for supper. The thought of finally being with Seamus kept her going during the emotionally cold, miserable evenings in the cottage. Seamus made her so deliriously happy, her heart skipped a beat whenever she saw him and he treated her like a queen. They had discussed how she would seek a divorce, and what they would do in the meantime. Her heart was filled with trepidation at what she would have to do, and the dreadful repercussions afterwards. But she had to be brave and trust the wild Irishman who had stolen her heart totally. And given her another great love, James. She glanced fondly down at him, lying in his carry cot, regarding his tiny hands as though they were the most fascinating objects in God's creation. Motherhood, she thought. It was everything she'd hoped, and more.

A few days later, Mavis excitedly opened a pale pink envelope, it was a letter from Eiddwen,

Dear Mavis,

I hope this letter finds you well, and little James too. Well, you'll never guess! Archie and I will be coming down to Llannon next week, and we will be staying with Seamus! Isn't that wonderful? Archie has decided that it is high time we sorted out what is due to me regarding the house, as my sisters are being very difficult.

I wonder what it will be like to stay in the Richards house? I can't wait! We will be arriving in Llanelli station around eight o'clock in the night on the Friday of next week, so I expect it will be too late to see you that evening, by the time we hire a taxi to Llannon. But maybe the next day?

Anyway, must dash now, as I have to cook the dinner (they call supper dinner up here) for me and Archie.

Lots of love (and a big kiss for James)

Your faithful friend,

Eiddwen. Xxx

Mavis grinned happily as she folded the letter and replaced it in its envelope. Seamus' sister was expected on the Monday, so any illicit liaisons would have to take place prior to her arrival. The pair had earmarked Sunday afternoon, as Ernest had once more excused her from Sunday School duties since having the baby, and this Sunday's service would be an extended one, as certificates were being awarded for good attendance. She would be able to enjoy a good two hours with no chance of Ernest returning. A secretive smile curled around her lips, she was looking forward to the meeting very much indeed. Adding the onions to the pot, she washed her hands and bent down to pick up James.

Mavis and Seamus lay curled up in bed, warm and replete. Little James was wearing just a nappy and lay on Seamus' naked chest, gently nuzzling and grabbing handfuls of hair. The midsummer sun streamed in through the window, bathing the little family in its summer rays.

"I could lie here forever." Mavis cuddled up closer to Seamus. "That was wonderful... I feel so sleepy!"

"Sleep if you need to." Seamus ruffled her hair, fondly. "I'll have a wee chat with my son and heir while you snore a while!"

"I do not snore!" Mavis poked him playfully in the ribs before closing her eyes and giving herself up to a few precious minutes of slumber. Seamus watched her.

Her smooth olive skin was already turning golden with the summer sun, and her glossy, dark hair was spread out over the pillow. How he longed to have her completely, to live with him, to wake up with him, to laugh and talk each day with him....but maybe, very soon?

The invitation to dinner was propped up on the parlour mantelpiece, having been slipped through the letterbox the previous evening. Ernest had scoffed at it initially, but couldn't find a good enough reason to decline. Mavis was uncertain whether she should mention the presence of Eiddwen and Drummond. The scandal of the elopement was only just subsiding in the community of Llannon. Better say nothing, she reckoned. As only two days remained – to decide what she should wear, Mavis began to rummage once more through her wardrobe. Although she'd regained her trim waist, and lost all her pregnancy weight, her chest was still rather spectacular, which ruled out any of her more glamorous dresses. Also, she would need to take James along as well, so he would need swift and discreet access to his evening feed. Her scowl of frustration was replaced by a gleeful smile of inspiration as she pulled out an ancient dress from the depths of her cupboard. Just the thing, she thought, as she tried it on. Looking in the mirror, she sighed happily. The white cambric dress fitted perfectly, as it had puffed sleeves and a ruched bodice, which accommodated her bountiful breasts easily. In fact, if she felt like, she could wear it off the shoulder, showing off her smooth, tanned skin. It made her look like a dark-haired Brigitte Bardot. She hadn't worn it since she was in her twenties, but it seemed just the thing for the dinner party, and when the baby demanded his feed, she could slip it down easily enough. And to hell with the boring scaffolding provided by her nursing brassiere, she was pert enough to dispense with that!

Seamus had invited her to drop by to see his sister before the party, to get to know her. Mavis wasn't sure what he had meant by this. Had he told her anything – - everything? She supposed she would just have to wait and see...

Ernest had left for Llanelli soon after lunch on Friday, and Mavis was looking forward to a quiet afternoon, playing with the baby and generally lazing about. Somehow, she always felt guilty being idle in front of her husband. He didn't actually say anything, but his expression said it all. She put James' baby blanket on the floor of the kitchen, having shooed Dai into the outhouse. Lifting the baby out of his carry cot, she placed him on the blanket, and started to sing to him, playing with his toes and tickling his tummy as she sang.

"Gee ceffyl bach, yn cario n'in dau
Dros y mynydd i hela cnau..."

She got no further, however, as there was a knock at the kitchen door, and a loud Irish voice called out,

"Hello, there! You in there, Mavis? 'Tis Bridget!" Mavis hastily scrambled to her feet, scooped up James and rushed to the door. Bridget stood there, larger than life, her bright red hair tied up in an emerald green scarf and her lips painted a vivid scarlet.

"Goodness! You've caught me on the hop!" Mavis was only too aware of her untidy hair and her old pinafore. "But do come in!" Nearly asphyxiated by Bridget's lavishly applied Tigresse, Mavis led the way into the kitchen, hoping the unwashed dishes and the unironed laundry would go unnoticed.

"Do you mind if we sit in here?" She hastily shoved the nappy bucket under the table with her foot. " I was just playing with the baby."

"Oh, to be sure! That's just grand! I can't wait to have a cuddle of him anyway!" Bridget sat down on the only comfortable chair in the room, taking off her long, purple cardigan.

"Tea?" Mavis moved over to the sink.

"I'm gasping for a cuppa, Mavis m'dear! Just hand me that wee fella and you'll have both hands free!" Bridget held out her arms, and enveloped James to her chest, smothering his blond head with kisses as she did. Surprisingly, he didn't seem to mind at all, and rewarded his new admirer with a beaming, toothless grin.

"Oh, look at the wee snipey! Look at him smile at his poor aunty Bridget! He's gorgeous! Mwah!" And James was subjected to yet another volley of crimson kisses on his cheeks. Mavis looked over at Bridget in astonishment. Had she heard correctly? Aunty? However, Bridget seemed unconcerned. With James safely back on his blanket, the two women were able to relax and talk. And talk they did, about the weather, village life in Llannon, and then...

"You know, he has the most stonning blue eyes, Mavis!" Bridget drank her tea noisily. "And there's you with brown eyes like Maltesers!" Mavis blushed furiously, not knowing where to look.

"Um, my husband has blue eyes. It's a recessive gene, according to the midwife." Bridget looked at her slyly, a small smile curling around her lips. "Now why d'you think I waited for Mr Watton to be out before calling by?"

"What on earth do you mean?" A wave of panic swept over Mavis. She felt as though her world was about to disintegrate. She bent down and picked up the baby, hugging him to her protectively.

"Oh, please don't worry!" Bridget got to her feet and moved closer to Mavis, bending down and putting her arm around her. "Seamus has told me everything. He couldn't keep it from me any longer. But I'm the only family member to know, he wouldn't trust the others. And I am so, so fecking delighted for him, for you both!"

Tears sprang to Mavis' eyes. "Oh, for God's sake, please keep it to yourself. Ernest would kill me if he found out!"

"Do you really think he would, Mavis? Hurt you?" Bridget voice was full of concern. "Because if he's in the habit of hitting you or anything, you should come away right now."

Mavis shook her head slowly."He hasn't hit me since I had the baby, and he has only ever done it once - that night of Seamus' party – do you remember how angry he was?"

"Yes, I do. But you must promise me that if you are ever fearful for your safety, you will rush over to Seamus?"

"I promise." Mavis hugged Bridget. "It's a relief to be able to talk about it with another woman. My best friend is coming back with the Professor tonight, but she is not known for her ability to keep quiet about things! And she would be so shocked."

Bridget resumed her position in the armchair, pulled out a nail file from her enormous patchwork bag and started to attend to her long, fuchsia fingernails.

"I'm gasping for a fag! I left mine over at the house. D'you have any?"

"Oh, I'm sorry. Ernest disapproves of cigarettes, he won't allow it in the house or anything! And the midwife mentioned that some experts think it isn't good for the baby's lungs, or something." Mavis blushed furiously.

" Oh, no matter! I'll survive! You know, I'm glad beyond belief that Seamus and you have got together – well, of a sort!" Bridget laughed quietly. "He's never settled down with a woman, not since, well, you know." Mavis nodded silently.

"And I am envious beyond belief as well," she continued, pausing her manicure briefly, "I'd have loved a wee baby, but it's too late now, and Mr Right never came along. Plenty of Mr Wrongs, mind you!" She threw back her head and roared with laughter at her own joke.

"Well, you can come and cuddle James whenever you want,"said Mavis firmly, "now, how's about a slice of bara brith?"

By four o'clock, Bridget had departed. Mavis somehow felt at peace with herself. It had been a cathartic experience to say the least. What an exuberant woman Bridget was, such carefree flamboyance. What a wonderful sister-in-law she was going to make. As she cleared away the tea things, Mavis breathed in deeply, feeling relaxed for the first time that day, watching the sun filter prettily through the branches of the apple tree and smiling at Dai rolling on his back on the lawn.

Her reverie was rudely interrupted, however, by the kitchen door opening and Ernest stalking in, his habitual scowl on his face.

"Well, what's for supper? Pass me my slippers!" He kicked off his shoes without undoing the laces and settled down in the armchair, opening the Evening Post, ignoring Mavis and the baby.

"And good evening to you too." Mavis replied, acidly. This was not lost on Ernest, unfortunately.

"Enough of your sauce, woman. Treat me with the respect I deserve, as any man deserves from his wife." He crumpled up the newspaper and threw it at Mavis. Tears sprang to her eyes, and her cheeks burned, but she was damned if she would let him see how much he had upset her.

"There's plenty of bread and cheese in the pantry. Help yourself. I'm taking James for a nap." Picking up the baby, she hurried from the room, before Ernest would have the satisfaction of seeing the tears pouring down her cheeks.

At nine o'clock, the sun was still visible above the hills at the back of Llannon, and it was still warm. James had had his very late nap, also on account of being thoroughly over-stimulated by Bridget, so was now quite wakeful and alert.

"I'm taking the baby out for a walk, Ernest." Mavis fetched the Silver Cross from its place of honour in the hallway. "Maybe the fresh air will help him settle. Do you want to come too?" She hoped he wouldn't, for she had other plans, which did not include him. Thankfully, he shook his head, peering at her over his spectacles.

"No, I want to listen to the radio. There's a programme about Pentecostal chapels on soon. Don't be long, will you? I want to go to bed before ten."

Joyfully, with a spring in her step, Mavis pushed the pram out of the cottage and into the lane. She had spied the taxi arriving half an hour ago, but hadn't wanted to impose herself on the men's reunion too soon. But she was longing to see Eiddwen.

Timidly knocking on Seamus' front door, she waited excitedly. After what seemed to be an interminable delay, the door was finally opened, and Seamus stood there, a delighted smile on his face, and a glass of whisky in his hand.

"Bejesus! Now this is a lovely surprise! Come in, sweet Mavis!"

"I'll leave the pram outside, it's too awkward to bring it in, and James is awake anyway!" Picking the baby up, she followed Seamus into the house, but got no further than the hall before he turned around and kissed her swiftly on the mouth.

"Couldn't resist it," he whispered, wickedly.

There in the kitchen stood Eiddwen and the Professor, each holding a glass of whisky as well.

"Mavis!"

"Eiddwen!"

The women shrieked at each other simultaneously. Mavis handed James to Seamus and rushed over to hug her friend. How much Eiddwen had changed. The tight curly perm was gone for good, the sleek bob had remained. She must have lost almost a stone in weight and was wearing a chic, black dress. Her once chubby face now had visible cheekbones and was discreetly made up. An air of happy confidence radiated from her. She was a woman deeply in love and well-loved. Eiddwen had finally become the woman she should have been years ago.

"Well, holding that wee bairn certainly becomes you, Seamus," chuckled the professor, "if I didn't know any better, I'd say you were an old hand at it!" And he bellowed with laughter. Seamus looked over at Mavis and grinned at her.

"Oh, I've seen this little fellow out and about on my travels quite a bit! I feel as though I have got to know him pretty well by now!" Mavis stifled a giggle.

Many "oh my goodnesses" and "how wonderfuls" later, Eiddwen was curled up on one of Seamus' squashy sofas, cuddling and cooing over James. Having declined a glass of whisky, Mavis sat next to Seamus on the opposite sofa, demurely sipping a glass of lemonade. Even though he was a good couple of feet away from her, she felt her skin tingling at the thought of being so near him.

"So what will you be making for us tomorrow night, Seamus?" Mavis smiled discreetly over at him.

Before he could reply, there was a rush of perfume, a swish of coppery silk and Bridget swept into the room.

"Brace yourselves, my angels," she laughed in her husky voice, "he's making you -wait for it - a curry!"

Eiddwen clapped her hands together in excitement. "Ooh! I've eaten curry before! In Edinburgh! Isn't it, Archie?" She turned to gaze adoringly at her husband, who patted her on the knee. "It was lovely! We went to an Indian restaurant, oh, it was all velvet seats and flocked wallpaper, and red lights everywhere. And the curry wasn't hot at all!"

"Oh, to be sure, this won't blow your heads off!" Seamus smiled reassuringly at Mavis, who was looking quite horrified, never having eaten a curry in her life. "It's an original recipe from the Punjab that I actually picked up in South Africa, of all places!"

"Is there anywhere in the world you haven't been?" Mavis laughed. "And do you think Ernest will like it? What shall I tell him?"

"You tell the old gobshite feck all!" giggled Bridget, saucily. "Let him enjoy the surprise!"

At a quarter to ten, Mavis reluctantly bade them farewell, not wanting to leave the little party, which seemed ready to go on carousing into the small hours.

"Much as I love you, Mavis," called Bridget as she left, "I can now be having a fecking ciggie!" More roars of laughter followed her and Seamus into the hall. As he bent down to kiss her a swift goodnight, Mavis stroked his cheek gently.

"Nos da, dear Seamus, I love you."

"And I love you, sweet Mavis. Until tomorrow, then." He stood at the door, watching her pushing the pram into the deepening twilight, unable to believe his luck, that soon she would finally be his.

Muffled squeals of mirth echoed along the dark landing just after midnight.

"Don't, Archie bear! Ssh!" Eiddwen opened the guest bedroom door slightly to see if anyone else was about. Thankfully, she could still hear Seamus and Bridget chatting away downstairs. Swiftly closing it, she locked the door hastily and resumed her place on the rug in front of the fireplace, which Seamus had filled with roses and ferns as it was summer.

Archie lay back on the bed, wearing a black satin dressing gown, lustfully watching his wife as she turned her back on him and writhed slowly, up and down, slipping the shoulder straps of her red silk nightgown down over her bare, white arms. Eiddwen peeped coyly over her shoulder at him, all the while easing the nightgown down, always down, over her hips and thighs. Still with her back to him, she swayed to and fro, dispensing with the nightgown altogether, stepping out of it with practised skill. Archie stared in undisguised appreciation at her curvaceous body, now clad only in red silk French knickers and stockings.

"Keep your shoes on, ya wee hussy! Keep them on!" His voice was thick with desire. "Dance some more for Archie bear!" Slowly, deliberately teasing him, Eiddwen turned around, cupping her big breasts in her hands.

"Do you want to see them, Archie bear?" she asked in a little girl voice.

Archie could only grunt his assent.

"Shall I show you my titties, Archie bear?" She moved closer to him, still hiding her assets in her hands. "Well, here they are!" And with a flourish she flung her hands apart, treating her husband to the sight of her bare, bouncing bosoms, which she rotated enticingly in front of his face.

"Ooh, come here, ya brazen woman!" He grabbed her and flung her on the bed. "I'm going to ravish you now!" Off came the knickers, then off came the black satin dressing gown. Archie gave a roar of delight as he plunged himself into her.

"Shush, Archie! Seamus will hear us!" Eiddwen could hardly get the words out as Archie pumped away with all his might.

"Ha ha ha!" He laughed rakishly. "The way I am gonna see to you, Missy, it'll be that stuck up Ernest Watton who'll be running over to complain about the noise!" Eiddwen gave up any pretence at silence and joined in the carnal game with great gusto, which cause many giggles and smirks in the lounge directly beneath them.

Lighting yet another cigarette, Seamus poured himself a final glass of whiskey. Bridget was stretched out with her feet up on a sofa, puffing away contentedly on a recently rolled reefer. Only a few candles remained lit, providing a subdued light to the dark room.

"They seem happy enough." She smiled through the haze of pungent smoke which hung in the air in an intoxicating cloud.

Seamus laughed. "Indeed they do. Who'd have thought it? Drummond, the eternal bachelor, married and as happy as a pig in muck. Eiddwen, the perpetual spinster, finally hitched and blossoming beautifully. And the best of luck to them."

"Talking of eternal bachelors," Bridget looked at him slyly from under her false eyelashes, "Mavis has certainly got you hooked, hasn't she? She's under your skin good and proper."

He gazed into his glass. "She's my world, Bridget. I can't do without her. You know, when I first set eyes on her, I thought she was the most gorgeous little thing, you know? But a pain in the fecking arse! Jesus! Feisty, opinionated, straight-laced beyond belief. But as I got to know her, I saw this vulnerable side to her, a wonderful softness. I saw the real woman, saw into her soul, saw the sadness in her heart. And someone like her is stuck with that miserable, cold-hearted bastard."

"But not for much longer, I hope. I am sure she'll make you incredibly happy, Seamus old boy. Now I'm off for my beauty sleep." Stubbing the reefer out in an onyx ashtray, she blew her brother a kiss and tripped rather drunkenly from the room, leaving him sitting at the window, gazing over at Mavis' cottage, unable to stem the waves of longing which kept breaking over him. Reluctantly dragging himself away, he blew out the candles and went upstairs, but not to bed. Instead he opened the door of the room where he stored all his completed canvases. Switching on the light, he walked over to the painting of Mavis, the unofficial one. Removing the dust sheet, he stood back to look at it. He had captured her so well. That glint in her eye, that look of seduction, yet of innocence. A promise of more to come, of secrets withheld, the fur coat slipping teasingly over her shoulders. Seized with inspiration, he took it down, a plan forming itself in his mind. He would get a taxi down into Llanelli first thing in the morning. Seeing as Mavis was about to become his officially, it was high time this painting was sent elsewhere. And he knew exactly where to send it.

Saturday. The end of another week. But every day was like another for Mavis, no longer going out to work, and spending her time looking after James, and doing housework. At least it was summer time, and she could go out and about, pushing the pram for miles along the track, enjoying the sunny weather. But there was no time for a long walk today. How on earth was she going to find time to accomplish everything? She sighed, pushing a stray strand of hair out of her eyes. She would need to wash her hair as well, and allow time for it to dry. Gone were the days when she could titivate and spend time on herself. No leisurely baths for her any more, it was all she could do to pop in and out of the water within a few minutes. And there was still the cleaning and ironing to be done. At least when she was feeding the baby, she had to sit down and relax.

Time, she thought, so little of it when there were things to be done, yet how slowly it went when there was something she was longing for. Like Seamus. Rebelliously, she decided that the housework could wait. And so what if tomorrow was Sunday, and a day of rest? She would wait until Ernest had gone to Sunday School and tackle it then.

A heat haze hung over the hills in the distance, and there was no breeze whatsoever. The day was sultry and hot, the sky a vague, unattainable blue, as though it hadn't quite made up its mind what colour it was going to wear this morning. Mavis watched Ernest through the kitchen window, as he angrily dug the vegetable patch and stomped about in a general bad mood, despite the beauty of the day. Why had she never noticed his moods before? Maybe she had been oblivious to them, become used to them even, shrugged them off in her superficial way. But her eyes had been opened when Seamus arrived, when he burst into her life like a wild, crazy flame, lighting her up from within and illuminating the shallow path she was treading.

As the grandfather clock struck ten, she was surprised to hear a car roll up outside. Peering through the kitchen window, she saw a taxi turning around at the top of the lane, then stopping outside Seamus' house. Watching quietly, she saw Seamus get out and pay the driver, before walking around the side of the house to the kitchen at the back. Where could he have been? Maybe he'd been down into Llanelli to buy ingredients for the curry? But she hadn't seen any shopping bags....but all would be revealed, she expected.

"Do we really need to go to this thing at all?" Ernest grumbled as he brushed his thick, white hair into submission. "I have nothing in common with that artist fellow, and I'd much rather be staying home, concentrating on my sermon with a sensible supper of sausage and mash."

Swiftly dressing James in the romper suit given to him by Eiddwen, Mavis said nothing. To respond would instigate an argument and could easily prevent them going at all. The day had been extremely hot, yet Ernest insisted on wearing his best suit, and his navy blue striped tie, which was as frivolous as he ever got.

"You're going like that?" He looked at his wife disdainfully, who looked as pretty as a picture in her sweet white dress, her shining hair cascading in casual ringlets over her bare shoulders.

"It's hot, cariad." Mavis didn't look at him, and continued packing a spare nappy and some Vaseline into a bag. Ernest snorted in annoyance and dismissed the thought from his mind that his wife actually looked very beautiful indeed.

By a quarter past seven, Mr and Mrs Watton were making their way across the lane, holding the carrycot between them, its precious cargo fast asleep with a tummy full of his mother's milk. Mavis' tummy, on the other hand, was full of anxiety. She hoped fervently that Ernest wouldn't take umbrage at any sort of carefree behaviour or conversation this evening. She needn't have worried. Vaughan Williams' Symphony No. 6 was drifting out of one of the open windows, and Bridget appeared in the doorway, wearing a demure grey linen dress, with her russet hair skilfully coiled up on top of her head.

"Come in, come in!" She greeted Mavis with a kiss on the cheek, which Ernest regarded with slight distaste. He hoped she wouldn't treat him similarly. But Bridget merely looked him straight in the eye and shook his hand. "Lovely to see you again, Mr Watton."

"Where shall we put James?" Mavis looked anxiously down at the sleeping baby.

Bridget led them into the cool hallway. "We're all in the garden, it's so hot! Let's put him by the French doors, they're open wide, so we'll be able to hear him if he cries, but we won't disturb him with our chatter!" Ernest scowled. He very much doubted he would be indulging in idle chatter with this bunch of arty hell-raisers.

To Mavis' surprise, a table had been laid in the middle of the lawn. A snowy-white tablecloth had been spread over it, with jam jars full of wild flowers placed at intervals along it. Incense sticks had been stuck into the flower beds, filling the evening air with the powerful scent of jasmine. A chiffon-clad Eiddwen and her safari-suited husband were relaxing on the chaise-longue, which had been placed underneath the apple tree. Seamus was nowhere to be seen.

Seeing Ernest, the professor stood up.

"Hello, there old chap! Great to see you again!" He slapped Ernest on the back, who maintained his poker face, unconvinced that he felt likewise. Eiddwen remained seated, nervously clutching her Babycham. She had no idea what to expect from the stern preacher.

"Good evening, both." Ernest managed a faint smile. "I did not expect to see you here. I must congratulate you on your wedding. It must be getting on for nine months or so since you left Llannon, Eiddwen." He looked at her spitefully. "You took us all by surprise, I have to say. Your sisters were quite shocked."

Eiddwen looked up, defiantly, her fingers anxiously pleating the folds of her cream dress. "I am sure they have recovered from the shock by now, Mr Watton. They are, after all, grown women."

Well done, Eiddwen, thought Mavis in admiration. The Eiddwen of old would never have defended herself so valiantly. The professor also looked down on her approvingly.

"Yes, Mr Watton. We will be paying Eiddwen's sisters a visit tomorrow after they have returned from chapel. There are many financial issues to address."

"Drinks?" Bridget looked expectantly at the Wattons. "We have local beer, wine, fruit juices and, er, Babycham!" She winked at Eiddwen and they both laughed.

Ernest sat down stiffly on the straightest backed chair he could find.

"I'll have a glass of lemon squash." He glared at Mavis, who had made herself quite comfortable on a nearby sofa, which had been draped in white cotton.

Bridget looked at Mavis.

"I'll have a glass of water, I have to drink lots in this weather."

Bridget nodded, heading for the kitchen. "I'll see if Seamus has any ice in that fridge of his." Ernest raised a bushy white eyebrow. A fridge! Whatever next?

On cue, out marched Seamus. The conversation halted abruptly, everyone's mouth hanging open in surprise. For there he stood, dressed in a white tunic and baggy white trousers, with a purple turban on his head, a large blue gem shining in the middle of it. On his feet were the most curious gold coloured shoes Mavis had ever seen.

Seamus seemed very pleased indeed at the reaction he was receiving, and bowed theatrically, waving a white drying cloth with a flourish.

"Savagata hai! Welcome!" He moved over to Ernest in two easy strides, and shook his reluctant hand. "A pleasure to see you again, Mr Watton."

What an amazingly good actor he is, thought Mavis, smiling, anyone would think he actually was pleased to see the miserable Ernest.

"And Mrs Watton! How charming you look this fine evening! Motherhood suits you incredibly well!" Seamus bent forward, took her hand and raised it to his lips, treating her to a sly wink as he did so. Ernest looked as though he was about to implode in fury.

"Dinner will be served in a few minutes." Seamus beamed around at his guests. "Tonight, you will savour a taste of the east, and your senses will be filled with the flavour of exotic spices. I do hope you will enjoy the experience!"

Bridget returned with a tray full of drinks, laughing. "He's been busy at it all day! So you lot had better be hungry!"

Seamus had cunningly arranged the seating so that he was at the head of the table, but next to Mavis. Ernest was next to her, with Bridget at the other end of the table, and the Drummonds facing the Wattons. Beads of sweat were now pouring off Ernest's face, and he mopped his brow with his handkerchief.

"Why don't you take your jacket off?" Mavis suggested. Scowling, Ernest reluctantly removed it, feeling strangely vulnerable as he sat there in his shirtsleeves and braces.

The party was soon served with a selection of salads, vegetable curries, chutneys, fluffy rice and oven-baked chicken. The most tantalising aroma filled the air. The Wattons stared in disbelief, unsure where to start.

"Let me help you." Bridget leaned over and heaped food onto Ernest's plate, smiling innocently as she did. He had no option but to taste it. To his great surprise it was delicious, and he tucked in with enthusiasm. Seamus took the opportunity to assist Mavis similarly, his hand accidentally brushing against hers in the process. She took a mouthful of chicken.

"This is truly wonderful, Seamus!" Mavis took another bite. "Not hot at all — I mean, I thought that curries were supposed to be very hot indeed!"

"Not at all." Seamus covertly rubbed his foot up against hers under the table. "Authentic curries are flavoursome and spicy, and rarely blow your head off!"

Mavis smiled. "Well, this is an education for us both, isn't it, Ernest? I will have to learn how to make a curry myself! You seem to be enjoying it a lot!" She returned the pressure on Seamus' foot, Ernest all the while concentrating on shovelling the food as quickly as he could into his mouth.

Putting her knife and fork down on her empty plate, Eiddwen looked over in astonishment at Mavis, who, having finished her food, was busy helping herself to more chicken and chutney.

"Goodness, Mavis! You never used to have such an appetite! Where on earth do you put it?"

Mavis laughed. "Oh, that's because I'm still feeding James! I'm hungry all the time!"

On cue, a wail of protest burst through the French doors, and a small pair of legs could be seen kicking vigorously above the carrycot, flinging the sheet onto the floor.

"Perfect timing!" Smiling, Mavis got to her feet and went to fetch the loudly objecting baby. Ernest immediately stopped eating, his fork half way to his mouth. Surely Mavis wasn't going to feed the baby here? In front of all these people?

Returning to the table with a temporarily pacified James, Mavis glanced at Seamus.

"Would you mind if I go inside to feed him?"

Ernest heaved a sigh of relief. At least his wife wouldn't be making an exhibition of herself. However, with a wicked glint in his eye and intent on making subtle mischief, Seamus also got to his feet, and guided Mavis and the baby over to the chaise longue, turning it around to face away from the rest of the party.

"Oh, now then! There's no need for mother and child to be excluded from any pearls of wisdom, or wonderful conversation that may occur ! Sit here, Mavis, so you won't miss anything!" He grinned roguishly at his guests, thoroughly enjoying Ernest's discomfiture. Mavis was relieved she couldn't see her husband's expression, but the waves of disapproval were almost tangible as he sat in his seat and fumed silently, glaring at the back of Mavis' head.

Thankfully, the Professor was able to divert Ernest's attention by initiating a deep discussion about the true meaning of Easter and its pagan origins. This seemed to inflame Ernest almost as much as his wife breastfeeding in public, but at least he knew his subject matter (or so he thought) and was able to vent his annoyance publicly.

Eiddwen, having drained her Babycham, couldn't wait to rush over to Mavis.

"Can I see? I've never seen a baby feed like this before? Do you mind, Mavis?"

Mavis laughed. "Of course not, Eiddwen! Not that there's much to see!" With perfect timing, James pulled away from the breast and let out a resonant burp.

"Plenty to hear, though!" Seamus bellowed with mirth from the other side of the garden. "He's a right little trencherman!"

Professor Drummond joined in the laughter. "But infant manners aside, don't they remind you of the Madonna and child? Such a lovely scene!" Seamus nodded in agreement, trying valiantly to hide the pride on his face.

Ernest scowled, extremely irritated by the way his wife and child were being discussed by other people. She was his wife, and they had no business talking about her in this way. But there was nothing he could do about it, without seeming peevish and bad tempered.

Eventually, James completed his feed, and had his nappy changed, Eiddwen declining to participate, so the party settled down once more to enjoy Seamus' home-made lemon sorbet.

The sinking sun slipped behind the ancient trees which surrounded the garden, its occupants feeling relief as they welcomed the shade as the heat of the day abated.

"Look at that plane up there." Eiddwen pointed up at the sky. "I wonder where it's going? I've never been on a plane, I wonder if I ever will. Why does it make all that smoke?"

"Contrails, m'dear, contrails." Professor Drummond puffed out his chest importantly. "And judging by it's trajectory, I would say it's heading for America."

Eiddwen looked suitably impressed. "So not one of those new parcel holidays, then?"

Nobody had the heart to correct her, except Ernest, that is.

"Parcel?" He snorted in derision. "Surely you mean package?"

Mavis stared at her pompous husband in fury, despising his mean-spirited behaviour.

"Mr Watton," the professor's voice was dangerously low, "it seems not everyone has experienced foreign travel to the extent you have. Would you care to share your experiences with us?" Ernest clenched his teeth angrily. Of course, he had never been further than Birmingham in his entire life, and that was on a mystery tour with his second wife.

Keen to diffuse the situation, Bridget got up to clear away the dishes, eagerly assisted by Eiddwen, who was anxious to escape Ernest's spite and disapproval.

The conversation dwindled to a halt, with Mavis rocking James gently in her arms, Ernest and the Professor eyeing each other warily over the table, like two duelling cowboys, and Seamus enjoying himself immensely.

Over in the east, just visible over the old garden wall, a huge yellow moon was rising, challenging the sunset, gaining the ascendant minute by minute.

Just like a picture from Alice through the Looking Glass, thought Mavis.

"I'll just settle James down again." She carried him back to the carrycot. "I'll put him inside, if you don't mind, Seamus, the midges are everywhere now and my life will be a misery tonight if he gets a bite!"

"I'll help you move it." Seamus was on his feet in a trice, following her through the open French doors.

He watched her settle the sleepy baby, then, ensuring they could not be seen, he took her by the shoulders.

"I can't keep my hands off you," he whispered. "it's torture for me to watch you looking so lovely and not touch you. I adore you, my gorgeous woman, and soon you will be all mine!" He bent down and kissed the top of her head.

"Oh, Seamus, it's hard for me too. I can't wait much longer. I love you so much." She hugged him hard, then sprang from him as the door opened, but it was only Bridget, looking for her brother to ask him to put some music on. She smiled, retreating discreetly.

"I'd better go back." Mavis reluctantly let go of his hand, and rejoined the others, Seamus following at a respectable distance.

Ernest and the Professor were still sitting at the table, glowering at each other, the latter nursing a glass of whisky, surreptitiously acquired during a pretended trip to the bathroom.

"So!" Seamus rubbed his hands together. "Music! What's it to be? My record player is ready and waiting. The Beatles? Tchaikovsky? I even have a record of the Treorchy Male Voice Choir, Mr Watton, if you would like me to play that?"

Somewhat mollified, Ernest nodded his assent, so Seamus disappeared once more into the house.

Bridget and Eiddwen soon rejoined the others, vowing that the dishes could wait until tomorrow, that the night was too beautiful to spend at the kitchen sink. The silence was only broken by the lonely hoot of an owl and some late-shift bees in the lavender bush.

"Is Seamus still looking for that record?" Bridget looked puzzled. "Seamus!" Her yell echoed around the garden. But there was no reply. There was nothing at all.

Concerned, she got up and walked briskly into the house. Her anguished cry brought them all running inside.

Seamus was doubled up in pain, his face ghastly pale, he seemed to be gasping for breath.

"What is it? What's the matter?" Mavis could hardly get the words out.

"Let's lie him down!" The Professor tried to take charge. Seamus' face was now contorted with agony, and he clutched his chest, unable to speak, his turban falling to one side, revealing an unhealthy sheen on his forehead. Mavis felt the blood drain from her face as she watched the man she loved sink to his knees, a livid purple replacing the pallor.

"Ring for the doctor!" Eiddwen sobbed, hysterically, besides herself with fright. Ernest, glad to escape the scene, rushed from the room to use the phone.

Somehow, between all of them, they managed to get Seamus onto the floor.

"Seamus! Speak to me!" Bridget tapped his face in terror. Mavis dropped onto the floor beside him, unable to believe what was happening.

But there was no response from Seamus. Frozen with fear, Mavis watched as the Professor started to press hard on Seamus' chest, then breathe into his mouth. Unconsciously, she reached for Seamus' hand and held it tightly. A slight pressure by way of return told her he knew she was there. However, within a few seconds, his hand relaxed. Seamus was dead.

Chapter Twenty-eight

Survival

Dr Hodges closed his medical bag with a sigh, hating these situations that occurred only too frequently in his profession.

"I'm so very sorry," he looked around at the stunned faces before him, "it appears to have been a massive heart attack. There was nothing anybody could have done, nothing at all. There will need to be a post-mortem, I'm afraid." Eiddwen sobbed quietly into her handkerchief, the Professor holding her closely. Bridget got up abruptly, and walked outside, fumbling in her pocket for her cigarettes, her face rigid with shock and grief.

Mavis sat perfectly still, enveloped in her own silent world, unable to process the events that had unfolded with horrifying clarity in front of her eyes. She looked down at her hands; they didn't feel like her hands at all. Did they belong to someone else? This could not be happening, it must be a dream, from which she must surely wake up. Ernest sat stiffly next to her. Seamus' body lay where he had fallen, on the moth-eaten carpet before the fireplace, a totally inappropriate orange bed sheet covering him, everyone too shocked to exercise enough common sense to fetch one of the many dust sheets that lay in abundance in the portrait room. James slept blissfully on, unaware of all the drama.

"One of you needs to ring the funeral director immediately, so that arrangements can be made. I will contact the coroner and Mr O'Brien's body will be collected as soon as possible, probably this evening." Dr Harries moved towards the door. "If any of you need anything to help you sleep, I can prescribe you something."

"That will not be necessary." Ernest got to his feet. "We will pray to the Lord for our departed friend, and accept solace that he is now at peace."

"I'll be the judge of that." Bridget returned, drawing deeply on her cigarette, ignoring Ernest's obvious disapproval. "I'll take whatever's on offer, doctor, or there's a good chance I may hit the bottle tonight." Dr Hodges hastily wrote out a prescription, and handed her two small pills in a tiny brown bottle.

"These are for tonight. If you need more, you can take the prescription to a chemist on Monday morning. I am sorry to leave so quickly, but I have another call, a sick baby, down in the village. Good evening, and please accept my deepest sympathy." And he was gone, leaving the sorrowful group to their own devices.

Mavis still hadn't moved or spoken a word, her face remaining expressionless. I can't move, she thought to herself, I can't do anything. Ernest seemed quite unaware of her total immobility.

"I'll phone the undertaker, if that's acceptable." He smiled stiffly at the others. "I have regular contact with Tudor Morris down in Llanelli. Miss O'Brien ? If I may?"

Bridget nodded, stubbing out the cigarette. "That'll be fine. But Seamus will be going home to Ireland to be buried. Of that I am certain. The family would want that. Now, I suppose I had better be ringing home soon to tell them the news..."

"Would you like me to do that for you, my dear?" The Professor leaned forward solicitously, as Ernest headed for the hallway.

Bridget smiled apologetically. "If you wouldn't mind, Drummond. I think all I'm capable of right now is going to bed to cry my fecking eyes out. Poor Seamus." She kneeled down beside his body. "Dear Seamus. My fabulous, kind, loyal big brother." And, pulling back the sheet, she put her arms around the cold, stiff shoulders and hugged him tightly, bursting into tears.

I want to do that, Mavis thought, numbly. I want to stay here and never leave. I want him, I want him, I want him....

Ernest returned, rubbing his hands together as if he had clinched some lucrative deal. "Well, that's that then. Mr Morris will be up in half an hour. My condolences once again. Come along, Mavis. We must leave these people to come to terms with their bereavement." He picked up the carrycot, and pulled Mavis to her feet. The room swayed before her, and she stood up shakily.

"Goodbye, Mavis." Bridget smiled at her in anguish. "I'll see you very soon, I'm sure." Mavis could only nod, but Bridget could see the agony in her eyes.

"Come here. I could do with a great big hug!" She pulled Mavis close to her, and the two women clung to each other, feeling each other's heartache and distress, yet deriving a small amount of comfort from the embrace.

Mavis didn't remember walking home, when she woke up at three o'clock to feed James, she didn't remember undressing and going to bed. All she could remember was the look on Seamus' face as he fell. Agony, disbelief and extreme panic all featuring in quick succession on that dear face before he fell to the floor. The scene would be imprinted on her mind forever, and would be replayed over and over again. It was unbearable for her to think that the man she loved so fiercely had suffered so dreadfully, and she had been unable to help him. And to have known such intense joy, to have her future all mapped out, only to have her dream snatched away so abruptly. Mavis also vaguely remembered peeping out of her bedroom window around midnight, seeing a dark van, and some men carrying Seamus away. Away from her forever. Tears poured down her face as she held James tightly to her breast, the baby suckling contentedly, oblivious to his mother's devastating grief.

"My poor Seamus," she whispered , "come back, come back. Don't leave me here, come back and take me with you." James pulled away from her, looking up at his mother with a beaming smile, milk dribbling out of the side of his mouth..

"Ah, if only you knew, my little one," she stifled a sob, lest Ernest heard her, "and if only you had known him better." She smiled at him through her tears, rocking him gently in her arms until he fell asleep.

Sundays in Llannon were always sombre and quiet, but to Mavis this Sunday morning was as grey and cold as the walls of Bethel Chapel itself, despite the warm sunshine. She felt angry at the sun for its lack of respect, and wondered how the birds could possibly sing so sweetly when Seamus was dead. Mavis became aware of a heightened sensitivity, the smell of the meat cooked the previous day, the sound of the grandfather clock ticking away, the rough fibres of the drying cloth as she finished doing the breakfast dishes. These sensations would remain with her forever, and would always remind her of the intense sorrow she was feeling.

"Well, aren't you getting ready for chapel?" Ernest put on his best jacket once more, it having remained on the bannister overnight.

"I don't feel well at all, Ernest." She did indeed look completely washed out, with huge dark circles under her eyes. "I can't possibly go to chapel this morning. In fact, once I have bathed James and sorted him out, I think I will go back to bed."

"As you wish." He put on his shoes, his hat and coat, picked up his prayer book and left the cottage without another word. She watched him making his way down the path, his jaw set. He didn't even look across at Seamus' house as he passed it.

Mavis slumped down into the armchair, unable to carry out any more mundane household tasks. Now that Ernest had gone, she could let her guard down and allow her grief full rein. James looked up in bewilderment as his mother wept loudly, her head in her hands, the agony of her loss taking complete possession of her. Dai wandered over to her, and put his paw on her knee, his head on one side as he gazed at her in puzzlement with his big brown eyes.

"Oh, Dai," she sobbed, stroking him gently, "what am I going to do?" The dog whined softly, putting his other paw on her lap as well. Mavis lifted her head, and cast her sore, red eyes at the apple tree in the garden. The apples were plentiful this year, tiny and immature as yet....they would grow and ripen, but Seamus would never see them. Seamus would never see his son grow up, he would never hold her in his arms again, he would never see another sunrise or paint another picture.

She was snapped out of her misery by a knock in the kitchen door, which was then opened as Bridget entered the cottage.

"Oh, Bridget." Mavis started weeping again. "Come in, sit down. I'll put the kettle on. Ernest just left for chapel." Bridget sat down cautiously on a hard kitchen chair.

"Hardly slept a wink." She took off the sunglasses she was wearing. Her eyes were bloodshot, with rivers of dried, black mascara staining her cheeks. "Those pills didn't work. Yeah, I know Ernest is out, I watched him walk down the lane, so I took my chance."

"Seamus has gone then." Mavis picked James up and cuddled him. Bridget took out a cigarette, then remembered where she was, and replaced it in the packet.

"Yes, he's been taken down to Llanelli, to the hospital there. The undertaker came up last night, quite late. No offence, my dear, but it's no wonder that Mr Morris is such a close colleague of your husband's. Talk about kindred spirits. Miserable fecker."

Mavis tried to smile, but her mouth wouldn't work, it was frozen forever, it seemed, in a sad, downward curve, like those clowns one saw in the circus. She got up, handed the baby to Bridget, before filling the kettle.

"At least we've got this little chap," Bridget hugged him tenderly, "we have a little bit of Seamus right here with us." She kissed him softly on his downy head.

Over the tea, which neither of them really drank, Bridget told Mavis that as soon as the post-mortem was done, Seamus' body would be taken back to Ireland for burial.

"Will you come?" Bridget looked expectantly at Mavis, already guessing what her answer would have to be.

"Oh, I would give anything to be there. But it would be impossible. My situation has altered in the blink of an eye. I am stuck here now, Bridget, this is to be my life after all." As she spoke the words, Mavis felt as though a thick, black cloud was starting to envelop her, smothering any hope she may have cherished.

"I wanted to give you something. Well, a few things, actually." James was handed back to his mother, as Bridget delved deep into her handbag. Pulling out a small package wrapped hastily in brown paper, she gave it to Mavis. "You should have these."

Using her one free hand with difficulty, Mavis unwrapped the package, finding inside the silver cigarette case she had bought Seamus for Christmas, and, encased in tissue paper, the small portrait he had done of her whilst she had been asleep in his garden. It now bore the title, Rhiannon.

"Oh, my." She whispered, softly, holding the drawing against her chest. "Where did you find it?"

"In his wallet. He carried it everywhere, he said. But he told me he never used the case – well, not for cigarettes, anyway, not after the twenty you included ran out." Mavis looked crestfallen as Bridget continued. "He kept something inside it that he stole from you one day."

"Stole from me?" Mavis looked puzzled. "I don't understand."

Bridget smiled sadly. "While you were asleep one day (I think maybe the day he did the drawing) he took a cutting of your hair, just a tiny one, you wouldn't have noticed, then he kissed you on the lips as you lay sleeping, so the stolen kiss and the lock of hair were carried around with him wherever he went."

In spite of the great sadness she was feeling, a new warmth filled Mavis' heart. To have been loved like this, to have meant so much to Seamus, it made her weep afresh, but this time with tears of gladness.

They talked about Seamus incessantly for the next half hour, funny stories about his childhood and how happy he had been here in Llannon.

Bridget got up. "I had better go now. That uptight husband of yours will be home before long. I'll be leaving for Ireland the same time as Seamus, but I have to return to London first. Are you sure you won't come with me? Leave Ernest and bring James over to Ireland? We'd make you welcome, and the family would love you, once they'd got used to the shock of it all!"

Mavis raised her eyes slowly, afraid to meet the challenge.

"I can't, Bridget. I suppose I am a coward. Seamus gave me courage, I would have followed him to the ends of the earth. But he's gone. I'll have to make the best of things here now. I have had my brief moment of joy, my moment in the sun, but now it's gone. At least I have James. But we can write, can't we?"

"Of course!" Bridget hugged her hard. "Take care, sweet Mavis." Sweet Mavis. His name for her. Mavis blinked away the tears that were threatening once more to pour down her cheeks.

"Goodbye, Bridget," she said, quietly, "and thank you."

Somehow, Mavis got through the next few days, mechanically doing the housework, her only conscious activities revolving solely around James. Eiddwen and the Professor had called by to say an emotional farewell, before leaving once more for Scotland, followed a day later by Bridget, heading for London. As she watched their respective taxis leaving, bumping down the uneven lane, she thought to herself that now she really was all alone. She felt she would explode with grief, having to keep it hidden all the time, even from Eiddwen. Her heart was leaden, she had no appetite, couldn't sleep and could see no future for herself.

Hearing James stir, anticipating his hungry cry, she glanced at the clock. Ten o'clock. He had only fed an hour ago. How could he be hungry so soon? Automatically she felt her breasts. Usually she would start leaking when the baby cried. Nothing this time. How strange, she thought. Putting a squirming James to her left breast, she wondered why he was being so uncharacteristically difficult. He kept pulling away and crying, then returning to the nipple and sucking voraciously. After a few minutes she realised that her let-down wasn't happening. Nothing was happening. There was no milk. In horror, she tried the other side. Nothing there either. What on earth was she going to do? In despair, she hastily dressed James, put him in the pram and set off down the lane, fervently hoping that Eva would be at home. The motion of the pram seemed to pacify James momentarily, and he stopped crying, which was just as well because Eira Jones was out in her garden pruning her roses.

"Hello, Mrs Jones!" Mavis walked even faster. "Can't stop, sorry, have to catch Eva!" And without waiting for a reply she hurried down to the main road and the shop.

Mavis could have shouted with relief when she saw the Griffiths' car parked directly outside the sweetshop. It seemed she was just in time, as Eva, dressed for her day off in a pretty, floral dress, was putting on her white, lace gloves and looking for the car keys in her bag.

"Eva!" The distress in Mavis' voice startled the midwife, and she swung round.

"What's the matter? Is the baby OK?" Eva rushed over to the pram, where a disgruntled James was busy chewing his fists.

"He's fine, Eva. But my milk has gone! What am I going to do? Help me, please!" For what seemed the hundredth time that week, Mavis burst into tears.

"Come inside." Eva calmly took charge of the pram, and ushered them inside and to the back room, leaving a surprised Mr Griffiths staring at them.

"Now sit down and let's talk about this." Eva pulled up a chair opposite Mavis. "Your milk has gone, you say?"

"Yes, oh yes! Since this morning! There's nothing there any more, and James is hungry!"

Eva considered the situation. "There's no need to worry. If worse comes to worse, I have some Cow and Gate powdered milk here, I keep it for emergencies just like this. But sometimes events can cause your milk to go. Do you feel ill? A temperature?"

Mavis shook her head dumbly. Eva sighed, but pressed on.

"A shock? Anything like that? Because that could affect your supply quite dramatically."

"Well, yes. I have had a shock." And Mavis proceeded to tell Eva about Seamus' death the previous Saturday.

"I see." Eva's face registered concern. "What a terrible thing to have witnessed. But that could explain it. I'll do what I can to help you, but you may need to give James a bottle until your milk returns. The body is a strange thing, and sometimes reacts in ways we don't expect. But remember, he has had a good twelve weeks and more of your milk, Mavis. You have done so well."

Eva resigned herself to the fact that her excursion into Carmarthen would have to be postponed, and settled down to spend the next hour fruitlessly attempting to help her friend.

"It's no good, Eva! There's nothing there!" Mavis' voice was pathetically forlorn. "Can you give him the bottle for me? I don't think I could bear it."

There was nothing for it. James was hungry, so Eva complied with Mavis' wishes, watching her sit there like a statue, with tears rolling down her face, as she watched Eva struggling to get James to take the bottle, which he did, eventually.

"Now he's been fed, you take him home and get some rest. I'll pop down to the chemist in Llanelli and pick up some more powdered milk and some bottles for you. I'll call up later with them and show you what to do. He should sleep for a couple of hours now, anyway. But when he wakes up, make sure you keep holding him close, next to your skin. Let him try feeding if he wants to, yes?"

Mavis nodded silently, feeling as though everything was closing in on her, crushing her.

Eva watched Mavis push the pram across the road, her shoulders rounded and her head down, no spring in her step.

"Something is seriously wrong here," she murmured to herself.

At five o'clock that afternoon, Eva pushed open the garden gate of the Wattons' cottage, expecting the kitchen door to be opened by either Mavis or Ernest, as she would have been spotted coming up the path. But there was no-one to be seen. Knocking on the door, she peeped in through the window. There was no movement at all, and the pram was visible in the kitchen. She supposed Ernest was out. Still, her mission was important, so she tried the door, and it opened. The baby was crying.

"Hello!" Her voice echoed through the cottage. "Mavis! It's me, Eva! Are you upstairs?" No response..

"Mavis!" Her voice was louder now, and an ominous feeling of unease crept over her. "I'm coming up." She put the basket of baby milk down on the table.

As she ran up the stairs, the baby's cries grew louder and more frantic. Opening the bedroom door, she was horrified at the sight which met her eyes.

James was lying in his carrycot, dressed just in his nappy, which badly needed changing, and he was clearly distressed. Mavis was lying on the bed, wearing a grubby dressing gown, staring out of the window, her eyes were glazed and unseeing.

"Mavis!" Eva sat down on the bed and took Mavis by the shoulders. "What's the matter? Are you ill?"

Slowly, Mavis turned to look at Eva, seemingly deaf to the baby's cries. "I can't cope," she whispered, "I can't do anything."

Eva picked up James, and started to hand him to Mavis, but she turned away again. "I can't. Don't make me. I just want to be left alone."

With a sinking heart, Eva saw to the baby, changing his nappy and consoling him. Just at that very moment, she heard the kitchen door open.

"Mavis! What's for supper?" The door slammed, and Ernest could be heard pulling off his shoes and flinging them under the table. Eva had never been so relieved to see the dour, miserable Ernest Watton in her entire life.

"Up here, Mr Watton, as quick as you can!"

Ernest was up the stairs in a flash. "What's going on?"

Eva stared at him challengingly. "Mavis is not well. Not well at all. Now I will stay here with her, and I want you to go down to the shop and ask my husband to ring Dr Hodges. Tell him to come as soon as possible."

"But what's the matter with her? What illness is it?" His demanding manner only served to infuriate the normally calm Eva.

"I'll explain later. Now, will you do as I have asked?" She drew herself up to her full height, and looked him directly in the eye. "Go and call the doctor." Along with scores of student nurses and midwives before him, Ernest looked away, abashed, and murmuring assent, left the room quickly.

Eva sat on the dressing table stool, nursing the baby, watching Mavis anxiously.

Her concern was shared by Dr Hodges when he arrived half an hour later.

"I think this is more than a simple case of baby blues." They spoke quietly on the landing. "I think Mrs Watton is severely depressed. Sr Griffiths, I have given her a mild sedative – I don't think she's been sleeping much - and I really think the baby should be looked after by her family. I doubt Mr Watton is up to it, so what do you think?"

Eva nodded sorrowfully. "I have to agree with you, Doctor. I don't agree with separating mothers and babies usually, but it would put the baby at risk if Mavis was just left to get on with it. Her sisters have no experience of babies, so there's no point in me contacting them. But I think, from what Mavis has said, that the extended family down in Llanelli is more than able. Shall I make the arrangements?"

"Please do. I will leave it to you to advise Mr and Mrs Watton what we propose. I very much doubt there'll be any objection. Although I cannot understand what has triggered this." He shook his head in puzzlement. "I know they all had a terrible shock last week when that fellow collapsed and died in front of them, but she hardly knew him. No, it must be a form of post-natal depression. You must tell Mr Watton that she needs looking after now. I'll call again in a day or two, I won't start her on any regular medication yet, let's see how things go."

And with that he left, a subdued Ernest holding the door for him as he left.

"Thank you for calling, Doctor. What exactly is wrong with Mrs Watton? When will she be back to normal? I mean, who will do the cooking and the cleaning?"

Dr Hodges looked at him sharply. "Your wife has severe depression, Mr Watton. She needs careful looking after. Sister Griffiths will explain everything to you." And he was gone.

"Mr Watton!" Eva came down the narrow staircase, holding a restless James in her arms. "Sit down. We need to have a little chat."

Mavis never had any proper recollection of the days which followed. Mostly she slept, unaware if it was day or night, not bothering to wash or dress, drinking water and attempting to eat only if cajoled by a rebuked and dutiful Ernest. Her normally petite frame now became fragile in the extreme and her rosy beauty was a thing of the past.

James had been taken down to stay with Gwyneth Baker and her husband, in Llanelli. Mavis had put up no fight when the little child was put into his carrycot and bundled into Mr Baker's car with all his belongings, she had made no objection at all. It was Mrs Baker who was doing all the weeping, while Mavis stood quietly by, not reacting or saying anything.

Her sleep was dreamless, a dark chasm which swallowed her up and rendered her numb, allowing her an escape from reality. The days ran into each other, having no meaning or structure. Mavis was gradually fading away, retreating into herself, where no-one could reach her.

It was on the fourth night that she had the dream. She was walking on the beach, the wind lifting her hair, the seagulls were shrieking in their usual way. The sun was shining down warmly, the sand felt smooth beneath her bare feet. Then a voice said quietly, "Why are you here? You're not supposed to be here. You must go back. You must wake up, Mavis, you have to go on..."

"But it's so nice here," she replied, "I don't want to go back..."

She became aware of the voice once again. "Go back, sweet Mavis, go back...."

She woke up with tears pouring down her face. Sweet Mavis. Of course, she would have to go on. If the owner of the voice was telling her to go on, then she would. Looking at the clock she saw that it was only six o'clock, but the sun was already shining through the window of the box room where she was spending most of her time. Slowly, she got out of bed. Her legs felt like jelly, but her mind was clearer and more alert than it had been for many days. She breathed in deeply. A little bit of the old Mavis started to return.

After a quick wash (something she hadn't done for nearly a week) she got dressed. Ernest was still asleep in the next room, so without making a sound, she crept downstairs. On impulse, she put Dai's lead on him and headed out of the cottage and up to the track.

The day was already warm, but there was no-one else about. The silence was broken only by a tractor in the distance, a few birds singing sweetly and Llanelli Town Hall clock striking the half hour a few miles away to the south. She walked slowly on, until she came to the "thinking stone." Sitting down, she buried her face in her hands, but would not allow the tears to spill from her eyes. The tractor stopped its work in the nearby fields, the birds stopped singing. Time seemed to stand still. She became aware of a great sense of peace and calm.

"Mavis?"

Slowly, she looked up. Who had spotted her so early in the morning? Then she blinked, unable to believe what she was seeing. Was it him? Was it really him? The dog seemed to notice nothing.

Seamus seemed to come and go, in a haze of sunlight. He was smiling. Oh, that dear, lovely smile.

"Seamus? Is it you?"

He continued to smile. He didn't open his mouth to speak, but she could still hear him.

"Sweet Mavis, you must try hard to keep faith, now. I have left you for now, and time will pass in a flash for me, until I see you again, but you have your life before you, many years to live. And our son, ah yes, our darling son. He needs his mother."

Mavis stood and moved closer to him, her arms open. As Seamus drifted closer to her, she felt herself enveloped in a golden warmth....and then he was gone, and she was all alone on the track once more. But no longer alone in her heart.

Calling Dai to her, she cuddled him tightly. "He was there, Dai," she whispered, "he was really there." An emotion she had forgotten ever existed returned at that moment. Hope.

Thoughtfully, she returned to the cottage, filled with a new strength. Appreciating the beauty of the early summer morning, she descended the steps which led from the track to the lane. She stopped and forced herself to look squarely at Seamus' house. The house of so many happy memories for her, a house of love, of promise and hope. She must never forget that.

Whatever she had just experienced up on the track, whatever it had been, it was surely a message, an instruction, guidance. She may indeed have lost the love of her life, but she was still a mother, and the only mother James should ever have.

Over the next few days, Mavis tried her hardest to look after herself. Ernest had proved a fairly reliable, if mechanical nurse, but he was relieved to see that Mavis was slowly returning to her usual self. She made an effort to eat properly, had a bath, washed her hair, but she was dismayed to see how loose her clothes were on her when she put them on.

All in good time, she told herself, I will recover and get well.

About a week later, and a full three weeks since Seamus had died, Mavis got up early, had breakfast, and to the surprise of Ernest, started to clean the kitchen.

"I'm supposed to do that," he made a feeble attempt to take over, "that's my job now." Mavis gave him a wry smile, retrieving the mop from his hands.

"I think it's time I took over, don't you? But if you don't mind, I want you to take me down to Mrs Baker's this afternoon. I'd like to see James."

"Yes, of course. Whatever you say, Mavis." His manner was solicitous and deferential. Privately Mavis thought that maybe Eva should have had a "little chat" with Ernest years ago...

They set off after lunch, the windows of the Reliant Robin fully wound down, as once again the weather was hot and sultry. A heat haze shimmered on the road as the car made its way over the brow of the hill which led down to Felinfoel. The Gower peninsular seemed very far away, and the tide was out, leaving a burnt umber stretch of sand reaching out to Whiteford lighthouse. The sun beat down relentlessly on the countryside, bleaching the fields and scorching the grass on the roadsides. Mavis weather, she thought to herself, fondly, Seamus used to call this her type of weather. She smiled dreamily.

"Mrs Baker doesn't know we're coming, you know." Ernest didn't take his eyes off the road. "I hope she won't mind us dropping in like this." Although Mavis was fond of and respected Gwyneth Baker, at this precise moment, she had no concern about social etiquette and was focusing solely on her own agenda.

"It'll be fine, Ernest," she murmured, "it'll be fine."

When they arrived at the Baker's street, there was no-where to park, as the street was so narrow and a lorry delivering cement was taking up most of the road. Ernest decided he would drop Mavis off while he secured a parking place.

Taking a deep breath, Mavis walked purposefully to number ten, and knocked firmly on the door.

Gwyneth Baker opened it, her face registering surprise and pleasure.

Mavis smiled at her nervously. "It's time for James to come home, now."

Chapter Twenty-nine

Resolution

From Bridget.(Sent to the shop in Llannon)
August 1st
Dear Mavis,

I sincerely hope you are well, and that little James is thriving as well as ever. He is such a gorgeous little chap, so sweet and loveable.

The funeral was yesterday. The sky was blue and the sun was shining as we said farewell to my wonderful brother. It was a beautiful service, and despite Seamus and I being complete and utter heathens, it did make me think that maybe, just maybe there is a God or something somewhere. There has to be, when you consider everything. How can a man as vital and loving as Seamus just suddenly cease to be? I wish you could have been there to say goodbye, I think it would have helped you. I honestly hope you have had some closure by now. It must have been so hard for you.

I have some news. Apparently, Seamus was not as disorganised as we assumed. He had set up a trust fund for James, and I am the trustee. It is unlikely James will want for anything while he is young and lives at home with you, but when the day comes that he leaves home, there will be money available to fund whatever higher education he chooses. I will send the details in a separate letter, again to the shop in Llannon, just in case. You can tell them that I don't know your actual postal address or something, and that I am mad Irish woman. You have plenty of time to concoct a story as to the source of the money – eighteen years in fact! - or even to have "saved " it up yourself.

My invitation to come over to Ireland remains. If your husband should ever raise his hand to you, or harm you in any way whatsoever, then you must ring the number I will add at the bottom of the letter. That is my flat in London, in

Norwood, but I can get on a train in a jiffy and be with you within a day and we could then get the train to Fishguard and sail over to Ireland.

I expect you still have the key to the house. When you have a moment, do go over there and have a look round. If you see anything that you would like to keep (although that could be difficult for you to explain away) then please take it. When you have finished, pop the key through the front door. The house will be going on the market in a month or so.

Take care of yourself, Mavis. My brother adored you and you were the love of his life. I just wish things could have been different for you both, but at least you had a year of knowing each other, loving each other and of course, your adorable wee baby.

I hope we can meet each other in the not too distant future.

Yours sincerely,

Bridget.

01-698-425

Mavis folded the letter carefully, before storing it away in her underwear drawer. A lump in her throat heralded more weeping, but she swallowed hard. No time for crying now. Ernest had gone to Carmarthen to buy some tools for the garden, giving her the perfect opportunity to go over to the house. She wrapped James next to her in a shawl so she could carry him easily yet have one hand free.

Walking into the house was so hard. The silence was different this time. There was a stark finality about it. This would be the last time she would ever enter the building of her own accord.

The smell of dead flowers hung miserably in the air. A vase of drooping, brown gladioli stood forlornly on the telephone table in the small room off the hallway. Instinctively she went to empty them into the bin, then stopped herself. No point, she thought, no point at all. The estate agent could deal with that.

Going from room to room, she closed her eyes, remembering all the happy times she had spent in each one, wondering which one James had actually been conceived in, unless of course, his conception had taken place over at Llangennith, in the dunes....what a glorious day that had been. She smiled.

She wandered into the portrait room. The painting of the notorious Gladys Williams had gone, thank goodness, probably to that Sheik in London. Who would sort out all the remaining pictures, she thought, as there were about five of them, of various sizes. She carefully removed the protective sheets; there were two of Parc Hardd's gardens, one of Bridget in her nun's outfit looking surprisingly innocent, another of the view of the Gower from the top of the hill, and a tiny one of Dai when he was a young puppy. She hadn't known he had done it.

Picking it up, she hid it in her pocket. But where was the unofficial portrait of her? It was nowhere to be seen. Maybe Bridget had taken it back to London for safekeeping, in case anyone found it.

Moving onto the landing, and into Seamus' bedroom, she found a half-used bottle of M.E.M. English Leather cologne. She unscrewed the top and inhaled it, remembering the times when she had laid her head on his bare chest and breathed in that distinctive scent. Replacing the top she added it to the picture in her pocket.

There was nothing else here for her now. All her memories were in her head, and she would see Seamus every day when she looked into her baby's eyes. She turned to go.

Towards the end of August, the Wattons took a trip down to Llanelli. Mavis left James with Eva for the excursion, handing him over to the midwife with a pile of clean nappies and his little pot of baby food.

"He's had a feed from me only a few minutes ago, although I had to top him up with a bottle as well. And his tea is due around three o'clock. We won't be long. Oh, and he likes to be rocked to sleep, and - "

"Off you go and enjoy yourselves," Eva said smiling, "It'll do you both good. And this little scamp will have lots and lots of Aunty Eva's attention for the next couple of hours!" She took the gurgling James from his mother, waving goodbye to them from the door of the shop.

One of their first stops was at the florist in Llanelli market. Mavis chose a beautiful bouquet of pink roses and gypsophila as a thank you present for Gwyneth Baker, who had looked after James so well during Mavis' illness. As the assistant wrapped the flowers up in cellophane and tied it all up with ribbons, Mavis got out her purse, first asking,

"Do you sell plants as well? For the garden?" Ernest looked at her in surprise. Mavis had never been much of a gardener.

"We have a small selection." The assistant pointed to half a dozen plants in pots at the back of the stall. Mavis thought for a moment, then pointed to a small rose shrub.

"I'll have that one. Roses do well in our garden, and they don't take too much looking after." The single red bud on the plant had drawn her eye, it would open soon, and there were others likely to follow shortly after. Due to its thorns, the assistant put it in a sturdy brown paper bag.

Happy with both her purchases, Mavis led the way out of the market and on to the Bakers' house.

The following day, when Ernest was down at the farm, and James was having his nap, Mavis found a trowel in the shed, and set about digging a hole in which to plant the shrub. Dai looked on with great interest, maybe he could help too? She had decided to plant it under the apple tree, the one where she used to sit and dream, the one where Seamus had caught her asleep one day. Even though the boughs were shady, the rose was positioned facing south, so that it had the sun all day.

"This is for you, Seamus," Mavis whispered, "I can't visit your grave in Ireland, so I will come here to talk to you. Sleep well, my dear love." She patted the earth around its base with her hands, standing back to admire her work.

Satisfied that she now had her own special place to remember Seamus, she walked back to the kitchen, and the rest of her life.

Chapter Thirty

The Finale.

Mavis settled down once more into motherhood and her role as a housewife, for what else was there she could do? The months, and then the years crept by, and James grew into an engaging little boy, displaying a great deal of his natural father's wit and merry nature, which made him popular with his classmates. He attended the local primary school, which was Welsh medium, ensuring he could converse fluently in both Welsh and English.

Mavis and Ernest trundled along fairly amicably, Ernest having realised how close he may have come to losing his efficient wife, although he would never know just how close that had been, and for a very different reason. His daughter Audrey returned to Llannon the following year, to marry her dashing Canadian fiance. The wedding ceremony was held in Bethel chapel, followed by the reception down in the Stradey Park Hotel in Llanelli. The whole event was a bitter sweet experience for Mavis – joy at seeing her delightful step-daughter get married, yet tinged with sadness that she, Mavis, would never be able to fulfil her secret dream of being with Seamus for the rest of her life. Each wedding vow seemed to strike a harsh blow into her heart, in spite of the gladness she felt for Audrey.

Seamus' house was sold to a property developer, and remained empty for a long time, before being converted into three holiday flats, but these were only ever occupied in the summer. Perhaps it was just as well, as it signified the end of that chapter of Mavis' life; there would be no going back, no returning to those idyllic days of love and romance.

Eiddwen remained in close contact by letter, but gradually the letters between the two friends grew less and less, Mavis being wrapped up in James and also because Eiddwen and the professor embarked on a world tour, visiting different universities in each new country. Post cards arrived every few months from

America, Hong Kong, Budapest and even Tasmania, but with just a short, scribbled message.

Bridget wrote faithfully every few months, and Mavis replied promptly, also enclosing photos of James at various important stages in his life: his first Christmas, his first day at school, riding his first bike.

Mavis would often go for walks along the track, taking an ageing Dai with her for company, when James was in school. She needed these private moments to be alone with her thoughts, her memories of the past and to daydream of what might have been. Sometimes she thought she would catch a glimpse of that familiar tall, lanky figure in the distance, only to find it was just her imagination. And when the wind blew from the west, she would hear him whispering her name, "Sweet Mavis." Somewhere, far away over the western horizon, her one true love lingered, amidst the glorious red sunsets and the starry nights of summer. Seamus was never far from her thoughts, he remained part of her very soul. The little rose shrub was now a sturdy bush, which flowered several times a year, beautiful crimson blossoms glowing brightly under the apple tree. Just like our love, Mavis would think. She would watch James as he played, his coltish legs still delicate with childhood, his blond hair turning darker year by year, but his eyes remaining as blue as the Irish Sea on a sunny, spring day. And when James smiled, her heart would stop, for it was the wicked, disarming smile of Seamus.

Ernest was a stern, distant parent, never hugging James, or praising him when he did well in school. His sole aim was for James to behave himself, attend chapel three times each Sunday, familiarise himself with the Bible and settle down in a respectable career, like Fred and Audrey. His discipline was rigid and unforgiving, his motto "spare the rod and spoil the child," so James soon learned to give Ernest a wide berth if a transgression had been revealed, to avoid a thrashing with Ernest's belt. But it was never Mavis who gave the show away, it was usually Eira Jones, or the parents of one of his many friends. Mavis saw James for the child he really was; affectionate, kind, naughty and lively. Little James could never quite understand why his mother was so warm and loving, but his father seemed so remote and cold. If James' personality had been of a more sensitive nature, he would have suffered considerably, but, having his mother's resilient streak and more than a little of Seamus' pragmatic character, he simply brushed it aside and tried not to think about it.

Shortly before his ninth birthday, James witnessed a confusing and highly unexpected event when he was sent down to Bethel Chapel on an errand for Mavis, to call Ernest for supper. It was almost six o'clock, and the evening meal was due to be served shortly. Ernest had been down at the vestry for over two hours, going over the accounts and sorting out some paper work; the supper would be ruined if he wasn't back soon. Braving the heavy rain and sleet, the little boy ran down the lane as quickly as he could.

It was getting dark as James tried to open the vestry door, but it was locked. He shouted out, but there was no response. Where could his father be? Standing on an old bench directly below the vestry window, he wiped the dusty glass with his sleeve and peered in. There was no light on inside, except for an old oil lamp which was kept in the chapel for emergencies. However, James could make out two figures rolling around on the floor. Had his father been attacked? In panic, he started screaming and hammering on the window. The figures got to their feet hurriedly, there was a scuffling and James could hear some panicked conversation between them.

The vestry door opened, and James, springing down from his viewing point, rushed to see what was going on.

Ernest stood there, in his shirtsleeves, with his braces still down, his face like thunder. Behind him in the dim light stood a plump, blond woman, hastily zipping up the black trousers she was wearing.

"M-m-mam said it's time for supper," the little boy stammered, "the potatoes are mashed and ready, but the sausages will burn if they're in the oven any longer." He reeled this off parrot fashion, having rehearsed it all the way to the chapel, as he was unable to take his eyes off this strange woman. What on earth could have been going on?

Ernest cleared his throat. "Run along, now. Tell your mother I will be home very soon. I am just finishing off some important business here with the temporary organist." James was sure he heard a snigger from the woman but he nodded obediently and turned to run back up the lane to the cottage, where the welcoming yellow lights were now shining through the windows. Had they been wrestling or – kissing? Mavis was standing at the kitchen door, looking out for Ernest and James.

"Dad's coming soon!" He was out of breath, he had run so fast. "He has to finish business with an organist, but, Mam? They were wrestling on the floor! Why were they doing that?"

Mavis tightened her lips. "Why indeed, James?" Here we go again, she thought furiously, that damned woman is back to try and worm her way into her life.

James looked up at her, puzzled. "Were they kissing, Mam? I thought they might have been kissing? But Dad's not supposed to kiss any other lady, is he?"

"No, James, he isn't. But don't worry, I will have a little chat with Dad later on tonight, and I am sure he won't be wrestling with any more ladies in the vestry." Mavis thought grimly that she would have great pleasure in putting things to rights that evening. After all, Ernest would certainly not want it spread around the village that he had been caught in flagrante delicto with the infamous Gladys Williams.

James, however, never forgot what he had seen, and stored it away at the back of his little mind.

When James was ten, and about to take his eleven-plus exam, a phone call came from the Bakers down in Llanelli. Ernest had decided it was necessary to move with the times, and the Wattons were now the proud owners of a cream coloured telephone, which graced the hall table, along with James' plastic Star Trek money box, as each phone call would require a two pence piece by way of payment. Ernest may have mellowed slightly, but his frugal streak was as strong as ever.

Mavis took the call from an excited Gwyneth. Wendy had exceeded all expectations in her ballet training and had managed to secure a scholarship at the Royal Ballet in London, after auditioning there the previous month. At the age of seventeen she would soon be leaving Llanelli to pursue the vocation she had always longed for. Ernest couldn't understand the great excitement at all, until Mavis patiently explained the prestige of such an opportunity, and how Wendy had had to compete against hundreds of other hopeful ballet dancers to win her place. Mavis felt a tremendous pride and sense of achievement when she heard the news. She was no dancer, and her knowledge of ballet was equal to her knowledge of human anatomy, but Wendy as a child had displayed that certain something, which was evidently being recognised elsewhere.

James was a clever little lad, and sailed through his eleven-plus, which allowed him to attend the Llanelli Boys' Grammar School, where he drove his teachers demented with his constant japes and disruptive behaviour. However, his sunny nature saw him through, and luckily for him, Ernest never got to hear the half of his pranks. If he had, the punishment would have been harsh. Their relationship continued to remain almost formal, lacking any warmth or spontaneity. James, knowing no better, assumed that all fathers were like that.

Unsurprisingly, James shone in Art, winning award after award at prize-giving evenings.

"What's the point in Art?" Ernest would grumble irritably, after a particularly tedious prize-giving. "Why can't he win an award in woodwork or something useful like that? Or Maths? He could work in a bank!"

Mavis smiled serenely. "He's a talented boy, Ernest, and we should encourage him. You never know, he could become famous." Ernest snorted in disapproval, and they made their way through the throngs of proud parents to meet the fourteen year old James, who was holding court with a group of friends, hanging on his every word as he regaled them with an account of how he had put potassium in the toilet bowls in the staff toilets, and how Evans Physics had nearly had a fit when he saw the lilac flames shooting up to the ceiling.

Tricks and playing the fool aside, James managed to get straight 'A's in his O-levels, and went on to study Art for A-level, along with History and French. However, he still found time for other pursuits, soon finding himself the star attraction amongst the girls at sixth form dances. His popularity was the envy of many of his classmates, but such was his comical attitude to life, they forgave him easily. Unlike Ernest, that is.

One balmy spring evening, James was loitering with adolescent intent at the bus stop on the main road just outside Llannon. It was eight o'clock, there was a glorious sunset and James was looking forward to sharing it with Sian Howells, whom he was expected to meet off the Cross Hands bus. The bus duly arrived, and there she was, as pretty as ever, with her blond hair flicked back, just like Farrah Fawcett-Majors, her face gleaming with skilfully applied fake tan and her tight jeans leaving nothing to the imagination. Steering her into the far corner of the bus shelter, James took advantage of her willingness to engage in low-level hanky-panky, and embarked on a marathon of kissing, shoving his hand inside her angora jumper at the earliest opportunity. Such was the ferocity of their passion, neither of them noticed the furious face of Ernest as he drove by, the passenger in Mr Bowen's farm van.

At nine o'clock, James returned home, having seen Sian safely back on to the return bus. Mavis was out, attending a Mothers' Union meeting down in the Sunday School hall.

As he quietly removed his shoes, James felt a stinging slap on the back of his head. Ernest stood there, bright red in the face and spitting with fury.

"Don't you ever behave like that in public again! Do you hear me? How dare you behave like that with that little trollop? It was disgusting!"

James rose to his feet, rubbing his head gingerly. Straightening up, he stood eye to eye with Ernest.

"Sian is not a trollop. She is a very nice girl with a healthy libido."

Ernest looked as though he was about to explode, and raised his hand, as if to strike James again. However, James quickly intercepted him, and grabbed the descending hand forcefully. His blue eyes blazed with indignation and anger.

"And don't you ever hit me again, Dad. I'm not a small boy now, you can't bully me any more. I can hit back. Do you hear me? And talk about double standards! You're so full of shit! I remember you in the chapel that night with that organist. Don't take me for a fool! And I bet you hit Mam as well, you're such a domineering bastard." And with that, James rushed from the room, slamming the door of his bedroom and locking it, fearful he had gone too far. But all remained quiet downstairs. And Ernest never hit him again.

James had his own agenda regarding his future. His burning desire, his absolute ambition was to study Art as a vocation. Despite the pleas of his History and French teachers, James applied to art college in London. Mavis was secretly delighted, and only told Ernest what was strictly necessary, afraid he would try and prevent James from following his dream. Any university or college prospectuses and letters that arrived through the letter box were swiftly intercepted and hidden by Mavis, to be given to James when he arrived home from school. Ernest would have been obstructive if he'd realised how determined James was, so the slight subterfuge was unfortunately necessary. Like the bully he was, and too afraid to hit the boy any more, Ernest would resort to verbal taunts, heavy sarcasm and the removal of privileges, which, unfortunately for Ernest, had as much effect as snow falling on an open fire.

The A-level results were outstanding, once again straight 'A's. Mavis felt so proud she thought she would burst. It was all around the village in a flash. However, the icing on the cake was when James, after several trips to London for interviews, which he determinedly made alone, managed to win a scholarship to study Art at St Martin's School of Art in King's Cross. So the trust fund would not be needed just yet.

Mavis thought her heart would break as the day approached when James would leave home to start his higher education. Ernest was now in his early seventies, and had no intention of driving all the way to London, so James travelled up by train with a couple of friends who were also going to universities there.

The cottage was so quiet without him. No more loud rock music (which Ernest detested), no more messy pots of paint left around, no more posters of Debbie Harry and Kate Bush on his bedroom wall, no more caricatures of Mavis, Ernest and his teachers littering his bedroom when he was suffering from teenage angst. As she tidied up James' room, the old box-room where she had nursed him as a baby, she caught a glimpse of herself in the mirror. At sixty-one she was remarkably well-preserved, but there were more silver hairs now, and the lines around her eyes had deepened, as her face had weathered all the traumas and struggles that life had thrown at her. Tears filled her eyes as she held a sweater that James had discarded on the floor (the FloorDrobe, as Mavis called it) and breathed in. Teenage sweat, Brut anti-perspirant and her son's own particular smell filled her senses. How she would miss him. Then she remembered doing exactly the same thing when Seamus had returned to Ireland all those years ago. Was she destined always to grieve after those people she loved the most? Sighing deeply, she opened the window to let the autumn air into the room, watching the sun sink slowly behind the hills, as she had done so many times before....

James had been away in London for a couple of years when an invitation arrived at the cottage to attend Wendy's debut as principal dancer in the Royal Ballet's production of Giselle. Even the disinterested Ernest had to admit that this was indeed a great honour, all the more so as Wendy had hinted that the Princess of Wales may be present. Therefore plans were made for the whole family, including Wendy's parents and her grandparents the Bakers, to travel to London for the performance.

Together, they commandeered almost an entire railway carriage. There was Mavis and Ernest, Margaret and Fred, Mr and Mrs Baker, with Audrey joining them in Cardiff, as well as Wendy's old ballet teacher, Miss Daphne, who was now well into her sixties, yet still wearing that bright red lipstick and her usual tight black clothing. Julie had decided not to come, as she was "too busy" with her secretarial studies, and had scoffed at the invitation, which stated that Wendy Wainwright – Wendy Wainwright? – would be dancing the lead role. Mavis thought to herself that there was more than a little jealousy at play there.

As the train pulled in at Paddington Station, the party alighted, the February day being bitterly cold, so Mavis was glad of her fur coat, defiantly ignoring the glances of disapproval from several young people passing by. The station seemed enormous, would they even find their way around? But there was James, excitedly waving a map of the Underground at them, and he pushed his way through the milling crowds to greet his family.

"Over here! This way!" He laughed delightedly, hugging his mother, Margaret and Gwyneth in turn. Audrey stood back to admire him. Her baby brother was now over six feet tall, with nut brown hair and bright blue eyes, totally at ease with himself and as enthusiastic as a young puppy. How like Seamus he is, thought Mavis with a lump in her throat.

"Hey! Look who's grown then!" Audrey punched him playfully, "Now, are you going to lead us out of this jungle?"

With all the exuberance of youth, James led the way to the tube station, shepherding the family, which was behaving like a flock of unruly sheep, down the scores of staircases until they got to the platform they needed.

They stayed at The Nadler Hotel in Covent Garden, with which Wendy had been able to negotiate a fifty percent discount. There was hardly time to do any sightseeing as they had to be at the theatre by seven o'clock, and after much grumbling by the men, who'd been forced into suits and bow ties for the event, the party set off at half past six for the short walk to see Wendy star in the performance of her life. James, also in a suit and bow tie, met them at the entrance, and soon they were all settled in the box that had been booked for them. To their delight, (all except Ernest's, that is) several bottles of Champagne waited for them in ice buckets, and a waiter hovered nearby attentively.

Mavis relished the atmosphere – jewels sparkling on white décolletages, programmes rustling, being scanned and remarked upon, beautiful people sitting on red velvet seats, whispering to each other, and fabulous, ornate artwork on the walls. She was glad she had worn her fur coat, it certainly didn't look out of place here, and her little black satin dress suited the occasion perfectly. Against the sheen of the satin, the tiny brooch from Seamus twinkled discreetly, and the linen handkerchief lay folded and hidden in her handbag, delicately sprinkled with Shalimar, the scent he had loved.

Then the lights dimmed, the crowd fell silent, and the curtain rose.

Wendy floated onto the stage for her first solo, looking every inch the innocent, young country girl that Giselle had been. Not only could she dance, she acted the part with passion, immersing herself in the emotion of the story of Giselle, winning the hearts of the audience completely. Miss Daphne unconsciously dug her red talons into Mavis' arm in her intense excitement, not that Mavis noticed, as she too was transported by the grace and stunning artistry of her niece.

Even Ernest sat transfixed as he watched his granddaughter leap through the air as though she had invisible wings, and execute pirouette after perfect pirouette as the ballet unfolded.

There wasn't a dry eye in the house as the ballet came to an end. Wendy had a standing ovation, with so many curtain calls that everyone lost count.

"I helped make this happen," thought Mavis, happily, tears rolling down her face, "I helped her get there!"

Eighteen months later, James graduated with a first class Honours degree from St Martin's. However, being as ambitious as ever, he applied to several art galleries in Paris, succeeding in gaining a position in the Musée de l'Orangerie as a museum exhibition officer. Now he was well placed to hone his craft, learn about the practical and financial aspects of art, as well as continuing to paint his own pictures. It was during these years in Paris that he met his future wife, the gamine Simone Lavisse, who was a trainee journalist for the Revue Noire. Falling hopelessly in love with her Bambi-like features, the pair married quietly one Easter – the following year in one of the small chapels of the Sacré-Cœur, arriving back in Llannon to break the news a week later.

Mavis was delighted with her new daughter-in-law, who was quietly deferential and obviously besotted with James. Ernest, on the other hand, wondered what James could possibly find attractive about his wife – she appeared much too thin, wore extremely tight jeans, had a diamond stud in her nose and, the worst sin of all – she smoked.

Mavis was delighted with her son's good fortune. Happily married, secure in his position in the museum and following his heart's desire as a painter, what more could a mother wish for her son? So Mavis thought her cup would overflow when, after a couple of years, James and Simone had their first child, a little girl, whom they called Mavis-Claire. She was fortunate that the little family returned to Llannon on a fairly regular basis, and she even went over to Paris a couple of times herself. Ernest never accompanied her, however, as he was now nearing eighty and preferred his own home comforts.

It was shortly after his eighty-third birthday that, like his mother before him, Ernest suffered a stroke. He was admitted to the newly-built Prince Phillip Hospital in Llanelli, but was soon transferred to Mynydd Mawr Hospital just a mile or so outside Llannon. He was bed-ridden now, not even able to get up in a chair, he had no speech and had to be fed through a tube, as his swallow reflex had also been affected. Mavis would catch the bus every evening at half past six, in order to visit Ernest, but in bad weather, Eva would offer her a lift.

Ernest lingered in this state for another six weeks, until one day, the ward sister rang Mavis at five o'clock in the evening to say that he had taken a turn for the worse, that it seemed he had suffered another stroke. It was thought advisable that Mavis should come immediately.

Eva arrived to pick her up.

"I think you need to prepare yourself for the worst, Mavis," she warned, the windscreen wipers making no impression on the unexpected thunderstorm which had suddenly burst upon the village. Mavis said nothing, but wrung her hands in worry. Ernest had never been a kind or loving husband to her, but had mellowed slightly with age. Her thoughts were in a turmoil, and she bit her lip, anxious to get to the hospital as quickly as possible, yet not wanting the security of sitting in the car to end.

Ernest had been moved to a side cubicle. The main light had been switched off and only the overhead bedlamp remained on. The young staff nurse smiled apologetically as the two women entered the room.

"Mr Watton is quite comfortable, now." She straightened the bed cover. "I'll leave you alone with him for a while, if you want?"

"H-how is he?" Mavis found it hard to say the words. "Will it be – you, know..."Her voice trailed away.

"Mr Watton may possibly be able to hear you very well,"the nurse replied, with a warning look on her face, "but it seems he is asleep. He is not in pain, and he's not distressed as you can see. I'll be outside. Just call me if you need me."

Mavis sank down into a chair next to the bed, while Eva remained by the door. How small and lonely Mavis looked, she thought. Even though Mavis was only a couple of years older that her, she suddenly seemed to have shrunk into herself.

Ernest's breathing was shallow and irregular, his cheeks sunken and his colour had developed an ominous yellow tinge. He didn't look like Ernest at all. The naso-gastric tube had been removed, thankfully. Mavis had always hated seeing that sticking out of his nose.

"Do you want to be alone, Mavis?" Eva whispered softly. Mavis turned to look at her friend.

"No, stay here, Eva. I don't want to be alone if he..." She stopped, remembering the nurse's words.

"Why don't you hold his hand?" Eva suggested. "And what about saying the Lord's Prayer? Ernest would like that, wouldn't he? In Welsh?"

Mavis nodded. Swallowing hard, she started to recite quietly.

"Ein Tad yn y nefoidd, sancteiddier dy enw..." But the words failed her, tears were coursing down her face as she held Ernest's gnarled hand. She allowed herself the luxury of weeping a little longer, then managed to pull herself together, and finished the prayer.

It seemed as though hours had passed, the two women continuing their vigil, but in reality it was only a few minutes before Mavis suddenly noticed that Ernest wasn't breathing any more. She looked at Eva, questioningly. Eva nodded, sorrowfully, her eyes bright with tears.

Ernest Watton, deacon of Bethel Chapel, had passed away.

A week later, the most well-attended funeral in living memory was held in Bethel Chapel. Fortunately, James had been able to return home in time for the service, although his wife, heavily pregnant with their second child, remained in Paris. The chapel was full to capacity, with scores of villagers standing outside as well. The coffin was borne by James, Fred, Audrey's husband John and their son, Nigel. The summer day was unseasonally cold, with a northerly wind blowing down from Scandinavia, so Mavis wore her fur coat, finding comfort in its familiar softness. Ernest was buried alongside his first wife in the graveyard which lay behind the chapel. It was a sombre, dour ceremony, the grey sky and chilly temperature doing nothing to relieve the morose mood of those present.

Back in the cottage, after an indifferent reception in the Sunday School Hall, Mavis and James said goodbye to the family members who had returned there with them. Mavis suddenly felt exhausted, worn out with having to be polite and accept condolences, and sank down into the old armchair next to the Rayburn.

"Mam." James' voice sounded strained. "I, er, need to talk to you about something." He was finding the words difficult, that was clear. Mavis looked up in surprise.

"What's the matter? You don't have to go back to Paris soon, do you?" She looked sad.

He smiled, reaching for her hand.

"No, Mam. I'll be staying the rest of the week, if you can bear to have me here!" He smiled, that wonderful smile so reminiscent of Seamus. Mavis relaxed.

"I need to ask you something," he continued, "it's about a painting." His mother looked up, puzzled. Why should her son, the art expert, want her opinion about a painting?

"The museum asked me to have a look at some work they bought from another gallery a few weeks ago. I came across, believe it or not, a portrait of you, Mam. It was painted by the same artist who did the one of you in the fur coat, the one in the hall, but in this one you're not wearing it properly. It's identical otherwise, well, more or less."

Mavis caught her breath, and avoided her son's eyes.

"It's even better than the one here," he went on, "the artist has captured something special, there's a glow about you that isn't there in the other one. And it's called Rhiannon. Tell me, Mam, who exactly was Seamus O'Brien? I know he was a celebrated artist, and well-respected - actually that portrait of you went for about three thousand pounds in London before it ended up in Paris!"

Mavis was dumbstruck, unsure what she should say. Slowly, she raised her eyes to meet James, still unable to speak.

James persisted. "I mean, did he actually live here in Llannon? Did you know him well? For you to have had your portrait painted with bare shoulders, when Dad was so bloody puritanical – it seems rather strange! I think that Seamus O'Brien sent the portrait off to London a few months after I was born, according to the information history. Can you tell me more about him, Mam?"

Tell him, a small voice inside her head advised her, tell him.

Mavis smiled bravely.

"Yes, James, I can indeed tell you more about him. You see, Seamus O'Brien was your father."

The old grandfather clock, which had witnessed so many emotional events in Mavis' life, ticked loudly and sanctimoniously in the otherwise silent kitchen. James then laughed quietly, shaking his head in disbelief.

"You know, I always thought that maybe I was adopted or something, there was something not quite right about the way things were between Dad and me. Did Dad know? Did Seamus O'Brien know? Mam, I need to know everything, everything you can possibly tell me!"

Taking a deep breath, Mavis got to her feet and walked over to the window, gazing out at the garden, at the apple tree where Dai, long gone, used to sleep and chase squirrels.

"I'll tell you everything, James, but first, are you terribly angry?"

She was relieved to see him shaking his head, a smile on his lips and his eyes bright with unshed tears.

"How could I be angry with you, Mam? You have always been such a great mother to me, you made me feel safe and secure, you were with me every step of the way as I grew up. Dad, on the other hand..." He got up and went over to hug her. "Everything, Mam. I need to know everything."

Mavis clung to him. "I'll tell you everything about my darling Seamus. I'll start by saying he was the most wonderful, kind-hearted man I have ever met in my entire life, and I was utterly destroyed when he died. Let's sit down, this will take some time."

"So there you have it." Mavis put down her empty cup of tea. "The story of how it all happened, and Ernest never knew – and there's only one other person who knows, and that is Bridget – your aunt – in Ireland, now. Seamus hadn't expected to die suddenly, yet he provided as best as he could for you. Remember me being able to pay for you to stay in that apartment in the Marais? Well, that money came from the trust fund I mentioned. I will give you all the details about it before you go back to Paris. You mentioned that I have been with you every step of the way as you grew up? Well, it felt to me, many times, when things were difficult, that Seamus was there with me too, every step of the way. He was the love of my life, James, and he would have been so proud of you. If he hadn't died, I would have left Ernest and we would all be together now, we'd have made a new life together."

James stared at his mother in wonder. "And you had to keep that secret all these years? You must have suffered so much."

Mavis smiled wryly. "Suffered? Oh, yes, I suffered. But there were times when I felt so very guilty as well. All the lies. All the pretence. But then, when Ernest treated me badly, I would think that I had nothing to feel guilty about. And if I hadn't had you, James, I don't know what would have become of me. Please forgive me?"

"Mam – there's nothing to forgive. I was a child born of love, you protected me and loved me. But it is such a relief to know that my father wasn't a cold-hearted, hypocritical, mysogynistic ....oh, Jesus!" He took his mother in his arms and hugged her. She felt like a tiny sparrow in his embrace, and he was afraid of crushing her.

"There's something I want you to have." Mavis delved deep into her handbag, into that inner zipped compartment that usually went unnoticed. "Here. Take this. You never know, it may be worth something one day." It was the small charcoal drawing that Seamus had done of her that wonderful evening when she had fallen asleep in his garden. Rhiannon. James took it reverently in his hand, staring at it for quite some time. This was the work of his father, the man who had adored his mother, the man he was just beginning to know.

They sat in silence for a long time, watching the rain beating down on the window, until it was quite late, mother and son, with the truth known at last.

The Brynglas Residential and Nursing Home building had hardly changed since Mavis had gone there to have James. However, the clientele had altered dramatically. No labouring mothers now, just the elderly who couldn't look after themselves any longer. So poignant, thought Mavis, when she arrived there at the age of eighty-five, that the place where she'd been delivered of her baby should be the place she'd come to in order to spend her final days.

She realised she wasn't the easiest of women to deal with, these days, but she was in constant pain with arthritis, and her leg ulcer just didn't seem to heal. It was lonely being old, she felt. Nobody wanted an old person around, they were too much work, they didn't understand the modern way of living, they couldn't work mobile phones and computers... We're in the way of progress, she would think, miserably. There were so few visitors as well. Her own sisters had gone into care homes up in Cross Hands, not they'd ever bothered much with her, anyway. James visited as often as he could, and Audrey popped in whenever she was in Llanelli. Fred and Margaret had their hands full looking after the Bakers, as Mrs Baker had developed dementia and kept wandering off all the time.

It had been wonderful beyond belief when Wendy had arrived the week before Christmas. Mavis had enjoyed that visit so much, and it had brought back so many memories for her.

Christmas came and went, and in March, Mavis became ill, developing a chest infection, which didn't respond to antibiotics. Slowly, her frail and vulnerable body succumbed to pneumonia. She slept most of the time, only waking to cough and drink water, or sips of tea, and when the carers came to wash her. The matron soon decided it was time to contact James in Paris.

He sat by her bed, holding her hand, telling her all about the new baby.

"Mavis-Claire and Patrice can't stop talking about him. He's the apple of their eye, although they can't quite get their little tongues around his name." He laughed. "Seamus doesn't really exist in French, so they just call him Mussy!"

He wasn't sure if his mother could hear him as her eyes remained closed. The radio was on, quietly playing music on Classic FM. The light outside was fading fast, although it was only half-past six. The clocks hadn't gone forward yet. The room became quite dark, yet James was loath to put on the light. Mavis looked so peaceful and calm, he didn't want to disturb her.

As the radio launched into Vaughan Williams' Symphony number 6, Mavis stirred slightly, and opened her eyes.

"James." He could barely hear her. "What a lovely boy you are." She squeezed his hand slightly. The whispering continued. "He's here, now, so I'll be going soon."

She's wandering in her mind, James thought, continuing to hold her hand, stroking her arm with his other hand.

But Mavis was smiling, and her eyes were now wide open. She felt so euphoric, the pain had gone and she could breathe easily.

"Seamus!" Her voice was stronger now. She looked at the doorway. There he was, laughing at her, holding out his arms. Without another thought, Mavis rose from her bed and walked towards the man she loved, into his arms, feeling the blissful joy of being reunited with him, forever. She looked back at the bed, where James was weeping silently, still holding the hand of the old woman she had been. But James would be fine, she thought. And she moved towards the light, with Seamus at her side.

Acknowledgments

Rhiannon has taken me the best part of ten years to write, and it has been an exciting ten years. For those of you who are not familiar with Carmarthenshire, Llannon is a tiny village about five miles north of Llanelli, which itself is a bustling town on the South Wales coast.
Bethel chapel is fictitious, and the only chapel that I am aware of in Llannon is Hermon.

I would like to thank my dear father, Eric, for generously giving me information about Llanelli in the 1960s, and for filling in the missing pieces of the jigsaw for me, when my own memory banks ran dry. I must also thank my mother, Joan, for correcting him when he got it wrong!

Ken McDermott proved immensely helpful when I almost lost my novel after my laptop crashed, and in his amazing assistance regarding the formatting. His wife Beth was my point of contact when I needed any Welsh translation. Thanks to you both! Diolch!

My husband Phil, and children Sally and Patrick, dogs Rosie, Bob and Red must have had their patience sorely tried when I would hide myself away in the dining room for hours, editing the story for the umpteenth time. Please forgive me!

I would also like to thank Susanne Lewis for her invaluable advice on legal matters, and drawing to my attention pitfalls I had not been aware of.

Lastly, a massive thank you to my childhood friend Christine Price, who designed the cover for the book.

I would like to dedicate this book to my late friend Julie Walters, who will never read it, and that is my deepest regret. Sleep well, dear friend.

About Author

Sonja Collavoce was born and brought up in Llanelli, South Wales. Her childhood was spent in the New Dock area of the town. Despite studying languages at A-level, she left home at eighteen to train as a nurse in Cardiff, qualifying as a Registered General Nurse, then a midwife and finally as a health visitor. She is married with two grown up children and has three dogs, whom she adores. Sonja has had several poems published, has performed some of them at the Dylan Thomas centenary festival in Cardiff and now plays keyboards in a rock band, Half Tidy. She also does a mean rendition of Wuthering Heights! This is her first novel.

Printed in Great Britain
by Amazon